CHILD

OF

VENUS

Also by Pamela Sargent

Novels

Short Fiction

CHILD OF VENUS

Pamela Sargent

An Imprint of HarperCollins Publishers

EOS

EOS
An Imprint of HarperCollins *Publishers*
10 East 53rd Street
New York, New York 10022-5299

Library of Congress Cataloging-in-Publication Data

Sargent, Pamela.
Child of Venus / Pamela Sargent.
p. cm.
ISBN 0-06-105027-X
I. Title.

PS3569.A6887 C48 2001
813'.54—dc21   00-046584

First Eos hardcover printing: May 2001

FIRST EDITION

10 9 8 7 6 5 4 3 2 1

www.eosbooks.com

To George

there for the long haul

From the personal record of Mahala Liangharad:

One of my earliest memories is still vivid enough that I can call it up at will, even though it was a simulated experience and not one I actually lived through myself.

No unprotected human being could have survived it.

I am standing on a wrinkled plain of black basalt, feeling the intense heat that surrounds me and presses in around me and an atmospheric pressure that threatens to crush me. In the distance, against a dark red sky, sits a pyramid so vast that it dwarfs even the shield volcano I glimpse in the distance. There is so little light that I can see only in the infrared; I wait, knowing what will happen, excited by anticipation and fear.

And then the ground heaves under my feet, and the sound of thunder strikes my ears with such a blow that I cry out in pain. A web of bright light appears along the pyramid's black sides as lightning dances at its apex. The ground shudders again, more fiercely this time, hurling me up into the clouds, and as I fly up, the planet below me begins to turn more rapidly. I can see it moving beneath me as I hover; the pyramid below me sweeps past as the planet turns, and after that the bright glow of the erupting volcano, and the wind screams at me as my world tears at itself.

This was a depiction of an event that happened long ago, nearly a century before I was born, on the world that was to become my home.

I try to remember when that world was no longer the imperfectly comprehended and often mysterious background of my young life, when it first became clear in my mind. Occasionally, I have the feeling that my environment was always in the foreground, that there was always some understanding on my part of what my world was and how I came to be in it, but that has to be an illusion. The time when I was beginning to discover my environment, exploring my surroundings and seeking out the place I might occupy in them—much of that is clouded for me now, as if I were viewing it through a heavy veil. Much of it is lost.

Lost to my own unaided memory, I mean, and not as easily recalled as things that happened to me later. All of the past is preserved in some form; I simply can't recollect it very easily by myself. I can no longer recall even whether my earliest apprehension of my world came from my actual experiences and the conclusions I drew from them or from the simulated events of a mind-tour, and maybe drawing such a distinction is irrelevant now. Those experiences have all become part of my past.

As a child, along with everyone else I knew, I often enjoyed the sensory entertainment of a mind-tour. By putting my band around my head, reaching out to our cyberminds, and asking for a particular tour—those that I was allowed to call up, anyway, those that had no barriers to block access—I could travel into the past, participate in an adventure, climb Mount McKinley or the Matterhorn or one of the other mountains of Earth, go diving in the sunken cities of Venice and Miami, ride a horse, shoot a bow, or else move like a ghost through other times and places, untouched by any of the visions that I observed.

The most common of these mind-tours, ones that had been shared by nearly everybody around me, were various depictions of how people had come to live on our world, depictions framed by dramatic and often apocryphal scenes. There were the obligatory scenes of the Earth after the end of the last of the Resource Wars, scenes showing the white-robed figures of the first Mukhtars, the inheritors and new rulers of humankind's ruined home planet, wandering through the rubble-strewn streets of Damascus and Tashkent and Samarkand and the other great cities of the New Islamic Nomarchy that was soon to become the center of Earth's culture. There were the moving scenes of Karim al-Anwar, one of those early Mukhtars, gazing out at a great sea with a visionary look in his intense dark eyes as he imagined creating such a body of water on inhospitable Venus, of making a new home for humanity.

At this point, some of the mind-tours would place the viewer amid a group of Mukhtars, all of them nodding their kaffiyeh-clad heads as Karim spoke eloquently of his dream of terraforming Venus; others would sweep the mind-tourist into a panoramic view of the dark tesserae of Venus, expanses of bizarrely wrinkled land veiled by thick clouds of carbon dioxide, and then to a view of Baltis Vallis, the longest of the many long, thin channels that meandered for thousands of kilometers over the Venusian surface, channels that had all of the appearance of ancient riverbeds and deltas. In the first such mind-tour I can recall experiencing, I felt extreme heat and a pressure that seemed great enough to crush me, while a low voice reminded me that an unprotected human body would be crushed by a barometric pressure ninety times that of Earth's atmosphere. In another, I flew over a blue-green ocean toward the burgeoning green jungles of the landmass of Aphrodite Terra—a vision of Venus as it would be.

Such mind-tours always inspired me with awe and pride, as they were intended to do, for I grew up as one of the Cytherians, as we called ourselves, one of the children of Venus. My childhood's Venus was no longer the hellish planet that Karim al-Anwar had dreamed of transforming, but it had also not yet become the green and fecund world he had hoped to bring into existence. We lived on the surface of our world, but only in domed settlements, gardens that were protected from the harsh and still lethal environment of Venus. We lived there in order to stake a human claim to that world, but a heretic might have said that we were prisoners, living out our lives in those enclosed places solely to make a point, to insist that Venus would eventually become habitable, whatever the obstacles that lay ahead.

Some believed that Karim al-Anwar had easily won the support of his fellow Mukhtars for the terraforming of Venus, while others thought that it had taken most of his life to inspire them with his dream. Over six hundred years had passed since his death, so there was much that the adults who taught me and the other children in my settlement did not know about him, many parts of his life that remained hidden. But Karim had lived to see Earth's Nomarchies finally at peace, and each of those regions ruled by a Mukhtar, with a peace guaranteed by the armed force known as the Guardians of the Nomarchies. He had also seen that Earth needed a new dream, one that would inspire Earth's people.

The mind-tours considered appropriate for children gave little indication of any motive for Karim's ambition other than a desire to dedicate himself and the people of Earth to the service of a great project, a desire fueled by his fear that Earth, with its rising oceans, steadily increasing average temperatures, and increase in levels of carbon dioxide, might eventually have great need of the knowledge terraforming would yield, in order to repair the damage to its own biosphere. Only later did it become evident to me that Karim and many other Earthfolk also saw his Venus Project as a way to challenge the Associated Habitats.

The Habbers: That was what the people of Earth called them, the descendants of those Earthfolk who had abandoned a planet that they saw as a worn-out husk, who had fled from the aftermath of the Resource Wars into space instead of staying to rebuild their damaged Earth. The Habbers: The term had begun as an insult and a curse, but over time it lost its sting and became only another name for the Habitat-dwellers.

The earliest Habbers had made their first homes inside the two satellites of Mars, Phobos and Deimos, before going on to construct larger Habitats using hollowed-out asteroids and all of the resources the solar system offered. They had been content to leave the wounded world of Earth to others, to build a new human civilization away from the surface of the home world. That was another reason for Karim's dream, the fear that without a great enterprise to inspire the people of Earth, humanity's future might belong entirely to the Habbers. And because the Habbers had in effect staked their own claim to Mars, preferring to keep that planet in its natural state as an object of study, Karim could not hope to transform the Red Planet. Venus would have to become a second planetary home for humankind, and the focus of his hopes.

Anwara, the satellite that circled Venus in a high orbit, had begun as a place to house the Venus Project's earliest scientists and workers and eventually grew into a vast ringed space station. The giant shield of the Parasol, constructed by thousands of Earthfolk at the cost of many lives, became an umbrella of immense fans with a diameter as great as that of Venus; in the shade of this giant metallic flower, Venus had slowly grown cooler. Frozen hydrogen from Saturn was hurled toward Venus in tanks, so that the hydrogen would combine with

Venus's free oxygen to form water. The Cytherian atmosphere was seeded with new bioengineered strains of algae that fed on the poisonous sulfuric acid and expelled it as iron and copper sulfides.

One mind-tour that I viewed in childhood conveyed the misleading impression that our surface settlements had been built not long after the construction of the Islands. In fact, the Islands had come into existence centuries before there were any settlers living inside domes on the high Maxwell Mountains of the Ishtar Terra landmass. The ten Islands where scientists and workers were to dwell, and an eleventh to be used as a port for both the dirigibles that carried people between the Islands and the shuttlecraft that traveled to Anwara, began as platforms built on rows of gigantic metallic cells filled with helium. Ten of the Islands were covered with soil and then enclosed in impermeable domes. These Islands floated in Venus's upper atmosphere slightly north of the equator; it was expected that in later centuries, as they slowly dropped through the altered atmosphere, they would come to rest on the planet's terraformed surface. In one mind-tour, I sat with the pilots of an airship as they left the Island port we called the Platform, bound for Island Eight; I gazed at sensor readings that told me of the fierce winds that raged below the Islands. In another mind-tour, I flew on a shuttle toward the rings of the great space station of Anwara.

Nowhere in any of these mind-tours was there any hint that the Habbers had been responsible for some of the Venus Project's successes. These scenarios never touched on the fact that Habber technology had been responsible for bringing needed hydrogen to Venus from Saturn, that Habber engineers had helped to design the Islands, that the Habbers had given us the formula for the ceramic-metallic alloy of the domes that protected our settlements. Earth, even before embarking on the Venus Project, had accepted many gifts from the Habbers, among them asteroids brought into Earth orbit to be mined. One might wonder—if one cared to venture into such dangerous theoretical territory—whether the Venus Project itself, Earth's bid to lay claim to the future of our species, would even have been possible without Habber aid.

Why did the Habbers wish to help Earth? Why had some among them willingly come to Venus to aid the Project, asking for nothing in return? They wanted only to learn, to test new technologies, to remain close to those whom they still considered their sisters and brothers; that was as much as the Habbers would claim. Perhaps they sought gratitude from those they helped. Instead, they garnered resentment, and Venus became the arena for the contest between Earth and the Associated Habitats, where one or the other would gain control over humankind's destiny.

Even as a child, I was aware of the role that my own family and line had played in this contest. My great-grandmother, Iris Angharads, and her bondmate, Liang Chen, had been the first of my family to come to Venus and labor for the Project. Iris had become a martyr for the Project, and a few scenes from her life, many of them sentimental inventions, were occasionally included in mind-tours of our history. During her time, the most powerful of the Island Administrators had confronted Earth and the Council of Mukhtars with his demands, in an effort to win control over the Project for himself and a closer alliance with the Habbers. His actions had precipitated a blockade of the Islands and a desperate attempt by a few people to threaten death to the hostages they had taken and the destruction of a dome on the surface where their captives were being held. Iris Angharads and her colleague Amir Azad lost their lives in saving the hostages, managing to get them to freedom aboard an airship before the dome was destroyed with the small nuclear charges the rebels had set around its perimeter, but their courageous example inspired the Mukhtars to come to an agreement that had both preserved the endangered Project and granted a measure of freedom to all Cytherian settlers.

So most of the official histories claimed, although I came to believe that much was left unsaid, that matters had been far more complicated than that.

But the martyred and honored Iris Angharads was only one member of my line. There were other members of my family who had left me with a more ambiguous heritage. One was Benzi Liangharad, the son of Iris and Liang Chen, who had abandoned the Venus Project to join the Habbers. Another was Malik Haddad, who had fled from Venus during the time of the Revolt, when many Cytherians had become misguided followers of the movement and cult known as Ishtar. I was genetically linked to both of them, as well as to the parents I never knew, who were dead before I was born and who had left me their own dubious legacy.

They all had been caught up in the battle for control of the Venus Project, in the struggle between Earthfolk and Habbers for the human future, in the fight of Cytherians for control of their own society. And all of them had largely been tools in the hands of others more powerful than they, who had probably seen them only as pawns whenever they were aware of them at all.

But I was only dimly aware of all of this as a child, when my world was still largely a mystery and I was just coming to glimpse my place in it.

The memory I can so easily call up now, that cataclysmic vision of a planet beginning to turn beneath me, depicts the event that marks the true beginning of the human-made history of Venus, or so it has always seemed to me. Before then, even with the creation of sterile oceans on the surface, the seeding of algae, the steady cooling of the planet under the Parasol's shade, the tanks of Saturnian hydrogen that flared like candles against the Cytherian darkness as they fell toward the thickly veiled planet, humankind still had only a tenuous hold on Venus. Increasing Venus's rotation, pushing against that planet's inertia with the gravitational forces of powerful man-made devices, had been the true start of a new era.

The vision comes to me once more: I stand on the black plain and gaze at the pyramid in the distance. That structure, one of three massive pyramids along the equator, has been built by Island engineers guiding their equipment by remote control. Each of the pyramids houses a gravitational pulse engine; rods anchoring those engines have pierced the basaltic mantle of Venus to penetrate to the planet's nickel and iron core. The ground heaves under my feet and thunder slaps my ears as the pyramid, veins of light bulging from its metallic walls, releases its pulse of energy. Venus, assaulted by the release of the powerful antigravitational pulse of the three engines, begins to turn more rapidly.

Other sights appear: Lightning bolts dance in the thick black clouds as the wind rises. A tidal wave rushes toward a shore as slabs of basalt are sheared from the sides of mountains. I fly up through the clouds to glimpse the colorful bands of aurorae flare over the northern pole, a sign of the magnetic field being generated. Venus turns more rapidly, and the increased rotation promises to provide my world with Earthlike weather patterns in later centuries, when people would at last walk the surface unprotected and look up through whatever remained of the Parasol at the sun.

That was the promise I saw in that vision, in those scenes of the past captured by sensors and preserved in our records, a pledge that out of the forces that had torn at my world, from the terrifying energies that my people had loosed upon it, that out of that destructive power something new would emerge, a world that would shake off the darkness of the past and emerge into the light.

Ishtar Terra

There were three routes Mahala could follow home from school. One led toward the lake at the center of Oberg's west dome. The second led past the rows of flat-roofed houses nearest her grandmother's, while the third route took her past the park area and community greenhouses to the road that circled the dome.

The third was her favorite. Traffic along the road was sparse, only an occasional cart of cargo with a few workers on board, or else one of the two passenger carts that continuously circled the west dome in opposite directions, stopping to pick up people or let them off along the way. Standing by the road, Mahala would peer down the long gray stretch of track until she spied a square vehicle on treads in the distance, appearing on the road's long curve, the heads of the passengers poking above the sides of the roofless cart. Her schoolmates often raced after the carts, shouting at the passengers, who waved back at the children from their seats. She would follow the cart and its passengers at a distance until she came to the glass-walled structures of the community greenhouses. Her grandfather, Sef Talis, who was taking his turn on duty there, usually left work at about the time she went home from school.

Mahala felt safer walking home with Sef. If she was with her grandfather, her schoolmate Ragnar Einarsson would not leap out at her from behind a shrub or other hiding place, then chase her all the way home. During her first days at school, she had gone home along the pathway that led past the lake, but a few days ago, from the slope of a gentle hill overlooking the mirrorlike surface of the water, she had seen Ragnar near one of the docks. A few people were usually fishing from the docks; she liked to sit near them as the golden surface of the lake faded into greenish-blue and then a darker blue as the wide disk of haloed bright light in the dome far overhead faded.

The lake had become a source of wonder for her, now that she was learning even more about her home. Streams of water, collected from the poisonous acidic rain falling steadily outside Oberg's domes, were cleansed to feed the streams of the settlement. People had made this lake and stocked it with fish, had made topsoil to cover the regolith and had seeded the land, had built the protective domes and their disks of light that glowed from a height of over a kilometer above the land, had even made the rain that fell outside the domes on the dark and barren surface of Venus. Once, she had felt awe while sitting by the lake and listening to the trilling of birds and thinking about what people had made here. Now her awe had become fear—of Ragnar, of others, of the secrets others kept from her, of the dark and dangerous world that lay outside the domes of Oberg.

The other children her age never seemed afraid. They pestered the teacher with questions, huddled together in groups, and were at ease with one another. Their world seemed unlike the one she had learned about from the screen and the teaching images that answered her questions. Other five-year-olds lived in a world of rules, games, and secrets that Mahala had failed to master even after being in school for twenty days. Sometimes she wished that she could learn at home; the screen images might tutor her as well as the teachers did.

But her grandmother would never allow that. "You're a Cytherian," Risa would say. "You're part of this community, making a new world, you can't just be off by yourself. You can't be a child for long. You have to learn how to get along with people, how to work with them—that's part of what school is for."

Mahala often chafed against her grandmother's rules. "Don't wander around alone in the main dome" was one rule. "Don't talk to people you don't know, especially new arrivals" was another. Mahala had worn her tracer, the bracelet that could alert her household to her whereabouts, longer than most of the other children. She had begged Risa not to force her to wear one to school, where her schoolmates were sure to make fun of her if she did.

Mahala came to the edge of the road and looked around for her grandfather. The glass walls of the three community greenhouses were just up the road, and past them she glimpsed the lighted cave of the entrance to the tunnel that led under the ground and into Oberg's main dome. Oberg seemed huge to her, its west dome a world in itself. When she walked to school, the disk of light far above would brighten until the darkness shrank to a black band just above the wall at the bottom of the dome. The flat green land, with only a few small hills, was a garden of trees and flowerbeds over which the prefabricated blocks of dwellings had been scattered and the facets of small greenhouses glittered like jewels, where the air was always warm and smelled of grass and leaves and growing things. Mahala never felt enclosed unless she was near the black wall that encircled the dome or inside one of the tunnels that connected the four domes of Oberg.

Her teacher Karin Mugabe had spoken of how the Cytherians would live outside the domes one day, when the world outside had changed enough for people to be able to survive there. Kolya Burian, one of Risa's housemates, sometimes walked with Mahala to the edge of the dome and then lifted her up in his strong arms so that she could see over the wall. Outside the transparent ceramic material of the dome, misted over by droplets of acid rain, a hazy glow marked the domes of the al-Khwarizmi settlement; when lightning flashed, it was possible to see the rocky shelf on which that settlement had been built. Most of this region of the Maxwell Mountains, the high cliffs that jutted up from the Ishtar plateau, was hidden in blackness, because Venus lay in the shade of the Parasol, the vast orbital umbrella that hid it from the sun. No solar light would fall upon this planet again until Venus had cooled.

A few people stood by the road, waiting for a cart. As Mahala walked toward them, her grandfather emerged from a greenhouse door.

"Sef!" she called out. The tall broad-shouldered man halted, then hurried toward her. A dark-haired woman followed him out of the greenhouse. Mahala had not seen her before and wondered who she was. The woman's long black hair was pulled back from her golden-skinned face; she gazed at Mahala, then turned away.

"Mahala—I thought you might have taken another way home," Sef said as he approached. Mahala shook her head. "You don't have to meet me after work every time."

"Don't you want to walk home with me?"

"Of course I do." Sef smiled, but his eyes searched the space behind her. "I was only saying you could walk home by yourself if you like." He took her hand and led her toward the road. Usually Sef lingered to talk with his friends, but this time he only nodded at them as he passed.

The strange dark-haired woman was leaning against a tree near the road, arms folded across her chest. She glanced at Sef, but did not speak. Mahala felt her grandfather's large hand tighten around hers; he strode past the woman in silence.

"Who is she?" Mahala asked. He did not reply. "She's awfully pretty. Is she a new settler?"

"No." Sef was silent for a bit. "She used to live here a few years ago—she just moved back to Oberg."

"Then why didn't you say anything to her?"

"Because I wish she hadn't come back, and she knows I feel that way. It doesn't matter, Mahala. Sometimes we have to work with people we'd rather avoid."

She struggled to keep up with her grandfather's long strides. At last he slowed and loosened his grip around her hand.

"Why don't you want her here?" Mahala said.

"She's very troubled," Sef replied. "Some hard things happened to her when she was only a girl. She'd be better off in another settlement, away from old memories—that's my feeling, anyway. Your grandmother did what she could to advise her family, but they didn't want our help."

People were always asking Risa for advice; Mahala wondered why the woman's family had refused it. Risa was important, a member of the Oberg Council that was elected by residents of the settlement, someone respected even by Administrators and Linkers.

"What happened to her?" Mahala asked.

"I've said enough, child. That's all you have to know. We don't have much to do with her, and it would be best if you didn't, either. Just stay away from her."

This was so unlike her grandfather that Mahala did not know what to say. He rarely took a dislike to anyone.

They were nearing the tunnel entrance. Their house, a rectangular flat-roofed one-story building, was near the path that led from the entrance. Through the trees set back from the road, Mahala saw the panes of her grandmother's small greenhouse.

Sef stopped and knelt next to her. "Come on," he said, "I'll give you a ride."

She climbed onto his broad shoulders, content.

✻   ✻   ✻

Risa sat on a cushion in the common room, at the low table where her household gathered for meals, going over the household accounts on a small screen. At least Mahala assumed that was what her grandmother was doing. Risa, on her days off from work, usually visited other households on Council business or to find out if anyone had problems or complaints, then came home to do chores there. If she wasn't in the greenhouse or repairing something in the house, she had to be doing something practical, such as the accounts. Risa was not the sort to sit around reading or playing screen games.

"Are you the only one home?" Sef asked as he lifted Mahala from his shoulders.

Risa looked up and nodded. "Paul's delivering a baby. Barika mentioned this morning that she and Kristof might stop at his family's house on the way home."

Mahala wondered if that meant they would eat later, when her grandparents' other housemates got here. Risa would not wait for Paul, who might not get home until long after last light, but she would certainly delay the meal for the others. "Kolya went to the lake," Risa continued, "but I'm not counting on his catching any fish for dinner." She frowned at her screen. Mahala could see part of it now, enough to know that her grandmother was not doing the accounts. The screen was covered with letters, not numbers, and the tiny image of a face was in one corner.

Risa had to be looking at someone's public record. Before Mahala could get a better look at the face, her grandmother had blanked the screen. Risa had not even greeted her or asked about school; she was still gazing up at Sef, as if waiting for him to speak.

"I'm almost done with my project," Mahala blurted out.

Risa turned toward her. "What project, dear?" she asked.

Mahala sat down on a cushion near her grandmother. "Karin gave us a project."

"Then you must tell me all about it," her grandmother said.

Sef seated himself on one of the cushions near them. He still had a worried look on his face, with his eyebrows drawn together and his mouth set in a straight line.

"Well," Mahala began, "Karin was telling us about how people came here to Venus from all over Earth. Then she said that we should know about our heritage, where we come from, because you should know about yourself and other people and respect their ways, so you can get along with them better."

Risa sniffed and said, "That's all very well, but I sometimes think a lot of old ways are best forgotten."

"Anyway, Karin told us her people come from both the Arctic Nomarchy and the Southeast African Nomarchy, and we're supposed to do reports about our own people and where they're from."

Risa was frowning even more. "Exactly what are you supposed to do?"

"I told you—find out things and do a report. Call up a map of Earth and show the places our people came from, and then tell something about those places." Mahala and her schoolmates already knew how to ask the cyberminds questions through their screens. She could call up an image of a person who would explain a subject to her, but often preferred wearing the band around her head that linked her directly to the minds. With the band, she could take a mind-tour and feel as though she was in the places where her people had lived on Earth. "I found out a lot about my people already, so I'll give my report day after tomorrow."

Her grandmother's hand was suddenly around her wrist, gripping it hard. "Exactly what did you find out, Mahala?"

"Risa." Mahala tried to pull away. "It was just public records. What's the matter?"

"I'm sorry." Risa let go. "I'm just tired. Why don't you go to the kitchen and get us some juice, and then you'll tell us all about your report."

Mahala had the feeling that Risa did not really want to hear about the report. She got up, went into the kitchen, and rummaged in the cooler, listening to the low murmur of the voices in the common room. Her grandparents were speaking softly, as if they had a secret. Mahala poured juice, climbed onto a stepstool and stretched to put the empty glass bottle up on the countertop, arranged the cups on a tray, then crept toward the doorway.

". . . didn't say anything," Sef muttered. "She just stared at me and walked away. Then I saw her again, on the way home with Mahala. I could feel her staring at us. Mahala started asking who she was. I said she was somebody who'd had some hardship and that it would be better to stay away from her."

They were talking about that woman, the pretty one Sef had called troubled. Mahala held her breath, trying to hear more.

"You're a Councilor," Sef said. "Isn't there anything you can do?"

"She has a right to live here. I would have thought she wouldn't want to be in Oberg, but—" Risa sighed. "I pity her. She has every reason to keep her distance from us, so I doubt—"

"Mahala may ask more questions."

"Yes, she will. And I don't know how much to tell her."

Everyone seemed to have secrets from her. Mahala lingered near the doorway. They would wonder what was taking her so long. She hurried out, set the tray on the low table near her grandparents, then sat down again.

"So how about this project of yours?" Sef asked.

"Well," Mahala replied, "I started with your names first, even if I do know about you already, and there's a lot about great-grandmother Iris in the historical records."

"Yes, there is," Risa said, as if happy to admit to something.

"I'll have lots of places to show on my map." Mahala gulped down some juice. "I mean, your people came from China and the North American Plains, and my mother's father was born in Damascus, and the records say my father had parents from Nueva Hispania but that one of his grandparents was from Central Africa. And Sef's from the Pacific Federation." She had included Sef in the project, even though he was not her biological grandfather. "I come from people who lived all over Earth!"

"That doesn't make you any better than anyone else." It was like her grandmother to say that. Risa usually had harsh words for people who, as she put it, got above themselves.

"It'd be easier if they came from just one or two places." Mahala finished her juice. "I wouldn't have so much to put in my report."

"Learning about your heritage—what nonsense." Risa gestured with her cup. "You're a Cytherian—that's what matters. That Karin ought to be spending more time on practical subjects."

"Risa." Sef leaned toward his bondmate. "The teacher's only doing her job. There's no harm in—"

"Time enough to learn about the past when she's older. Right now, she'd be better off learning things of more use to the Project."

Risa had said such things before, but did not usually sound this upset. Mahala set down her cup. "Is that why you put a block on my parents' public records?" she asked, feeling that it was time to ask.

Risa lifted her brows. "What?"

"I found out when I was doing my report. I wanted to ask about them, and the screen said the minds couldn't tell me because you put a block on their records."

"I'm your guardian," Risa said. "I have the right. Sef and I thought it best that you—"

"But why?"

"You already have enough information for this report, don't you?"

The birthdates and deathdates of her mother and father, the origins of their parents and other forebears, the fact that Mahala's mother had once been the Guide and leader of Ishtar's believers here—the screen had readily yielded all of that. Mahala had often called up images of her parents and knew some of the important facts about her mother's life. But this time, she had asked other questions, and the minds had refused to answer. Risa Liangharad, they had told her, had put a block on answering certain questions.

"You don't understand." Mahala let out her breath. "You won't let me hear part of the public record, something everybody else can find out except me—it isn't fair."

"You know what you need to know," her grandmother said. "You'll find out more when you're older."

"Everyone else knows. I'm the only one that doesn't." Mahala felt the truth of that statement as soon as she spoke. Certain things were suddenly clear; the occasional silences of other children when the name of Mahala's mother was mentioned, the worried or cautious looks of adults. They all had a secret, and it had something to do with her parents. "Everybody knows except me!"

"Mahala—" Risa slid closer to her. "Please listen. There's no reason for you to—"

"If the minds won't tell me," Mahala said, "I'll get one of the other kids to find out for me." Risa could not block others' access to public records. "I'll tell them what to ask, and—"

"You won't."

"I will."

"If you do, I'll have to punish you for disobeying me."

"I don't care."

Risa opened her mouth; Sef shook his head at his bondmate. "We knew this would come," he said. "Maybe we should give her some answers before someone else does."

Risa gazed at him for a long time, then slowly got to her feet. "Grazie and Kolya will be home soon," she said. "I'll talk to Mahala alone." She reached for her granddaughter's hand. "Come with me."

✳   ✳   ✳

They went to Mahala's room, which was at the end of the short corridor in Risa's wing of the house. The room Risa and Sef shared was separated from Mahala's by a bathroom; the three rooms on the other side of the corridor were empty. Mahala's great-uncle Benzi and her uncle Dyami used those rooms when they visited, and new arrivals in Oberg often stayed there until they found another place to live. Barika Maitana, one of Risa's housemates, had come there as a new settler when Mahala was still a baby and had decided to stay. Sooner or later, Barika and her bondmate Kristof Anders would have a child, and then one of the two empty rooms in Paul's wing of the house would be filled. Her grandmother would have liked to have Dyami living here, too, but Risa's son made his home in the Turing settlement, up in the Freyja Mountains to the north.

The house was too empty; her grandmother often said that. The extra space was wasteful, a failing high on Risa's list of offenses, and it also wasn't good for Mahala to be the only child in this house.

Mahala sat on her bed, feeling the silence of the house as Risa settled herself on a cushion in one corner.

"I knew we'd have to have this talk eventually," Risa murmured. "I hoped it could wait until you were older, but—" She sighed. "It's painful for me to talk about your mother, even after all this time."

Mahala had been born after the deaths of both her parents; that was part of her record, a fact she had always known. Her mother and father had stored their genetic material, and the embryo that had grown into Mahala had begun to gestate before the deaths of her parents in 631, during that troubled time people here called the Cytherian Revolt, although Mahala had not entered the world until two years after the uprising. Risa, after keeping the embryo of her grandchild cryonically stored for nearly two years, had finally chosen to rear Mahala.

As it happened, Mahala and her grandmother had started life under similar circumstances. Risa had also gestated inside an artificial womb after her own mother's death, and her father, Liang Chen, had brought her up. Risa's mother, Iris, held a place of honor in Venus's history; a monument to her stood in Oberg's main dome. The legacy of Mahala's mother was more ambiguous.

She would never know her parents; Mahala had accepted that. Risa had never known her mother, either. But now, for the first time, she was beginning to wonder why she knew so little about her mother and father.

"You have a right to some answers, child." Risa brushed back a lock of her graying black hair. "What is it you want to know?" she asked, and Mahala felt her reluctance to tell.

Mahala considered what to ask. Her mother's name had been Chimene Liang-Haddad, and her father's Boaz Huerta, but she had been given her grandmother's surname of Liangharad. While still a young woman, Chimene had become the leader of the Ishtar cult, believers in a Spirit that was coming to life on this once-lifeless world, with whom all Cytherians would someday be united. Ishtar had dreamed of ruling Venus, with the help of Earth's Council of Mukhtars, but the cult's followers had become so repressive that many had finally turned against them during the Cytherian Revolt. Chimene had been misled by some of those close to her, but in the end she had sided with the people who had defied Earth's Mukhtars. Sef had told Mahala all about that.

Chimene and Boaz, she knew, had died before all the hearings were held to judge those who had committed the worst offenses against their fellow Cytherians. There had been no chance for them to defend themselves against possibly unjust accusations. But she did not know how her parents had met their deaths.

"How did my mother die?" she asked.

Risa took a breath. "I didn't want you to know. It's why I put a lock on that part of her public record."

"But everyone else must know."

"Yes. My daughter recorded her intentions before carrying them out and placed the speech in the public record. I didn't want you to see that—I was afraid it would be too upsetting. Chimene took her own life, Mahala. She chose to die."

Mahala was not sure she understood. "But why?"

"Because she felt that she could no longer be Ishtar's Guide. She'd made a lot of mistakes, you see, and many other people suffered for them. I didn't understand then why she took her life, but now I think she saw it as the only way to atone for her deeds, to show people how sorry she was for her actions. That's what I believe, anyway, that she finally saw what was right, that it was best to leave the future of Venus to others. Some loved her, and some hated her. Maybe it would have been harder for people who took different sides back then to be reconciled now if she were still living among us."

Risa's head drooped, and the lines around her mouth and eyes seemed deeper. Mahala suddenly felt how old her grandmother was. Her thoughts were on death now. How could anyone choose to die? It seemed to her that anyone alive would struggle against death for as long as possible.

"There was a time, after your mother's death," Risa continued, "when I wondered if my own son could ever forget what her followers had done to him, if he would ever forget the suffering the people around his sister caused."

Mahala thought of her uncle Dyami. He had been a prisoner in Turing during the darkest time of the Venus settlements and had organized an uprising against his captors in the early days of the Cytherian Revolt. She knew this only because she had picked it up from others, since Dyami himself never spoke of his experiences. He was a quiet man; with his chestnut hair and tall frame, he looked much like his father Sef, but he lacked Sef's quick smile and easy manner. Kind as Dyami was, he held himself apart from others during his visits, and Mahala had sensed that he would not welcome questions about his time as a captive.

"Your mother believed," Risa went on, "that there was something beyond death, that it wasn't the end, that another life would follow this one. I've always found such notions foolish, but maybe that was another reason she decided to die. If I had known what she meant to do, maybe—" She bowed her head. "Her last message is in her public record. I didn't want you to see it—I've read a transcript of what she said, but I've never been able to listen to it. But when you're older, it might help you to understand why she acted as she did. She spoke of her regrets, of her shame at being misled by those she loved and trusted."

This was too much for Mahala to absorb. If Risa understood what Chimene had done to herself, then why had she been so secretive about it?

"How did she do it?" Mahala asked.

"She was found with a knife. She'd slashed her throat. She bled to death before she was discovered."

Mahala shuddered. "And my father?"

"He died a short time before your mother did. His record will tell you that his body was found in Chimene's house and that a drug of some sort killed him. A physician who was with my daughter at the time confessed that she was responsible for his death, and that woman took her own life soon after that, so a hearing was never held." Risa sounded as if she were rattling off a statement at the start of a public Council meeting. "Your father was the enemy of many here, and I didn't mourn his loss, but maybe he was also sorry for his deeds at the end."

Risa got up, sat on the bed, and drew Mahala to her. "What they did," she said, "whatever suffering your parents caused, has nothing to do with you. Don't ever feel that you're less because of it. It was all over before you took your first breath—never feel that you have to share any of your parents' guilt. We can't help where we come from."

But it wasn't over. Had it been over, Risa would not have felt the need to keep so much hidden. If it was over, why did the people around her suddenly look guarded when her mother's name was mentioned?

"Chimene was such a beautiful child," Risa continued. Mahala had seen images of her mother; with her large dark eyes, long black hair, and golden-skinned face, she looked so perfect that she hardly seemed human. "She took after her father Malik. She was so beautiful it frightened me sometimes—I used to wonder how she could ever have come from my body." Her arm tightened around Mahala. "It's past, child. What happened is over. I'm grateful I have you."

"Risa?" She nestled closer to her grandmother. "Is that why people don't talk to me about her, because she killed herself?"

"It's part of the reason. It's useless to talk about those days, during the Revolt and before—there's so much bitterness still."

Mahala tried to imagine her parents dying as they had. That such a beautiful woman and her handsome lover could have died so horribly did not make sense. She thought of her mother's delicate features and her father's warm brown eyes; they had seemed perfectly matched in their beauty. While staring at their images, she had often wished fervently that she looked more like them.

Risa said that they had died because they were sorry for what they had done, that they had believed they were going to a better place. Mahala clung to that thought, hoping that it might be true.

2

Mahala was to give her report to her schoolmates after Ragnar Einarsson finished his. Ragnar's people came from a part of the Arctic Nomarchy called Iceland, and he had shown many images of volcanoes spewing black ash, green hillsides below rocky gray cliffs, and mist rising from hot springs. Other scenes showed people in boats on a white-capped sea, and then a market where there seemed to be enough fish to feed everyone in Oberg.

An image of an Icelandic bay faded from the large screen on the classroom wall. Ragnar had given his entire report only on Iceland, since he had no people from anywhere else, but Mahala wondered if her report would be as interesting as his. Iceland was a place with few people, which made Ragnar and his family unusual, and only a few families of Icelanders had come here as settlers. Yet Ragnar had made it seem that the Icelandic people, whose Scandinavian ancestors had sailed west long ago to make a home for themselves near the slopes of smoldering volcanoes, were not so different in spirit from Cytherians.

"That was fascinating, Ragnar." Karin Mugabe glanced around the room. "I'm sure we all enjoyed learning about this most unusual part of Earth. Does anyone have any questions?"

Devaki Patel waved her hand at the teacher. "Didn't your people come from a place near Iceland?"

Karin nodded. "Some of my mother's family came from Norway. It might be that, a long time ago, some of my distant ancestors found their way to Iceland." She shifted on her cushion. "People have always reached out for new places to settle, for lands where they could make new lives. In the old days, they often fought those who had already settled there and took the land from them. Here, we can make a new world together without having to fight anyone."

"Except Earth and the Mukhtars," a boy near Ragnar said.

"That dispute was settled." Karin narrowed her brown eyes, then smiled. "We Cytherians have an agreement with Earth now."

"Maybe the Habbers'll want to take over someday," Ragnar said, looking at Mahala as he spoke.

"They have their own worlds," the teacher replied, "their Habitats. There's no reason for them to want our world. Habbers are on Venus only to help us." She paused. "Perhaps we can have Mahala's report now."

Mahala looked around the room. The other children sat on their cushions, small screens on their laps, faces turned toward the large wall screen. Her report might not seem as interesting as Ragnar's. She sighed, then whispered to her screen to call up the report.

"My grandmother, Risa Liangharad," Mahala's recorded voice began, "and my great-grandfather, Liang Chen, were with the very first group of settlers who came to the surface of Venus." Her cheeks burned. What she had said was true, but hearing it from the screen, as an image of Oberg's main dome was shown, sounded like bragging. "My great-grandmother, Iris Angharads, came here all the way from the North American Plains in the year 543 of the Nomarchies to work for the Project on the Islands." An image of the domed settlements sailing in the thin upper atmosphere of Venus appeared, blurred greenish beacons of light against the darkness, seeds of life. The Islands floating on their platforms of helium cells had been humankind's first outposts here and were still the homes of some fifty thousand Cytherians. "Chen and Iris came from Nomarchies that were very far apart on Earth, but wanting to come here brought them together."

This is awful, Mahala thought as her voice continued and a map of Earth appeared. Why couldn't she have stayed at home when her report was shown, instead of having to sit through it here? Shanghai's impossibly crowded streets, where Chen had grown up while being trained as a mechanic, were on the screen now. The other children gaped at the sight of so many people gathering at markets and jostling one another in doorways; one street in that city could probably hold more people than the almost twenty-five thousand who lived in Oberg.

The scene changed to one of a windswept plain, a vast expanse open to the sky; someone gasped.

Mahala looked away from the wall screen to the smaller one on her lap. Risa had told her stories of how Chen had been sent to a small Plains town in North America, where he had fallen in love with Iris, but she couldn't have fit all of that into her report. There was barely time to show a bit of Shanghai and to say a little about the customs of the Plains, where the women lived in towns, farmed, and reared their children by themselves while the men traveled from place to place. Now she was gazing at a vista of pastel-colored houses crowded together amid olive trees on rocky hills; towers loomed in the distance. This was Amman, where her biological grandfather, Malik Haddad, her grandmother Risa's first bondmate, had once taught in that city's great university.

No wonder Ragnar's report was so good, she thought bitterly. He had to show only one place, while she had to find out things about a lot of places and leave out much of what she knew.

Someone whispered behind her during the part of the report that showed the homelands of Boaz's forebears. The tropical landscape disappeared, to be replaced by a view of Puget Sound, where Sef had spent his boyhood. By the time the scene had shifted to the Great Salt Lake of New Deseret, the home of Sef's ancestors on his mother's side, Mahala wished that she had found an excuse to stay home. Instead of seeming to have learned about a lot of different places, she sounded as though she didn't know very much about any of them.

The report ended with a view of the monument to her great-grandmother, Iris. On the pillar, which stood in Oberg's main dome, Iris's sculpted face gazed out at the settlement that she had not lived to see. She and Amir Azad, the man whose image was next to hers on the monument, had given their lives to save others; people now lived inside domes on the surface of Venus because of them. Everyone knew the story in one version or another, but Mahala had not seen how she could avoid showing the monument, given the prominent place Iris held in Venus's history. Now she wished that she had concluded with something else, maybe a view of Oberg as an approaching airship would see it. Reminding everyone that Iris Angharads was her ancestor seemed like boasting and getting above others.

"That was very interesting, Mahala," Karin said as the screen image faded. "I'm sure we all appreciated seeing so many parts of Earth. You deserve some praise for organizing and putting together such a large amount of material." Karin, Mahala thought, probably wouldn't say anything bad about anyone's report, since one of her duties was to encourage her students. "Any questions?"

Ragnar spoke first. "She's got Habbers in her family." The blond boy frowned as he looked toward Mahala. "She didn't say anything about them."

"We were supposed to tell where our people came from," Mahala said, "not where they went afterward."

"That's because the rest of our people came here and stayed. Yours didn't, at least not all of them. They came here first, and then they left Venus."

"Just my grandfather Malik and my great-uncle Benzi, and they—"

Ragnar scowled. "They must not have wanted to be Cytherians."

"That isn't fair," Mahala burst out. "Benzi's here, living on Island Two."

The teacher held up a hand. "Ragnar, without the help of Habbers, our Project would have been much harder. We wouldn't be living here on the surface if it weren't for their engineering contributions, and we wouldn't have won an agreement from Earth without them. Mahala's great-uncle might have gone to a Habitat long ago, but he came back here to aid us."

Ragnar opened his mouth; Karin shook her head at him. "Every one of you probably has at least one family member who didn't set the best example," she continued. "The purpose of your reports is to give you a sense of your past, a feeling for your differences while you see that you're all Cytherians now. What's important is what brings you together, not what might divide you from one another."

Ragnar was silent, but Mahala could tell he was furious; his face was paler than ever, and the hands holding his screen trembled slightly. It had to be embarrassing to have the teacher scold him, however gently, after he had given such a good report.

Karin motioned at a boy sitting near Mahala. "Shing, we'll have your report now."

Mahala rushed from the classroom when Karin dismissed them, slowing only when she reached the end of the hall. Usually few students left by this side door, but this time three girls were loitering outside on the path. One of them was Solveig Einarsdottir; Mahala's heart sank. It was just her luck to run into Ragnar's sister.

Ah Lin Bergen motioned to her. The small round-faced girl was Mahala's age and lived in a house near Risa's, but Ah Lin had started school a year earlier, when she was four.

"Come to the lake with us," Ah Lin said. "We're going to play there and then go over to Ellie's house."

Mahala eyed the others uncertainly. Ah Lin was all right, but she did not know Ellie Ruiz that well, and Solveig made her nervous. She was tall and had her brother's white-blond hair; at seven, she was two years older than Ragnar, but seemed even older than that. She moved slowly and gracefully, the way an older person might, and her broad-boned, attractive face was so still and expressionless that it was impossible to tell what she was thinking.

"Come on," Ellie said.

"We found a great spot to go wading," Ah Lin added. "Nobody ever fishes there." Solveig said nothing.

"Uh, I have to meet my grandfather," Mahala replied, "or he'll worry about me." That lie would only make the others think of her as even more of a baby, but she could not think of any other excuse.

Ellie shrugged. Solveig stared past Mahala. "Maybe some other time," Ah Lin muttered as they walked away.

Mahala wandered toward the park that bordered the school, already regretting her decision. Why couldn't she be more like her schoolmates? Maybe it was her family. Risa could talk all she wanted to about how one Cytherian was as good as another, but her grandmother and her family were still unusual. Risa was influential enough as a Councilor to have Jamilah al-Hussaini, who was an Administrator and the Liaison to the Project Council, consult her, and even if Risa had not been on the Oberg Council, she was still the daughter of Iris Angharads.

Risa was respected, but her first bondmate had seized the chance to flee to the Associated Habitats, those hollowed-out asteroids and artificial worldlets inhabited by the people who had abandoned Earth long ago, and her daughter had caused her such pain that Risa had wept after telling Mahala about her. That had frightened Mahala, seeing Risa weep; her grandmother was usually impatient with tears and crying. Why couldn't her people have been more like other folk? Instead, they seemed to produce heroic sorts, such as Iris, or else people like Chimene, whom everyone seemed embarrassed to mention.

That was what it came down to, Mahala supposed. She was different from her friends because of her people and what they had done, and there was nothing she could do to change that.

She was turning from the path toward the greenhouses when she heard a muffled sound among the trees. Mahala spun around. Ragnar Einarsson was sprawled on the ground, as if he had tripped over a root.

"Are you hurt?" she asked.

"What's it to you?" He got to his feet. "I was waiting for you."

"Leave me alone." She backed away, afraid.

"You little bitch. My report was better than yours—admit it."

"Yours was a very good report, Ragnar."

"Yours was shit. Even Karin knew that."

"You didn't have to say those things about my family."

"Why not? It's true. Those Habber people of yours aren't even the worst. There's your dead parents my mother says we shouldn't talk about when we're around you, but I know what they did to my father. They had him beaten because they knew he hated them. He might have been killed if the Revolt hadn't started when it did, and then my mother would have been all alone with Solveig."

"Leave me alone or—"

"What?" Ragnar stepped toward her; his pale blue-gray eyes were wild. "What'll you do? Go running to your grandmother to tell on me?"

She turned and ran toward the road, then fell. Something heavy was pressed against her; a hand grabbed at her long hair, pulling it hard. Mahala struggled, but the boy had her pinned. He yanked her hair again, making her whimper, then pushed her face against the grass.

"Stop it," a woman's voice called out.

Ragnar let go; Mahala lifted her head. The strange woman Sef had warned her about was walking toward them along the road.

Ragnar got to his feet. "It's none of your business," he shouted.

"Maybe it's none of my business if it's a fair fight, but this didn't look fair to me. You're a lot bigger and heavier than that little girl, and it didn't look as if you were giving her much of a chance to fight back."

Mahala stood up, her knees shaking. Ragnar glared at her, then suddenly raced toward the trees.

The woman stared after him, then moved closer to Mahala. "Are you all right?" she asked.

Mahala nodded.

The woman smiled, looking even prettier; for a moment, she looked almost exactly like one of the images Mahala had seen of Chimene. "I'll walk you to the road if you like," the woman continued, "but I don't think he'll be back."

"He'll just come after me again tomorrow."

"Outrun him, then—you probably could. Just head for the road or the greenhouses. He's not going to come after you while a shift's ending and people are going home."

They walked toward the road. "What's your name?" the woman asked.

"Mahala Liangharad."

"You're Risa Liangharad's granddaughter, aren't you?"

"Yes."

"I thought you were."

In the grassy space beyond the trees, Sef was talking to a few men by the road. He caught sight of Mahala, then strode toward her.

"There's my grandfather," Mahala started to say, but the woman was already hurrying away from her across the road.

"You're a sight, child," Sef said as he came to her. "You've got dirt all over yourself." He knelt and wiped her face with a sleeve; she winced as he rubbed her right cheek. "And you've got a bruise there. What—"

"Somebody tried to beat me up."

"Who—"

"One of the boys. It doesn't matter." However frightened she was of Ragnar, she did not want Risa confronting the boy's parents. "Anyway, that woman came along and scared him away."

"So that's why you were with her."

Mahala nodded. "She helped me, Sef. She can't be as bad as you say."

"I said she was troubled, not bad." He took her hand as they walked along the edge of the road. A cart rolled past them, then slowed to pick up the men waiting for it. "Still, there's no reason to go out of your way to have anything to do with her."

"Sef?" She paused, then asked, "Was Einar Gunnarsson beaten and almost killed, before the Revolt?"

"That's an odd question," Sef said. "What made you think of that?"

She did not answer. "A lot of people suffered then," her grandfather continued. "Einar could have been one of them. I don't know him that well—he and Thorunn moved here from Tsou Yen when their daughter Solveig was still an infant, and he isn't a talkative man." Sef sighed. "Better not to think about those days, Mahala. Anyway, I have some good news. Dyami's going to be here in three days."

"Really?" The last time her uncle had visited, he had brought her a doll he had carved himself. He might bring her another present this time, and Risa was always in high spirits when he was in the house.

"He's only staying for five days, but luckily I have some time off. Maybe I can even talk your grandmother into postponing some of her Council business while he's here."

"Maybe I can miss school, too."

"No, you mustn't fall behind."

"I can do the work at home. The screen can teach me as much as—"

"You will go, Mahala. When you're older, you won't be able to take time off from work whenever you like. You're very lucky to be in a school, to have that chance. I sometimes wish I'd had a chance at more schooling myself, but very few kids on Earth get chosen for a school or have parents powerful enough to get them into one."

She would not be able to avoid Ragnar, who seemed to hate her because of things that had happened long ago. Mahala was beginning to see why her grandparents did not want to talk about the past. They would definitely not want her asking questions around her uncle Dyami, who had suffered more than most during the time before the Revolt.

"I wish—" Mahala began.

"What?" Sef asked.

Mahala glanced up at the slowly darkening dome. "I wish I already knew everything I had to know."

"No, you don't," Sef said.

"Why?"

"Because then there'd be nothing left for you to find out."

Her grandfather made it sound as if there would always be secrets. No, Mahala thought; every secret grasped and understood meant one less unknown that might rise up and hurt her, as Ragnar had tried to do. Maybe when all of the secrets were gone, she would no longer have to fear anything.

3

Mahala managed to evade Ragnar for two days. She got up early, before first light, gulped down bread and fruit for breakfast, and was on her way to school by the time the rest of the household was awake. After school, she ran as fast as she could to the community greenhouses to meet Sef. So far, Ragnar had not come after her, but she wondered how much longer she could keep avoiding him.

"Mahala."

She started, then looked up from her schoolwork. Karin had come over to her table and was leaning over her, a worried look on her face. "Are you feeling all right?" the teacher asked.

"I'm fine," Mahala replied.

"You looked as though you were about to faint."

Mahala tried to stifle a yawn, but failed. "It's nothing."

Karin frowned, then walked away. Ragnar was staring at Mahala from across the classroom. She gazed at her screen, trying to concentrate on the arithmetic lesson.

"Wrong," a gentle voice said from the screen. "Please add these numbers again." Mahala obeyed, then traced another set of numerals on the screen with her stylus. Ragnar would be waiting for her after school. She could take the usual way home, but Sef, with time off that he had earned coming to him, would not be working any shifts at the greenhouse during Dyami's visit.

"That is correct," the screen voice said. "Very good, Mahala." A new column of numbers appeared. Even after her uncle Dyami left, Sef would return to the west dome's bay and his usual job of repairing and maintaining the diggers and crawlers used for surface operations. He would not be able to walk home with her after school anymore.

She yawned again; the numbers seemed to float on the screen. Before she could trace out her answer, the soft chime marking the end of the school day sounded.

Mahala jumped up from her cushion, ready to run for the door. "Farewell, children," Karin called out. "Mahala, please stay—I'd like to speak to you."

The others scrambled around cushions and tables toward the door. Ragnar shot her a look of triumph as he left the room. Her only chance had been to leave the school ahead of him, and then to run home as fast as she could.

Mahala sidled around a table. "Is something wrong?" Karin asked. "You look tired. Have you had a checkup lately?"

"Paul checked me," Mahala mumbled as she approached the teacher's console. "Paul Bettinas, one of my grandmother's housemates—he's a paramedic."

"Yes, I know."

"He gave me a scan before I started school. I just haven't been sleeping enough. I'll try to go to bed early." She waited to be dismissed, but the teacher motioned to her. Mahala sighed as she sat down on a cushion near the console. Ragnar might already be waiting for her outside.

"I don't think it's just lack of sleep," Karin murmured. "You've been nervous, too—looking around as if you expected somebody to bite you. Is there some sort of problem?"

"It's nothing." She couldn't tell Karin about Ragnar. If the teacher reprimanded the boy, Ragnar would hold it against Mahala and blame her for any black marks Karin added to his record.

"Does it have anything to do with that assignment I gave you, that report on your family? Did Ragnar upset you with his questions?"

Mahala was afraid to look up; Karin was getting too close.

"It's the kind of project we always assign our new students," Karin went on, "but I should have seen that it might present a few problems for you. Your immediate ancestors were—well, much more interesting than most people."

"My grandmother told me about my mother," Mahala said, "that she killed herself. Risa said she did it because she was sorry about a lot of things."

"A lot of people besides your poor mother had reason to be sorry," the teacher said softly. "Some didn't think about anything back then except protecting themselves. It was hard to know whom to trust then or who might betray you. Your grandmother Risa was one of the courageous ones who stood up for what was right. You can take pride in that."

"I have to go," Mahala said. "My grandfather'll wonder where I am—I'm supposed to meet him." She tried to think of something more compelling to add to that lie. "My uncle's coming to visit—my uncle Dyami."

Karin smiled. "Then you must greet him for me. I was one of his schoolmates—he's welcome to visit at my house any time."

"I'll tell him."

"Are you sure you're all right?"

"I'm fine."

"Then you'd better go meet your grandfather," Karin said, still looking concerned. "Maybe I'll call your household later and speak to Dyami myself."

"Peace, Karin," Mahala said absently, then got up and wandered from the room.

Down the hallway, three doors to classrooms had been left open. Some of the older students often stayed after hours to do extra work or tutor younger students. In one classroom, Eugenio Tokugawa sat with three children. Mahala could not see the point of asking another student for help when a teaching image on the screen could offer guidance, but some students preferred a tutor. Eugenio, according to rumor, planned to become a teacher. In a way, his mother, Lena Kerein, was a kind of teacher herself.

Lena was Ishtar's Guide. The story was that Mahala's mother, her close friend, had chosen her for that position, even though Lena had turned against much of what the Ishtar cult had tried to do during Chimene's time. The Guide occasionally put one of her speeches to her followers on the public channels. The speeches were about sharing possessions with others, being honest and truthful, and the dangers of being secretive or of lusting for power. Ishtar's followers were encouraged, through good deeds, to work toward making their world the perfect world it could be and also to seek to know the will of the Spirit that was slowly coming to life on Venus. Mahala had sometimes wondered what the appeal of the cult was; Lena was a kind, easygoing woman, but not much of a speaker. Those in Ishtar had once hoped to bring everyone in the settlements to their beliefs, but many had fallen away from the cult, and few people were members of the group now. Those who wanted spiritual solace were Muslims, Buddhists, Christians of various sects, or followers of other faiths imported from Earth. Some, like her grandmother, did not look beyond the world they knew for meaning.

She came to the side doorway, then halted. Ragnar knew that she used this exit. Mahala steadied herself. If he was outside when the door opened, she could duck back inside; he wouldn't chase her down the hallway with teachers and students still in the building.

She pressed her hand against the door; it slid open. Outside, a tall girl with white-blond hair was sitting near the path. Mahala tensed, wondering what Solveig Einarsdottir was doing there. She was about to retreat inside when Solveig lifted a hand.

"Hey," the blond girl called out. "Hey, Mahala. If you're looking for my brother, he isn't here."

Mahala walked slowly toward Solveig, ready to escape back to the school if necessary. "I know he's mad at you," Solveig went on. "I saw him head into the woods." The tall girl gestured toward the trees near the school. "He's waiting somewhere along the path between here and the greenhouses. That's the way you always go, isn't it?"

Mahala was suddenly suspicious. "Is this some kind of trick?"

"It isn't a trick—honest."

"Ragnar tried to beat me up a couple of days ago."

"I know." Solveig got to her feet. "It couldn't have been much of a fight. You're so much smaller."

"This woman came along and scared him off. I didn't tell my grandparents about it. My teacher asked me what was wrong with me today, and I didn't say anything. I won't tell on him, but if he keeps it up, somebody'll find out, and it won't be my fault if he gets a black mark and a bad name."

"If anybody's going to get black marks and a Council hearing, it's Ragnar," Solveig said; her husky voice made her sound like an adult. "He is an awful bastard sometimes, isn't he?"

Mahala gaped at her, not knowing what to say.

"Oh, I care about him." Solveig took a step toward her. "He is my brother, but he does act like a shit sometimes. Anyway, he's getting tired of being mad at you. He'll give up soon, and if he bothers you any more after that, I'll fix him."

"Maybe that'll just get him madder at me," Mahala said.

"I told you—he'll get tired of this." Solveig brushed some grass and dirt from the back of her pale green tunic. "I'll walk with you, if you want. If Ragnar sees us together, he'll leave you alone. We don't have to go through the park—we can take another way."

"I'll go this way."

They strolled toward the trees. "Why is he after you, anyway?" Solveig asked.

"We had to give those reports, the ones about our people and where they're from. Ragnar said I should have put Habbers in mine, because of my uncle and grandfather joining them, and then our teacher scolded him for saying mean things about them. He tried to beat me up afterward. He said his report was better than mine and that I made him look bad. He said my parents and some other people in Ishtar had your father beaten and almost killed."

"It wasn't right of him to say that."

"His report was better than mine, though. I told him that, but it didn't help."

"He's smart," Solveig said. "He could have started school sooner than he did, but our mother thought he needed more time in the nursery learning how to get along. He likes to be alone a lot, with his screen and any wood or clay he can get his hands on."

"Why?" Mahala asked.

"So he can draw and whittle and make things out of clay. He made a model of our cat once, but he smashed it later. He gets angry."

"I know," Mahala said.

"But you don't know why he's angry." Solveig was walking more slowly. "It's because Ragnar already knows what he wants to do, and he knows he can't ever do it here."

"What does he want?"

"To do that—to make things. To draw and carve things out of wood and make clay models."

"But he can do stuff like that." Mahala turned her head and looked up at the taller girl. "My grandmother has some of the carvings her father made, and my uncle Dyami makes all kinds of things."

"I know," Solveig said. "I've seen images of that monument in Turing he made." Mahala knew that Solveig meant the monument honoring all of those held as prisoners in Turing before the Revolt. "My mother says it's the only thing on Venus she'd call real art." The blond girl sighed. "But it's still something your uncle does on the side, when he isn't doing his real work. Ragnar doesn't want to do any other kind of work except his carvings and models, and he knows that's impossible."

"We all have to do things we don't want to do." That was something Risa would say, and Mahala suddenly did not like the way it sounded.

Solveig stopped and leaned against a tree. "Maybe it'd be easier if the Habbers weren't around. They help us, but they're here mostly because they want to be, doing what they want to do when they're here and then leaving when they feel like it. Ragnar won't say so, but I think he'd rather be one of them."

"But he hates them."

"That's just what he says."

Mahala thought about Ragnar's report. She was beginning to see why it was about the best one any of her schoolmates had given, and it wasn't just because he had only one part of Earth to show. Every scene had been visually striking in some way; the report had not really needed his words. The images alone would have told the story of his people.

"Anyway," Mahala said, "even Habbers can't just do whatever they like. My grandmother's brother Benzi isn't staying on the Islands because he really wants to be there—he thought he should be here, working for Venus. That's what Risa says." Benzi spoke to them occasionally, and she dimly recalled a visit from him. He and Risa might share some genes, but Benzi Liangharad was a Habber, apart from any family he had here. He had already lived a century, as many years as most people ever did, yet age had left him unmarked. Mahala had seen his eyes change when she looked up into his face, as if he had suddenly forgotten her or was gazing beyond her at something else.

They walked on. As they were coming to the road, Mahala glimpsed Ragnar's blond head among the trees. "I was right," Solveig said under her breath.

"I didn't say anything to anybody," Mahala said hastily. "I don't want him coming after me because he thinks I told."

"I'll tell him that. He won't bother you—I'll see that he doesn't. I have to go."

"But—"

Solveig hurried toward her brother; the two quickly vanished among the trees.

Why was Solveig being so kind? The blond girl barely knew her and had no reason to look out for her. Mahala came to the road, still tired, and decided to wait for a passenger cart.

"Greetings."

Mahala looked up, surprised; she had not seen the pretty dark-haired woman near the road.

"I thought I saw that boy who was fighting with you the other day," the stranger continued. "He didn't try to hurt you again, did he?"

"No, and he isn't going to—at least that's what his sister says." Mahala walked on; the woman kept at her side. "I'm not supposed to talk to you."

"Oh?"

"That's what my grandfather said."

"I can't imagine why. I knew your parents, child. In fact, I knew them extremely well."

Mahala was intrigued. "You did?"

"I lived in their house. I was one of those closest to them."

Neither Sef nor Risa had mentioned that. "Who are you?" Mahala asked.

"My name is Lakshmi Tiris. You look very much like your mother, Mahala." No one had ever told her that. She had Chimene's long black hair and Boaz's large, almost black eyes, but Mahala knew that she was far from being a beauty. Risa would tell her that people were not responsible for their looks and that character was much more important than appearance, but Mahala had sometimes wished for more of her mother's grace.

"Perhaps we can talk," Lakshmi went on. "My house isn't far—it's just over there." She waved a hand at a cluster of houses set back from the road. "There are things I've wanted to say to you."

Mahala was curious. "I can't," she managed to say. "My uncle's coming to visit. I should get home—he might already be there."

The woman raised her brows. "Your uncle?"

"My uncle Dyami."

"Yes, of course. He never did move back to Oberg, did he?"

"He lives in Turing."

"Strange, isn't it, how many of those who were imprisoned in Turing chose to stay there after the Revolt, after they were free again." Lakshmi was silent for a while, then said, "We have something in common, you and I. Chimene took me into her household when I was only a girl. My parents were so honored when she asked if I could live with her and her companions—they were thrilled that I would be so close to the Guide. Our family had been part of Ishtar almost from the beginning, you see, and when Chimene and Boaz singled me out, my mother and father were terribly pleased. In a sense, I was your mother's first child, although I thought of her more as an older sister. You may carry her genes, but I was the child of her spirit."

"But my grandmother never—"

"Your grandmother didn't want me to come back here," Lakshmi interrupted. "I've been living in the Tsou Yen settlement between shifts, with an aunt, but I wanted to come back to Oberg. It was time for me to come back." Lakshmi's voice was hoarse, as if she had to force herself to speak. "I was close to your father, too. Has your grandmother told you much about him?"

Mahala shook her head.

"I thought not. They were enemies, your father and Risa. She probably thinks it's wiser not to talk to you about him or about your mother, either. She knows plenty about Boaz and Chimene that others don't know, things that will never be part of their records."

"Risa told me about my parents," Mahala said.

"I wonder if she told you everything. In Ishtar, we were taught to share all of our thoughts and feelings. I have never felt that secrets were necessary."

Mahala knew that she should not go any farther with this woman, but could not pull herself away. Lakshmi had turned from the road and was following a path made of flat rocks toward the nearest houses. These were new dwellings, set closer together than most of the west dome's older houses, with greenhouses that were extensions of the residences, since there was so little space for separate structures. Mahala did not see anyone around, but people would be coming home before last light. Someone might mention having seen Mahala with Lakshmi, and that piece of news could easily find its way to Risa; her grandmother had a talent for finding things out.

Lakshmi halted in front of one house. "You may come in if you like," the pretty woman said. "My housemates are all at work today, so we'll have the common room to ourselves until they get home. We can talk about your parents. It isn't right for your grandmother to keep secrets, especially from you about your own mother and father. But Risa Liangharad's probably used to doing as she likes."

"She told me everything about my parents," Mahala said, still drawn to this woman in spite of herself.

"I'm certain she didn't. You didn't know about me, did you? Risa must think keeping secrets is best for you, but all it means is that everyone here is hiding things from you and that you'll never know what they really think. Even your schoolmates probably know more than Risa ever told you. And I can tell you a lot more, things even your grandmother doesn't know."

Mahala was frightened now. Her grandparents did not want her talking to this woman, and she had promised to be home early to greet Dyami. Yet Lakshmi drew her. Didn't she have a right to find out what others already knew? Was it fair to have others whispering behind her back? She would find out sooner or later; why not now?

"I have to go home," Mahala said faintly.

"Then go, child. I'm not about to drag you inside—you may do as you like." Lakshmi stepped onto the short path that led to the house's main door.

Mahala hesitated, then followed her.

Lakshmi settled Mahala on a cushion in the common room, then sat down across from her. "Would you like anything?" the woman asked. "Some tea or juice—or perhaps a cookie?"

"I'm not hungry." Bad enough for her to be talking to the woman; she would not eat her food. This common room was much smaller than Risa's, with only one small table and a few cushions on the floor. Judging from the size of the house, Lakshmi could not have more than a couple of housemates. "What's your job, anyway?" Mahala asked.

"I'm just a greenhouse farmer at the moment, but one of the botanists has taken me on as an assistant in his lab. I much prefer it to Bat duty."

Mahala leaned forward. "You're on Bat duty?"

"Not anymore. I moved here after finishing my last shift, but I might go back to it in a couple of years if they need me. I did fairly well up there—didn't mind it as much as some."

Mahala was impressed. Those who volunteered for Bat duty earned a fair amount of respect. The Bats were the two winged satellites above Venus's north and south poles, and duty there had its risks, since the workers had to service the robot scooper ships that ferried excess oxygen from the surface installations at the planet's poles to the Bats. The process of terraforming had released much of Venus's oxygen and was continuing to do so. Some of the oxygen was combining with hydrogen to form water for the Venusian oceans; some would remain locked in rock, but the rest of the excess oxygen had to be removed if the Cytherian atmosphere was ever to support life. The oxygen was compressed inside the massive structures at the north and south poles, then brought to the Bats in tanks; some of it was used there for Bat operations, and the rest was hurled into space. There was always a chance that, during this process, the volatile oxygen might explode; Bat duty had claimed a number of lives.

Dangerous as the work was, many young people volunteered to do it. Workers on the Bats were admired for their courage, and the chance to earn more status, in addition to the extra credit, drew more than enough volunteers.

Risa, Mahala knew, had worked on the northern Bat in her youth. Surely she must know that Lakshmi had taken on the risks of Bat duty; that would be part of the woman's public record. Risa was quick to praise those who volunteered, so why was she so wary of Lakshmi Tiris?

"I'd be afraid to work on a Bat," Mahala said. Maybe, she thought, she should not have admitted that. "But my grandmother'll expect me to volunteer if I don't get into an Island school."

"I once hoped to study there." Lakshmi's dark eyes glittered, and her low voice sounded even huskier. "None of the Island schools would take me. I was a good student as a child—some even called me gifted, but studying got harder for me after that, after—" She paused. "I volunteered for the Bats as soon as I could."

Mahala stirred restlessly on her cushion. "But we didn't come here to talk about me," Lakshmi said. The woman was playing with her long dark hair now, twisting the locks around her hands, piling hair up on her head before letting it fall down her back. "I met your mother when I was a girl. I'd seen her on the screen, of course, and we often listened to one of her recorded speeches during the fellowship's weekly meeting, but there was nothing like seeing her in person. I went to live with her and her household when I was twelve."

"You told me that already," Mahala said.

"I wanted to be just like Chimene someday, beautiful and kind and loved by everyone. I longed for someone just like Boaz to love me as much as he loved her. Boaz was an older brother to me at first. He told me that someday, if it was the will of the Spirit, I might be chosen as Ishtar's Guide." She stared past Mahala, her arms still; it was almost as if Lakshmi had forgotten she was there. "I dreamed of that, but at the same time hoped it would never happen, because it would have meant living in a world without Chimene." She plucked at a strand of hair. "The fellowship isn't the same with Lena Kerein as the Guide, but then I left it some time ago. I suppose you could say that I lost my faith, as so many others did, after Chimene took her life."

"My grandmother told me why she did that," Mahala said.

"Because she was sorry? Is that what Risa Liangharad told you?" Lakshmi's mouth twitched slightly. "Oh, she was sorry, all right. She also didn't want to face a hearing, one where she might have been accused of murder, among other deeds."

Mahala wanted to run from the house. I shouldn't have come here, she thought; I should have listened to Risa.

Lakshmi said, "You don't know how your father died, do you?"

Mahala tensed. "Yes, I do. Risa said a physician gave something to him, so I guess he wanted to die, too."

Lakshmi folded her hands. Mahala could simply get up and leave, but had the feeling that the woman might stop her. Tell me, she thought; tell me everything and get it over with. It was strange that she could be so frightened, so certain that Lakshmi would tell her something horrible, while still wanting to hear it.

"I was with your father when he died," Lakshmi murmured in her husky voice. "I loved him, and he loved me—that was our secret, that we were lovers. I didn't want it to be a secret, but Boaz said we would keep it to ourselves for only a little while, that people wouldn't understand if they found out. I was only a child, you see."

Mahala shook her head in protest. She had a vague idea of what lovers did with each other, but to use a child that way was one of the worst offenses an adult could commit. "But my mother—she wouldn't have—"

"She shared herself with other men, just as Boaz did with women, but she never knew what had happened between us. I was still a child in her eyes, too young for such things. How I longed for the day when Boaz and I could be open about what we felt."

Mahala said, "I don't want to hear any more."

"Even about your father's death? Your grandmother lied to you about that. She knows the truth, and so does her friend, that Councilor Yakov Serba. Only a few others know, but they're fearful enough of Risa Liangharad to keep quiet, and you won't find the truth in Boaz's record." Lakshmi was motionless, except for her trembling hands. "Not all of the truth, anyway, just the fact that a drug brought him his death."

Mahala tried to get up. Lakshmi lifted a hand; Mahala shrank back. She could not tell what this woman might do; Lakshmi scared her more than anyone she had ever met.

"Your grandmother probably didn't tell you I was in Chimene's house when Boaz was found. I loved him, I thought I knew him, but he had many secrets, even from me. All I knew then was that Chimene had found out he was planning to betray her, that he had plotted with others to surrender all control over our world to Earth, that he was a traitor to Venus and the Project. Some think that Chimene was brave for standing against the traitors in the end and noble for taking her own life out of shame for what was done in her name, but I know better. She didn't want to answer to others for what she allowed to happen. Her own brother Dyami might have been one of the witnesses against her."

Mahala said, "I'm going."

"Leave, and you'll never know the truth. Your grandmother will never tell it to you."

Mahala's ears throbbed; her mouth was so dry that she could not swallow. It had happened long ago, Risa would say; it had nothing to do with her.

"I was in Chimene's house when Boaz was brought to her," Lakshmi said. "We'd been hiding for days during the uprising, afraid to go outside. Chimene wept when she saw Boaz—she kept telling him how much she loved him. I still didn't quite understand what was happening. She was saying that she knew Boaz was plotting her death, that he'd been using her for his own ends, but that she would give him a chance to repent. She had to forgive him—I was certain she would, that it would all turn out to be a mistake. She was my sister in Ishtar, and he was my lover—it would all work out in the end."

Lakshmi leaned across the table; her hand snaked out and closed around Mahala's wrist. "Galina Kolek, one of Chimene's housemates, was with us. Galina was a physician. She was the one who gave Boaz the drug, but it was at your mother's orders. She gave him something that produces a kind of paralysis. The men who brought him to her had to hold him down while Galina—"

"It isn't true!"

Lakshmi's fingers dug into her arm. "It's true. It took him a long time to die. I don't know how long, because Galina gave me an injection to keep me tranquilized, but I was still awake, I saw it all. Chimene kept talking to him while he struggled for breath, while he lay there knowing that his lungs and heart would eventually fail him. Chimene was telling him that she forgave him, that his death would bring him peace, that his child and hers was already growing in an artificial womb, that—"

Mahala screamed.

"Be quiet! You wanted to know the truth. I hated Chimene for tormenting him like that, for taking his life. Later, I came to hate him, too. Those were your parents, child. They were everything I loved, everything I thought was beautiful and fine, and they ruined me. It was all deception and lies, just an illusion, and when it was gone, I had nothing left. And your grandmother's gone on hiding what really happened with her own lies. I don't care what others believe, but you ought to know the truth."

Mahala struggled to her feet. "You look like them," Lakshmi whispered. "It's strange—you don't have any of their beauty, but I see them in you. It's as if you're a distorted image of your mother. You shouldn't be alive at all; Risa should never have chosen to bring you up. She should have let every part of them die. Then maybe all of those people your mother and her cult wounded so deeply could forget."

Mahala ran from the house.

She came to the road and stumbled along it until Risa's house was in sight. The dome was growing darker; people in the nearby houses set back from the road were calling to children or greeting returning bondmates. Her grandmother and grandfather were probably inside their house with Dyami, assuming his airship had arrived on time and had not made any unscheduled stops. They would be sitting around and talking, as if everything was the same as before.

She could not go home, not now. Mahala turned toward the tunnel that led to the main dome.

She walked through the long lighted passageway. A knot of people had gathered near one wall to talk; others were hurrying home. A cart carrying two workers and tied-down stacked crates rolled slowly toward her; Mahala moved to the side. A woman's voice called out her name; she kept going, past a stretch of wall covered with graffiti written in Arabic and Anglaic, following the gentle upward slope at the end of the tunnel into the main dome.

She boarded the first passenger cart that rolled past, heedless of where she was headed until the entrance to the airship bay was in sight. The entrance, twenty meters wide and thirty meters high, was open, revealing two cranes and groups of workers hovering over consoles. Clusters of tents for new settlers sat in the small grassy space outside the bay. Oberg's main dome was more crowded than any of the other three, with large buildings that held laboratories in addition to the houses that nestled near the wooded park areas. There were so many houses on the flat land that stretched to the External Operations Center that Mahala could barely glimpse the distant lighted windows of the large three-story building.

The cart rolled to a stop to let off passengers near the new community greenhouse; a gray-haired woman lingered near Mahala. "Excuse me, child," the woman said. "You look distressed. Is there anything I can do?"

"No. I'm fine."

"I take this way home all the time, and I don't think I've seen you before. Shouldn't you be—"

"I'm all right," Mahala said.

The woman climbed down from the cart. People outside the tents were kneeling on prayer rugs; others moved toward the large, walled-in courtyard that served as Oberg's mosque as the call to prayer sounded from the mosque's minaret.

She was alone. Oberg's night, its darktime, had come; a disk of silvery light glowed far overhead. Mahala had always felt secure inside Oberg's domes, protected from the dangers of the planet's surface. Now she felt trapped, unable to escape the past.

You shouldn't be alive, Lakshmi had told her. It was all very clear now, the whispers, the silences, the secrets that had been kept. Ishtar's followers had made prisoners of many, even of Dyami, but Mahala had always believed that her mother must have been misled by those around her, that she had not known what some of her followers were doing. Maybe that was just another lie. No wonder Dyami had never moved back to Oberg, even though Mahala knew that Risa and Sef wanted him there. He probably saw her the same way Lakshmi did, as part of everything he wanted to forget.

Mahala stood up; the cart halted to let her off. She was near a grove of slender trees; in the shadows, she could make out the memorial pillars that honored Oberg's dead. Several globes of light had been set in the nearby trees to illuminate the area; two mourners knelt near one pillar to lay down a wreath. She did not want to go there, where a holo image of her mother's beautiful face gazed out from the top of one pillar. There was no image of Boaz. There was no memorial to him because he had not wanted one; Risa had told her that lie, too. Now she was certain that no one had wanted her father, the traitor, commemorated.

She hurried through the trees until she came to the monument honoring her great-grandmother, then froze. A man nearly as tall and broad-shouldered as Sef stood there, a duffel at his feet. He turned his head; before she could conceal herself, he had seen her.

"Mahala! It is you, isn't it?"

The light from one of the lanterns hanging from a branch overhead had given her away. She wandered toward her uncle, her eyes down.

"Greetings, Dyami," she said. A lump rose in her throat; she had kept from crying ever since leaving Lakshmi's house, but tears were threatening to come.

"What are you doing here so late?" Dyami asked. "Did Risa send you to meet me? I didn't tell her I'd stop at Iris's monument, but she must have guessed that I would."

"I thought—" She swallowed hard as Dyami knelt next to her. "I thought you'd be at the house already."

"The airship needed repairs at the last minute. I got a message to Risa and Sef saying that I'd be late, but when did you ever know an airship to be right on time?" He touched her hand lightly. "Do they know you're here?"

"No."

"Didn't you tell them where you were going?"

"No."

"Then Risa will be worried sick. She'll be calling friends and asking who might have seen you, even putting a message on the public channels about you."

"A woman told me all about my parents. She said Chimene was a murderer and Boaz was a traitor. She told me everything about them. Risa lied to me."

Dyami drew her to him. "Who told you this?"

"Her name's Lakshmi—Lakshmi Tiris. She said she used to live with my mother. She told me I shouldn't even be alive."

He scowled. "That's a hateful thing to say."

"My mother killed my father—that's what she said. She hates them and she hates me. You were a prisoner—maybe you hate me, too."

"No, Mahala—you mustn't think that." He held her more tightly. "Please believe this—without you, everything would have been much harder for Risa and Sef. Risa thought for a long time about what she should do, but she's never regretted choosing to bring you home. My parents love you, and if they didn't tell you everything they knew about your parents, it was only because they were trying to protect you."

A sob wrenched itself from her, and then she was crying as she clung to him. Dyami held her until her sobs subsided. "Mahala." He wiped her face with his sleeve. "Let me ask you a question. What woman does this monument honor?"

"That's silly." She sniffed and rubbed at her eyes. "My great-grandmother, of course."

"Your great-grandmother. Iris Angharads. You should remember that, Mahala. There's something of her in you, too." He sat down and draped an arm over one knee. "Some people in our line are admirable, and others did shameful things, and that only makes you very much like everyone else. You can take pride in some of your people and feel ashamed of others, but in the end you have to make your own life. What your ancestors did may cast a shadow, but you can choose to move into the light."

"Dyami?" She looked up at him. "Why didn't you ever move back to Oberg?"

"Most of the people I was imprisoned with live in Turing. We have other settlers, of course, but they're the ones I'm closest to. I'll be honest—I feel easier around such people. I trust them, because I know what they are, how they behaved when we were prisoners. They had some courage. You can't say the same about some of the people here. A lot of them may be sorry for what happened, but they didn't stand against it at the time."

"You don't live in Turing because of me?"

"No, Mahala. I'll admit that, in the beginning, I wanted nothing to do with any child of my sister's. Everything in me seemed dead after I was freed—maybe you'll understand why someday, when you're old enough to view the records of the hearings held after the Revolt. I felt little after learning that Chimene and Boaz were dead, only relief that they would no longer trouble us, and then Sef told me about the child they had stored, who was gestating. I was bitter about that, angry that Risa and Sef would even consider bringing such a child into their household. Risa waited before having you brought to term because she was afraid that, if she took you in, she would lose me." He sat up and slipped an arm over her shoulders. "That bitterness left me when I first saw you. That was when I knew that Risa had done the right thing."

They were silent for a while. At last Dyami nudged her. "It would be good to sit here all night and settle everything, but if I don't get you home right away, Risa will be even angrier with me than with you."

"Dyami, are you sure—"

"That you're my favorite niece?"

"I'm your only niece."

"You're also my favorite child, which is why I absolutely insist that you visit me as soon as you have time off from school. That's one of the things I came here to discuss with Sef and Risa."

He picked up his duffel, took her hand, and led her away from the monument.

4

Mahala expected to be punished, not only for being late but also, somehow, for what she had learned while being late. Risa, after greeting Dyami, gazed at her for a long time in silence. The rest of the household, all of them gathered in the common room, seemed subdued. Mahala felt then that she had become someone else.

"I know where you went after school," Risa murmured. "When you didn't come home, I called some friends and found out you had been seen near Lakshmi Tiris's house."

"I'm sorry. I know I wasn't supposed to, but—"

"It's all right, Mahala. I'm not going to punish you. I know what was said, and Lakshmi won't bother you again. Let's set this matter aside."

Kolya and Barika brought out the food as the others settled on the cushions around the table. Mahala poked at her fish and vegetables, unable to eat, still feeling like a stranger. Dyami had made her feel a little better on the way home, but now the truth was pressing in on her again. The truth! Maybe she would find out that almost nothing she believed was true.

"I'll tell you what I've heard," Grazie said. "It isn't on her record, but they say that Lakshmi Tiris had her tour of Bat duty cut short because so few people wanted to work with her. They say she was needlessly reckless, a danger to—"

Risa shot the other woman a warning glance. Grazie tucked a loose strand of graying hair behind her ear, then turned her attention to her food.

Kolya was the next to speak. "Saw Andy Dinel today," he said to

Risa. "He hinted that he wants to talk to you about getting his record straightened out."

Risa lifted her brows. "What is it this time?"

"I'm not sure." Kolya reached for the bread and tore off a piece. "He probably got another witness willing to affirm that Andy was actually on the side of the resistance to Ishtar all along."

Paul shook his head. "I haven't forgotten how well he was doing with Ishtar, how much whiskey he was selling and sometimes even giving away to members of their patrol. Does he really think people will believe some public statement made by people he probably bribed?"

"Some will believe it," Risa said, "and what's said might even be true. Andy's just the sort to have whispered to some resisters that he was sympathizing with them even while he was profiting from Ishtar."

"And if he can clear his record," Paul said, "he'd have a better chance of winning if he ran for the Council."

Mahala had heard talk of problems with records ever since she could remember. Some people claimed that they had been falsely accused of betraying others during Venus's time of troubles, others that they had been blackmailed or were only trying to protect their families. Whenever any of these complaints became, as they occasionally did, the subject of a public hearing, people often ended up more confused than ever. A highly respected Cytherian might find his name on a recently uncovered list of those trusted by the traitors; someone known to have served on Ishtar's patrols might suddenly be revealed as a secret resister. Many people had become obsessed with cleansing their records of any black marks dating from those times.

How many people were actually what they seemed? Mahala wondered. How much of her world's history was lies or stories that might be only a part of the truth? Her own mother had been transformed by Lakshmi Tiris's story into a murderer. Her uncle, despite his kind words, might still be feeling anger at his dead sister whenever he looked at Mahala.

"Better eat your fish, Mahala," Kolya said, "before it gets cold."

"I'm not hungry."

"Shouldn't waste food," Grazie said.

"Then you can eat it," Mahala muttered.

Paul frowned at her. "Maybe I'd better take a look at you."

"Please." Mahala got to her feet. Dyami, by now, was probably sorry he had come here. "I just want to go to my room." Risa nodded at Barika; the mahogany-skinned woman quickly stood up.

Mahala left the room, Barika right behind her. "I'll read to you if you like," the young woman said. "Maybe you need a story to take your mind off things."

Mahala pressed her door open. A voice on her screen could narrate a story and punctuate the tale with images whenever she got tired of following the words, but Barika would interrupt her reading with anecdotes about the previous lives of the characters, their customs, and with digressions even about insignificant details. Mahala suspected that Barika made most of these accounts up, but her asides were often more interesting than the story itself. She felt a flicker of longing for a new story, then sighed as she sat down on her bed. "I don't think so."

"You mustn't brood on what that woman said," Barika said as she sat down on a cushion near the bed. "Risa had a talk with her."

"Risa talked to her?"

"Over the screen, as soon as she found out you'd been there. You don't think your grandmother would just let it pass, do you? Risa didn't even excuse herself to talk in private, just called the creature right from the common room. The woman admitted she had spoken to you and told us what she had said. That somebody could say such awful things to a child—"

"Then everybody else knows." Mahala bowed her head, ashamed and miserable. Her only consolation was that no one could possibly tell her anything worse about her parents than what Lakshmi had already told her. Others would no longer have to whisper behind her back.

"We're not going to say anything to anyone else, believe me," Barika said. "Anyway, Kolya was in the kitchen at the time, and Grazie was in our greenhouse." That was some comfort, Mahala supposed, since Grazie was the member of the household most likely to relate the story to other people. "Your grandmother was quite restrained, considering."

"Lakshmi said I shouldn't be alive."

"That's a horrible thing to say."

"It's true, isn't it? Everything she said about my parents was true."

"I haven't been here long enough to be sure." Barika paused. "When I was a student at the university in Harare, one of my professors used to say that the trick with history was learning how to live with it and learn from it without having it overwhelm you. Many people came here hoping to escape the past altogether. That's probably part of the reason your grandmother always wanted people to put what happened here behind them."

Barika seemed to be saying that people could not run away from what had already happened. "I wanted to find out," Mahala said. "Now I wish I hadn't."

"It's over, Mahala. The only thing to be done about it now is to try to understand why things happened as they did, so that you can think of how to make them better."

"Maybe things'll never be better."

"People came here because they thought they could be better."

Mahala's head drooped; she covered her mouth and yawned. "You're tired," Barika continued. "Time to go to sleep." The young woman helped her off with her clothes and slipped a light tunic over her head. "Are you sure you'll be all right?"

Mahala nodded. Barika covered her with a sheet, then left the room.

Exhausted as she was, Mahala could not sleep. She did not know what disturbed her more, that her parents had done what they did or that Lakshmi had been so anxious to hurt her. A woman who did not even know her could hate her because of what her parents had done.

At last she got up and went into the narrow hallway. In the common room, Risa was saying good night to Paul and Grazie. For a moment, there was the familiar silence, and then she heard her grandmother's voice again.

"It was eerie," Risa said. "Sometimes that young woman seemed quite rational, and then I'd glimpse that mad look in her eyes."

"She needs help, if you ask me," Sef said.

"She needed it years ago," Risa said. "I could have tried to do more for her."

Mahala moved toward the light. Her grandparents and Dyami were still sitting at the table. "You should be asleep, child," Risa said.

"I can't sleep."

"Then come and sit with us."

Mahala went to them. Sef held out what was left of the bread; she shook her head.

"I suppose you heard us talking about Lakshmi Tiris," Risa murmured. "I'm sorry you spoke to her and furious with her for what she said to you, but I'm partly to blame for that. Her parents sent her to another settlement not long after your mother's death and told me Lakshmi only wanted to forget what was past. Since I wanted the same thing, I was content to forget about the girl. I was relieved that there would be no hearing for Chimene, that almost no one would know what my daughter's last days were really like."

"Was it true, what she said about my mother and about what happened with Lakshmi and my father?"

"The story about your father's death is true. As for Lakshmi and Boaz and their dealings, I had no knowledge of any of that at the time, but hardly think she'd make a story like that up." Risa glanced at her bondmate, then reached for his hand. "Maybe if there had been a hearing, Lakshmi Tiris could have put her experience behind her. I should have tried to do more to help her, but I was thinking more about those close to me. Many others had suffered. I couldn't be bothered with worrying about one girl."

"You couldn't have known," Sef said.

"I should have guessed."

Dyami was silent. He had been a prisoner; that was another fact Mahala had always known without really feeling what it meant.

"What are you going to do?" Sef asked.

"Encourage her to seek some help," Risa replied. "Lena Kerein might be able to counsel her. Or, if she can't bear to speak to the Guide, there are others who might—"

"I'll speak to her," Dyami said.

Risa tensed. "You? But I don't expect you to—"

"Some in Turing meet occasionally to talk about the past. Sometimes one needs that kind of emotional support. I never cared for dwelling on such matters myself, but maybe this woman would find it easier to talk to me. If she doesn't, you've lost nothing."

"But—"

"I'll also be sure to tell her not to bother Mahala again." Dyami's voice seemed colder. "I don't expect that she will, given that the Council has ways of dealing with those who harass children, but perhaps it wouldn't hurt to emphasize that fact."

"I won't talk to her anymore," Mahala said. "I wish I hadn't talked to her at all."

No one spoke for a while, and then Risa said, "Mahala, you must go to sleep." Her grandmother leaned toward her and put a hand on her shoulder. "Make me this promise—if you have any questions about your parents, come to me with them. And I'll make this promise to you—I may not know the answer to every question, but I won't hide what I do know from you."

Mahala nodded, then stood up. Dyami rose and held out his hand. "Come on," her uncle said. She thrust her hand in his as they moved toward Risa's wing of the house.

Mahala was yawning by the time she was getting into her bed. Dyami covered her, then smoothed back her hair.

"Sleep well," he said. His voice was warmer again, but she heard sadness in it.

Ragnar Einarsson gazed sullenly at Mahala in the classroom, pointedly turned away to stare out the room's wide window whenever she looked toward him, avoided coming anywhere near her during lunch, and left school in the company of three other boys without even a glance at her. Apparently Solveig had been right about saying he would not come after her again.

Dyami was standing just outside the school's main entrance, waiting for her. She ran toward her uncle. "Why are you here?" she asked.

"To ask something of you." He looked around, but the few children outside the square school building were wandering away. "I'm going to speak to Lakshmi Tiris now. You may come along with me, but I won't insist that you do."

"But why?"

"Maybe if she sees you, she'll understand what she's done. It might make her more willing to talk to me. But the choice has to be yours."

"I'll come with you," she said.

"Good."

They walked in the direction of the greenhouses, Dyami shortening his strides so that she could keep up with him. When they reached the road, she pointed out the way to Lakshmi's house. Greenhouse workers were leaving for their homes; Mahala soon saw the dark-haired woman outside one doorway.

"That's Lakshmi," she said, pointing. Others were walking in twos and threes or in groups, but Lakshmi was alone. Maybe she did not have many friends. Mahala felt a surge of pity for her.

They waited near the stone path until Lakshmi was near them. The woman's hands were inside the pockets of her tunic, her head down.

"Greetings," Dyami said.

Lakshmi looked up; her eyes narrowed. "I know who you are," Dyami continued, "but please allow me to introduce myself. My name is Dyami Liang-Talis—I'm the son of Risa Liangharad and Sef Talis, and—"

"I guessed it," Lakshmi said in her raspy voice. "You look just like your father. I know about you."

"Then maybe you'll understand that I have some sympathy for you, in spite of what you said to my niece. I'm here to tell you that I'm willing to help you. If you talked with someone who could understand what you've gone through, you—"

"Spare me your false compassion," Lakshmi said. "I see what's going on. You want to make sure I don't talk to anybody else. That might be embarrassing for your mother the Councilor. If people find out how much she's hidden of what happened during her daughter's last days, they might wonder what other secrets she's kept."

"Do you think she cares anything about that?" Dyami lowered his voice. "If coming to terms with the past requires that you go on all the public channels with everything you know, no one will stop you. A great many people have made quite a hobby of raking over the past and revising their records." He paused and took a breath. "Maybe you should find someone here, another former member of Ishtar in whom you might confide. You could go to the Guide. Lena didn't let her faith blind her to what was going on before the Revolt, when she stood with the resisters, and she might be able to show you—"

"She can't show me anything. Neither can you." Lakshmi's mouth twitched. "Why did you bring that child here?"

"So that you could apologize to her."

The woman's eyes widened. "Apologize for what? Telling her the truth?"

"What you told her about her parents was one thing." Dyami had let go of Mahala's hand; his own, hanging at his side, was clenched in a fist. "I don't blame you for hating them. But you have no right to pass on your hatred to my niece or to make her suffer for what her parents did."

"I suppose I might have told her more gently." Lakshmi gazed at Mahala, then looked away. "But you have no right to tell me what to do. Bring a complaint against me before the Council if you have a grievance against me. Your mother would have to disqualify herself from judging me, given the circumstances. See how Risa Liangharad likes having this child testify in public after I've told my story. Otherwise, leave me alone."

"I thought you might listen," Dyami said. "My mother was sorry that she didn't do more to help you. She's willing to help you now. But if you'd rather pick at your wounds instead of trying to heal them, there isn't much we can do. We'll leave you alone, as long as you don't trouble Mahala."

"I'm not afraid of her," Mahala said, "not any more."

Lakshmi's face froze. She took a step back, then shook back her hair. "I have no reason to speak to the girl again." Her lips curved up. "The Guide, your sister, taught me a few truths amid all the lies. One was that people like you were an offense to the Spirit. How she must have hoped to bring you to the right way, to give up your perversions. But I no longer believe in the Spirit, so I can't feel a little love for you even while praying that you might turn to the true path. I can only despise you."

Dyami said nothing. Mahala, peering up at his face, could not read the expression in his brown eyes; it was almost as if he had not heard the woman's words. Lakshmi turned and left them.

"Dyami?" Mahala tugged at her uncle's sleeve. "Why did she say that? What did she mean?"

"She hates what I am. That's one of the things my sister and her comrades taught her, to hate people who find lovers among those who are like themselves. She hates me because I love men. The people in that cursed cult were taught that men and women have to come together in their embraces, that this is part of bringing life to Venus and its Spirit, and that someone like me is an offense to their beliefs. It served their purposes, having a group of people to hate, and there were enough people here from the more backward regions of Earth who already shared some of their prejudices." He sighed. "It doesn't matter, Mahala. I no longer care what such people think as long as they haven't got the power to harm me."

He took her hand and led her toward the road. "You may have learned one lesson today," he went on. "It's one of those lessons that makes me wonder if we can ever be better than we are."

"What lesson?" she asked.

"That some prefer to nurse their hatreds, to cling to old pains and past hurts even when they poison the mind holding them, even when they would be better off letting them go. The poison of the past has a way of living on, in spite of what we do."

Dyami seemed to be saying that their efforts here might be futile. If they could change a world, why couldn't they change themselves? She looked toward the dome, but saw only darkness there.

5

Long scars that might have been clawed by a giant marked the rocky cliff. As lights swept through the blackness, Mahala made out the faint yellow glow of al-Khwarizmi's domes. She seemed to feel the tanklike body of the crawler around her as she gazed through its screens and sensed the movement of its treads under her feet, but was careful not to try to direct the vehicle herself. Diggers had clawed rock from the cliffside to the west and now sat at the base of the cliff, giant slugs of metal huddled there. Two crawlers carrying mined minerals rolled slowly through the dark.

Mahala felt a hand on her arm, then reached up to remove the band around her head. The vision of the world outside abruptly vanished. Sitting in front of the screens, consoles, and panels that constituted their stations, workers wearing thin silvery bands around their heads were guiding the diggers and crawlers on the surface. Mining was not the only task of the west dome's External Operations Center. Other workers would be checking the bunkers that held the dome's life-support installations, monitoring and repairing sensors, or inspecting the distillers that extracted nitrogen from the ammonia-filled rain falling outside. At least one seismologist was always monitoring readings of seismic activity; bringing water to Venus and increasing the planet's rotation had unlocked tectonic plates, making quakes a frequent occurrence.

"Well, Mahala," Noella Sanger said, "you've put in enough time on this shift to have earned some credit."

Mahala rubbed at her shoulder, ran her hand through her short mop of hair, then stretched. "I ache all over," she said. "I wonder how Risa can stand it for so many hours."

"You're only eight years old," the engineer replied. "Risa's older, and she's trained to sit still for longer periods of time. She also gets her breaks and handles different operations to keep from getting tired and bored. Boredom can be costly—it keeps you from being attentive."

"I don't see why people have to do this." Mahala, unused to sitting in a chair, stood up and shook out her legs. "Machines and cyberminds could do most of it."

The gray-haired woman smiled. "Strictly speaking, you're right. But it costs the Project less to use people, rather than machines and cyberminds, for this kind of work."

Karin Mugabe had left Mahala and her schoolmates with Noella. The engineer had taken the children through the Center to show them the stations where people worked and to answer their questions. There had not been that many questions; most of the children were impatient to put on the bands, as if a work station were no more than a place to take a mind-tour and indulge in synthetic sensory experiences.

Now, except for Ragnar, the others had already left. The children had already known, in a general sort of way, what the people in external operations did, and there were mind-tours of the Cytherian environment that were a lot more exciting than anything they could see here.

Maybe, Mahala thought, they should have been more attentive to this work, work that kept them alive. There had been another reminder of how precarious life here could be less than twenty-four hours ago. An accident in ibn-Qurrah's airship bay had killed three technicians and two workers. Kolya's daughter Irina, who lived in that settlement with her bondmate and son, had called him with the news, although she had not been able to tell him any details.

"Your friend's still enthralled." Noella gestured at Ragnar, who was sitting at another station, a band around his head, his eyes staring sightlessly at the screen. "I'd better pull him out." She reached over and touched Ragnar lightly on the shoulder. The blond boy tensed, then lifted the slender golden circlet from his head.

"Seen enough?" Noella asked.

"I guess so." Ragnar moved his broad shoulders. "It's stupid, having it take so long."

"Having what take so long?"

"Changing everything."

"Terraforming takes a long time," Noella said. "You can't just make it happen all at once."

"We'd better go," Mahala said. "Thanks for showing us around, Noella."

"Glad to do it. Oh, when you see Nikolai, do tell him that we're expecting him after supper. We're going to borrow a cart, so we can move my things over in one trip."

"I'll tell him." Mahala followed Ragnar from the room. The short hallway was silent, the workers hidden behind doors.

"She's really moving into your house?" Ragnar asked as they stepped outside.

"Yes," Mahala replied. Noella had lived with Risa when both of them were young women, before leaving to set up her own household with her bondmate Theron Hyland. She had taken up residence with her children and grandchildren after the death of her bondmate. Theron, who had died during the Revolt trying to protect his students in the west dome's school, was another of the uprising's heroes. "Noella's moving back to our house now because of Kolya." The engineer, in front of others, persisted in addressing Kolya as "Nikolai" even when the two lovers were joining the rest of Risa's household at breakfast after a night in Kolya's room. Everyone else had been surprised at the sudden romance between the two old friends, but Mahala had suspected that something was up as soon as Noella had started using Kolya's formal first name; the woman would roll the name around in her mouth, as if tasting it. "I'll bet they make a pledge sooner or later."

Her grandparents' house, Mahala thought, was definitely getting more crowded. She had come back from her first visit with Dyami in Turing three years ago to find that Risa had acquired two new housemates, a young woman named Ching Hoa and a man, Jamil Owens. Since the two new settlers intended to become bondmates, everyone had assumed that they would eventually form their own household. Instead, Hoa and Jamil had gotten along so well with Risa's housemates that the couple had decided to stay on after making their pledge. By then, Barika and Kristof had been expecting their first child.

Now Kyril, their son, born in 640, was nearly a year old according to the Earth calendar the Cytherians continued to use, and Hoa had recently announced that she and Jamil were trying for a daughter. That meant that Hoa would almost certainly be pregnant soon, given that she and her bondmate were healthy and young. Paul, after examining them both and doing their gene scan, had practically guaranteed an immediate pregnancy.

The External Operations Center lay near the main road, and a passenger cart was rolling over the bridge that spanned the small creek, but Solveig had said that she would meet Mahala and Ragnar at a bridge farther upstream. The creek was one of the many small streams created from the cleansed and purified water collected from the acidic rains outside, streams that fed the lake in the center of the west dome's settlement. Mahala often thought of the rain and what it meant and found it beautiful.

"When's your Habber uncle supposed to get here?" Ragnar asked, interrupting her vision of the rain.

"Benzi? He said tomorrow."

Ragnar was fascinated by her uncle and her great-uncle, although he would not admit it outright. He had learned to get along with her over the past couple of years partly because of that and because Solveig had become her friend. Whenever either Benzi or Dyami was visiting, Ragnar found an excuse to come over, usually tagging along with Solveig. It was odd that, given his interest in her relatives, he was so quiet and distant when in their presence. Dyami's old friend and housemate Amina Astarte, who had come with him during his last visit, had tried to draw Ragnar out, but even she had not penetrated his barriers. Ragnar could watch Dyami do a carving for hours, but had not, despite his sister's urging, shown any of his own sketches and carvings to him. He was usually silent around Benzi and had offered no opinion to Mahala about the Habber.

"He doesn't visit very much," Ragnar said.

"My grandmother says that might be because when Benzi went to the Habbers, he probably thought he'd never see the people he left behind again. Now here he is, and for him to come and see Risa, and know she's his younger sister when he doesn't look any older than Dyami—"

"It's weird," Ragnar said.

"For him," Mahala said, "two visits in the past three years must seem like a lot. After all, he has a Link, so he can visit with people whenever he wants to without going anywhere."

"As long as they have Links, too." Ragnar thrust his hands into his pants pockets. "That stuff about all of the Habbers having Links—maybe that's just what they tell us. We don't really know if it's true—maybe it's just the Habbers who come here who have them. We can't go to their Habitats to find out for sure, we only have their word."

The Linkers of Earth and Venus had a small glassy jewel in their foreheads, the outward sign of their implanted Links, but Habbers did not wear such ornaments. That could account for some of Ragnar's doubts about them, along with the fact that the Linkers of both Earth and Venus still kept their own Links closed to those of Habbers, while the channels to the minds of the Habitats were closed to Cytherians and Earthfolk. No communications would pass between them or their nets of cyberminds. Even after all that had happened, distrust of the Habbers had not entirely died.

"Benzi wouldn't have lied about something like that," Mahala said.

"How do you know? Just because he's your uncle? Seems to me nobody really knows that much about Habbers. The new settlers are put in suspension if they make the run here from Earth with Habbers, so they never get to see very much of the Habber ships—makes you wonder if the Habbers are trying to hide something by making sure they're asleep and stored away and not able to poke around. The Habbers got the Mukhtars to back down during the Revolt, but how do we know if they could really have shut down Anwara or not if they didn't get their way?"

Anwara, the satellite and space station that circled Venus in high orbit, where shuttles from the Islands docked and freighters and torchships from Earth arrived, was also the port of any Habber vessels carrying passengers to Venus. Had Anwara been disabled, Earth would have been cut off from Venus completely, and the Islands and the settlements would have suffered the effects of a prolonged siege, might not even have survived.

"Oh, Ragnar." Mahala shook her head. "You know what the Habbers helped us do, how much help they still give to Earth. They're keeping one of their ships in orbit to study the changes here. I don't think they'd have a ship nearby unless they knew they could protect it."

"And there's another thing." The blond boy slowed his pace as they moved down a grassy slope toward the creek. "They send Habbers here, and their pilots spend time on Earth before they come back with more settlers, but nobody from here or Earth ever gets to go to one of their Habs."

"What are you talking about? Those Islanders who escaped to one of the Habs came back. Benzi went there, and my grandmother's first bondmate is still living in a Hab. The Habbers always said they'd welcome anybody. We're the ones who don't want to go, and it's the Mukhtars who won't let people from Earth go there."

"I haven't seen any Habbers going out of their way to invite us," Ragnar said, "and your uncle and your other grandfather don't count. They're Habbers now, not Cytherians. And those Islanders—can you really trust anybody who ran away when things got hard and then came back when things here were settled? Nobody goes to a Hab and comes back without being different. Maybe they don't let some people ever come back."

The boy had probably been hearing such talk from his father. Einar Gunnarsson had suffered at the hands of traitors and might have paid for his resistance to Ishtar with imprisonment or worse if the Habbers had not intervened ten years ago, during the Revolt. Einar should have been grateful to the Habitat-dwellers, yet he was still suspicious of them.

Mahala thought of her grandfather Malik Haddad, who had fled to the Habitats with the group of Islander specialists. Why hadn't he returned with the others? What had happened to him in the over twelve years since then? Risa had asked Benzi, who had said only that Malik was reasonably content with his life and spent much of his time in study. Mahala had never asked Benzi for more details about her biological grandfather; maybe it was time she did.

Four new prefabricated houses with white sides, small windows, and flat roofs had gone up near the stream they were approaching. Small greenhouses next to them had been built since the last quake a couple of months ago, a quake that had been strong enough to level a few houses. No one had been seriously injured, largely because of the lightweight materials used in the construction of their residences. They did not need to construct durable houses of sturdy materials here. The climate of the settlements was always the same, with warm air that seemed slightly heavier and more humid near the larger artificial bodies of water; they did not have to build against bad weather, for no storms ever raged inside the domes. Dwellings could be enlarged or taken down easily, as necessary, but lately it seemed to Mahala that even more houses were going up. She had not felt how crowded Oberg was becoming until she had visited Dyami in the more sparsely settled domes of Turing.

Solveig was standing on the footbridge leaning against the railing, tossing pebbles into the stream below. She looked up as Mahala and Ragnar hurried toward her.

"You took long enough," Solveig called out. She rested her back against the railing. Solveig would soon be eleven, but already she was taller than Risa. She had let her pale hair grow long, and it hung down her back in two braids. "What did you see at the Center that kept you there so long?"

"That cliff," Ragnar said, "the one where the diggers are mining. I'd like to carve something on that. I was looking at the patterns the diggers made and thinking about what I could do with them." He flung his arms out. "A big face—I could carve a big face staring right into the dome!"

Solveig smiled. "You couldn't go out there to do it."

"So I'd use a digger." Ragnar frowned at his sister as she shook her head. "What good is that cliff going to be when all the ore's gone? Might as well do something with it."

"Maybe there won't be anything left of it," Solveig said. "Maybe it'll just become a hillside covered with trees."

"As if we're going to be around long enough to see any trees growing out there."

Solveig plucked at a braid. "I wish I could be around that long," she murmured. "Everything here could have been done without us. They could have just put more cyberminds inside the domes and had them manage everything."

"They wouldn't have needed domes at all," Mahala said, "just the Islands and Anwara. The cyberminds and the Islanders could have done everything from there."

"I don't care what happens here later," Ragnar said. "I'd just like to see some other places besides Oberg."

Mahala had heard the boy say that often. "So do I," she said fervently. Ragnar glanced at her; she had never admitted that to him before.

"Where would you go?" Solveig asked.

"I haven't really thought about it that much," Mahala replied. "The Islands, of course, and Anwara." Given that the Islands sailed in Venus's upper atmosphere and Anwara was the nearest space station, this did not sound very adventurous on her part. "I'd want to see Earth, too."

"Earth's a big place," Ragnar said. "You'd never be able to see it all."

"Well, I could see some of the places my people came from. And then—" Mahala paused.

"You'd come back here," Ragnar said, "because there isn't anywhere else to go."

"There are the Habs," Mahala said, "and maybe—" She turned toward the others. "But I'd come back."

"You've been to Turing," Ragnar muttered. "That's farther away than I've been."

They followed the creek toward the lake, walking between two rows of elms with boughs that formed a canopy overhead. Her teacher Karin had told Mahala that the trees here were not like those of Earth, however much they resembled them, that the elms and oaks and willows had been bioengineered to mutate into trees that produced more oxygen than did their Earthly counterparts. Mahala loved these elms and knew that they would be preserved by the people of Oberg; they were needed to maintain the dome environments, but more settlers were now encroaching on the open spaces near them.

Clusters of houses covered the land near the water; the lake's silvery surface was almost as smooth as a mirror. "Did Karin tell you which new teachers you're getting yet?" Solveig asked.

"Marina Delon," Ragnar replied, making a face; his new teacher was reputed to be strict.

"Kiyoshi Tanaka," Mahala said. According to rumor, Marina got the children who weren't doing as well as expected, and Kiyoshi was assigned those who showed intellectual promise. Mahala was not sure she believed that. The teachers believed in keeping each class together for about three years before breaking it up, so her classmates would have ended up with different teachers even if they had all been doing equally well. They had to learn how to get along with others, and that would not happen if they remained with the same group throughout their schooling.

"You'll be in my class, then," Solveig said.

"For a while, anyway." Solveig would probably soon move up to one of the smaller classes of older students, then divide her time among different teachers, depending on her interests and how well she did.

Everything was changing. With the new people in her grandparents' household, Risa and Sef did not have quite as much time for her.

Now there would be a new teacher and classmates to adjust to, and Risa would soon be expecting her to take on more household tasks.

Maybe she would not feel quite so uneasy if she had at least some idea of what her future work might be. True, she was only eight, with years ahead of her before she had to make any hard decisions, but she could already guess which of her schoolmates would leave school early to apprentice themselves and what kinds of further studies others might pursue. Unlike some of the more privileged children of Earth, who would be expected to assume positions of power and influence in adulthood, they did not have the luxury of postponing the biological changes of adolescence in order to concentrate on their studies.

Among their fellow students, only she, Solveig, and Ragnar seemed to have no particular direction. Ragnar neglected his lessons for his artistic hobby, while Solveig spent much of her time studying astronomy, a useless interest to pursue on their cloud-enveloped world. Mahala was unable to focus on any one subject. A lesson in the history of Venus would lead to curiosity about the engineering that had built the Parasol and the Islands, and that in turn guided her to readings and history mind-tours about the events on Earth that had originally led to the Project. Karin did not seem too worried about this tendency, but had mentioned it to Risa and Sef during conferences. "Your teacher made it sound," Risa had said later, "as if you want to swallow the universe."

She ought to have some sort of goal by now, even if it was still vague. She could aspire to an Island school, perhaps even fulfill her dream of seeing Earth by winning a place at its Cytherian Institute. If she did very well, she might be among the few chosen for Linker training, although she would have to show true brilliance for that. Yet whatever happened, she would eventually come back to Venus and live out her life on an Island or in a surface settlement. She might even end up back in Oberg, living in the west dome.

They came to a slope that led down to the lake. Three men were out fishing on one dock, while other fisherfolk had taken a boat out on the water.

"Maybe we can get a ride across," Ragnar said. Sometimes a couple of the fishers, if they were in a good mood, would row the children to the other side.

"I'd better not," Mahala said. "Risa was furious when she found out about the last time. She thinks I'll fall in and drown."

"Our mother's the same way," Solveig said. "Somebody ought to teach us how to swim. Then they wouldn't have to worry."

"They won't, though." Ragnar kicked a loose pebble along the path. "They'd just say it's a waste of time. You're supposed to use a boat for fishing, not to fool around, and if you're fooling around, you shouldn't be in a boat. So why learn to swim when you'll never use it except when you're doing something you shouldn't be doing?"

Risa would have agreed with the boy, although she would not have come up with such a convoluted argument. Mahala had a bond with Ragnar and his sister. He wanted to do his art, Solveig hoped for a glimpse of the stars, and she longed to see places that were impossible to reach. None of them would ever fulfill such dreams on Venus.

Risa's housemates seemed awkward in Benzi's presence at first, as they had the last time he had visited. Kristof and Barika showed off their son, Kyril, let him sit in Benzi's lap when the Habber showed no objection to that, then vanished with the child to their rooms in Paul's wing of the house, as if to ration his exposure to the Habber. Hoa was even quieter than usual, while her bondmate Jamil was completely tongue-tied. Only Grazie, content to fill Benzi in on the latest Oberg gossip, was at ease, chattering away as Benzi listened politely.

By supper, their shyness had passed, and Benzi, sitting next to Risa, seemed less distant. He laughed at Kolya's jokes, told Noella how pleased he was to see her again, and ate everything the others urged on him. Sef was relating the news of Earth he had heard in the airship bay during his shift there. Mukhtar Kaseko Wugabe, it appeared, was retiring and relinquishing control of Earth's Council of Mukhtars. After dropping from sight for several days, he had turned up in his homeland of Azania to announce that he was giving up his position to pursue a quiet life in a small town bordering the veldt. No one believed that his retirement was voluntary, and there was no word on who might be in control of the Council of Mukhtars now.

"This isn't good news," Risa said. "Any changes among the Mukhtars make things more uncertain for us."

"But Earth has no reason to act against your interests," Benzi said, "and our relations with them are still peaceful, even if strained. The Project's going well, and conditions in the Nomarchies seem calm. At the camp outside Tashkent, even the inmates and Guardians seemed remarkably free of rancor." The Habber had recently returned from Earth with new settlers from that camp, where those hoping to be allowed to come to Venus waited for passage. "A Guardian officer mentioned a few rumors he'd heard to me. Apparently some in power were worried that Mukhtar Kaseko might still be looking for a way to strike at the Habitats. The other Mukhtars didn't particularly care to give up the calm they have now for glory, so it seems that they decided to ease Kaseko out."

"Benzi met the Mukhtar after the Revolt," Grazie said to Risa's newer housemates. "He was part of the Habber delegation that went to Anwara to meet with Mukhtar Kaseko." The Cytherians had finally risen against those in Ishtar who were conspiring to seize control of Venus's settlements and ally themselves with Earth; a speech of Chimene's in which she had revealed that plot had roused the Cytherians to action. The Habbers had traveled to Anwara then to learn what Earth's intentions were. Happily, they had found out that Kaseko Wugabe, instead of coming to Venus's satellite to reassert Earth's control over the Project, had intended to deceive the conspirators once they revealed their plans to him.

Mahala had learned most of this from records recounting the events of the Cytherian Revolt. Chimene's speech had saved Mukhtar Kaseko from having to use his forces to crush the plotters; the Cytherians themselves had been roused to fight against them. Her mother Chimene's role in the rebellion made up a little for some of her more questionable deeds.

"Kaseko Wugabe was feared on Earth," Hoa said. "I used to wonder why a former Guardian Commander had chosen such a peaceful settlement of that crisis. It always seemed—" She gestured at Benzi with one slender arm. "When I came here, I began to think that you Habitat-dwellers had more to do with the agreement between Earth and Venus than seemed obvious. I wondered if Mukhtar Kaseko had agreed to go back to Earth only to plot ways to regain control." She gazed at Benzi silently for a moment. "I think we're all safer with him in retirement."

"I hope you're right," Paul said, "but if you'd lived here longer, you might understand why we get worried. Changes on the Council of Mukhtars often resulted in more problems for us and more uncertainty for the Island Administrators who have to deal with them."

Risa turned toward her brother. "I don't suppose," she murmured, "that you heard any gossip about who might replace Mukhtar Kaseko while you were on Earth."

"No." Benzi sipped his tea, looking unconcerned. Mahala suspected that her great-uncle would look the same way even if disaster loomed. She supposed that he cared about her grandmother and her household, or he would not have bothered to come here, but she had never been able to tell how deep his feelings ran.

When they finished their meal, Mahala helped Risa and Kristof clear the dishes, then returned to the common room. Benzi was already saying good night to the others. He was making excuses about being tired from his trip, having barely had time to rest up after returning to Venus from Earth. Mahala was doubtful. Habbers, with their youthful and rejuvenated bodies, did not seem the type to get weary after long journeys. Perhaps Benzi only wanted to be alone in order to commune with other Habbers through his Link.

He caught Mahala's eye and smiled; his eyes seemed warmer. Maybe she should speak to him now, before she changed her mind.

"Benzi? I have to ask you something."

"What is it?"

"Could I ask you in your room?"

"Of course."

Risa had put him in the room across from Mahala's; she followed him to the end of the corridor. Benzi pressed the door open and ushered her inside. There were still two empty rooms in Risa's end of the house, but this one had always been small, and the bed took up most of the space. She perched on the bed as Benzi sat down and leaned back against the wall. "What do you want to know?" he asked.

"About my grandfather—my grandfather Malik." She paused. "I know you can call other Habbers with your Link. Can you talk to him?"

"Yes, I can. It would take a little while—one doesn't interrupt someone's thoughts abruptly through the channels. If I wanted to speak to Malik, I would send him a message first, then wait for him to receive it and respond."

"Could you do that right now?"

"Certainly, if I needed to communicate with him."

"Then would you? Give him a message from me, I mean. I just want to know if he ever thinks about us, if he might come back sometime."

"I can't," the Habber replied.

"But why—"

"I can't because I already know that he won't respond to my message."

"Why not?"

"I'll try to explain. Malik was unhappy here. He wasn't one of those who came to Venus willingly—he came because he was in disgrace on Earth and there was nowhere else for him to go. He tried to make a life for himself on Venus, but he was unhappy here, and when a chance came to flee, he took it. I was younger than Malik when I became a Habitat-dweller, and I still found the adjustment difficult. For him, it's been harder still. He was a scholar on Earth and a teacher here, but he has no function now except that of a child who is still learning. The temptation is always there for him to retreat into the sensory experiences his Link can provide."

"But why won't he answer you?"

"Because he wants no messages from Venus," Benzi said. "He told me so years ago, after I sent a message telling him that Risa had brought his grandchild to her house. He's struggling with his new life. It's too painful to be reminded of the old, of the people he abandoned."

"Wouldn't he even have a message for me?"

Benzi shook his head. "Try to understand. Malik still wonders if he did the right thing. To hear from you or any of the others here would only reopen old wounds." He put his hand on her shoulder. "Maybe, after enough time has gone by, he'll want to hear about you. It was many years before I could even think about the parents I left, but in time I volunteered to ferry settlers from Earth to Anwara. It took even longer to bring myself to come here."

"Do you think he'll ever come back?" she asked.

"I can't say."

"Well, if he doesn't, I'll have to go see him."

Benzi sat up. "You'd be willing to do that?" A smile flickered across his lips. "You wouldn't be afraid we'd keep you there and refuse to let you come back?"

"No. I wish—" Mahala drew her brows together. "I wish I could see other places."

"Maybe you will. In the meantime, there's always a mind-tour. Many prefer that to actual travel."

"I don't. I know they're not real, however they look and feel, that they're only something somebody else put together. You're only seeing what they want you to see. I want to be in a place and see it for myself."

"I'll confess something to you," Benzi said. "One of the reasons I left the Project was that I didn't want to be limited to one world. I thought—" The distant look had entered his eyes again. "Yet here I am. Apparently I still have my own small contribution to make to this world. Risa would expect me to remind you that you have a new world to build."

"But I'll never see it. We'll still be living inside these domes when I'm old."

"Things could change, Mahala. Maybe—" Benzi stiffened and held up a hand. He would be opening his Link to a message from another Habber. Maybe he was wrong about her grandfather; perhaps Malik had suddenly decided to send a message after all.

Benzi's eyes closed; except for an occasional twitch of his mouth, she would have thought he was in a trance. He opened his eyes and focused on her.

"The message was from Balin," he said. Balin, who was also a Habber, lived with other Habbers in Turing, but often stayed with Dyami at his house. The two men had been lovers for some time. Once, some people would have disapproved of their relationship because it involved one man loving another. Now others were more likely to be critical of the pair because it was a Habber whom Dyami loved.

"Was it about Dyami?" Mahala asked.

"Yes. He didn't tell me much, only that Dyami would be coming to Oberg as soon as possible. He might already be calling Risa about that. It seems he has something very important to discuss with my sister."

"What could it be?"

"It concerns Amina's niece. Amina's sister and her bondmate were among those who died in that airship bay accident in ibn-Qurrah." Benzi's voice was steady, but his hand shook as he clutched Mahala's shoulder. Risa had said that Habbers had trouble dealing with any death, knowing as they did that their odds of an accidental death increased during the course of their long lives. Even a death that came at the end of a long and happy life disturbed them, and Amina's sister could not have been that old.

"How awful for Amina," Mahala whispered.

"Her sister left a daughter who's about your age. Apparently Amina and Dyami have already brought the girl back to their house."

"But then why would Dyami be coming here? Amina must need him there even more now."

Benzi released her. "I think Dyami is going to ask Risa to let you go back with him."

"But how can you—"

"Dyami's wanted to bring you there for some time, and so have I. We've discussed the possibility in the past. Now there's even more reason for him to bring you to his home."

She was about to ask him why he and Dyami had been considering such plans for her, and then the Habber rose to his feet. "I had better go to Risa," he said. "She'll be concerned about Amina when Dyami gives her the news, " he added, then hurried from the room.

6

"I can't do that," Risa was saying. "Don't get me wrong, I'd do almost anything for Amina. If you think it would do her and the child good to come here for a while, I can find room for them. Surely that would make more sense than dragging Mahala off to Turing."

Mahala sat in the corner of her grandparents' bedroom. Benzi and Dyami sat on cushions near her, while Risa and Sef were seated on the bed. They would have been more comfortable in the common room, but then everyone else in the household would have been offering an opinion on Dyami's proposal.

"I'm not dragging her off," Dyami said. "Amina's niece could use a young friend now, but Mahala has to decide if she wants to live with us or not." He glanced at Mahala. "This has always been your home, and I don't want you feeling that I pressured you into doing something you didn't want to do."

Mahala tried to imagine what it must be like for the girl. Amina's niece Frania, in the space of a few hours, had suddenly lost a mother and father; that had to be much worse than never knowing one's parents at all. Amina and her sister had lost their mother a couple of years ago, and their father was now an old man. Amina had, according to Dyami, promised her sister that she would become Frania's guardian if anything happened to both of the girl's parents.

"You always say," Dyami continued, "that it isn't good for any child to be the only child in the house."

"So now you'll use my own words against me." Risa shook her graying head. "That girl wouldn't be the only child in your house if you'd had one of your own by now. You could have made an arrangement of some kind. You might have talked Amina into it—you could have done worse than making that good young woman your bondmate and giving her a child by whatever means you could."

Dyami scowled, but Risa had said the words gently, and at last his face softened. "Amina's my friend, but she was never sure if she wanted a child of her own. I wasn't about to use her simply to give you another grandchild." He looked around at the others. "But we have a child to care for now, and we're prepared to welcome her. I also think Frania and Mahala might both benefit by making a home with us."

Mahala sighed. This whole business concerned her, so naturally she had to be present, but it did not look as though the matter would be settled very easily.

"Forgive me, son." Risa rested her elbows on her folded legs. "I'm getting to be an old woman, and I've picked up the bad habit of repeating myself even when I know it won't change anything. I'd miss Mahala terribly, but I can understand why you want her with you now. What I don't understand is how you and Benzi could have been plotting to steal her from me all this time, with no thought of—"

"Stealing her!" Dyami raised his brows. "Isn't that a little harsh? We admitted that we've discussed her future in the past. We weren't about to do anything without speaking to you first."

"This isn't just about Amina's niece. You're using that as an excuse."

"Helping that child," Benzi said, "would be a good enough reason by itself for Mahala to go, but I'll admit that it isn't the only reason. She would have more chances in Turing. Even in just a few years, it's clear that the students there are far ahead of those in the other settlements. She'd have better teachers and a better school, as well as a chance to meet more of my people—Turing is still the only one of the surface settlements where we Habbers feel completely at ease."

"That's all very well," Risa said, "but she can learn everything she needs to know here, and I can't see what she would gain by meeting more Habbers."

"Risa." Sef put his hand over hers. "It's unkind to say that to your brother."

"It isn't that I have anything against them, but even Benzi would admit that they're very different from us." She gazed steadily at her Habber brother and said, "I've had people come to me, just a few, worried that their children look at your people and see how free they are and how much longer their lives are than ours, and then wonder why they can't have an easier life doing what they like instead of settling for the harder lives we have to live. Maybe it's better if you keep your distance."

Benzi held up a hand. "Isn't it pointless to go on about this until we've asked Mahala what she thinks?"

"Mahala," Risa said, "is only eight years old."

"Almost nine," Mahala interrupted.

"She's still a child."

Dyami rested his back against the wall. "She's old enough to make certain choices, and this one isn't irreversible. She can always come back to Oberg if she decides that's what she prefers." He turned toward Mahala. "What do you think?"

All of them expected something of her, and she could not fulfill the hopes of one without hurting another. Why did so many of their hopes have to rest with her? Maybe it was just as well that her grandfather Malik had not come back; he would have been yet another adult making demands on her, waiting for her to measure up to his expectations.

"I don't know what I think." Mahala got to her feet. "Hearing all of you arguing about it isn't helping me to decide." She moved toward the door. "I'm going over to Solveig's, if it's all right with you."

"It's almost time for supper," Sef said.

"I can eat there. Solveig and Ragnar probably owe me for all the meals they've had here. Maybe I'll get a chance to think." She left the room.

Einar Gunnarsson's household was already eating when Mahala arrived, but they made a place at the table for her. Ragnar pushed a large bowl of beans toward her while his mother went to the kitchen to fetch a plate.

"Do your grandparents know you're here?" Einar asked. He was a tall, rangy man, with hair nearly as blond as his son's.

"I told them where I was going," Mahala replied.

"Just wanted to make sure, since nobody called to say you were on your way. Maybe I should call—"

Thorunn Ericsdottir returned and set a plate in front of Mahala.

"Let the girl eat in peace," she said to her bondmate. "You can call her grandparents afterward."

Mahala helped herself to some beans. This family was a lot quieter at meals than her household. Thorunn began to speak to her brother Ingmar about a new strain of cabbage she wanted to try in their family greenhouse; Einar was silent. Solveig had told Mahala that her father thought a lot of talk at meals was bad for the digestion. Even Lars, resting in a cradle at his mother's side, let out only a occasional whimper.

"Thank you for supper," Mahala said when they had finished eating.

Einar grunted. "You're welcome anytime," Thorunn said as she stood up. "We always have enough for one more, especially someone who eats as little as you do."

"I've seen her eat a lot more than that," Ragnar said.

"Well, I hope you had enough, then." A look of concern crossed Thorunn's fine-boned face. "Did something disagree with you?"

"Oh, no." Mahala tried to smile. "It was delicious, Thorunn. I just wasn't that hungry."

"I'll call Sef," Einar said, "and tell him Mahala's here. Ought to find out when he expects her back home."

"You'll want some fresh fruit for breakfast," Solveig said to her mother. "We'll go out and get some." She motioned to Mahala; Ragnar followed them outside.

"What is it, Mahala?" Solveig murmured as they hurried toward the family's small greenhouse. "Something's bothering you."

"Dyami's been arguing with Risa ever since he got here."

"What about?"

"He wants me to go back to Turing with him. He says it's because of Frania, Amina's niece—because it'd help her to have a friend now, someone else living with her who also doesn't have a mother and father."

Solveig pressed open the greenhouse door. "He may be right. Losing both her parents—that must be hard. I can't see why your grandmother would mind." They walked past shelves of cabbages, tomatoes, and sprouting potato plants until they came to a row of dwarf peach trees. "You can do your lessons in Turing just as easily as here, and we're getting another break from school soon anyway."

"You don't understand. Dyami wants me to live there, at least for a while. He and Benzi have been talking about it. That's why Risa got so upset—because they admitted they were thinking about it all along. It isn't just because of Amina's niece."

A few cloth bags hung on the wall near them. Solveig pulled one off its hook. "Frankly, I think you're lucky." She studied the peaches, then reached for one. "I wouldn't mind going to a school in Turing for a while. They say some of the Habbers there even come to the classes sometimes." She slipped the ripe peach into her bag as Ragnar picked another. "I'd like to talk to a specialist who really knows something about astronomy."

"You always said you wanted to see other places," Ragnar said. "Even Turing's a start."

"You don't understand." Mahala sat down on the floor. "It isn't that simple. My grandmother acts as if my uncle and great-uncle want to take me away from her, and in a way, they do. I think Dyami's hoping I'll get into an Island school, and Benzi—" She sighed. "I'm not sure what he wants . . . but he expects something from me. He sort of said that living in Oberg might hold me back."

Solveig handed her brother the bag, then sat down next to Mahala. "But your grandmother must want what's best for you, too."

"Oh, she does, but she would be just as happy if I apprenticed myself in a few years and settled down in Oberg."

"Maybe you'll end up doing that anyway." Ragnar picked another piece of fruit, then bit into it. "Just because you're going to Turing doesn't mean you'll do well in school later. You might mess up."

Solveig made a face at him. "That's a great thing to say."

Mahala said, "I don't know if I'm going."

"But why wouldn't you?" Solveig asked.

"Nobody's going to force me. I'm the one that has to decide. Risa and Sef need me, too, you know—I'm the only grandchild they have." She could not explain her feelings to them. Dyami and Benzi had all the best arguments on their side, and even if they did not, she ought to do what she could for Amina's niece. Risa and Sef would miss her, but she would visit often, and they would have their housemates and their other obligations to occupy their time.

She was afraid. That was what she could not tell Solveig and Ragnar. To leave meant uncertainty. Mahala was beginning to see why it might be easier to settle for what she already had.

"I'll miss you," Solveig said.

"You sound as if I've made up my mind to go."

"You'll go, Mahala. You're a fool if you don't. You should do any-thing you can that might give you a chance at what you want. We won't get that many chances."

"What do you mean?"

"You know perfectly well," Solveig replied. "You'll have better teach-ers in Turing, and that'll give you a better chance at an Island school later. You might find some kind of work you really want to do. Stay here, and it still might happen, but it isn't as likely." The blond girl drew up her knees and rested her arms across them. "You said it yourself. Your uncle thinks living here might hold you back, and your grand-mother would be happy if you lived the way she does. Is that what you want?"

"I don't know."

"You do know, Mahala. They tell us about the Revolt and how it made us free. We're not free. The Project still owns us."

"We can decide what we want to do," Mahala objected. "We elect our own Councils instead of the Island Administrators or the Mukhtars or somebody else telling us what to do."

"We can decide what we want to do as long as it helps the Project. We live inside these domes and dream about a world we'll never see." Solveig sighed. "Sometimes I wonder what the Administrators would do if they thought the Project might not succeed."

"What do you mean?" Mahala asked. It was something she had never heard said.

"Even if they knew things wouldn't work out, they couldn't come out and admit it. I'm not the only one who wonders about that—I've heard older kids talking about it, when the teachers aren't around. What are they going to do, tell people that all their work's for nothing?"

"But the Habbers are helping," Mahala said. "Why would they bother sending their people here and keeping a ship in orbit if they thought the Project would fail?"

"That's a good question," Solveig murmured. "Maybe we need more help from the Habbers than the Administrators will admit. Maybe their help is the only thing keeping us going. And ask yourself this—why's your Habber uncle so interested in getting you out of Oberg? Why was he talk-ing to Dyami before about what you ought to do? Maybe he knows some-thing we don't."

Mahala shook her head. "I'm the only child in our family. Who else can he look out for here? That's all it is."

"Maybe you're right," Solveig said, "and everything's going along fine. Still, you should think of yourself and what you might want later."

Mahala glanced up at Ragnar. The boy had been so quiet that she thought he might not have been listening, but he was leaning against a shelf, the bag hanging from his hand, his pale eyes on her.

"What do you think?" Mahala said to him.

"Do you really have to ask?" Ragnar's mouth twisted. "You know what I'd do. Make up your own mind, Mahala. I know you want to leave—you're just afraid."

"I can't just think of myself." Risa was speaking through her.

"You wouldn't be," Solveig said. "You'd be doing something for yourself and maybe helping that girl, too—look at it that way."

"Yeah," Ragnar muttered. "You can have it both ways."

"I'd miss you, Solveig. You're the best friend I have."

Ragnar snorted. "That isn't much of a reason to stay."

Solveig wrinkled her nose. "And getting away from you is another good reason for her to go."

Ragnar hefted the bag. "We'd better go inside."

They moved toward the door. As they stepped outside, Mahala saw Dyami coming toward them along the path. "I was going to come home in a little while," she called out.

"I'm sure you were," her uncle said. "Einar called Sef and said he and Thorunn had fed you. I thought I'd come over and walk you home." He paused. "We were worried about you."

"I'm fine."

Dyami nodded at the other children. "What's in the bag?"

"Peaches," Ragnar said, "for our breakfast. How soon are you going to go back to Turing?"

"As soon as possible. Tomorrow, or the day after at the latest."

"Then Mahala has to make up her mind fast if she's going to go along."

"I see she's been discussing things with you." Dyami glanced from the boy to Mahala. "You can have more time to think about it. Maybe you should wait until your school break. You don't have to travel back with me now if you'd rather—"

"Why think about it any more?" Mahala gazed up into Dyami's face, but could not read his expression in the darkness. "If I stay here, it'll just give Risa and everybody else more time to talk me out of going."

Dyami's lips curved into a smile. "Have these two been trying to convince you to stay?"

"No. They think I should go, too. But you better not say that to Risa."

"I won't." Dyami held out a hand. "I'll take that inside if you like — I should greet your parents before we go."

Ragnar handed him the bag. "So you're going after all," he whispered as the door to the house slid shut behind Dyami.

"Yeah." Mahala swallowed.

"Maybe tomorrow?"

"Yes."

He turned away without speaking and went inside. "It's good you're leaving," Solveig murmured, "but I'm still going to miss you. Promise you'll call or at least leave messages once in a while."

"I promise." Mahala clutched her friend by the elbows. "Maybe it won't work out. I might want to come back."

"Don't go there feeling like that, Mahala, or it probably won't work out. Look forward to it. You have to do the best you can." There was a tremor in the tall girl's voice. "You'll be visiting here, anyway, during breaks."

"And maybe you can come to Turing."

"Maybe."

"I'll call you when I know what time we're leaving."

"No." Solveig wiped at her face with the edge of one sleeve. "I'll say good-bye to you here. It'll just be harder later." Mahala heard a choked sound and realized that the other girl was crying. She threw her arms around her friend, afraid she would cry herself.

The door to the house opened. Solveig freed herself from Mahala as Dyami came outside, then ran toward the house. "I'll call you as soon as I get to Turing," Mahala said.

"Call me after you're settled." Solveig disappeared inside.

Dyami was silent as they walked toward the wide stone path that led to the road. Birds chirped from the nearby trees as they settled down to rest; Mahala heard the sound of voices through a house's open entrance before the door closed. Then, for just an instant, the silence pressed in around her until a distant shout and the howl of a cat dispersed it. She had sensed the silence before, a stillness that made her feel as if the dome that enclosed her could also suppress all sound. Could there be such a silence on Earth, where people were free to move across its surface and breathe its air? It seemed to her that there would always be something to hear there—the wind she had heard only in mind-tours of distant places, the roll of thunder, the crashing of waves against the dikes built to hold back the risen sea.

They came to the road and stopped under one of the lanterns to wait for a cart. "Is Risa still upset?" Mahala asked.

"A little. She's saying that it probably makes sense for you to live with me for a while and that you can always come home when Frania's over her loss. Risa's not really upset with you—she's a lot angrier at Benzi and me. Given that we've just about admitted that your life here would be more limited than it might be somewhere else, I can't blame her. It's as if we're saying that her efforts aren't good enough."

"What if—" She hesitated. "What would happen if the Project didn't work? What if it turns out we can't ever make Venus what we want?"

"Well, there may be some obstacles that turn out to be more of a problem than expected. Even so, we have to assume that we can find a way around them."

"But what if we can't?"

"How can I answer that?" Dyami's voice sounded strained. "To be honest, I haven't thought about it that much. I doubt many people have, especially those who had to live through the time before the Revolt. Better to avoid thinking about it. We have to believe that a new world's possible here, or else we're throwing our lives away."

"Dyami!" a voice called from behind them. "Mahala!"

She turned to see Ragnar running toward them, a cloth bag slung over one shoulder. He slowed to a stop, then set down the bag.

"What is it?" Mahala asked, wondering if he had come after her to say farewell.

Ragnar said, "I have to ask you something."

"What?"

"Not you, your uncle." Ragnar squatted by his bag. "Tell me if this stuff's any good." He pulled a wood carving from the bag and handed it to Dyami. Mahala had seen it before; the carving was of a stretching cat with an arched back.

"Why do you want my opinion?" Dyami said.

"Because you'll know if it's any good. If you think it's shit, tell me— I don't mind." Ragnar pulled out another carving of a girl's head and shoulders. Mahala recognized Solveig and felt a bit annoyed that the boy was showing the carving to Dyami when he had never shown it to her. "And here's some sketches."

He pulled out a pocket screen. Dyami knelt; Mahala peered over Ragnar's shoulder as he called up his sketches. There was one of a few boys playing outside the school and another showing two men fishing from a boat. A third showed a square, simple house like those in Oberg, with a greenhouse and a stone path leading to the front door. Ragnar had drawn a low wall in the distance, yet the house was surrounded by a grassy plain, with no other dwellings in sight.

"Why aren't there any other houses?" Mahala said.

"I was thinking about being alone, having a whole dome to myself, so I drew it that way." Ragnar set the screen down. "I can show you more if you want."

"I'd like to see more," Dyami said, "but I've seen enough already to know you have talent. If you keep at it, you'll create some beautiful things."

"I'm going to keep doing it. I wish I could do it all the time. Whenever I'm in a mind-tour, I keep thinking of things that would make it better. Then I get some wood or I draw, and it's like I'm thinking with my hands. Is that what it's like for you?"

"Something like that." Dyami rested a hand on the boy's shoulder. "I used to think, when I was a boy, that I noticed things other people didn't see—a certain cast to the light, for instance, or the way a man walks when he's happy. Often they were just little details, but I'd see them and feel as if the people around me were partly blind, because they didn't see them."

"It's like that for me," Ragnar said eagerly.

"I think we're all like that in the beginning," Dyami said, "and then we lose it. When I was still a child, I started to grow afraid of what I might see instead of being open to it. The Habbers, from what I can tell, never lose that quality—my friend Balin tells me that, in a way, many of his people are artists of a kind throughout their lives."

"Benzi isn't like that," Mahala said.

"Benzi came to his Habber life later, so maybe he'd already lost some of that vision. I didn't find it again myself until I went to live in Turing. That was when I first saw that I might have the makings of a craftsman—started with carvings and worked up to casting sculptures at the refinery. So you, Ragnar, are way ahead of where I was at your age."

Ragnar rose and picked up his bag. "I have to ask you something. If I gave you some credit, could I be kind of like an apprentice to you?" He seemed to hold his breath as he waited for an answer.

Mahala smiled. "You can't be an apprentice for something like that—it isn't real work."

"I didn't ask you, I asked Dyami. Well? I've got some credit saved up. All you have to do is look at things I do and tell me what I'm doing wrong. You're about the only person I know who can teach me things like that."

"I'd be happy to teach you what I can." Dyami got to his feet. "But I won't take any payment for it. Seeing you develop your talent will be payment enough. You may rapidly get to the point where you'll be a lot more accomplished than I am—I may not have that much to teach you after a while. You may even end up with me as your apprentice."

Ragnar grinned, then pulled another piece out of the bag. "Take this." He pressed the object into Dyami's hand. "At least I can give you a present. I'll send you a message when I have more to show you."

"I'll look forward to it. We'll set up a time for screen sessions, and the next time I'm in Oberg, we'll have to get together."

Ragnar lifted his bag to his shoulder. "Thanks, Dyami. Have a safe trip back to Turing." He started to walk away, then looked back. "Good-bye, Mahala."

"Good-bye, Ragnar." Here she was, going away tomorrow or the day after, and Ragnar had been more interested in talking to her uncle. She glared after him as he hurried toward his house. Solveig had been after him for ages to show his sketches and carvings to Dyami, and Ragnar had waited until now to pester him with them. Mahala looked up at Dyami; he was peering at the carving the boy had given him. Even her uncle had forgotten about her.

"He didn't give me anything," she said. "I'll bet he doesn't even care I'm leaving."

"You mustn't say that. I think he meant this for both of us." Dyami held out the carving.

It took her a few moments to recognize herself; Ragnar had made the face more delicate than the one she saw in mirrors. Her mouth was still too wide, and the large eyes of the image bulged slightly, as her own did. Yet the carved face framed by short, feathered hair might almost have been called pretty. Was that how Ragnar saw her? When had he done the carving, and why hadn't he shown it to her? She took the carved face from Dyami and held it, marveling at the skill and effort the boy had put into it.

"That boy's an artist," Dyami said.

"He was happy you liked his things."

"But I suspect that if I'd told him they weren't any good, he would have said I didn't know what I was talking about."

"That's Ragnar," Mahala said. "When he thinks he's right about something, he doesn't care what anybody else thinks."

"He'll need that kind of conviction, Mahala. A lot of people are going to tell him he's wasting time in useless activity or that he should turn his talent to something more practical."

"Why are you teaching him, then?"

"Because we have to make a place for people like him if this world's going to be worth anything. That's why I'll do what I can for him. It's also why I'm taking you to Turing."

"I'm not like Ragnar," she said, wondering if Dyami wished that she were.

"You'll get a chance to find out what you are in your own way." A passenger cart was approaching; he stepped into the road. "That's what Benzi wants for you, too—we're one on that."

7

Oberg was the northernmost of the ten settlements in the Maxwell Mountains and the closest to the large and striking circular impact crater of Cleopatra to the east, the only impact crater in that region of Venus. The other nine settlements in that mountain range, except for the nearest, al-Khwarizmi, which lay to the west of Oberg, were sited to the south, all of them named after prominent scientists of the past. Here, the Venus Project had not kept to the old custom, one that predated the centuries of Earth's Nomarchies, of using only female names for Cytherian locations, and in fact the Maxwell massif had been named for a male scientist before the custom of using female nomenclature had become established in older times.

"Not that it matters, really," Noella Sanger had once said to Barika and Risa in Mahala's hearing. "The geological features are named for women and goddesses and other female figures, and they'll still be here when our settlements are long gone." That had bothered Mahala, thinking of that distant time when the domed settlements would no longer exist, which was foolish of her; the settlements were meant to be only an intermediate stage, a way for people to inhabit the surface as the planet was transformed. But for a moment Noella's comment had made her feel as though she was flitting through her world as insubstantially as she moved through the synthetic settings of a mind-tour.

Tsou Yen, named for an ancient Chinese scientist and developer of elemental theories, lay to the southeast of Oberg, not far from ibn-Qurrah; Curie, Galileo, and Kepler had been built in the middle regions of the massif, with Hasseen, Lyata, and Mtshana to their south. Each of them was home to anywhere from fifteen thousand to twenty thousand people, although Oberg, the oldest and largest, now had more than twenty-five thousand inhabitants. A long time would pass before Venus had a population center that came close to the size of one of Earth's great cities, but the Project Council had reasons for keeeping the settlements near their present size. Smaller groups meant that people would be more accountable to one another and also allowed Earth more control over what was still the great and rare privilege of immigrating here. When a settlement had constructed four connected domes and grown to about twenty thousand people, it was time for the inhabitants to consider moving to a less crowded place or into a new settlement, which was why new settlements were being constructed in the north near Turing. But occasionally Mahala, even after a few tension-filled and frightening mind-tours of Earth's great cities of Tashkent and Beijing and Nueva Las Vegas, wondered if there might be advantages, even pleasures, in living amid such hordes; in such a city, she could be anonymous in a way that she could never be in Oberg or in Turing.

She was headed for Turing now, leaving the long curved ridges of the high Maxwell massif, the highest range on Venus, behind as the airship floated over the eastern part of the flat volcanic plain of the Lakshmi Plateau, north toward the Freyja Mountains and Dyami's home. Even if Venus were eventually flooded with oceans that covered most of the surface, the Lakshmi Plateau, twice as large as Earth's Tibet, smooth-surfaced except for the wide deep craters of the dormant but awakening volcanoes Sacajawea and Colette, would remain above water, with a sheer scarp nearly six kilometers high to the south. During her first trip to Turing, she had been fascinated by the screen images, but distracted by the thrill of worrying that the dirigible might crash, unlikely as that was. Now the view of the landscape held her completely.

Black cliffs surrounded Turing's three domes. On the airship's screen, above the console where the pilots sat, the new settlements to the west of Turing in the Freyja Mountains, Ptolemy and Hypatia, were pinpoints of light atop walls of black rock. The screen, of course, was showing Mahala and the other airship passengers only what they would have seen if light from the sun could penetrate to Venus's surface. Had the image been completely true to what lay outside, the rust-colored sky would have been black, and the bright orange scars gouged in the cliffs by Turing's diggers would have been only dimly illuminated by the settlement's light. High as the ridges of the Freyja Mountains were, they did not match the majestic height of the Maxwell Mountains, nor did they have the sharply steep cliffs of the Maxwell massif on its southwest sides.

Droplets of moisture, more of a mist than a rain, sifted down over the ground to make rivers of the thin sinuous channels that veined the plateau and to fill the ocean basin in the lowlands below Ishtar Terra. The planet had greatly cooled over the more than five-century duration of the Project, to the point where the temperature outside had dropped to about ninety degrees Centigrade, but the air was still thick with carbon dioxide, and the atmospheric pressure could still crush an unprotected human body.

The airship had a few passengers and a lot of cargo. Crates had been lashed down in the aisles and smaller boxes were tied to unclaimed seats. Mahala released her harness, stretched as she got to her feet, then followed Dyami off the ship, down the ramp from the airship's cradle, and through the bay, where two of the workers on duty greeted him. Both of them wore identity bracelets, as everyone did when traveling, so that scanners would record that they had arrived safely. Beyond the wide entrance at the end of the bay lay Turing's south dome, now filled with a soft yellow light. All of the settlements on Venus kept the same time as the Islands, and the airship had left Oberg after dark; it would be first light here and everywhere else under the domes.

A wide paved road about five kilometers long ran north from the airship bay toward the tunnel entrance to the dome where Dyami lived. They walked up the road, with Dyami shortening his pace so that she could keep up with him; to Mahala's right, the front side of Turing's refinery was a vast metal wall. Across the road, the small glassy dome of the ceramics plant glittered, catching the light of the much larger dome overhead. Unlike Oberg, the less populated Turing had not crowded its main dome with houses and residents and tents to house new arrivals; to the west, the tunnel that led to a newly constructed dome was hidden by trees. Turing's residents preferred giving over large areas of their domes to woods that were wilder and more overgrown than the tended parks of Oberg.

"Can you walk the distance to my house?" Dyami asked.

"Yes," Mahala replied.

A cart loaded with crates and carrying two men in gray workers' coveralls came toward them from the bay. Dyami stepped into the road and the cart slowly rolled to a stop. He handed his duffel to one of the men, then reached for Mahala's. "Could you take these for me?" he asked.

"Of course," one of the men replied.

"Thanks—just leave them at the side of the road." He turned to Mahala as the cart rolled away. "I'm glad you're not too tired to walk home—I can use the exercise."

The walk would give her time to think. By the time they reached her uncle's house, she might be prepared to face the orphaned girl who would be living with them. Mahala had already been introduced to her over the screen, but the other child had said nothing after murmuring her name. Frania Astarte Milus was a wisp of a girl with dark brown hair and hazel eyes; she had clung to Amina's hand throughout the brief call. She was a year younger than Mahala, but seemed even younger than that.

Mahala kept near Dyami. From time to time, his stride lengthened, and then he would slow down again. More carts passed them, then turned onto the narrower road that wound through the woods to the west dome's tunnel.

Now that her journey, during which she had felt removed from the passage of time, was over, everything seemed to be happening too fast. Dyami had arranged to leave for Turing as soon as it was agreed she would come with him. She had been impatient to go, feeling somehow that she might change her mind and decide to stay in Oberg if they waited too long. During the trip, she had thought of the people she was leaving behind, but had eased herself with the thought that she could always go back to her grandparents' house.

Now, for the first time, it occurred to her that she might be content here, yet still have to leave if Frania did not take to her or get along with her. After all, she could always return to Risa's household, while Frania had nowhere else to go; her grandfather was too frail to look after her, and none of her dead father's family had followed him to Venus.

"You're being awfully quiet," Dyami said as they entered the lighted tunnel, following the gentle downward slope of the passageway.

"What if Frania doesn't like me?"

"There's no reason why she shouldn't."

"But what if she doesn't?"

"Isn't it a bit soon to be worrying about that?"

Mahala was about to reply when another man called out from behind them. "Dyami! Hold on—I'll walk back with you." She turned around to see a slender brown-skinned man with dark eyes, thick black hair, and a mustache. She had met him before, and searched her mind for his name: Suleiman Khan.

Suleiman greeted her. The two men were soon deep in discussion about an upcoming task at the refinery, where Suleiman had been putting in darktime shifts. Suleiman was a man who liked to talk; he did not fall silent until they were through the tunnel and inside the north dome.

The memorial pillar Dyami had designed stood at the top of the rise outside the tunnel, a few meters from a second, more conventional pillar. This monument, unlike those in Oberg, did not simply honor the dead, but also commemorated the suffering those once imprisoned here had endured. Around the base were twisted human bodies, their heads bowed, their backs bending under the assault of disembodied fists. Above them, other nude figures stood with upraised arms; near the top of the pillar, skeletal figures with distended limbs clutched wands and other weapons, while bodies lay at their feet. There were no holo images of the dead here; instead, their sculpted faces were framed by the distorted bodies, and the plaque listing their names was near the monument's base.

Dyami had known them all. He must have wanted to forget what had passed, yet he had made this monument for the people who were imprisoned with him, for those who had died trying to free themselves. He had said something about the poison of the past, Mahala recalled, during his confrontation with Lakshmi Tiris three years ago. Here was part of his poisonous past, preserved by his own hands. Often Dyami had told her that it was necessary to remember what had happened on Venus, lest it happen again. At other times, he had murmured that he would be grateful if no one ever gave the monument a second glance.

Her parents had caused such suffering; her uncle's pillar always reminded her of that. Perhaps they had not meant to do so, but they had all the same. She nodded at Suleiman as he made his farewells, then followed Dyami past a cluster of houses toward the creek.

✳   ✳   ✳

Hills sloped gently up from where the creek flowed into a large lake. Dyami's house stood on one small grassy hill; below, a few boats lay along the shore of the lake.

A bridge spanned the creek. Their bags sat on the opposite bank, just below a narrow dirt road; Dyami hurried across the bridge to fetch them. Mahala looked up at the house's glassy walls, wondering if Frania was peering out at her, already making judgments about her.

Dyami came back with the duffels slung over his broad shoulders. "Ready?" he asked.

"I guess so."

"Don't worry, Mahala. Frania's probably just as nervous as you are."

They climbed the hill. Mahala's reflected image and that of her uncle floated on the house's mirrored surface as they approached. As Dyami was about to press his hand against the door, it slid open.

Amina and Frania were sitting on cushions in the center of the large common room. Mahala took a step forward as the two got to their feet; Amina came to her and took her hand. "I know you must be tired," she said, "so after you've met Frani, you can rest."

Dyami set down the duffels. Frania hung back, looking even smaller than she had on the screen.

"Greetings, Frania," Mahala murmured.

"Salaam," the other girl said softly.

"You may call my niece Frani," Amina said. "Everyone else does."

"Everyone did in ibn-Qurrah," Frania said, with a harder edge to her voice.

"Maybe you'd like to show Mahala to your room," Amina murmured, sounding uncertain.

Frania shrugged. Mahala picked up her bag and followed the other girl across the wide floor. The common room took up much of the space of Dyami's house, and its walls were transparent on the front side and the side facing north; there, the house seemed to have no walls. Dyami had designed the dwelling himself, and many other residences in Turing also varied from the simple rectangular house designs of Oberg.

Frania pressed the door open. Two futons lay on the floor, and clothes hung from one of the rods set against the walls. Mahala would, it seemed, have to share the room with the other girl. She had used this bedroom before when visiting. It had been Dyami's room, but he always slept on a futon in the common room whenever she or anyone else was staying here. Another room had been added to the house since her last visit, but maybe her uncle meant to claim that room for himself.

"They put us both in here," Frania said.

"I can see that." Mahala looked around. Dyami often admitted that he liked having space around him, and for a bedroom, this room was large. "Well, I'll still have more space here than in my old room in Oberg."

Frania said, "Look, it wasn't my idea to come here. Amina only brought me to Turing because my grandfather didn't want me. He didn't say so, but I knew. He's old, and he wants to stay with his housemates, and they don't have any more room, and Amina won't move to ibn-Qurrah because she and my grandfather always end up arguing about something sooner or later."

"Oh." This was news to her, but Amina had never spoken very often about her father. Mahala rummaged through her clothes. "I don't mind sharing a room, really."

Frania sat down on a cushion and was silent as Mahala unpacked. "Sometimes I hate this place," the brown-haired girl said at last.

"Turing? But why?"

"Not Turing—Venus." Frania shook her head. "My aunt told me about you. She said you didn't have any mother and father, either. Maybe that's supposed to make us friends."

"I never knew my parents," Mahala said, trying to be kind. "It must be worse for you."

"Maybe you should be glad you didn't know them. My parents told me about your parents, about how they used to have to sneak around being afraid of them, worrying about Amina and wondering what the Guide and her friends and all those people in Ishtar might do to her when she was a prisoner. I'll bet they wouldn't have wanted me here if they knew you'd be living in this house."

"It's not my fault," Mahala said.

"A lot of people here had a hard time because of your mother. I don't know why your uncle even wanted you to come live with him."

Mahala stood up. "I don't have to stay here, you know. I can go home to Oberg—I've got grandparents who would be happy to have me back, unlike you." She turned her back to Frania and hung up her clothes, furious, as she added, "Dyami says the kids at my level here don't go back to school for another eight days. If you can't get along with me by then, I can tell him I want to go home."

Footsteps pattered across the room. From the corner of her eye, Mahala saw the bedroom door open, then slide shut.

When she came back into the common room, Dyami was working on a small screen. Amina sat at the table with him, nibbling at a piece of fruit.

"Have some food," Amina said to Mahala.

"I'm not hungry." Mahala went to the table, which was next to one glassy wall. Outside, near the bottom of a hill that sloped toward the shore of the lake, Frania sat above three small rowboats that had been pulled out of the water. "This isn't working."

Dyami said, "You haven't given it much of a chance."

"Things aren't going to get any better."

"Sit down," he said. "Let me sketch you." She sat down on a cushion, keeping still as Dyami's stylus moved over his screen. "Our shifts at the refinery begin again tomorrow," he went on, "so Amina and I won't be home until nearly last light. You'll have some time alone with Frania, and all I ask is that you tidy up your room and check the greenhouse. You might find that you get along after all."

"But what if we don't?"

Amina reached for her cup. "Then Frani and I will move," the yellow-haired woman said.

"Move? Where?"

"To Tasida's house. She has more room now, with Lorie deciding to move out. She's always wanted me there anyway, and she'd welcome another child in her house."

Mahala looked down. "I thought you liked it better here."

Tasida Getran was Amina's lover, but Amina lived with Dyami because, as she put it, she needed more solitude than she would find in Tasida's house, among the physician's housemates and the patients and friends who often called on her. Dyami would offer temporary quarters to new arrivals with no place to stay, but most of the time, he kept to himself. Even his lover Balin did not stay with him for more than a few days at a time.

Dyami glanced up from his screen. "I'd miss you," he said to Amina.

"I'd miss you, too, Dyami, but staying with Tasida and her housemates might be good for me, and you may be ready to have other people live with you here. Maybe we've both been too reclusive for too long."

"I agree—that's why the girls should stay."

"But if they can't get along—" Amina pushed another cup toward Mahala. "If you're not hungry, at least have some juice."

Mahala stared at the cup. Dyami and Amina might have to disrupt the peaceful life they had made for themselves because of her. Their peace, she knew, had been hard-won and was precarious even now; the suffering they had endured as prisoners before the Revolt still marked them. During her previous visits, she had occasionally been awakened by the screams Amina's nightmares evoked or had left her room in the night to find Dyami sitting up, brooding, unable to sleep.

She said, "If we can't get along, I'll go back to Oberg."

Amina's blue eyes widened. "You're homesick—is that it? Do you want to go back?"

"No, but it's better than having you move out of Dyami's house."

Dyami set down his screen. "I wanted to have you here. I thought being here would be good for you. Maybe I was wrong."

Mahala got to her feet and went to the door, then stepped outside. A slender man with curling black hair was walking toward her; she recognized Balin. On the opposite side of the creek, a group of about twenty young people was coming in this direction. Some were older children, while others seemed to be in their early teens; they were massed together, keeping pace with Balin. Apparently Frania had already noticed them. The small girl was hurrying up the hill toward the bridge.

Mahala went down the grassy slope toward Balin. "Greetings," she called out.

"Mahala." The Habber raised his hand, but his smile seemed hesitant. The crowd of boys and girls had halted by the bridge, but did not come across it; three were carrying what looked like long rolls of cloth under their arms. Frania watched them for a few moments, then turned toward Balin and Mahala.

"That's, uh, Frani Milus," Mahala murmured, remembering the other girl's nickname. "Amina's niece," she added.

"I know. We've met." Balin held up a hand in greeting. Frania nodded at him, but he was staring past her at the crowd on the other side of the bridge.

"They're here again," Frania said as she came to Balin's side.

He said, "There are more of them this time."

"Who are they?" Mahala asked.

"Children who want us to do more for them than we can," Balin replied. Some among the group were unrolling the cloth they had brought with them; the sheets were covered with lettering. They sat down, holding up the cloth signs; one was in Arabic, the other two in Anglaic.

THE WORLD WE WANT IS NOT HERE, one sign read. Another said: GIVE VENUS LIFE SO THAT WE CAN HAVE OUR OWN LIVES. Mahala had been studying Arabic on her screen, but did not know enough to be sure of what the third sign said.

"Habitat-dweller, help us!" one boy shouted. Others took up the cry. "Habitat-dweller, help us!"

"What is it?" Mahala said.

"Don't be afraid," Balin said. "They won't hurt us. All of these demonstrations have been peaceful so far."

"You mean it's happened before?"

The Habber nodded. "They've been calling on my people to terraform this planet as quickly as possible, to speed up the process somehow—as if we could somehow magically shorten the time needed to make this world live. I've never been sure if, after that, their wish is to stay here or to come to live with us."

" 'We are slaves of the Project, in bondage to Earth's dreams,' " Frania said tonelessly. Mahala glanced at her, startled. "That's what the sign in Arabic says."

She had not known that the other girl already read Arabic. She thought of what Solveig had told her the other night, about the chance that the Project might fail.

"This group's larger than the last one," Dyami said behind her; Mahala had not heard him come down the hill. The children fell silent.

"What are you going to do?" Balin asked.

"Nothing," Dyami said, "as long as they just sit there and they're peaceful. Their families have to handle this. I'm not about to make a formal complaint about children expressing their opinions." In spite of his reasonable words, he sounded angry, his voice low and strained.

"They've come here before?" Mahala said.

"Yes," Dyami said, "when Balin comes to visit. They'll go away."

"They used to come to the Habber residences here," Balin said, "and sit there with their signs. Lately, they've taken to following some of us around."

Dyami linked his arm through Balin's. "Come inside." The two men climbed toward the house. Mahala was about to beckon to Frania when the other girl sat down.

"Maybe they're right," Frania said.

"About the Project?"

"The Project killed my parents."

"It was an accident," Mahala said. "That doesn't make it any easier for you, but—"

"This planet killed them. Maybe it killed your parents, too. Maybe they would have been better people somewhere else." Frania turned; her hazel eyes were filled with tears. "Some of your people went to live in the Habs, didn't they?"

"Just my great-uncle and my other grandfather."

"And they're still alive, aren't they? They'll be alive for a long time. They'll be alive when all of us here are dead. Maybe they'll be alive forever."

"You don't know that for certain. Habbers can die—Balin will tell you that. So would my great-uncle Benzi." Mahala paused. "I guess I can understand why you hate this place."

"I didn't used to hate it. Once I wanted to stay in ibn-Qurrah forever. I didn't—" She let out a sigh, then bowed her head.

The children across the bridge were getting to their feet, rolling up their long pieces of cloth. They drifted away slowly, in groups of two or three, some moving alongside the creek, others wandering toward the lake. These demonstrations could not have been going on for very long; she had visited Dyami less than a year ago and had not seen anything like this.

She could understand why Dyami had sounded so angry and even a bit frightened. Perhaps the Ishtar cult her mother had led had started the same way, with just a few people who dreamed of something beyond the Project.

"I shouldn't have said what I did to you," Frania said. "Before. In our room."

"It's all right," Mahala replied. "I shouldn't have been so mad at you, either. I'm not angry with you anymore."

"I'm lucky I've got Amina." Frania slowly got to her feet. "I'd better go back inside and show her I'm not still angry at you."

Mahala stood up. "I'll come with you, Frania. Friends?" She extended her arm.

"Yes, friends," Frania said as she clasped Mahala's hand.

8

Mahala struggled to breathe in the heat. The entire species would die out, all of the small furry creatures that huddled near her feet. The air was close and warm, the few plants inside the small dome wilting. Leaves and stalks had been eaten by the animals, chewed down to their roots; little was left except the lichens and moss. A small rodent clutched at her foot. They might survive for another two generations, but their grim fate was certain after that; the air would be unbreathable, the plants that fed them gone.

She removed the slender band from around her head. Wilhelm Asher, her teacher, was talking to one of the other students, but Balin was assisting him in the classroom. She beckoned to the Habber; he rose and came toward her.

"Well?" Balin said, settling on a cushion next to her.

"They're going to die."

"All of them?"

"Look at this graph." She held out her screen. "If everything stays the same, in two generations there'll only be about six to twelve of them left, and by then they won't have air to breathe or food to eat." Mahala sighed. "I made a mistake somewhere."

Balin took the screen from her. The graph faded as another appeared. "If it was one of our domes," she went on, "we would have built another one before things got so bad, and then moved out, and then worked on this one, starting all over with new topsoil and microorganisms if we had to."

"Indeed."

"I cut the birthrate this time, but there's still too many of them for the environment, and they can't build a new dome for more space—it isn't allowed by the program. And even if they could, it would be a while before that dome was ready to support life, so a lot of them would die anyway."

"Maybe you didn't make a mistake," Balin said. "Perhaps this is the way it has to come out."

"Why?"

He smiled. "Ask yourself that." He stood up and went to Wilhelm's side. Gino Hislop-Carnera had taken off his band and was scowling at his screen; apparently his projected ecology had turned out as unsuccessfully as hers.

Mahala set down her screen. She had been in Turing for nearly six months now, and for much of that time had wondered what the teachers in the north dome's school were trying to teach them. Most of their lessons and projects seemed to raise more questions than they answered. She could usually guess at what her teacher in Oberg was trying to convey, while Wilhelm Asher rarely gave her a straight answer to anything.

She picked up her screen, calling up an image of her mind-tour's doomed rodents. The problem was that her assumptions were too limited; she was beginning to doubt that there was any way, given the restrictions built into the problem, to solve it. The rodents could be given some rudimentary intelligence, but their dome was the whole of the environment she was allowed to construct, with nothing outside of it for her creatures to use as a resource. Maybe that was what she was supposed to discover, that there was no solution to this problem.

In that case, she would have to break the rules in order to find a solution. Was that what Wilhelm was trying to teach them? Was that what they were supposed to do?

Frania, seated just in front of her, removed her band and rubbed at her head. They had both been assigned to the same class when starting school here. Mahala had been happy about that at first, since it meant having at least one person she already knew amid the crowd of strangers.

Now she sometimes wished that Frania had been assigned to another teacher. The other girl clung to her, keeping near her throughout the day and doing schoolwork with her at night. Since they lived in the same house, Mahala could hardly invite other schoolmates over without including Frania in their activities. There had to be a way she could encourage Frania to go off on her own once in a while without hurting her feelings.

A break from school was coming up soon. Dyami and Amina had not said anything about their plans for the girls, but Mahala assumed that she would go to Oberg and visit Risa and Sef during that time. She could have a real talk with Solveig, instead of just sending messages or saying what she had to say quickly, so that Dyami would have more time to talk to Ragnar about his drawings and carvings. Solveig and she had not spoken to each other for almost a month, and the last time, Solveig had mentioned that her parents were in the middle of what she called a "big decision," one she could not discuss with anyone outside the family, even Mahala, until Einar and Thorunn had made up their minds. Maybe Frania would be sent to stay with her grandfather for a while, but if not, some time by herself while Mahala was in Oberg might be good for the other girl.

"I think," Frania said, "that I'm ready to give up on my dome."

"Aha!" Gino grinned as he glanced in their direction. "They could have a war. That's one way of settling things."

"No one said anything about a war," Frania said.

"And nobody said we couldn't have one. I think my creatures are going to start fighting." Gino put on his band. Mahala smiled, admiring the boy just a little.

Balin and Wilhelm were talking. Sometimes it seemed that Balin, during the days he was here, was as much their teacher as Wilhelm was. Maybe it wasn't such a good idea for the Habbers to spend as much time as they did at the school. Less than a month ago, some of the older students had protested outside the school itself, attaching a banner to the front door before two teachers hastily pulled it down. The message, in Anglaic, had been a simple one:

YOU OFFER US HELP
NOW GIVE IT

The demonstration had cost all of the protesting children a black mark in their records, the first time anyone had received such a penalty for this particular offense. The Turing Council had to become more severe, since the other settlements were now aware of the protests and the young people were becoming bolder in staging them.

Maybe they would stop, Mahala thought as she picked up her

band. Some of them probably wondered why she had not joined them, given that she had two relatives who had made the choice the students presumably wanted to have. That, of course, was exactly why she could not join the protests. "Don't you have anything to do with that nonsense," Risa had told her over the screen during their last conversation.

Mahala closed her eyes, trying to concentrate once more on the dilemma her virtual rodents faced.

"It works," Gino said to Mahala. He was talking about the warfare he had programmed into his project. "I mean, it works in a way."

"What do you mean, in a way?" Frania asked.

"The problem is that they have to have a new war every couple of generations. I'm not sure if Wilhelm will allow that."

"I don't believe it," a girl said behind Mahala.

Mahala lifted her head. Down by the lake, a banner fluttered from a tree. GIVE US A CHOICE, this one said.

"I wonder who put it there," another girl said, "and how they did it."

"They must have sneaked the banner out during our free time," Gino was saying, "then waited until everybody else was back inside."

"Which means," Mahala said, "that the teachers can find out who did it. All they have to do is figure out who was late getting back to class."

Gino shrugged. "No one's going to admit doing it, and a few kids are always late. They can't blame them all."

The other children stopped by the tree to stare up at the banner; someone would have to climb the tree, or fetch a ladder, to get it down. Mahala walked toward the path that skirted the lake, Frania trailing her.

"They really took a chance," Frania said.

"They could have been caught so easily," Mahala said.

"Gino was late getting back. But Wilhelm was late, too, so I don't think he noticed."

Mahala frowned. Children her age were not involved in the demonstrations as far as she knew—not that she actually knew much more than what she had heard others gossip about and whisper. Some said that the older children who were protesting publicly were only a small number of those who were involved in the demonstrations, that many others sympathized with them.

She was not even sure of what they wanted. Did they think that the Habbers could really do much more for the Project than they were already doing? Or were they hoping that the Habbers would suddenly send for their ships and take them all away to their Habs? If they kept it up, eventually the Turing Council would have to hold hearings, before the protests spread to other settlements.

"I can see," Frania said, "why they do it."

"It won't do any good," Mahala said.

"Maybe not, but—" Frania paused. "You want to see other places, you're always saying you do. I do, too. What's so strange about other kids wanting the same thing?"

"I'm not so sure that's all they want."

"Maybe it is. Maybe it'd be easier to live here if you knew you could go somewhere else later."

"But we can do that now," Mahala objected.

"If you're smart enough to get into an Island school, you can go. If you get into the Cytherian Institute, you can see Earth. That's about it, Mahala. Most of us will never get those chances."

"People come here from Earth because they think it's better here, don't they?"

"But that's their choice. What about us? Nobody asked us if we wanted to be here. What if we want something else?"

Mahala glanced back at the school building. The other children were still looking up at the banner. Wilhelm strode toward them with another teacher. She saw Balin then, up in the tree's lower limbs. The Habber shook the banner from his hands; it fluttered to the ground.

Dyami, she realized as she watched Balin, had more reason than most people to worry about such protests. If it seemed that the presence of the Habbers was provoking the demonstrations, the Project Council might consider asking them to leave the domed settlements, even the Islands. Earth's Mukhtars might have less power over them now than in the past, but the Island Administrators could not ignore their authority altogether, and the Mukhtars might welcome a chance to reassert their authority here.

If that happened, Dyami might lose Balin for good.

*   *   *

"Seven days," Amina said, "is about the limit, I'm afraid." She smiled at Frania. "But we'll be in the east dome, so you'll be near your old friends, able to see them as much as you like."

Frania smiled back at her aunt. Amina had announced her plans for the school break just as they sat down to dinner. She had some days off owed to her, so she was going to take Frania to ibn-Qurrah. They would stay with friends of Amina's, in a house not far from that of Frania's grandfather, which meant less opportunity for Amina and her father to get into arguments.

Frania's hazel eyes glowed; she was obviously looking forward to the trip. Mahala poked at her plate of beans. She had expected to spend the entire break in Oberg, but Dyami had mentioned that she would not be going there until Frania and Amina left for ibn-Qurrah. Many of her schoolmates here would be clearing deadwood from the wooded land on the lake's eastern side with the aid of some adults or helping out in the Turing community greenhouses; Dyami wanted her to spend some of her free time helping with those tasks.

She could plead with him to change his mind, to send her to Oberg sooner; her uncle might give in. He might understand if she told him that she had to talk to Solveig about the big decision her parents would soon make. Could they be thinking of severing their bond? Mahala thrilled at the thought. Separating from a bondmate was extremely unusual, given all the obstacles to such a decision, but separations weren't unknown.

It was a silly idea. Thorunn and Einar got along so well that they hardly ever fought, and somehow she could not imagine Einar getting excited enough about anything to have such a monumental disagreement with his bondmate.

Mahala finished her beans and reached for some fruit. Balin got up to carry empty plates into the kitchen. Dyami had excused himself from the table early, saying that he had to speak to someone over the screen privately. Mahala shifted on her cushion. Maybe Risa was calling, to argue with Dyami about keeping her in Turing during part of the break; her grandmother would have wanted her to stay in Oberg for as long as possible.

The door to Dyami's room slid open. "I just spoke to Einar Gunnarson," he said as he came toward the table. "He had some interesting news." He sat down on his cushion as Balin returned from the kitchen. "I called to ask him if it might be possible for Solveig and Ragnar to stay here for a few days during their break."

Mahala sat up straighter. "Oh, Dyami." She felt ashamed of herself for doubting him; he had been thinking of her after all, planning to bring her friend Solveig here. "Are they coming?"

"Einar and Thorunn say it's fine with them, but I think Frani should have something to say about it, too, since she's a member of this household."

Frania looked down. "I don't mind."

"You can be honest with me," Dyami said. "If you think it might be a problem, we can make other arrangements."

The brown-haired girl lifted her head. "But I really would like to meet them."

"I know you'll like Solveig," Mahala said, "and if Ragnar starts bothering you—well, there are three of us and only one of him."

"Einar worries that his son's spending too much time on his hobby as it is," Dyami said, "but he seemed happier about the boy coming here when I mentioned that he could probably sell some of his work before long."

"It's that good?" Mahala asked.

"He's much more skilled than he was." Dyami paused. "Anyway, Einar told me that he and Thorunn have decided to move to Hypatia—says Oberg's getting just a bit too crowded for them. So the children will stop here while the parents go on to get their new home ready."

Mahala clasped her hands. Solveig would be closer to Turing then, up here in the Freyja Mountains and only two hours away by airship in the new settlement of Hypatia; and they would be together soon.

Mahala got up, went to her uncle, and hugged him hard. "Thank you, Dyami."

Mahala and Frania went together to the airship bay to meet Solveig and Ragnar. Solveig had grown taller; she crushed Mahala to her chest, then drew herself up as Mahala introduced Frania. She and her brother were carrying duffels, but Ragnar also had a smaller bag.

Mahala led them out of the bay, then reached for Ragnar's small bag. "I can carry that."

He handed it to her; the weight of it was more than she had expected. "What did you bring?" she asked.

"Chisels and blades and clay. Some carvings I made. I gave away a lot of them, but my father said he wasn't going to drag the rest to Hypatia." He took the bag back. "My duffel's lighter—take that."

She carried the duffel toward the main road. A passenger cart was rolling along the wide flat road toward the north dome; they climbed aboard and sat down in adjoining seats in the back. Solveig was soon talking about the move to Hypatia. Their parents would leave for that settlement tomorrow, after a last round of farewells. Thorunn's brother Ingmar and his family were staying in Oberg, but Einar, after learning that there was a shortage of maintenance workers in Hypatia, had decided to move. Thorunn had already been assigned to Hypatia's new chemistry laboratory.

"We'll have to live in a tent for a while," Solveig said, "until we get the house up." The wisps of blond hair over her forehead fluttered in the light breeze created by the open cart's motion. "They've only got four teachers in the whole settlement so far, but there should be twice that many in a year or so, and anyway, there aren't that many kids in Hypatia yet. Besides, with the screen lessons, we'll keep up with the work."

"Aren't you going to miss Oberg?" Mahala asked.

"I suppose." Solveig grinned. "But I'll like Hypatia, I know I will. I just wish you were living there, too."

The cart stopped to let off two passengers near houses where a small flock of sheep were grazing in a fenced-in enclosure. The sheep were a new altered breed that was becoming more popular in the settlements. They were about half the size of their merino ancestors, so needed less grazing land, but their fine silky wool grew so rapidly that they had to be shorn every forty days. The light but durable fabric of Mahala's blue shirt had been woven from the wool; Dyami had traded some of his credit to a refinery worker who sewed garments from the cloth and sold them during her time off.

"It's beautiful," Frania murmured from the seat behind them.

Mahala turned her head. Frania was holding a wooden carving of a cat.

"This one's better," Ragnar said as he reached into his bag. Frania smiled as he thrust another carved cat at her. "You can keep them if you want."

Frania's smiled widened. "Thank you, Ragnar."

Mahala turned back to Solveig, wondering why she felt so annoyed.

* * *

Solveig would sleep in the room Mahala and Frania shared, while Ragnar would use Amina's former room. Mahala assured him that Dyami often slept in the large common room anyway and that Amina would not mind giving up her room for a few days. They would soon have more space; Dyami had already started putting up walls for a third room in the corner next to Amina's.

Dyami and Amina would not be home until last light. Mahala led her friends down to the lake after they had eaten. "Some of the kids in Oberg had a protest a few days ago," Solveig said as they climbed over the rocks. "They went over to the Habber residence in the main dome with a sign that said 'We didn't sign up for this Project.' Your grandmother was furious—she was coming out of the Administrative Center when she saw them."

"Really?" Mahala was surprised. "Risa didn't tell me anything about that."

"It only happened a couple of days ago, just before we left. They all got notations in their records, and Risa said she'd call for a hearing if any of them did it again."

"For a protest?" Mahala shook her head. "Here, they would have just had a warning. The only ones who got black marks were these kids who protested in front of our school, and that's because they'd all been warned before."

"Turing's different. Everybody knows your Council is—well, easier on people. But if these protests start spreading to other settlements, all the settlement Councils will have to act."

"I wonder why they bother," Mahala said. "Protests won't do any good."

"How do you know?" Ragnar called out. He and Frania were just above on the slope, sitting together on a large flat rock; Frania had hardly left his side since his arrival. "How do you know it won't do any good?"

"You can't even tell what they really want," Mahala replied.

"Sure you can. They want to be able to leave the domes and live on the surface someday. They want to decide for themselves whether to stay here or not. The Habbers might be able to help with all of that. What's so hard to understand?"

"Protests won't make it happen."

"At least they're saying something about what they want instead of just putting up with everything the way it is."

"You sound like you want to do the same thing, Ragnar."

"Maybe I would."

"You're an idiot."

Ragnar shrugged. Frania murmured something to him. The boy seemed more interested in talking to her anyway.

"Come on," Mahala said to Solveig. "Let's walk over to the docks."

Frania's futon was empty when Mahala awoke. She went into the common room to find Dyami and Ragnar doing sketches on their screens while Frania watched. By the time Solveig was up, and Dyami and Amina had left for the refinery, Ragnar was sketching the brown-haired girl.

"You'd better eat," Mahala told them. "We're supposed to go over to the community greenhouses to help out."

"We ate our breakfast before," Ragnar said. "We'll be ready."

"Some of our schoolmates will be there," Mahala went on. "You'll get a chance to meet them." Ragnar did not respond. "It'll be more fun tomorrow when we clear the woods. It's just breaking up the bigger branches and dragging the deadwood to the road so it can get loaded into a cart, and we won't have to do that all the time—they'll let us wander around and take breaks."

Ragnar gazed at his screen. At last Mahala led Solveig to the kitchen.

On their way to the community greenhouses later, Mahala heard Ragnar promise Frania that he would make a carving of her before he left. At the greenhouse, they put on their face masks and rebreathers to protect them against the carbon dioxide enriched air in which the gardens thrived before they were put to work weeding some of the tiers of hydroponic vegetables. Ragnar, with Frania at his side, was soon fooling around with the other children, making honking sounds at them through his mask. By the time they were packing broccoli and miniature heads of lettuce and other produce, Ragnar was going out of his way to help Frania load her small crates.

At home, after supper, Frania seemed content to sit with the boy and Dyami while Mahala played screen games with Solveig. Somehow, this visit was not going as she had expected. She had supposed that Ragnar would spend a lot of his free time learning what he could from Dyami; that was obviously one of the reasons for his visit. She had thought her main problem might be having a chance to talk to Solveig alone without Frania tagging along.

The next day, when they were clearing deadwood, it was Frania who guided the boy along the paths through the forested land. The day after that, Ragnar and Frania disappeared for nearly the whole day, returning just before last light. The next morning, they had vanished again.

"Ragnar likes Frani," Solveig said to Mahala as they followed the creek away from Dyami's house.

"I guess so." Mahala did not want to talk about Ragnar and Frania. Solveig would be here for only three more days, and Mahala had promised to show her around the south dome. There would be more tasks for them tomorrow; the settlements did not want the children to get used to too much idleness during their break.

"What's bothering you?" Solveig asked.

"Nothing."

"Well, you haven't been acting like yourself."

"I'm sorry, Solveig."

"Is it Frani? Haven't you two been getting along?"

"Actually, we have. The only thing that's been bothering me is that it's almost impossible to do anything by myself—I mean, she's always there, tagging along." She followed Solveig across a small footbridge. "With Ragnar around, I guess I don't have to worry about that."

"He may like Frani, but he wanted to see you again."

"What?" Mahala slowed her steps. "Did he actually say that?"

Solveig smiled. "Of course not. He'd never admit it, but I can tell."

Ahead, in the hollow, stood the long rectangular building that was Turing's Administrative Center. Above it, on the gentle slope of a hill, was the round glassy dome of the Habber residence. Houses lined the white stone paths that wound up the hills and through copses of trees; Dyami's monument and the memorial pillar next to it were visible near the tunnel that led to the south dome.

A woman with long reddish hair and clothed in a long green tunic and pants was leaving the Habber residence. Mahala, recognizing her, waved; the woman lifted a hand.

"What's her name?" Solveig asked.

"Tesia." Mahala had not known the Habber woman was back in

Turing. She had come to Dyami's house with Balin four months ago, to say that she was going to one of the Islands for a while, but might leave Venus for good after that. Maybe Tesia had changed her mind.

A small group of children clustered around the monument. Most of them seemed older, but Mahala spotted Ragnar's blond head among them, and then the small, slight form of Frania. She gritted her teeth, suddenly annoyed with them both.

"Looks like Ragnar's found some more friends," Solveig said.

Before Mahala could respond, two of the boys were moving away from the monument, unrolling a banner between them. The other children sat down.

"A protest," Mahala whispered. Tesia froze along the sloping path; more Habbers had come outside their residence, Balin among them. Tesia was motionless, her arm still raised; Balin hurried toward her. A cart carrying two men and crates of supplies rolled out of the tunnel, slowing as it neared the monument.

Mahala moved toward the protesters, then broke into a run. She could read what the banner said now.

YOUR LIVES ARE LONG, OURS ARE SHORT
YOU CAN WAIT
WE CANNOT

The cart rolled to a halt as the men jumped out. "Damned kids!" one of them shouted; he was a big, brown-skinned man, moving swiftly in spite of his bulk. Mahala slowed down as Solveig caught up to her. A passenger cart was leaving the tunnel with seven people aboard; the protestors would have even more of an audience.

The big man ripped the banner from the hands of the boys holding it. "What do you think you're doing?" he called out as his companion grabbed at another boy.

"Stop!" A Habber Mahala did not know, a muscular, golden-skinned man, was hastening toward the demonstration. "Let them go—they're only children."

The children were already scattering. "You'll get marked for this," the smaller man shouted after them. "Don't think you won't. You there, Josef—I'll pay a call on your parents later and tell them what you did. Hama, don't think you'll get off easy."

"It's all right," the Habber said. "We won't make a complaint."

"Maybe it's time you did," the big man replied. "I'm going to make one. Disturbing the peace—that's good for a start. Desecrating the space around our monuments with that sign."

Balin had his arms around Tesia; the other Habbers had come down the hill to her. Ragnar and Frania were walking away, trailing the other children.

Mahala went after the pair, Solveig just behind her. "Why did you do it?" Mahala asked, grabbing at Ragnar; he shook off her hand. "Why? Did you have to do it right next to Dyami's monument? How do you think he's going to feel about that?"

Ragnar kept walking, then abruptly halted; she nearly bumped into him. "It had to be done, Mahala." His blue-gray eyes were cold.

"You're not even sorry." She turned to Frania. "And you—how did you get dragged into this?"

Tears spilled from Frania's eyes. "I asked her to come with me," Ragnar replied.

Mahala glared at him. "I guessed that. She wouldn't have dared do it by herself."

"Frani pointed out some of the kids who'd done this stuff before. We went to them and said we agreed with what they were doing. They told us we'd have to prove it, and so I came up with the idea of protesting here and said we'd come along. Trouble is, we should have waited until the end of this shift—more people would have been coming home then. More people would have seen us."

"Idiot," Solveig muttered. "You're going to get it."

"After all my uncle's done for you," Mahala said, "you go and do this. I hope he throws you out of his house and never speaks to you again."

Ragnar spun around and walked away. Frania was crying now, covering her face with trembling hands. "I didn't want to do it," she sobbed.

Mahala wanted to strike her. "Then why did you?"

"Ragnar must have pushed her into this." Solveig draped an arm over the small brown-haired girl. "Come on, Frani—let's forget about it for now."

Mahala said, "There's going to be a lot of trouble over this."

"I know," Solveig said.

*　　*　　*

Dyami had heard about the incident from Balin on his way home. He was silent, his face pale, as Frania admitted to her aunt that she had introduced Ragnar to the troublemakers. She was accepting her share of responsibility, not trying to blame most of her actions on Ragnar.

"And you, Ragnar?" Amina asked.

"I'm sorry," the boy said, not sounding as though he meant it.

"I can understand pranks, but this—"

"I'm not sorry about that." Ragnar lifted his head. "I shouldn't have done it here, maybe, because I'm just a guest in Turing. It'd be different in my own settlement."

"I see," Dyami murmured.

"I guess you don't want to give me lessons anymore," Ragnar said.

Dyami shook his head. "No, Ragnar—I won't punish you that way. But if there's a hearing here and the others get a reprimand, you'll have to share their punishment. Maybe that doesn't seem like much to you now, but a bad record will affect how you're treated later. Some people won't trust you as much. You might not get as many chances for certain types of training or study. That would be a pity for someone with your talents."

Ragnar looked away. "You had to protest right next to Dyami's monument," Mahala burst out. "At least you could have picked somewhere else."

"It was near the Habber residence," Ragnar responded. "We figured—"

"Enough." Dyami leaned forward on his cushion, resting his arms on his knees. "Let me explain something to you. One of the Habbers who saw you today is a woman named Tesia. She was in love with Sigurd Kristens-Vitos for many years, the Administrator who once held the position Jamilah al-Hussaini holds now, Liaison to the Project Council. And Sigurd loved Tesia, too, despite the disapproval of many who thought he might be compromising his position by being so close to a Habber. You may know Sigurd's name—it's one of those on the monument. I came to know him here. He died here in Turing as a prisoner."

Frania bit her lower lip. Ragnar lowered his eyes.

"Sigurd could have escaped, with Mahala's grandfather Malik and the others who were able to get away with the Habbers when they were expelled from the Islands. He could have gone with Tesia. He chose to remain behind instead, to stay and do what he could to save the Project, because he thought it was his duty, and that decision cost him his life. Imagine how Tesia must have felt, remembering that, when she saw your sign."

"I didn't know," Ragnar said.

"She went back to her Hab after she learned about Sigurd's death," Dyami went on. "Balin didn't think she'd ever come back here. She did, but it's been hard for her. I don't know if she'll want to stay now."

"I'm sorry," Ragnar said. This time, he sounded sincere.

"They're doing what they can—all that they feel they can do, anyway. The ones who grow closest to us know they'll live long enough to eventually lose anyone they come to love here. They might decide that it's easier in the end, less painful, to have nothing to do with us. These protests will certainly encourage them to think that way."

"And we just have to get along the way we are," Ragnar muttered.

"And hope things might change." Dyami sighed. "I sympathize with you, Ragnar, and with all of those young people, but what you did won't accomplish anything."

Ragnar glanced at Mahala. She tried to smile, to show him that she was not angry with him now. In a way, what she wanted was not all that different from what the protesters were demanding—a chance to do more, an opportunity to escape the domes, at least for a while. Even Dyami had admitted that he sympathized with the protesters.

Dyami stood up. "Now I'll have to call your parents. They'll find out about this eventually, so they might as well hear it from me. I'll have to apologize to them for not supervising you more closely."

"It wasn't your fault." Ragnar got to his feet. "I'll talk to them, too, and tell them so."

"Then come along."

At their next meeting, the Turing Council decided to enter a reprimand on each child's record, along with assigning the children the task of tending the gardens around the Habber residence for the next month. Since Ragnar would be going to Hypatia soon, his punishment was to weed the gardens before he left. None of the children, or their parents, asked for a hearing to challenge the punishment, and no one thought Ragnar had gotten off more easily than the others. He might not have to lose as much free time working in the gardens, but he would be moving to a new settlement with a black mark on his record, something not likely to win him new friends there quickly.

Frania offered to help Ragnar with the weeding; he refused. He no longer sought her out and spent the last two days of his visit working at a carving he refused to show anyone. He gave it to Dyami on the morning he and Solveig were to leave; it turned out to be a carving of Dyami's face.

"Why, thank you," Dyami murmured.

"I didn't do such a good job on it," Ragnar said.

"But you did."

"Your cheekbones are a little broader."

Solveig hugged Mahala, then Frania. "I'm going to miss you," the blond girl said.

"We're coming with you to the bay," Mahala said.

"Don't. It'll just make it harder."

Amina and Dyami were to walk with them as far as the refinery. Dyami shouldered the children's duffels; Mahala and Frania followed them as far as the creek. Solveig turned and waved one last time after crossing the footbridge. Mahala stared after the four until they rounded a bend and were hidden by trees.

"He said he'd make a carving of me," Frania said, "but I guess he forgot."

"It's all right, Frani. He probably thought he should do something for Dyami first. I'll bet he'll do one of you next time."

"If he comes here again."

"He will." He would, Mahala thought, if only to learn more from Dyami, who had promised to show him how to make and cast molds. It irritated her to know that was Ragnar's main reason for wanting to come here at all. She glanced at Frania and caught the look of longing in the girl's large hazel eyes.

Both Sef and Risa came to Oberg's bay to greet Mahala. She kept silent when Risa told her of how much everyone had missed her and of how the entire household had made a special supper for her. It seemed that Benzi had decided to visit as well; he had arrived only a few hours earlier.

Hoa was pregnant, and Kyril just as noisy as ever, except when his mother, Barika, was holding him. Noella and Kolya mentioned that Irina, Kolya's daughter, would soon be visiting them, traveling there from her home in ibn-Qurrah. Paul and Grazie were planning to go to Kepler to see their son Patrick. Risa was muttering about retiring from the Oberg Council, but the others were soon arguing with her to stay on and run for reelection.

Mahala ate her fish and vegetables and munched on Sef's baked bread while the others chattered of Oberg's affairs. Oberg did not feel like her home anymore. She wondered if Frania was feeling the same way about ibn-Qurrah and already missed the other girl's quiet, gentle presence.

Benzi, who had been nearly as silent as she, was the first to excuse himself. "Think I'll take a walk," he said. "Mahala, why don't you come with me?"

She smiled at him, happier than she had expected to be for a chance to get away from the others. "I'd like that."

"Go ahead," Risa said. "It's your first night home—I won't ask for any help with chores until tomorrow."

Mahala followed Benzi outside. They walked along the pathway that stretched past the neighboring houses. She could see the blurred images of people inside greenhouses; a few boys raced past her toward the lake. The houses seemed too close together here, the darkness alive with muffled conversations and distant shouts, without the silences and spaces of Turing.

"Have you been happy in Turing?" Benzi asked.

"Yes, I have." The words sprang to her lips quickly. "I think Frani's happier there, too."

"I heard about the latest demonstration, the one your young friends were involved in."

"They got black marks for that," Mahala said.

"I know. I think your people feel we should be more upset about those protests than we are." He slowed his pace. "Mahala, I haven't told this to Risa yet. I wanted to tell you first. I'm returning to my Habitat soon, but I will come back to Venus—I promise."

"You're leaving?"

"Temporarily."

"But why?"

"That's hard to explain." He was silent for a while. "Part of it is that staying among you for too long is disorienting to us—I need to go back for a while. But I also think that, at the moment, I can do more for you Cytherians there."

"How?"

"That's something I can't tell you yet, but—let's just say that I miss some of the times I spend communing with our cyberminds."

"You sound almost as if the minds are your friends."

"They are. They are much more than friends." He stopped and turned back toward Risa's house. "If you ever need to get a message to me, go to Balin. I'll respond as soon as I can."

Something in his voice disturbed her. He sounded almost as if he were worried, or afraid. He, along with Dyami, had taken a hand in shaping her life. Benzi had tried to guide her family in the same way his people were trying to guide the Project, for some mysterious purpose of his own.

"Maybe you'll forget us," she said. "You don't think about us all that much even when you're here. How often do you see us? Why can't you—"

"Mahala." He knelt and took her by the arms. "Please trust me."

"That's what you all want us to do—trust you. We're supposed to think that all you want is to help, that you know what's best for us. How do I even know you'll come back?"

"Because I'm promising you that I will."

"Benzi." Her voice caught. "I don't know what I'm supposed to do."

"Don't think of what you're supposed to do—think of what you want."

"I can't have what I want here."

"What is it that you want?" Benzi asked.

"To leave. Not for good, not for the rest of my life, just long enough so that I can see other things and then come back and want to stay, long enough so that—I don't know how to say it."

"You may be able to have what you want."

"You're just saying that, Benzi."

"I'm not. We're more alike than you think. You might be surprised at how many others have hopes much like your own. Follow your path, Mahala, but don't look so far ahead that you miss seeing too much of what lies along the road. Do you understand?"

"You're telling me not to get impatient."

"That's part of it. That was one of the more difficult things I had to learn when I was first living among Habbers."

They walked back to the house. "I'll miss you," Mahala said as they approached the greenhouse. "That must sound funny—it's not as if I see you all that much anyway." She paused. "Are you going to tell Risa now?"

"Tomorrow. It'll be easier to tell her and Sef alone."

"Farewell, Benzi." Mahala swallowed. "I wanted to say it now."

"Farewell, Mahala—only until I come back."

She reached for his hand, clasped it tightly, then heard him sigh as they walked toward the house.

Islands

9

The airship carrying Mahala from Oberg to Turing was one of the newer dirigibles, with walls and a sliding door to separate the pilots from the passenger and cargo section. The design struck her as both useless and as an affectation. People traveling on airships knew better than to distract the pilots while they were monitoring their controls; all such a barrier did was increase the psychological distance between the pilots and the passengers. We may all be fellow Cytherians in the settlements and on the Islands, the wall seemed to say, but on this airship, your lives are in our hands and we are much too important to be bothered with you.

That she now could not view the Venusian landscape on the large screen above the pilots' console was a minor inconvenience. She had opened a channel to the airship's sensors and was picking up their data and images on her pocket screen.

Mahala had noticed a few small patches of lichens and moss on her way back to Turing. Six months ago, during the trip to Oberg, the brown and olive-green patches had been even smaller against the rocky landscape, not visible at all except with a magnified image. Ishtar Terra was still barren, but thin layers of a genetically engineered moss, nourished by the heat and able to survive in darkness, now clung precariously to the sides of hills and ridges and the cliffs below Turing.

The Cytherian environment outside the domes had continued to change during the fifteen years of Mahala's life. If a way could be found to lock more of Venus's excess oxygen into the surface rocks, instead of having to ferry it up to the Bats, more seeding of the outside might be possible. For now, the shallow oceans fed by the constant acidic drizzle remained sterile, and the only life except for the moss that could survive was the algae that fed on Venus's clouds of sulfur dioxide. The Project ought to get more aggressive, she thought, whatever it cost and however many life-forms failed; eventually more would evolve on their own and thrive.

In the Freyja Mountains, the domes for two more future settlements, al-Farghani and Yang, were being constructed. With a steadily dropping surface temperature and atmospheric pressure, these domes did not have to be quite as strong as the older ones, but would be built to the same specifications anyway; the engineers were taking no chances. This world was still hostile, seismically active, and with more newly awakened volcanoes; better to have as much protection for the settlers as possible. Their home, as Dyami often said, required constant intervention, constant vigilance, underlined by the assumption that there would always be a human civilization capable of maintaining the Cytherian biosphere. In the meantime, all they had were their embryonic biospheres, the environments of their domes.

Mahala released her harness, then followed the other airship passengers to the exit. A woman who had come aboard in al-Khwarizmi had pestered her with questions for a while, with inquiries about Risa's latest meetings with the Island Administrators, as if Mahala would know anything about that, and whether or not there was any truth to the rumor that fewer Cytherians would be allowed to study at Earth's Cytherian Institute in the future.

The other passengers had soon been eavesdropping on the conversation, although Mahala had no answers to offer the woman. Meetings with Administrators, she had explained, were not a subject her grandmother would discuss with her fifteen-year-old granddaughter, but Risa Liangharad could be counted on to defend the interests of the settlers. Mahala hoped that the number of students traveling to Earth remained the same, or even increased, since she still harbored hopes of studying at the Institute herself.

She had been truthful in admitting that ambition. What she did not say to the woman was that she wanted to go to the Institute largely because that was probably the only way she would ever see Earth. She was doing well in biology, a specialty that would become increasingly important during the next stages of the Project. If she got into the Cytherian Institute and did well, she could even hope for Linker training. She might return to her world to become an aide to an Island Administrator, about the highest goal an accomplished graduate could reach, and then—

She could not see what might lie beyond that for her. It was probably better not to dream of too much past that point. The more highly trained she was, the more she would owe to the Project, and the more she would be expected to contribute to her world.

Odd, she thought, to think of the end of her training as possibly being the end of her dreams as well.

Frania had come to meet her in the bay. The brown-haired girl shrieked a greeting, threw her arms around Mahala, then led her through the bay's wide doorway.

"I really missed you," Frania said, reaching for Mahala's duffel. "I think I enjoyed having our room to myself for about two days. After that, it got very tiresome."

"I know what you mean," Mahala said. "My grandparents put me in the smallest room in the house, and after a few days I was wishing you were there—I didn't care how crowded we'd be."

"Dyami had a couple of new arrivals stay with us for a while, but the place still seemed empty without you."

"I had the opposite problem—people all over the place. Noella's children and grandchildren come over all the time, and Barika and Kristof's daughter was born just before I started packing to come back. It's too much family!" Mahala was suddenly sorry for those words. Except for Amina, the other girl had no family now; her grandfather had died two months ago. "I didn't mean—"

"I know." Frania was still smiling. "Look, as far as I'm concerned, you and Dyami are my family, too—you know that. So's Tasida, in a way—even Balin is like an uncle." Frania was still as slender as she had always been, but she had grown taller during the past months, and her green shirt was tighter across her breasts. Her thick brown hair fell nearly to her waist, and her hazel eyes dominated her delicately boned face. During the past couple of years, she had become a beauty, but seemed unaware of it.

"I forgot to tell you," Frania continued as they walked along the wide road toward the refinery. "Tasida's thinking of moving in with us.

She's been spending a lot more time with us as it is—about the only time she's over at her own house now is to see patients."

"You mentioned that in your last message."

"She's still getting along with everybody there, but she's always wanted to live with Amina. She told me that maybe it's time for a change."

Risa had said much the same thing to Dyami, while trying to convince him to send Mahala back to Oberg for an extended visit. Dyami had understood, and Mahala, despite a few qualms, had quickly agreed to go. For a while, the more crowded confines of Oberg had diverted her, and she had happily taken over many of the chores in her grandparents' greenhouse. Kolya had often taken her to the lake while he fished, teaching her how to bait the lines, and Sef always made time to talk to her, as he had when she was a small child.

Her first day at her old school was more disappointing. Three of her former schoolmates had shown enough promise to be chosen for Island schools. Two had moved to other settlements with their families, and Ah Lin Bergen was still in school, hoping to become a teacher; she had come back from Island Four only two months earlier.

Their other schoolmates, Ah Lin informed her, had left school to apprentice themselves. "At least a few of them could have gone on with their studies," Ah Lin said when Mahala expressed her surprise. "But I can understand why they left. It doesn't make sense to be too ambitious here."

"Most fifteen-year-olds in Turing are still in school," Mahala had replied.

"That's Turing. It's different there. People there seem to want more than the rest of us—that's what everyone says."

"Well, isn't it better to do as much as you can and try for as much as possible, even if you fail?"

Ah Lin's brown eyes warmed with sympathy. "Oh, we can try, but it's easier to give up." She sounded resigned. "Settle for what you can get, and you save yourself a lot of disappointment later on."

Mahala shook her head. "You wouldn't want to be a teacher if you really believed that."

"Sure I would. A teacher's job isn't just to encourage students to learn all they can. It's also to get them to accept what they have to be in the end, to understand that they owe something to their world, to think of Venus instead of just themselves."

"I don't think you completely believe that, either."

Ah Lin had a half-smile on her round face. "Look, I'll push any students of mine as far as I can, Mahala, and as far as they want to go. But I know I'll probably fail with most of them."

"So what have you been doing?" Frania asked, breaking in on Mahala's thoughts.

Mahala wrenched herself back to the present. "Doing?"

"In Oberg. You didn't send any messages, so I figured you had to be busy."

"I guess I was." Mahala felt a twinge of guilt. She might have made time to send Frania more messages or called more often, but she had not known how to convey her sense of unease and disappointment. After several attempts at setting down messages in writing, or speaking them aloud to the screen, it had been easier not to try.

"So how was it?" Frania asked.

"Except for my friend Ah Lin, there was hardly anybody my age or older still attending my old school. I put in some time being a teacher's aide." Eugenio Tokugawa had asked her to assist in his classroom occasionally with the younger children. "And there was plenty of work to do at my grandparents' house." Mahala paused. "I should have called you, Frani. I tried, but every time I got ready to call, I started thinking about Oberg and what's happened to some of my old friends, and then I just—"

"I understand. I could see it in your face when I called, your disappointment."

Her former schoolmates had given up. They would do what they could for the Project and find whatever happiness they could in their work, even if they had once dreamed of a different kind of life. Such resignation seemed contrary to the spirit of the Project, to the dream of creating a new world. Maybe Benzi had given up, too. That might be why he had not returned or even sent her a message.

It was foolish to think that way. Risa had left school at an early age, and Sef could barely read his own name, but no one could claim that they had not contributed much to the Project. Yet their lives seemed constricted, and she knew that they both had regrets about what they might have learned.

"Have you heard anything from Solveig?" Mahala asked.

"I got a message from her yesterday," Frania replied. "She's going to Anwara. It's just for a week, but she's really excited about it—says one of the astronomers there is going to show the students around. She said hello to you." Solveig had been admitted to a school on Island Two nearly a year ago and would be there for at least another year. "That reminds me—Ragnar's going to be here in a couple of days."

Mahala slowed as they came to the ceramics plant. Solveig had come to Turing alone during her last two visits; Ragnar still spoke to Dyami over the screen, but Mahala had not seen him for almost two years. She frowned. Solveig had sometimes hinted that she was worried about her brother, but had avoided saying anything more specific.

"He probably just wants to get more instruction from Dyami," Mahala said.

"I don't know. He was kind of mysterious about what he's coming here for, and I didn't ask."

"I would have asked, especially with his kind of record. How many black marks does he have now, anyway?"

"That's not fair, Mahala," Frania said in her gentle voice. "His reprimands were only for being in protests, and he hasn't been involved with any protesters for a while."

Frania, she thought, would always stand up for Ragnar. "I'll enjoy seeing him anyway," Mahala murmured, a bit surprised that she meant it.

Frania filled her in on the doings of their schoolmates as they approached the tunnel to the north dome. All of them were still in school, although a few would be apprenticing themselves soon. In a couple of years, some would probably be volunteering for Bat duty; Frania was betting that Gino Hislop-Carnera would be the first to do so.

Mahala looked toward the Habber residence as they came out of the tunnel. She should go there right now and do what she had never been able to bring herself to do; tell Balin that she wanted to send a message to Benzi. She had put it off for too long, afraid that Benzi might not want to receive her message. But Balin probably wasn't there now anyway; he would be waiting at her uncle's house to welcome her home.

Turing was truly her home now. She welcomed its stretches of empty land after the clutter of Oberg; at the same time, she felt as if she knew Turing too well, that she had already exhausted it and would never discover anything new here again.

*   *   *

Dyami greeted her with Balin at his side. Her uncle and Amina had made her favorite vegetable soup and dark bread, and Tasida soon arrived to share the meal with them.

She would not ruin their evening by pestering Balin for news of Benzi. If he had any sort of message from her great-uncle, he would have conveyed it to her by now; so she told herself, while wondering if that was the case. In all the time that she had been living with Dyami, Balin had been practically part of her uncle's household, yet she could still feel that she did not truly know the Habber.

She also knew little of his and Benzi's society or of its limits. Benzi might be unable to return; the Habbers might be more restricted in their comparative freedom than she assumed.

"Frani told me Ragnar's coming to visit," Mahala said after she had finished her recitation of recent events in Risa's household.

"Actually, he isn't just going to be visiting," Dyami said.

Frania glanced at Mahala, apparently as surprised as she was. "I found out today," Dyami continued. "Ragnar's planning to live in Turing. More digger and crawler operators are needed for the work on Turing's new east dome, now that the topsoil's laid down. Turns out that Ragnar can run the machines—he apprenticed himself a year ago. I don't know why he never told me, but I suppose he thought it was his business and not mine."

"Oh," Frania murmured. Mahala set down her cup; Solveig had not told her that Ragnar had left school.

"Anyway, Ragnar put himself on the list," Dyami said, "and the engineering team seems happy to have him. His record shows that he's a hard worker and that he also has the understanding of spacial relationships that a good operator needs. I guess that's not surprising, given his artistic gifts, and—"

"How could he?" Mahala burst out.

Amina lifted her brows slightly; Tasida sat up and wrinkled her nose. "How could he what?" Dyami asked.

"Give up like that. In Oberg, at our old school, he'd do as well as anybody whenever he bothered to work. He could have gone to an Island school if he'd tried. How could he settle for being a crawler and digger operator?"

Dyami frowned. "I'll remind you," he said softly, "that Risa doesn't consider running diggers and crawlers beneath her, and that Sef earns some of his credit repairing them. Your great-grandmother, in spite of her climatology degree from the Cytherian Institute, had a bond with a laborer—you're his great-grandchild, too."

Her grandmother would have said almost exactly the same thing. Amina might be a metallurgical engineer, with training at an Island school, but she was capable of running a crawler. Dyami himself, who had once hoped to make mathematics his specialization, seemed content to do his mining and engineering tasks at the refinery and the ceramics plant while limiting his mathematical pursuits to what he could pick up from files in the net of minds, journal articles transmitted from Earth, and what he could learn from Balin.

"I'm sorry," Mahala mumbled. "I didn't mean—" She paused. "Most of my old schoolmates in Oberg aren't in school anymore. It isn't that what they're doing now isn't important, it's just that maybe they're settling for less than what they might have done. And now Ragnar—"

Dyami's brown eyes grew warmer. "I understand. But if Ragnar's making a mistake, he's the one who has to live with it. He might not be wrong, you know. He'll have his choice of sites in the east dome when it's finished, if he wants to live there, and there's nothing to stop him from pursuing more education with screen lessons. I'd like to ask him to stay here with us, as long as it's all right with you. I'm sure his parents would rather have him in this house instead of with strangers or living in a tent."

Frania cleared her throat. "That's fine with me."

Mahala set down her soup spoon. "Of course he can stay." Solveig must know of Ragnar's plans by now; her parents would have told her about them even if her brother had not. Ragnar would not follow his sister to the Islands. Mahala felt a pang of regret; she had assumed that they might all be there eventually—she, Solveig, Frania, and Ragnar—dreaming together of other places they might see and deeds they might accomplish.

She gazed across the table at her uncle. For a moment, she thought she saw her regrets hiding in Dyami's eyes before he turned to murmur a few words to Balin.

Mahala and Frania went to meet Ragnar at the airship bay. He had grown much taller during the past two years and wore his long blond hair pulled back in a braid. His face was as chiseled as one of his sculptures, his shoulders broad; he looked like a man now.

Frania blushed as she greeted him. Mahala murmured a few words of welcome as she picked up one of his three duffels.

"I won't be with you for more than a few days," Ragnar said. "One of the engineers said they'd get a temporary shelter up for anyone who doesn't have a place to live."

"But you have to stay with us," Frania murmured. "Dyami will insist. You'll have to sleep in the common room, at least for now, but—"

"That's all right, then. I didn't want to ask Dyami myself, but I was hoping he might let me stay with him."

"You could have asked," Frania said, her blush deepening. "We all want you to stay, for as long as you like."

"I won't be in your way," Ragnar said. "I asked for a schedule of darktime shifts, so I can sleep when you're all out of the house."

"You asked for darktime shifts?" Mahala said. Most people took them only reluctantly, when their turns at them came around. "But why?"

"Why not? Anyway, they were glad to let me have them."

The two duffels the girls had taken were light enough to carry to the house. Ragnar lifted the largest one to his shoulder. "Have you heard anything from Solveig?" Mahala asked.

"Haven't talked to her in a while," Ragnar replied.

"I was just wondering what she thought about your coming here to work."

His eyes narrowed. "It was my decision." He turned and followed Frania toward the road.

"Exactly what kind of work will you be doing?" the other girl asked.

"They've assigned me to digging tunnels for now," he replied. "But with the dome up already, I'm hoping they'll move me to landscaping." He went on to speak of his training in both remote and manual control of the machines; apparently, unlike some operators, he had also learned something about repairing the diggers and crawlers. Frania gazed at him raptly whenever the three slowed their pace, as if the story of Ragnar's apprenticeship were the most fascinating tale she had ever heard.

Mahala was soon lagging behind them. They looked perfect together, the two of them, tall and graceful. The last time Ragnar had visited them, over two years ago, he had made a bust of Frania, modeling her face in clay for the mold Dyami helped him cast later at the refinery. Frania had kept still for hours while he worked, the perfect model; Mahala had never been able to stop fidgeting whenever she sat for him. Maybe he would try his hand at painting Frania now that Dyami, in a burst of uncharacteristic extravagance, had spent a huge amount of credit on imported paints and canvases from Earth.

Frania loved Ragnar. Mahala had known that for a while. Now she saw the longing in Frania's hazel eyes, a look that flared into joy whenever Ragnar so much as glanced at her.

A lump rose in Mahala's throat; she swallowed hard. She had never spoken to Frania of her own tangled feelings for Ragnar, partly because she could not be sure of what she actually felt. His emotional distance, the way he seemed to care for nothing but his art, had often convinced her that she disliked him. She had thought she was past her own emotional confusion, that mix of rage and yearning that melted into gratitude for his occasional kindnesses toward her.

But her own feelings for Ragnar did not matter. Frania would be deeply hurt if she ever saw into Mahala's troubled heart; better not to reveal her emotions. Ragnar would only mock her if he ever found out how she felt. He could not possibly care for someone like her when a girl as kind and beautiful as Frania adored him.

"Have you thought about what you want to do?" Ragnar was saying to Frania.

"I didn't know for the longest time," she replied. "Then, about a month ago, I realized that I did know, and then it was as if I'd known what I wanted to be all along and just hadn't seen it. I'd like to be a pilot."

Mahala faltered, stunned by this admission, then hastened to catch up with the two. "A pilot?" she said as she came up on Frania's left, bewildered that her friend had not even hinted at this ambition before revealing it to Ragnar. "This is the first I've heard of it."

"It doesn't surprise me," Ragnar said. "You always did want to see other places. If you're a pilot, you'll get to visit all the Islands and settlements eventually—and Anwara."

"Maybe even Earth," Frania said, "if I can train to be a torchship pilot—but there are enough of those from Earth, so a Cytherian doesn't have much of a chance at that."

"I thought you were going to try for an Island school," Mahala said, "and study biology."

"Oh, Mahala—I couldn't get in. I'm sure of that now. It's kind of a relief to know that, in a way."

"But we always talked of going together," Mahala muttered.

"I know we did, but—" Frania stopped and searched Mahala's face. "I don't think that's really for me, Mahala. Look, once you make it into an Island school, I can visit you. I'll have to come there anyway for shuttle training."

"That's if you make it into pilot training," Mahala said, "or get through it. A lot of people want to be pilots, so they can go here and there and not be stuck in one place most of the time. They can't accept everyone for the job."

Frania flinched. Ragnar shifted from one foot to the other, obviously annoyed. "I didn't mean that you don't have a chance," Mahala said hastily.

"I'll make it," Frania said, sounding more confident than she ever had before. "I've taken some tests, the ones you do with a band and simulations. I did very well. As soon as I try the next tests, I'll tell Amina if I pass them, too. I don't want to say anything to her until I know I have a real chance at becoming a pilot."

"Come on," Ragnar said. "I'm going to be starving by the time we get to your house."

They continued toward the tunnel. Mahala was silent as her two friends, their lives now seemingly mapped out, chattered of their plans.

Ragnar ate a meal of bread and cheese, then suggested a walk along the lake. Mahala followed the two down the rocky slope, feeling as though she was in their way and wishing that she had thought of an excuse to stay behind. But they were likely to run into other young people, since many of their friends spent their free time near the water. Mahala could go off with another group then and leave Frania and Ragnar to themselves.

But the shore was deserted; even the few daring young people who had recently taken up swimming were absent. Mahala searched the trees as they neared the forested land and saw no one.

They had said little while walking. Ragnar let out a sigh and sat down on a clear patch of land as Frania settled herself next to him. Mahala gazed out at the still surface of the nameless lake. No one had given the lake in Oberg's west dome a name, either. They left the landmarks in their environments without names or labeled them according to their functions; they continued to mark time by Earthly days and months and years, as if knowing that they and their artifacts and designations of time and place were only the prelude to the true Cytherian civilization, that nothing in their own culture was likely to endure.

"I like it here in Turing," Ragnar said then.

"Better than Hypatia?" Frania asked.

"Yeah." Ragnar shrugged. "Part of that's because of Dyami's house. He picked a good site for it, and I like its design more than that of most houses I've seen. About the only thing I'd do differently with my own house is maybe have it closer to the trees."

Mahala sat down and folded her legs. "Is that why you came here to work? Because you like it and want to build a house here?"

Ragnar leaned back, resting an arm on one raised knee. "That's part of it."

"I don't understand you." Mahala could not restrain herself anymore. "Is that all you want to do with your life, run diggers and crawlers and then go home to your house?"

Ragnar's face paled slightly. "It's what I want to do now."

"I guess I thought you were more ambitious."

"Mahala." Frania touched her arm. "Be fair. What's wrong with that?"

"I didn't say there was anything wrong with it." Mahala took a breath. "It's just—you could have gone to an Island school, Ragnar. You're smart enough that they probably would have admitted you even with your record. You could have done something else, and you just threw away all your chances."

"I didn't throw anything away." Ragnar sat up straight. "I know exactly what I'm doing. I don't much care what kind of job I have, as long as I'm good at it and can earn my credit doing it. The kind of work I'll be doing won't get in the way of my art, and that's what matters to me."

"Your art?" Mahala shook her head. "Is that all you really care about—your hobby?"

"It isn't just a hobby to me." Ragnar's eyes were cold, his face taut. "It's something I have to do. Don't ask me why—that's just the way it is with me. That hobby is my real life, it means the most to me—nothing else really counts. If I couldn't make the things I do, it would be like not being able to breathe. I thought you'd understand that by now."

"I do understand," Mahala said. "I know it means a lot to you, it's just—" She paused. "Dyami's like you. He needs time to do his sculptures and models, too, but it isn't his whole life."

"Well, that's one way we're different, then."

Frania was gazing intently at the boy, obviously ready to take his side. "Dyami's taught me a lot," Ragnar continued. "That monument he designed and made—I never asked him what it was like for him when he was working on it. I figured he probably wouldn't want to talk about it, given what he went through being a prisoner. But I'll bet that while he was doing that monument, it was everything to him, that it took up his whole life."

"That's probably true," Mahala said. "He used to say that he had to do it."

"Maybe he was thinking of his friends," Ragnar said, "the ones who died under torture and the ones who were killed in the final battle against their guards. Maybe it was the only way he could deal with what happened to him when he was a prisoner. It's possible he put so much of himself into that monument that there wasn't much left over, or maybe it was just that he had one great creation in him and no more. The point is that he's finished his real work—it's enough for him now to do his job and play around with sculpting and teach me a few things and maybe dabble in math with Balin. I want to do more than that."

"Then you should have stayed in school," Mahala said. "You still could have had your art."

"That's where you're wrong." Ragnar leaned toward her. "All of those studies would have just been in my way. Frankly, I probably wouldn't even have done well at them because I'd have known all along it wasn't what I wanted. This way, I can do my job and give the rest of my time to myself."

"I suppose that's why you asked for darktime shifts," Mahala said. "Most people are busy after first light, so they won't be bothering you."

"That's one reason."

"You'll have even more time to yourself and your little pastime."

Ragnar's hands fisted. "It isn't a pastime," he muttered. Mahala was suddenly sorry for her words, suddenly puzzled by what she had said to him.

"Please," Frania said, "do you two have to argue on our first day together?"

"I know why you're upset." Ragnar's eyes were still on Mahala. "You just want me to be with you, doing whatever you want me to do. You're mad at me because there's something else I want more than being around you—or being around anyone."

Mahala jumped to her feet, stung. "I can't stand being around you sometimes, and I don't care what you do, either."

"Then leave me alone."

"I'll be glad to." She walked away quickly, then made her way over the rocks toward the trees. He had struck at the source of her anger and disappointment, that she had hoped he might follow her dreams, become more closely bound to her life. Her cheeks burned; she felt both furious and ashamed. Maybe he had even guessed that, whenever she allowed herself to indulge fully in her fantasies, she had imagined that Ragnar would be at her side to explore the Islands and Earth.

She sat down and rested her back against a tree. Ragnar and Frania were on their feet; the boy was speaking, but she could not hear his voice. At last Frania wandered off, head down, as Ragnar climbed toward the trees.

I've ruined everything, Mahala thought. She had been meaning to put in her request to be considered for an Island school, and there was no point in putting that off any longer. Ragnar would have his art and Frania her pilot's training; the two were not likely to miss her once she was gone.

Ragnar was coming toward her. Mahala wanted to get up and walk away, but she would still have to deal with him back at her uncle's house later.

"Frani's upset," he said as he sat down next to her.

"I'm sorry."

"You should be sorry for that. She wouldn't do that to you."

"I'm sorry I said what I did to you. I just thought—" Mahala kept staring at the lake, refusing to look at him. "I only said it because I think you could do more."

"I'm doing what I want to do." He drew up his knees and rested his head on them. "I considered it for a long time. I have to do things this way now. I thought you'd understand."

"I understand that it's what you want, Ragnar. I just don't understand why you want it so much."

"Well, at least we can agree on that, because I don't, either."

She glanced at him and was surprised to see a smile flicker across his face. "You don't?"

"It's as if I really don't have any choice. It's what I have to do, whatever it means, whatever mistakes I make trying to do it. Maybe you think I've forgotten about how we used to talk about seeing other places or being more than we are, but I haven't. When I'm drawing or sculpting, it's as if I'm in another place then. I just feel—I don't know how to explain it—that this is how I have to find my way to something else."

"I think I see."

"I hope so." Ragnar sighed. "I've been arguing with my parents for the past year—I had to get away from them. Thorunn keeps saying that I'm wasting my time when I could be doing something useful and Einar was always after me to figure out how to sell my stuff and at least get paid some credit for it. And Solveig was always trying to act as if she understands what I'm doing, but I'm not sure she really does. I don't want you after me, too."

"I won't be. Anyway, I'm going to put in for an Island school, so if I'm lucky, you won't have to put up with me for much longer."

"Oh." He was silent for a while. "You haven't applied yet. So I thought maybe you'd changed your plans."

"I was putting it off, and I thought Frani and I could apply together, and then Risa wanted me to stay with her for a while, and—" Mahala looked away from Ragnar. "Well, it's silly to wait now. I'll have a lot of work ahead of me if I'm going to get into the Cytherian Institute."

"So you still want that. The story I heard was that Earth doesn't want as many Cytherian students there now. Makes sense—graduates from Earth who come here might have more loyalty to the Mukhtars. A lot of people think their main reason for having any of us there at all is so they can convince more of us to be sympathetic to Earth's interests back here."

She sat up. "Are you trying to get back at me?"

"I'm telling you that you might not gain that much from going to the Institute."

"So now you're telling me to do what *you* want."

"What you do is your business, Mahala. I'll admit I want you to stay. I don't think for one second that you will stay if a school accepts you."

"Ragnar, I—"

"Can't you see? For somebody intelligent, you can be awfully stupid. I moved here because of you, because you're here."

She averted her gaze, unable to look at him. "I didn't think—"

"Oh, part of coming here, an important reason, was so I could be around Dyami. He's about the only person I know who understands me at all. But it was mostly you, Mahala. I thought you would have guessed that by now."

She raised her head and met his eyes. "You don't make it easy for me. About all we've done since you got here is argue."

"I thought it'd be different, that maybe I wouldn't feel the same about you when I was here, but I did. Then you had to start in on how I was making a big mistake."

"I didn't mean—"

He grabbed her by the shoulders and pulled her toward him. His mouth met hers awkwardly, his lips too hard against hers. An arm slipped around her waist, cradling her.

Mahala drew back, then rested her head against his chest. "Now you know," he said softly. "If you don't feel the same way about me, then say so now, and I won't bother you again."

She could not speak.

"You don't have to worry, Mahala. I just want to know where I stand. I'll leave you alone if that's the way you want it."

A spark of joy flared up inside her. She had wanted this all along, had longed for it so much that she had found it too painful to contemplate. Now he had shown that he longed for her, but she could feel herself wavering. Why did she suddenly feel as though her life was no longer her own?

She thought of Frania, of how hurt the other girl would be to learn of Ragnar's feelings. Better to tell him that he could be no more than a friend. He would get over her in time, and her feelings for him would eventually fade. Older people said that to younger ones all the time.

"Ragnar," she whispered.

"You do care," he said. "You do."

"Yes." She nearly choked on the word. His arms tightened around her. A few children were scampering over the rocks below, climbing toward the trees. "Not here," she managed to say, overwhelmed by doubt.

"Later, then," he said. "After supper. We can find a spot. Everybody will think we're just taking a walk."

"You're forgetting about Frani."

"What's Frani got to do with it? You can tell her we want to be by ourselves. She won't say anything to the others."

Something twisted inside her. She could not bear to hurt Frania that way, but her only other choice was to lie to her. That was what Ragnar was offering, a chance to wound the girl she thought of as her sister, or else to deceive her. Telling him that Frania loved him would be a betrayal of her friend's secret, and she could not know how he would react.

Frania, of course, would be kind and understanding about everything, no matter how deeply she might be hurt. Mahala consoled herself with that thought.

They sat together for a while, not moving. Ragnar got up and held out his arm. She thrust her hand into his as he led her down the rocky slope.

10

He had made love to her as though he was practiced at it, his earlier awkwardness gone. He seemed to know when to wait and when to kiss her for long moments.

"I love you," Ragnar whispered. A hand brushed the hair from her face, then reached down to cup her hip. She could not see him in the darkness under the trees. She had shuddered under him, grateful he could not see her until the pleasure he was bringing her drove other thoughts from her mind.

I'm not ready for this, she thought, now that it was too late. Somehow she had expected these moments to be different. When she had gone to Tasida two years ago to get her contraceptive implant, as everyone did upon reaching puberty, the physician had offered to answer any of Mahala's questions. Mahala had loftily replied that she knew everything already and that she needed no more information. She would know when the time was right for her, when the boy was someone she could both love and trust, and then everything would be perfect. She had not been prepared for the melancholy that filled her now and the feeling that she might have made a mistake.

Ragnar had saved her the trouble of lying to Frania. "Mahala and I are going to take a walk," he had said after dinner. Amina had gone out to their greenhouse behind the kitchen; Dyami was at the other side of the common room, sketching. "You don't mind if we go by ourselves, do you?" Frania had flinched, her eyes widening with pain before her smile quickly reappeared.

She knows, Mahala had thought. Before she could tell Ragnar that she did not want to go with him, Frania had practically been pushing them out the door. "Go on," the other girl had said, still with that frozen smile on her face.

Ragnar's hand ran along her spine. Mahala twisted away from him and sat up, pulling on her shirt. Beyond the trees, a silvery disk, the reflection of the dome's light, floated on the glassy black surface of the lake.

"What's the matter?" Ragnar asked.

"When did you know? How you felt about me, I mean."

"I've known for a while—just didn't want to admit it to myself. There was someone in Hypatia. I figured if I found another girl, maybe my feelings toward you would change, but I still wanted you even when I was with her."

He had admitted it, just like that; she had not even had to ask him if there had been another before her. "Oh," she murmured.

"It didn't mean anything."

"If it didn't mean anything, then you shouldn't have done it."

"Look, it didn't mean anything to her, either. She was a couple of years older than me. I think she just wanted some fun before she left to go on Bat duty."

"We should go home," she said. "Dyami will be wondering why we're out so late." Her uncle had probably guessed why they had left the house, especially when Frania had stayed behind, but would naturally be concerned. He would undoubtedly still be sitting up, as would Amina, in case she or Ragnar needed to talk. If she said nothing, her uncle and his housemate would not intrude on their privacy. But she would have to face Frania, whom she had hurt.

"We'll come here tomorrow," Ragnar said. "I don't start work until the day after."

"Maybe we ought to restrain ourselves for a while."

His hand slipped into hers. "You're thinking of Frani, aren't you?" Mahala could not reply. "I saw it in her eyes, when we left. I honestly didn't know how she felt until then. We're all going to be living in the same house, so we can't exactly hide it from her."

"We don't have to rub her nose in it, either."

"I'm sorry, Mahala. If I'd known, I would have told Dyami I couldn't stay with him. That might have made it a little easier on her."

She slipped her hand from his, wondering if he meant that, if he had truly meant it when he had said he loved her.

*   *   *

Dyami and Amina stayed up just long enough to see that neither Mahala or Ragnar wanted to talk to them. Frania was already in bed. Mahala went to the bathroom to wash, then back into the common room.

Ragnar sat at a table, slouched over a screen. Mahala glanced toward his futon. "Aren't you going to sleep?"

"Might as well stay up. I'm going to be working late shifts anyway, so I should get used to that schedule." His stylus moved across the screen. "Sit with me while I sketch."

"Are you going to draw me?"

He shook his blond head. "You're not a good model. Frani's more cooperative—I never have to tell her to hold still."

"Then I'm going to bed." She pressed the door to her room open. Frania had left a small light on near Mahala's bed. She tiptoed across the room as the door closed, then heard a sigh as she was reaching toward her clothing rod for a shift.

Mahala turned. Frania was sitting up, but her long hair hid most of her face. "Tasida came over while you were out," Frania said in a toneless voice. "Moved in some of her things. She's keeping her office in her old house, though."

"Just as well," Mahala said.

"Dyami said Balin will be over tomorrow."

"Good. I promised myself that the next time I saw him, I'd ask if I could send a message to Benzi. Maybe he'll actually respond."

"I didn't tell them anything about you and Ragnar," Frania said, so softly that Mahala could hardly hear her. "Amina and Dyami don't know. If he doesn't care about me, there's nothing I can do about it—I'll just have to—" Her voice broke; she covered her eyes with one hand.

"Frani." Mahala went to her and sat down on Frania's bed. "I'm sorry. I shouldn't have gone with him."

"Don't be stupid. If he'd asked me, I would have gone and been happy about it, too, even if I knew you were in love with him. You are, aren't you."

"I guess I am," Mahala replied, not knowing even now if that was true.

"Then I won't ruin things for you. I can't force him to love me. I don't want him to know—I can't—"

Mahala held the other girl as she wept. It isn't worth it, she told herself; nothing was worth causing Frani such unhappiness and pain.

It was foolish to have such thoughts, when she knew that she would inevitably make love with Ragnar again.

"I've decided one thing," Mahala said when Frania's sobs had subsided. "I'm going to put in for an Island school right away, maybe tomorrow, and definitely before school starts again."

Frania drew away. "You don't have to do that for me."

"I'm not doing it just for you, Frani. It's something I always wanted, and I meant to do it anyway after I came back here. I have to apply as soon as I can now, because if I don't, I'll just keep putting it off. And the longer I do that, the more of a hold Ragnar will have on me."

Frania cleared her throat. "You really do care about him."

Mahala shook herself. "I wish I didn't. It makes me feel out of control. It makes me do something thoughtless like going off with him even when I knew how much that would hurt you."

"I'll get over it—being hurt, I mean. It isn't your fault that he feels the way he does." Frania smoothed down her shift. "If it had to be somebody else for him, I'm glad at least that it's you."

Mahala bowed her head. Had she been in the other girl's place, she wondered if she would have been so forbearing and forgiving.

Mahala did not go off with Ragnar the next evening, excusing herself by saying that she wanted to spend some time with Balin, whom she had not seen for so long. At last the boy went out by himself, telling her nothing about where he was going. She had meant to ask the Habber about Benzi, but Balin seemed more solemn than usual, and so she had contented herself with telling him about her hopes to study on one of the Islands. Balin had brightened a little when she said that; Dyami also seemed pleased by her plans.

Ragnar had still not returned by the time she and Frania were going to bed and was asleep on his futon when she got up for breakfast. Mahala spent the rest of the day with her screen, leaving messages for all her former teachers as she began to assemble her application for admission to an Island school. The Administrators in charge of the schools, once they had reviewed her public record and any recommendations her former teachers made, would ask her for an essay about her ambitions and how an Island school could further them, and she might as well get started on the admissions tests in the meantime.

The tests presented problems that could be solved in a number of different ways, much as her teachers in the Turing school had in many of their lessons.

Ragnar was shaping a piece of wood when she finally came out of her room into the common area. Frania sat near him, mending a shirt; she looked up. "Finished already?" the other girl asked.

Mahala shook her head. "I'm barely started. I'm just hoping I can finish all the tests before school starts. If an Administrator asks for an interview, then I'll know I had good recommendations." She glanced at Ragnar. He continued to work at his carving, apparently indifferent to her plans.

He said nothing to her until just before supper, when Frania went out to the greenhouse, Dyami and Balin were in the kitchen, and Amina was helping Tasida move a box of possessions into the room they would share. "I've got to go to work right after supper," he said. "My shift's over two hours before first light. Maybe you can meet me about half an hour later."

"Maybe I can't."

"You said you didn't want to upset Frani any more than necessary. We can get back to the house before anyone gets up. That might make things a little easier on her, not having to see us go off together."

"Oh." She was chagrined at not having thought of that herself. "I'll think about it."

"I'll wait down by the lake."

She slept uneasily that night, knowing she would go to him and angry with herself for that. The timepiece on her finger woke her with a slight shock; she pulled on a shift and pants, careful not to awaken Frania as she crept from the room.

Ragnar was sitting on a rock by the lake. As she hurried down to him, he got up and held out an arm. He seemed vulnerable at that moment, as trapped as she was by what he felt. She reached for his hand and followed him toward the trees.

They fell into a pattern. Every other night, Mahala slipped out before first light to meet Ragnar, then returned with him to the house before the others were up. Frania was not fooled, but Mahala had not really expected her to be, and they both avoided speaking of the matter. Dyami and Amina seemed aware of what was happening as well. Sometimes she would look up to see her uncle watching her, his brown eyes filled with concern.

When she and Ragnar made love, the pleasure he brought her and the happiness she felt at giving him joy were enough to quiet her doubts. Often they lay under the trees afterward, arms around each other as the dome slowly brightened. Sometimes Ragnar spoke of his team and his work; more often, he spoke of the tools he would need to fashion the objects he longed to make. He had greater ambitions than making small sculptures and paintings for people who might exchange credit for them; he dreamed of creating something on a larger scale, sculptures that might surpass Dyami's monument. She was in communion with him then, sympathizing with his desires even if she did not completely understand them.

Her uncertainty overtook her when they left their wooded refuge. If she won her way to an Island school, she would be apart from him, having to fear that his feelings might change when she was gone. Often, when she came home to find him at work on a painting or carving, it seemed that he had already forgotten her.

She grew more absentminded at school, slightly more careless in her work. Her teacher would let it pass for a while and assume that her application to the Island schools was distracting her, but too many such lapses would not help her chances. At home, she kept busy with any tasks she could find for herself in an effort to control her inner turbulence: weeding tiers in their greenhouse; checking the pipe of the toilet's waste dryer-compressor to make sure that it wasn't stopped up; mending her clothes; taking dishes out of the kitchen's cleaner and stacking them on shelves. It took the shock of receiving a message from Administrator Saburo Yamata to restore her to herself.

Administrator Saburo was in charge of the Island Two school, the one Solveig attended, and he wanted to interview her.

Mahala's teacher excused her from class for the interview. She spoke with Saburo Yamata in one of the school's smaller rooms. There was a moment of panic when his image appeared and she lifted her eyes to the large screen; she felt small and vulnerable, alone on a cushion in an empty room, as this Administrator prepared to judge her. He had put on his ceremonial white robe and headdress for the occasion, which was even more intimidating.

Administrator Saburo began by inquiring after her grandparents and her uncle, as if this were only a call from a friend of the family. By the time he was questioning her about her ambitions and what she hoped to gain from coming to an Island school, her unease was gone. She realized only four hours later, when she was leaving the room, that she had not thought about Ragnar at all during the interview.

The Administrator had promised a decision in seven days. It was possible that she might not be accepted now, but would be told she could apply again later. She was young; there might be a chance for her another time, when she was more mature. She wondered if she could live with that, or if Ragnar might convince her to surrender most of her dreams by then. She refused to think of what rejection might mean for her.

"Balin's coming by tonight, isn't he?" Ragnar asked as they left the trees.

"I think so," Mahala replied.

"I may give him a couple of my things to show to other Habbers. Maybe a few of his friends will ask me to do some drawings or carvings for them."

"I didn't think you were interested in earning credit for your pieces."

"I'm not," he said, "but it wouldn't hurt for some Habbers to know what I do and maybe take an interest in me. You've got relatives who joined the Habbers. Maybe someday more of us can do the same thing."

"What?" Mahala shook her head, surprised. "How can you possibly—"

"What would the Project be losing? A digger and crawler operator who dabbles in a few crafts—that's how most people here would look at me."

"You want to be a Habber?"

He halted, then sat down on a rock. "No. Not really. I just don't want to have to think of myself as a component in the Project. What do you think those protests were about? If I can have what I want by staying here, I'd be content with that, but if I can't, I'd rather be somewhere else." He turned toward her as she seated herself. "I can say that to you, Mahala. I wouldn't tell anybody else, not even Frani or my sister."

"You'd leave Venus for good if you got the chance. That's what you're saying."

"If that was my only choice, I would. I want my own life. You ought to understand that—you want the same thing."

That was true, she supposed, although she would not have stated her wishes quite as baldly as Ragnar had. "If I don't get into an Island school," she said, "I'll have to settle for what I can have and how I can be of most use here, not necessarily what I would prefer."

"You could teach," he said.

"But I wouldn't be as good a teacher as someone who wants to do that more than anything." She suddenly envied Ragnar for knowing what he wanted, for having something that might sustain him even if many of his other hopes were dashed.

"That Administrator said he'd give you an answer by today," Ragnar said. "He might already have left a message for you."

Mahala's hands tightened on her knees. "I can't look at his reply with everybody else around. I'll wait."

"Until after school? I don't know how—"

"I'm not going to school. I've never missed before—no one's going to mess up my record over one day. I'll wait here until they're all out of the house. Whatever Saburo tells me, I can handle it better if I'm alone."

"Well." Ragnar stood up. "I'll tell them you just need some time to yourself—they'll understand." His hand rested on her shoulder for a moment. "Hope you get what you want."

Dyami was the last to leave the house. Mahala saw him look back from the bottom of the hill and lift his hand, as if acknowledging that he understood.

She waited until he was across the bridge, then got to her feet and climbed toward the house. Ragnar was asleep on his futon in the common room. Mahala hurried to her room and let the door slide shut behind her, then moved toward her bed. A pocket screen lay on the small table between her bed and Frania's; she picked it up and saw that there were two private messages for her.

The first was from Frania. "Good luck," the girl's image said as Mahala sat down with the screen. "I don't know what else to say, but just wanted you to know I'm hoping for you. If they don't take you, they're idiots."

Frania's image disappeared as Mahala rested the screen on her lap. The other message was from Administrator Saburo. She took a deep breath as his face appeared.

"Congratulations, Mahala Liangharad," the Administrator said, allowing himself a brief smile. "I'm pleased to inform you that you have been accepted at Island Two's preparatory school, with a chance to advance to the university level if your preparatory work is satisfactory. Our next term will begin just after the New Year, and we look forward to having you among us."

She was very still, unable to move. Saburo's image was replaced by that of an older man, who went on to tell her that she would soon get a list of her courses and teachers and that living quarters would be found for her if she had any problem making her own arrangements. The names of people willing to have a student live with their families, and a list of other available quarters for individuals and small groups, were appended to this message. She was to let the school know her plans within two weeks and should feel free to ask any questions she might have at that time.

She turned off the screen. This message would be the same one sent to all those who were accepted; she would listen to it again later.

She went into the common room. Ragnar stirred under his coverlet as she walked toward him.

She said, "I got in."

Ragnar sat up and rubbed at his face. "What?"

"They accepted me."

"That's great," he said without hesitation, then reached for her and pulled her down to him. "I'm glad, I really am." She looked into his eyes and saw that he truly was happy for her. She had thought that he might secretly be hoping that she would not be admitted.

"Oh, Ragnar." She ran her fingers through his long, thick hair. "It's going to be hard, leaving you."

"You'll come back for visits, and maybe I can think of some way of getting up to the Islands myself." He pressed her hand between his palms. "Mahala, I've been meaning to ask you something. I didn't want to ask until this was settled, and now it is, and—" His throat moved as he swallowed. "You know how I feel. I want you to be my bondmate."

She looked away, deeply touched but also uncertain. "You mean that—" She slipped her hand from him. "You want me to promise that I'll make a pledge to become your bondmate later?"

"No, that you'll make a pledge now, before you go to Island Two. I need a bond with you, Mahala. You said you loved me, so why wait?"

"But I—" She swallowed. "We're too young, Ragnar. We can't make a promise like that."

"Why not? I'm sixteen now, and you will be soon. Some people who aren't much older than we are have bondmates. Your great-grandmother had a bond when she was your age. I know what I want. Does it matter if we make a pledge now instead of later?" He cupped her face in his hands, forcing her to look at him. "By the time you're finished with your schooling, I'll have a house ready for us. Maybe by then some of the things I was talking to you about can happen."

She suddenly knew why he wanted this bond. His life would be in order then, his personal desires met, his dreams still a possibility. He could do his work and then lose himself in his art; he would not have to worry about or be distracted by anything else. He must love her, she told herself, or he would not have offered her a pledge. Yet she wondered if he would actually miss her that much once they were bondmates and she left for Island Two.

He said, "I need this bond with you, Mahala."

That was the problem, she thought; he needed it too much, and yet not enough. Everything would be settled for him as soon as she accepted his promise, and with that uncertainty gone, he could give himself fully to the art he truly loved.

"I can't," she whispered. "I'm just not ready."

"If you think about it too much, you'll never be ready."

"I'm not ready now. Maybe I will be later. If we still feel the same way, we can become bondmates when we're older, can't we? And if we've changed our minds by then, that'll only prove we would have been making a big mistake now."

"Good reasoning, Mahala." There was bitterness in his voice. "Must be one of the things that got you into that Island school, being so logical. You haven't thought this through, though. Having a bond would be something we could hang on to, that could get us past any problems we have later. But without one, maybe our feelings will change. I'd always remember that you weren't sure enough of your feelings to make a pledge, and maybe that all by itself will change how I feel. Don't you know that a bond is something to build on? It's not something to wait for."

"Ragnar—"

"I asked you. Just say yes or no now—don't go on about how maybe we can be bondmates when we're older, because I'm not promising you anything if you do say no. Maybe I'll still want to make a pledge years from now, and maybe I won't. You'll just have to take your chances."

"That isn't fair," she said.

"It is fair. At least I'm not lying to you about what might happen."

"I can't," she said softly. "I can't make a promise when I don't know—"

"You told me no. You don't have to go on explaining." He stretched out and pulled the coverlet over himself. "If you get going now, you won't be that late for school. You can tell everybody there your good news."

"Ragnar." She wanted to tell him that she would make a pledge after all, but she could not say the words.

"I am happy for you, Mahala. You deserved to get in. You ought to call Solveig—she'd rather hear it from you first than from me."

"I'll call her from school." A lump rose in her throat. She was suddenly angry at Ragnar for making his proposal, for blighting this time with his entreaty.

Mahala's friends congratulated her. The teachers seemed pleased, but not overly excited; they had known that she had a good chance, and Turing had already sent a number of its children on to Island schools.

During a break, she called Solveig and left a message. Perhaps the other girl would give her some advice on where she might live. Only after that did she think of sending a message to her grandmother.

Frania walked home with her, as happy and excited as though she had won admission herself. "By the time you're on Island Two," the other girl said, "I should know about my pilot training. Have they told you anything yet about where you're going to live?"

"They gave me a list of places. Solveig might be able to help me out." Mahala slowed her pace as they neared the house. The dome was beginning to darken; accepting congratulations had kept her at school longer than usual, and she was not anxious to rush home. Ragnar would be there, reminding her of what she would have to leave behind.

Amina hugged Mahala as she came through the door. "I'm so pleased for you," she said. "We'll have to give you a proper send-off when the time comes and figure out what you should take with you." Amina had gone to an Island school herself.

Amina stepped aside; Dyami embraced Mahala. "I already have a message from Risa," he said. "She's ready to call everyone she knows on Island Two to ask about where you should live, and she also wants to talk to you."

Mahala smiled. "I can imagine. She probably has at least two hours' worth of advice to give me." She glanced past him at Tasida and Ragnar, who had just left the kitchen. Tasida was grinning; Ragnar's eyes, seeming more gray than blue, gazed at her steadily, betraying no unhappiness.

"Maybe you should call her now," Dyami said, "before Balin arrives. Supper will give you an excuse to cut things short if Risa starts giving you too much advice."

Mahala spoke to Risa on the large screen, while the others set out supper. As she had expected, her grandmother had counsel to offer. The school was offering some of the students single rooms, which might be more conducive to studying than living with a family. A couple of Administrators had offered to have Mahala reside in their quarters, which were certainly the most comfortable ones available, but Risa had politely turned them down; Mahala might otherwise be getting above herself. Sef interrupted to say how proud he was, and then the rest of the household offered congratulations. Grazie, according to Kolya and Noella, had done her best to spread the news to everyone in Oberg.

"I have to go," Mahala said as Dyami went to the door to greet Balin. "We're just about to eat."

"If there's any way you can visit us before you leave," Risa said, "we'd love to have you. Of course, you'll probably be too busy packing what you'll need there. Do take some of your best clothing with you—Islanders tend to dress up a little more than we do."

"I will."

"I really am happy for you, dear. Not that apprenticing yourself or learning a practical skill would have been anything to sneer at, but I know this is what you want."

Mahala said farewell and blanked the screen.

"I heard," Balin said as she went to the table. "Congratulations." The Habber's eyes seemed more solemn than usual, his manner even more subdued. "This is getting to be a fairly eventful time for all of us. I came over here with some news of my own."

Dyami lifted his brows. "What is it?" Amina asked.

"Benzi's coming back here, to Venus. His message came to me rather suddenly, just after he informed the Administrators of the fact. He said nothing about what he'd be doing here, only that he expected to stay for a while."

"It'll be good to see him again," Dyami said. Mahala clasped her hands together; Benzi was keeping the promise he had made to her after all.

"There's more I have to tell you," Balin went on. "Malik Haddad will be accompanying him to the Islands."

Mahala nearly dropped her spoon. Why, after all this time, had the grandfather she had never met decided to come back? She looked around at the others, who seemed just as surprised as she was.

"Well." Dyami set down his cup. "Is Malik Haddad coming here temporarily or permanently?"

"He chose to become one of us," Balin replied, "so I must assume he'll eventually leave Venus again, as we all do."

Dyami leaned forward; he and Balin gazed at each other in silence. Frania nudged Mahala. "Nothing happens for ages," the brown-haired girl said, "and then everything happens all at once."

Mahala poked at her food, too overcome to eat, uncertain about how she felt. Too much was changing, she thought, and too fast, before she had time to think about what it might mean. She felt that her future, whatever that might be, was hunting her, and there was nowhere to hide.

After supper, Ragnar sat down at his small table; Mahala had forgotten that he now had some time off from work. He beckoned to Frania, who quickly sat down in front of him. The boy began to mold clay with his hands, glancing from time to time at Frania's face. Mahala felt a pang as she seated herself near Ragnar, thinking of what lay ahead—her studies, a new place to live, expectations that she might fail to meet, and a grandfather who would be a stranger. It might have been easier to face it all knowing that Ragnar was waiting here for her.

The adults sat together, drinking tea as they murmured among themselves, and then Dyami led Balin to his room. Mahala stared after them as Dyami's door slid shut. Something was wrong; she could feel it. Her uncle never went to bed without saying good night, and he had not said anything about planning a celebration for her ever since Amina had suggested that idea at supper.

Frania yawned. "Can't you stay still?" Ragnar asked.

"I'm exhausted." The other girl blushed slightly, looking apologetic.

"Then go to sleep." He scraped at the clay with a chisel.

"Good night, Ragnar," Frania said as she stood up. He grunted, intent on his clay. Mahala lingered for a few moments, but he seemed unaware of her. He had not said whether he would meet her outside before first light.

At last she went to her room. As she prepared for sleep, she told herself that she could not expect Ragnar to wait in the absence of any promise from her. She had not given him the pledge he wanted because she was afraid she could not keep it, so she could not hope that he would wait patiently for her in the meantime.

Mahala slept, waking from habit at the time when she usually met Ragnar. Frania was asleep, her long hair fanned around her head. Mahala pulled on trousers under her shift, then crept toward the door.

Ragnar was not in the common room. Perhaps he was waiting for her in the usual place. She crossed the darkened room, hurried outside, and was halfway down to the lake when she saw him walking along the shore, shoulders slumped, his hands inside his trouser pockets.

He turned as she came toward him. "I wasn't expecting you to meet me," he said.

"I came anyway."

"Maybe you shouldn't have bothered. It might be easier if we break it off now."

"I thought maybe you'd try to make me change my mind."

"Shit, Mahala—don't toy with me now." He halted and stared out at the lake. "Balin's going back to his Hab."

"What?"

"He and Dyami must have thought I was asleep," he said. "I didn't mean to listen, but I couldn't help it. They came out of Dyami's room, and your uncle said something about always knowing Balin would have to leave, but not really believing that he ever would. Then Balin was saying he'd stayed too long as it was, that he was in danger of losing his balance. Dyami asked him if he was ever coming back, and Balin said he didn't know. I didn't hear what they said after that, because they were at the door by then. I figured I'd better go on pretending I was sleeping until Dyami went back to his room."

This news should not surprise her. Balin had already spent more years on Venus than nearly any other Habber. She had known that he would leave eventually, but had refused to dwell on that.

"Benzi's coming back," she said. "Balin might return later on."

"What's Dyami supposed to do in the meantime? By the time he sees Balin again, if he ever does, Balin will still be the way he is, but Dyami'll be older, maybe a lot older." Ragnar let out his breath. "That's probably one of the reasons Balin's leaving."

"Because it's hard for him to watch someone he loves age when he doesn't?"

"You sound more sentimental than I thought you were," Ragnar said. "That wouldn't be the only reason, maybe not even the most important one. The Habbers can't get too attached to us or they might think of changing the way things are for us here, and they can't let themselves do too much of that, because there's no way of telling where it might lead."

Mahala recalled what Balin had said a few nights ago. She had come in after weeding a few tiers of beans in their greenhouse to overhear Balin say, "Isn't it obvious why we're here?"

"Because of your curiosity, of course," Dyami had replied. "A way to remain connected with the home world and your own humanity. A way to keep an eye on Earth and the Mukhtars. That's what we've always thought."

"There are other reasons to involve ourselves with the Project," Balin had continued. "You're working to make this planet habitable. We build our Habitats in space. But the one assumption we share is that we believe we will always be able to maintain those environments, that the knowledge and civilization that created them will never be lost. Because if it ever is, our Habs would become dead shells, and Venus would grow hot and poisonous and unlivable again."

Balin's words had evoked a sudden vision of the Parasol falling into

a decaying orbit, of lava and hot gas melting the lithosphere and forming new crust, of domed settlements disappearing during a cata-
strophic resurfacing, of moss-covered cliffsides sinking into vast
subduction trenches. It came to Mahala then how shortsighted they
were, to think only in spans of hundreds of thousands of years, or millions, when the life of a planet had to be measured in billions. But the
Habbers; who lived such greatly extended lives, might be growing
more accustomed to such extreme long-term thinking. Balin might be
even older than she knew, with a mind becoming as layered as the
strata of an ancient cliffside.

"Perhaps we won't maintain them ourselves," Dyami had said.
"Maybe that task will pass to the children of our artificial intelligences."

Ragnar spoke again, interrupting Mahala's thoughts. "If I were your
uncle, I would have asked Balin to find a way of taking me with him."

"Dyami couldn't have gone with him, and you know it."

"I would have asked Balin anyway, faced him with it, made him
give me a yes or a no. Maybe Dyami did that, after they went outside."

"I doubt it," Mahala said. "He wouldn't leave Venus even if he
could. He went through too much to give up on the Project now."

"The Project." Ragnar spat. "I'm heading back to the house. I
should pick out something to give Balin as a farewell present."

"I'll come with you." She slipped her arm through his. "Ragnar, I
do care about you. I wish I weren't going to Island Two now."

"Don't tell me that, Mahala. You wanted to go, and you're going.
Don't ruin things for yourself by being sorry about it now."

They climbed toward the house in silence. As they approached, the
door slid open. Dyami stood in the doorway; Mahala went to him and
slipped her arms around him, pressing her head against his chest.

11

The airship bound for Island Two rose slowly from Turing's open bay through the still and stagnant atmosphere. There were few passengers aboard, only Mahala, two Linkers she did not know, and three Islanders who had been visiting relatives in Turing. They sat in the seats up front, just behind the two pilots; this was an older airship, with no partition separating the passengers from the crew.

The passengers had greeted one another politely but distantly, exchanged a few words, then settled down in their seats. In the back of the airship cabin, crates of cargo, most of them filled with bolts of merino wool to be traded on the Islands for imported goods from Earth, had been lashed to many of the seats; a few households in Turing had a profitable trade going with Islanders for the prized wool. Mahala checked the straps of her safety harness, then watched the large screen above the pilots as the airship climbed toward the Islands. By the time Turing's domes had shrunk to small bright spots in the misty blackness below, her fellow passengers were asleep.

The airship moved south as it rose toward the Islands that floated just north of Venus's equator in the upper atmosphere. Lulled by the silence outside the vessel, Mahala drifted into a dream: She was in Turing again, standing near Dyami's house on a slope overlooking the lake, knowing that she was leaving the settlement and would never return. She had to turn back, she suddenly realized; her place was there, not on an Island, not in a place far from her home.

It was the whine of the wind outside that woke her. The airship cabin shook, buffeted by the wind. The other passengers slept on, but Mahala tensed in her seat. The pilots, their bands around their heads, would be monitoring the sensors, alert to any sign of trouble. Outside, the wind just below the Islands would be shrieking, whipping around the planet at nearly three hundred kilometers an hour; riding that fierce wind earned the pilots their credit. Mahala forced herself not to think of the few airships that had crashed, crippled by failing pumps, leaking helium cells, or sensor malfunctions, ships that had failed to ride the wind, reminding herself that almost all of the vessels made it safely to port.

In the distant future, the wind would die, and the Islands would slowly fall toward Venus, finally coming to rest on the surface of a transformed world. But for now, the wind raged, and in its scream Mahala heard the cry of Venus as her child, the new world, struggled to be born.

Solveig was waiting for Mahala just outside Island Two's airship bay. She rushed forward and grabbed Mahala's hands.

"I just found out a couple of hours ago," Solveig said. "I'm going to be your student adviser. I didn't know if they'd put you in my group, but at the last minute, there you were on my list." She reached for one of Mahala's duffels. "You're the first one to get here. The other new students won't arrive until tomorrow."

Mahala hefted her other duffel to her shoulder. "Benzi said he would meet me."

"He was here, waiting for you, and then a Guardian came up to him and said Administrator Jamilah wanted to see him. So he asked me to take you to his quarters."

Mahala frowned. Her grandmother had often muttered bitter words about Guardians after returning from a meeting on Island Two. Getting used to the presence of those military forces on the Islands was one of the adjustments she would have to make while living here. There were few of the Guardians on the Islands now, fewer than there had been before the Revolt; even Risa would concede that they were largely a token force. But the Administrators did not care to provoke more bad feeling with Earth by asking the Mukhtars to withdraw their soldiers altogether.

She took a breath and noticed that the air here seemed drier that that of Turing and Oberg; perhaps that was because there were no large bodies of water on any of the Islands. There were also none of the familiar smells of cooking food, of leaves and pine needles, of the compost the settlers collected from their kitchen compacters to use as fertilizer for their gardens, only a slight scent of grass and traces of the fragrance of flowers. Near the entrance to the bay, a colorful banner celebrating the new year of 649 fluttered from a pole; apparently no one had yet bothered to take it down.

Dyami and his household had followed their celebration of Mahala's sixteenth birthday with a party to mark both the New Year and her departure for Island Two. She and her friends had sat outside Dyami's house to watch the traditional light show on the dome, which always ended with an image of a green and blue globe representing the terraformed Venus. Only after she had turned her attention away from the reflection of the globe on the mirrorlike surface of the lake had she noticed that Ragnar and Frania were sitting together, their heads close.

She and Solveig walked along a white stone path. Island Two was a landscape of tended gardens and expanses of grass clipped so short that the grass resembled a soft green carpet. Slender trees stood on either side of the path, and a few people were dining at tables set outside a pavilion near a small pool; a tiny apelike creature moved toward one group with a tray of teacups. Risa disapproved of such genetically engineered animals, feeling that their simple tasks of gardening and food preparation should be performed by people or machines and that their places might better be taken by new settlers. There had never been any such creatures allowed in the surface settlements.

In the spaces between the trees, Mahala glimpsed the ziggurat that housed the Administrators; a tiered tower reaching toward the soft yellow glow of the light disk in the center of the dome that enclosed Island Two. The Islanders marked their days as the surface settlers did, with twelve hours of light and twelve of darkness. She was in a tidy environment, a pruned and weeded and cultivated garden that made it easier not to think of where she actually was—on an Island that had been built atop giant helium cells and floated above thick acidic clouds, under a protective dome that bore the scars of small meteorites that had been able to penetrate the thin upper atmosphere where the Islands sailed.

"Have you seen Malik Haddad yet?" Mahala had almost called him her grandfather, but referring to him that way still seemed strange. Sef was more truly her grandfather than this man she had never met, whose only tie to her was genetic.

"I haven't seen him at all," Solveig replied. "The story is that as soon as he arrived, a couple of Guardians met him and took him and your great-uncle to the Administrators' residence. I saw Benzi briefly today, but there wasn't a chance to ask him what was going on."

Benzi, according to the message he had sent to Mahala before she left Turing, had arrived on Island Two from Anwara only three days ago. He had, much to his surprise, been given quarters in the pilots' residence instead of in the Habber dwelling; because there was the usual shortage of space on the Island, Mahala would be allowed to live with him there. He had said nothing about Malik Haddad, and she, distracted by having to notify the school authorities that she would not need a single room after all and by gatherings of friends in Turing to mark her departure, had not thought to ask.

"Some of the older Administrators might have known Malik before," Mahala said. "Maybe they just wanted to visit with him." She hoped that she was right. Being so abruptly taken to the Administrators, to the most powerful people here, those who negotiated with Earth and the Project Council members on Anwara to get the resources they needed, was not likely to make any new arrival feel at ease.

"You're probably right," Solveig said, "and he must have gone to the Habber residence afterward. I assume that's where he'll stay." She shortened her long stride; at eighteen, the blond young woman was taller than many men. "After we get you settled, we can do whatever you like. Tomorrow, I've got to meet an airship as soon as I'm up and then two others later in the day—that'll be the rest of our group. I'm supposed to share a meal with all of you and answer any questions you have. The day after that, I'll take you around the school, introduce you to some people, and give you some advice."

"What kind of advice?" Mahala asked.

"The usual do's and don'ts. Never greet Administrators unless they greet you first. Otherwise, just bow or touch your forehead with your fingers, then walk on. Don't be too friendly to any of the Guardians—that kind of thing." Solveig lowered her voice. "To be honest, except for some of the workers, Islanders are a bit haughty. Maybe that isn't the right word. What I mean is that they're always aware of what they are and who you are, and we're just a pair of grubbers, a couple of students from the surface.

"So Risa's told me."

"By the way, how's my brother doing?"

"He's fine."

"I was wondering. The only time I had a chance to say a few words to him were those times you called. He hasn't sent me any messages since he started living in your uncle's house."

Mahala had suspected as much. She had been worrying about how much to tell Solveig about what had happened between her and Ragnar. Solveig, who must know her brother better than almost anyone, might be able to advise her on what to do.

He had hurt her deeply by cutting things off as completely as he had. There had been no more meetings under the trees, not even a few moments alone to talk. He had wished her well before the trip here and had seemed sincere, but his words had been those of a friend, not someone who had wanted her as a bondmate.

Maybe it was better that way, and best not to tell Solveig what had passed. It was useless to hope that Ragnar might relent.

The pilots' dwelling had a large common room filled with a few low tables and cushions that looked well used and two triangular wings of residential rooms. Mahala and Benzi had been given two tiny bedrooms adjoining a slightly larger room equipped with cushions, a table, and a wall screen.

"I had more space in Risa's house," Mahala said as she looked around her small quarters.

"Most people here would call this roomy," Solveig murmured. The blond girl went on to tell her about the school. The teachers expected their students to take some initiative in designing their courses of study, so Mahala would largely be on her own. She was required to meet with each of her teachers at least once every fourteen days, but Solveig advised her to do so more often than that. Depending on which subjects she pursued, she would be assigned to classes that would include lectures by a teacher and discussion among the students; she could attend them either in person or by screen. She could work at what she liked, but eventually the faculty would have to assess her progress and decide if she would be allowed to remain a student and do university-level work or else encouraged to turn her thoughts to an apprenticeship. Mahala knew most of this already, but said nothing.

"What I'd advise," Solveig continued, "is that you go to the classes most of the time and miss a few occasionally. That way, you look as though you're taking the work seriously without seeming to be too dependent on the teachers and other students. Same goes for projects—do at least one by yourself and then try to interest a few students in working on another with you as a team." She sighed as she shifted on her cushion. "The trick is not to be either too solitary or too tied to a group—you want to show you can be cooperative, but still able to work alone. They want to see you show initiative without being domineering. After all, that's the kind of person we want on the Project."

Mahala heard a sardonic tone in her friend's voice. It sounded like some of the advice she had overheard others telling young people who aspired to the Cytherian Institute: It won't hurt you to learn Arabic, even if all the classes are in Anglaic. The Administrators will be flattered and impressed if you can master their official, ceremonial language; that will show you're serious and mean to rise. It's wrong to submit to a faith you don't truly hold, but if you're sincere about becoming a Muslim, submission to that faith certainly won't do your future prospects any harm.

If she weighed everything that way long enough, Mahala wondered, would she forget how to distinguish between what she genuinely felt and what was only pragmatic?

"I came here knowing I'd have to work hard," Mahala said. "If I have to worry about whether I'm missing the right number of classes or some of those other things—"

"Yes, I know. You're right—you can't really plan it out that way." Solveig sounded more like herself. "But I figured you should know how some of our more calculating schoolmates go about their business."

Mahala stifled a yawn, then smiled apologetically. "I'm more tired than I thought."

"Get some rest, then." Solveig got to her feet. "We can have supper together later, if you like."

"I think Benzi's expecting to dine with me." He had not told her that, but he would surely come to their quarters by last light to greet her. She wanted to find out more about Malik from him, and as soon as possible; better to be prepared in case she ran into her grandfather unexpectedly.

"If you're not doing anything after that, call," Solveig went on. "I'll introduce you to some of my friends."

"All right."

After Solveig was gone, Mahala went into one of the bedrooms. The drawers set into the wall were empty, so she assumed that Benzi had taken the other room. She unpacked one of her duffels, then stretched out on the bed.

Even though she felt tired, sleep was elusive. Mahala lay there, thinking of what she might have been doing now. Her grandmother would expect her to call up everyone on the list of Risa's Island Two acquaintances and leave messages saying that she had arrived and was looking forward to meeting them. She might also have been getting an early start on her studies.

A door whispered open, and then she heard footsteps in the outer room. "Mahala?" She recognized Benzi's voice. "Are you here?"

She slipped from the bed and hurried out to him. He was the same as he had been, his hair still black, his golden-skinned face that of a much younger man. She drew back slightly from him as he caught her by the arms.

"You've changed," he said.

"You haven't."

He smiled. "I have—it just doesn't show." He let go of her and looked down, seeming uncertain for a moment. "You were a lot shorter when we said farewell last time."

"I'm still short." Her head came only to his shoulder, and Benzi was not a tall man. "This is about as tall as I'm likely to get." She stepped toward a cushion and sat down.

Her great-uncle seated himself across from her. "I'm sorry I couldn't meet you at the bay," he said.

"That's all right. Solveig was there to greet me."

"I know you didn't expect to live here." Benzi crossed his legs and rested his hands on his knees. "I assumed I'd be living in the Habber quarters again."

"Why did you come back?" The words were out of her mouth before she could stop them. "What do you want, anyway—a chance to pretend you still have a family here before you go back to your Hab again?"

"Mahala—"

"Balin left Turing. Dyami doesn't know if he's ever coming back. Obviously it isn't a good idea to get too attached to any of you."

"You don't understand. Balin had to—"

"That's what he told Dyami, that he had to go. Dyami was probably just a diversion to him all along. He loves him—he deserved better than that from Balin."

"Balin loves Dyami, too."

"But not enough to stay. You must get bored after a while, living your long lives. After a while, it's time to move on."

Benzi's eyes narrowed. If she had not known better, she might have thought he was angry. He bowed his head; when he looked up again, he seemed calm.

"Your people would resent us even more if we stayed here too long," he said. "The time when people we know start noticing that we haven't aged at all and begin wondering exactly how long we can keep rejuvenating ourselves is often what strains the limits of their tolerance, and it's usually better for individual Habbers to make a departure earlier than that." He paused. "As it is, we have all those groups of young people demonstrating and making their demands. What kinds of demonstrations do you think they would stage if we—"

"Is that the only reason?" Mahala asked.

"No. It can be too easy to forget what we are here, that we're Habbers. And in the Habitats, we have to try to remember that we're human." He folded his arms. "Maybe you and Risa and Dyami are all that's kept me human."

"Why did you come back, Benzi?"

He quickly rose to his feet. "Let's take a walk."

She frowned, but uttered no protest as she followed him from the room. They passed through the pilots' common room on the way out; the main door had been propped open by a pole, and men and women sat around tables near the entrance, laughing and talking as they ate their evening meal.

Benzi took her arm as they left the building, guiding her along a path. Evening had come to Island Two; the dome's silvery light seemed dimmer than that of Turing's night. Others were strolling along the paths, and a few people sat at tables under trees, drinking from cups.

The path of flat white tiles ended at the bottom of a flight of stairs. They had come to the eastern edge of the Island; above them, a curving platform stood against the dome. Mahala climbed the steps, Benzi just behind her. They were alone; apparently few came to the observational platform at this hour. Venus was below, cloaked in the shadow of the Parasol, invisible. She leaned against the railing and gazed through the dome at the blackness.

"This may seem overly suspicious on my part," Benzi murmured, "but I'd rather discuss certain things here than in our rooms. It wouldn't be hard for the Administrators to eavesdrop, and I haven't had a chance yet to block any channels or devices they might use to monitor me."

"You are too suspicious," she said.

"Being ushered to the Administrative Center by Guardians upon one's arrival has the effect of rousing one's suspicions. They didn't keep me long, but Malik was still in Jamilah al-Hussaini's quarters when I left. Since then, I discovered, he hasn't been seen, and he hasn't answered any messages from the Habbers here."

Her hands tightened on the railing. "But what could anyone here want with him?"

"I told him that it might be unwise to come here now," Benzi responded. "He chose to become a Habber—that makes him different from the others who fled to our Habitat with him. The others came back here after the Revolt, showing that their true loyalties still lay with this Project and that they had sought refuge with us only out of desperation. They could be forgiven. But Malik stayed on when he could have returned."

"You did the same thing, Benzi," Mahala said. "How is he any different from you?"

"He still has relatives who are close to the Council of Mukhtars, and he shamed his family with his actions. The Linkers here may want to keep a close watch on him until they see if the Mukhtars are going to take his presence here amiss." He turned toward her. "He was the father of a woman who caused your people much suffering. His disgrace on Earth and his questioning of the official ideology were what brought him here, what forced him to come here as an exile, and he was never truly devoted to Venus or the Project. He was a coward who feared bringing even more trouble on himself. He escaped from this world when some who might have escaped with him remained behind instead to fight on."

"You're judging him harshly."

"I've said only what Malik says about himself," Benzi said. "He thought that maybe it wouldn't matter now, that he could come back here for a time, that he might even be of some use. What freedom you Cytherians have was hard-won, Mahala, and our presence here helps to guarantee it. But if some on Earth choose to view Malik's visit to the Islands as a provocation, there isn't much we can do."

"Do you really think—"

Benzi lifted a hand. "I'm saying that it may be in the interests of the Administrators, who have no reason to antagonize Earth, to convince him that he's not welcome here and to make that clear before the Mukhtars decide it might be worthwhile to make an issue of him. Malik fell into disgrace because he dared to hint that you Cytherians should be more autonomous, that Earth might benefit in the long run by letting you go your own way. He thought Venus might become a bridge between Earth and our Habitats, that this should be the Project's true purpose. For him to come here now, after the Mukhtars have given up much of their real authority here, might seem overly provocative to some."

"Then why did he come back?" she asked.

"To see you. To make his peace with the past. He was, after all, a historian once. The past means more to him than it does to many people."

Mahala said, "He made his choice. It's useless for him to come back now."

"How harsh you sound."

"All I'm saying is that, once you've made a decision, it's pointless to regret it." She thought of Ragnar. "What good does it do to look back?"

"You're young. You might feel different when you're Malik's age."

"Is that why you came back, to make your peace with the past?"

"Partly. We need you more than you realize, and you need us—" She waited for him to go on, but he was silent for a long time. "Let's go back to our rooms," he said at last. "You're probably tired."

She was about to say that she had not eaten yet, but she did not feel very hungry. Benzi led her down the stairs; they had gone only a short distance along the path when she saw him tense.

He was very still, not moving, his head slightly tilted as if he were listening to something. "It's Malik," he said at last. "He's at the Habber residence now. He wants to see you. He also says that—"

She was suddenly irritated with both Benzi and her grandfather. "If he wants to see me," she said, "he can leave me a message saying so. He doesn't have to go through you." She strode ahead of him before he could reply. Deciding to live with Benzi had been a mistake; she should never have agreed to it so readily. Solveig might be able to help her find new quarters, and it made more sense for Benzi to live with the other Habbers instead of among the pilots.

A hand brushed against her arm. "I'm sorry," Benzi said, catching up with her. "I just thought—" He paused. "I was right about one thing. The Administrators don't particularly want him to stay, but Malik doesn't know what they're prepared to do with him if he does stay. They seem uninterested in making a fuss, which is a bit surprising. Perhaps—"

"None of that matters to me."

"Don't be so merciless, Mahala. You may be more like your grandfather than you think. Otherwise, you'd still be down in Oberg, happily preparing yourself for the life Risa wants for you and telling yourself you don't need anything more."

The words stung, coming from him; Benzi rarely sounded that upset. "I'm tired," she said. "That's all. I'll be in a better mood when I've had some sleep."

The door to the common room was closed now; Mahala and Benzi went to their room. As they entered, Mahala saw a light flashing below the wall screen; someone had left a message.

Malik, she thought, and went to the screen, taking a breath before she spoke. "If the message is for me," she ordered, "you may deliver it now." What would Malik's voice be like, and how would he look? Probably much as he always had. Risa had often told her how handsome he was, and the images Mahala had seen had confirmed that.

The screen lit up. No image appeared, and she heard no voice. Malik had left a written message.

Mahala, the message began, *I long to see the grandchild I have never known. You may come to visit with me at the Habber residence here tomorrow, at any time you wish. If you desire no contact with the grandfather who has been absent from your life, you need not respond. I shall assume, if you do not seek me out, that you want nothing to do with me. Please do not feel that you owe me any explanation for your decision. I gave up the right to ask anything of you when I left this world and will not trouble you further. Malik Haddad.*

She sank to a cushion as the message flickered out. How clever of him to leave only those words, to reveal nothing of himself. He must have known that her curiosity would be roused and that she would have to see him.

12

The Habber residence was a round building made of gray stone, within sight of the ziggurat of the Administrators and surrounded by a small park of willows and flowering shrubs. The two black-uniformed Guardians on duty stood at attention as Mahala approached. Benzi had offered to come with her, but she wanted to meet Malik Haddad alone.

The Guardians, two young men who looked only two or three years older than Mahala, barely glanced at her as she moved toward the entrance. She pressed her hand against the door; it slid open, revealing a dimly-lit and empty room.

Mahala stepped forward; the door closed behind her. She stood in the large room, wondering where to go next, and then the wall to her right opened, sliding soundlessly across the floor. A curving hallway with closed doors on either side, hidden by the wall, was now revealed.

She had never been inside a Habber residence before, not even in Turing. It came to her then that the Habbers, even Balin and Benzi, had subtly discouraged such visits, that Cytherians had rarely been seen entering their quarters and that the Habbers had seemed content with that arrangement. She had assumed that their residences were much like anyone else's, but this empty room, obviously meant to be a common room, had no tables and cushions, while the retracting wall in front of the hallway seemed an unnecessary precaution.

Were the Habbers so fearful of their safety here that they needed to seal themselves off until assured that any callers were friendly? Dyami had told her of how Habbers and Cytherians had once felt free to visit one another at any time in Turing and had lived in much the same sorts of quarters while working together, but that had been during the time before her uncle's imprisonment there. The Habbers still had many reasons to be cautious, and having Guardians on duty outside this building probably added to their anxiety instead of reassuring them.

Mahala moved toward the hallway. A door near her opened and a dark-haired man in a plain gray tunic and trousers stepped through the opening. She recognized Malik Haddad immediately. His handsome beardless face was unchanged from the images of him she had seen, and his dark hair was only lightly touched with gray.

"Salaam," he said. She hesitated, unable even to utter a greeting. "Please come inside."

She followed him into the room. The only furnishings were two wide mats that covered much of the floor. Mahala sat down on one; the man who was her biological grandfather settled himself on the other, facing her. Most people would have set out some food and drink for a visitor, even if the provisions were only tea and bits of bread or pastry, but he offered her nothing. It was just as well, she thought nervously; she was too nervous to eat or drink anything.

"Forgive me," Malik said. She tensed, wondering if he was about to unburden himself now, without preliminaries. "For my lack of hospitality," he continued. "If you'd like something to eat—"

"No, thank you," she replied. Now that she was closer to him, he seemed more aged. His black hair had only a few strands of silver, his face was unmarred by lines and wrinkles, his body apparently firm and straight, yet in some indefinable way, he seemed as old as her grandmother. Maybe it was the trace of weariness in his eyes, the slightly hollow cheeks, or the barely detectable slumping of his shoulders.

"This must be awkward for you," he said. "It was my hope that, since you'd spent more time among Habbers than most here, with Benzi and with others in Turing, that you might be more at ease with me."

"Are you a Habber?" she asked.

"Your Administrators certainly consider me one. Benzi does, but then there are Habbers who continue to regard him as one who is still apart from them in some ways. And—" His voice trailed off.

"Have the Administrators asked you to leave?"

"They've told me that I'm not welcome. They'll make sure that

Earth knows they disapprove of my presence on Island Two. But neither the Administrators or the Mukhtars are likely to make an issue of me. I'm much too insignificant for either group to provoke the other."

"Benzi thought that your coming here might cause some trouble."

"Benzi," Malik said, "is sometimes too quick to assume the worst. Neither Earth or Venus will risk another conflict. That, in a way, is part of the problem."

"I don't see why that's a problem. Would you rather have us threatening each other?"

"You seem to think those are the only choices. Cooperation would be another, but that's most likely a futile hope."

"You seem to know quite a bit about what's going on here for someone who left years ago."

Malik smiled briefly. "It's not difficult to sense the difference between what someone like Jamilah al-Hussaini says and what she actually means. You also forget that I can easily commune with anyone here." He smiled again. "With any Habber who will allow me access through my Link, of course. That's what I meant. Linkers don't commune with Habbers. Most of what I know of recent developments here, I learned through Benzi, and my interest was roused."

Mahala drew back slightly. It was still easy for her to forget their Links, to forget that what she said to a Habber could be overheard by many others, and perhaps the Habbers were used to less privacy than were Linkers.

"And I am more of a solitary than most," Malik continued. "I'm not quite a Habber, not even now, and the Mukhtars had deprived me of my Link before I left Earth and came to Venus. One reason for joining myself to the Habbers was to regain a Link, but it isn't quite the same as the one I had when I . . . " His voice trailed off, and she had the feeling that he did not want to say more.

"If you're truly so interested in us," she said at last, "then why didn't you come back before, when you had the chance?"

"Because I was unlike most of the others who came here," he said. "They wanted to join the Project to win a new kind of life for themselves. They came here willingly, and some gave up much to do so. But I came as an exile. There was no place left for me on Earth after my disgrace. I would have preferred going to the Habitats even then, instead of coming here, but I didn't have that choice."

"In other words, you were always hoping you might get to the Habs eventually."

"Not exactly. I made my peace with your world when my daughter Chimene was born. I had high hopes for her, but she was destined to be—" He looked away for a moment. "A disappointment," he went on, "and perhaps that was partly my fault."

"That was why you left?" Mahala hesitated a moment. "Because of my mother?"

"I wouldn't quite put it that way, child. Chimene had simply robbed me of my one reason for remaining here."

"Then why did you come back?"

"To see you."

You're not part of my life, she wanted to say. You don't belong here; you have no right to come back and think you have any claim on me.

"Not that I expect you to have any feelings for me," he murmured, "or any sense of obligation. I wanted to see what has passed here since I left. In a Hab, one can easily forget that time is passing, that indeed there is any history at all."

She remembered that he had been a historian on Earth. That was what had brought him trouble; he had been accused of spreading dangerous ideas and questioning accepted historical theories. So his record said, at any rate. Mahala gazed at the man, trying to imagine him taking such a risk.

"In other words," she said, "you came here to see what's happened since you left."

"In a sense."

"You could have found all of that out from Benzi."

"But that wouldn't be the same as seeing it for myself."

Her irritation with him was warming into anger. Did the man have any strong feelings at all? He was speaking as though he had some regrets about his past actions, but she heard little emotion in his voice.

Mahala leaned forward. "Do you know what I most dislike about you?" She swallowed. "What I dislike in all Habbers? It's as if nothing's real to you, that what we're doing here is only a game. You come here whenever you like and then leave whenever you please. You pretend you care about us, and some of you even fall in love with some of us, but this isn't your world, and you can always leave Venus and the people here behind. We might as well be part of a mind-tour for you. You'd get just as much out of that, and you wouldn't have to be away from your Habs."

"There's some justice to what you say."

She leaned forward. "Then why are you here?"

"Did you ever ask yourself what might happen if all the Habs ever left?"

"Left Venus again?"

Malik shook his head. "I said Habs, not Habbers. I am asking what might happen if all of the Habitats departed from this solar system."

"But they couldn't. They—"

"But of course they could leave. Any Habitat is potentially a mobile world, as you should know, and humankind once had dreams of exploring interstellar space, dreams that were long postponed and then forgotten." Malik seemed to be gazing at her more kindly, but perhaps she was imagining that. "The possibility of leaving has been discussed. What do you think would happen then?"

"There are five Habs orbiting Mars," she replied, "two of them created from the Martian moons. If they left, the Mukhtars would claim Mars, I'm sure. Maybe they'd even begin planning another terraforming project there."

"And here?" Malik asked.

"You must know the answer to that." Mahala glared at him. "Earth and the Mukhtars would be in control of Venus again. There wouldn't be anything to stop them from tightening their grip. They wouldn't have to worry about what the Habbers might do. Oh, we could stand up to them for a while, but it wouldn't do any good. We couldn't hold out forever, and things would only be worse for us when it was over." She took a breath. "Why are you asking me this?"

"Because some who live in the Habitats are saying that we should leave this system. What would we do if Earth acquires the will, and maybe even the means, to strike at us? Someone may yet come to power who thinks such an attack would be worth the risks. Whatever the result, many on Earth, and perhaps in the Habs, would die."

"It couldn't happen," Mahala said, compelling herself to believe that.

"Not now, maybe not a century from now. But it's still a possibility, however distant, and Habbers are used to long-term thinking. It may be better to leave before there's a chance for such a conflict, to put ourselves well out of Earth's reach."

"All of the Habs wouldn't go," she said. "The people in your Hab and Benzi's—they've always been closer to us than the others, haven't they?"

"Benzi is one of those advising us that it may be time to leave."

The words numbed her. Mahala sat there, unable to speak, her body as still as stone while her inner voice shrieked at her. You lied, we mean even less to you than I thought, you came here pretending that we were part of your family, and all along you wanted to run away from us again. She wanted to rush from this dwelling and hurl the words at Benzi, who had intended to betray them all along.

"How can you—" Mahala struggled for breath. "Why are you telling me—"

Malik clasped her hands between his. "Because we can't simply abandon Venus."

"I think you could." She jerked her hands away. "It would be easy for you. After all, you've done it before, you and Benzi both. You didn't care what leaving here might cost others."

"Would I be speaking to you now if we weren't concerned? Do you think Benzi would have asked me to do so?"

"So you're here because he asked you."

"Partly. But I also wanted to come."

Mahala lowered her eyes, wondering what else to say to this man. He was here because he wanted to be; she did not know a lot about Habber customs, but was certain no one had compelled Malik to come here. Why had he told her that the Habbers were thinking of leaving the solar system? Surely they would be wiser to hide such intentions. If the Habbers left without warning, Venus could do little to stop them and Earth little more. The Habbers could be beyond the reach of the home world before the Mukhtars even guessed at their intentions. By telling her of their deliberations, he was taking a risk.

But Malik and Benzi would not be acting without the knowledge of other Habbers. Given their Links, and the presence of others of their people on Venus and its Islands, she doubted that the Habbers could keep secrets from one another for long. She could tell others what Malik had told her, but that might accomplish little. Who would believe her, one insignificant girl, in any case? Administrator Jamilah would have little reason to think a student here was more aware of future Habber intentions than she was, and the other Hab-

bers would probably deny that what Mahala said was true. Benzi—
and any other Habber, for that matter—could always say that Malik
had misunderstood, that he had not lived long enough among them
to understand their true intentions.

In addition to that, she would make matters much worse if others
did believe her. Relations between Venus and the Habs would be poi-
soned by suspicion and doubt.

Mahala finally broke the silence. "Why are you telling me this?"
she said softly. "You must realize I can't tell anyone else what you said
without causing a lot of trouble, assuming anyone would even believe
me in the first place."

"Benzi thought it was important that you know."

"Really," she muttered. "He's just given me more to worry about."

"You may have more of a role to play in this than you think," he
said.

She shook her head. "I'm here to study at an Island school. I mean
to work as hard as I can so that I'll be admitted to the Cytherian Institute."

"Why the Cytherian Institute?"

"One overwhelming reason," she replied, "is that it's the only way
I'm likely to see Earth, and I very much want to see it."

"And after that?"

She still did not know. "I suppose I'll figure that out later. I assume
that the Habbers will stay here at least that long."

"We'll remain as long as we have to in order to ensure this world's
future. Nothing has been decided anyway—possibilities are being explored and weighed. We have also devoted a lot of effort to the Project,
whether the Mukhtars care to admit that or not."

"You mean that other Habbers devoted that effort." She gazed directly at him. "You didn't." She folded her arms. "What were you
doing? On your Hab, I mean, before you came back here."

Malik's face grew solemn. "I suppose you could say that I was
adapting." He looked away from her. "I had been a Linker on Earth. I
thought that living with a Link among Habbers would be much the
same. It isn't." He was silent for a long time after that.

"Are you happy there?" she asked.

He made a sound that might have been a laugh. "I'm not unhappy." He lifted a hand to smooth back his hair. "I have a favor to ask
of you, Mahala. You may of course refuse to grant it."

"What do you want?"

"Only a chance to talk to you from time to time. I'll do my best not to be intrusive. I would also like to accompany you the next time you go to the surface to visit."

Mahala frowned. "But you can visit the settlements any time you like. The Administrators won't stop you. You could always let them believe that you regret what you did, that you might want to stay here permanently. The Project Council would love to hear from Administrator Jamilah that you're sorry for what you did."

"Are you saying that you would rather not have me travel with you?"

She flushed. "I didn't mean that." She had meant it, but was embarrassed to admit that now.

"It would be easier for me to see some of the people and places I used to know if you were my escort or my host, so to speak. I'll stay in the nearest Habber quarters if that's more convenient for everyone."

He would probably want to see Risa. Mahala wondered what her grandmother would say to that, how she would feel about seeing her former bondmate again.

"Well." Mahala rested her hand on her knees. "I don't see how I can refuse."

"You're free to do so. I can always—"

"No, I really don't mind," she said. "Besides, given what you told me, it probably wouldn't be wise to offend you." He averted his eyes for a moment. "There's just one thing, though—if somebody doesn't want to see you, there won't be anything I can do about it. I'm not going to bring you to someone's home unless I know you'll be welcome there." She was thinking of Risa and Sef.

"That's only proper."

"I really have to go." Mahala got to her feet. "There's one thing you never told me. All the Habbers here have some work to do, advising a team or working with the specialists and engineers or whatever. What's your work here?"

"I should have told you," Malik said as he stood up. "I only found out just before you came that the Administrators here had reluctantly granted my request." He led her toward the door. "I'll be teaching at your school."

*   *   *

Benzi was sitting at a table not far from the Habber residence. He looked up as Mahala approached; he had obviously been waiting for her.

"Well, now I've met Malik," she said as she sat down.

Benzi poured tea. "And what did you think?"

"I don't know." Mahala reached for a cup. "It probably isn't fair to expect too much after just one short meeting." She sipped some tea, then set her cup down. "You knew what he was going to tell me."

"Approximately."

"Maybe you even listened in."

"You said you wanted to see him by yourself. Don't you think I'd respect that?"

Mahala leaned forward. "You're all thinking of leaving. That's what he said. All of you may just—"

He shook his head slightly at her. No one was sitting near them, but two Guardians were strolling along a path in their direction. "You won't be abandoned," he said softly. "We haven't been blind and deaf to the demands some of you have made. We've done what we could for Venus in the past, and I promise you that won't change."

"Why did Malik have to tell me anything, then?" she asked.

"Are you saying that you would rather have remained ignorant?"

"What use is it to know about something you can't change or do anything about? I'd be happier not knowing. You Habbers seem perfectly content to have us know almost nothing about you as it is."

"That could change," he said. "It has to change. I wanted you to know because you may help to bring that change about."

Mahala sat back in her chair. "*I* might help? I'm not exactly that important. Why me?"

Benzi smiled slightly. "Maybe partly because you are my grandniece and Malik's granddaughter. That isn't the only reason, of course, and it's probably the least important one, but we're not entirely indifferent to genetic bonds." His smile faded. "You're more like me—and like Malik—than you may realize. That's another reason for telling you."

"You haven't even told me that much," she said, "just that you—"

He lifted a hand. "You know enough for the moment, considering that we Habbers are still wrestling with various choices ourselves."

"And exactly what am I supposed to do now?"

"What you've been doing—learning, working toward the goals you have for yourself, living your life, discovering what you find worthwhile."

Mahala said, "You make it sound like some sort of test."

"In a sense, it is."

Except that she did not know what she had to do to pass the test or even what his criteria were for judging her one way or another. What would she do, knowing that the Habbers were debating about whether they should abandon the rest of humankind altogether? That was the question Benzi had posed, and she did not know what answer he wanted.

It struck her then what the departure of the Habbers might mean. They had always been there, in their deliberate worlds. In a sense, everyone on Earth and Venus tended to look toward them—as a kind of help of last resort. She felt odd thinking in this way, but the insights seemed inescapable, and a part of her took pride in the fact that she was thinking for herself.

What it all meant was that the humanity of the solar system, Habber or not, was still more closely joined than it knew or wished to acknowledge.

13

She would not speak to anyone else about what Malik had told her. Mahala made that decision immediately.

Then it occurred to her that if Malik had so easily confided in her, others probably knew all about the Habbers' hypothetical plans. She might be Malik's granddaughter, but she was also a stranger to him. Either he was testing her to see if she was trustworthy, for some obscure reason of his own, or he had no reason to fear any of the consequences should she reveal what he had told her to others.

With her studies and her other responsibilities, she soon did not have much time to dwell on what Malik and Benzi had said. Malik might be teaching at her school, but his history lectures were something she considered an indulgence, not nearly as important as the other subjects she would have to master. It was easy enough to avoid her grandfather most of the time and to visit with him only briefly, usually in the garden near the small building that housed their seminar and study rooms; many of the students often gathered in the garden to talk and share a meal. Malik asked only innocuous questions about her friends and interests, ones she could respond to almost automatically. Sometimes she found herself wondering if he was even paying much attention to what she said or only pretending to listen out of duty.

As for Benzi, he was occupied with shuttling between Island Two and Anwara, meeting here with the Administrators and there with the Project Council. She was beginning to see that Benzi might be the Habber equivalent of a Liaison to the Council, and therefore perhaps a much more important person than she realized. There was, however, no point in asking him if this were so. The Habbers, it seemed, either had little hierarchy or else ignored any signs of differing status; one Habber was as good as another.

Biology had the most appeal to her as a subject and was a practical course of study as well. To pursue botany could lead to work in engineering new genetic strains of plants for the greenhouses, which meant in essence being a farmer, or to work on developing or modifying algae, lichens, and other life needed to seed Venus's surface. Physiology could lead to a position as a medical specialist or physician. It was much the same with other biological specializations; by the time she reached the point in her studies where they might become truly fascinating in themselves and suggest possibilities for further research, she would have to decide on what work she could do that would best serve the Project. Becoming a physician might be her best choice, and that work had its attractions; she would know that she was helping others directly, and there would be some variety in her routine while she served the Project.

It always came back to that in the end, serving the Project. She could not pursue a particular line of work solely because it interested her. Pure research barely existed here, even on the Islands. Even on Earth, research was a fragile enterprise, allowed to go on only at the pleasure of the Council of Mukhtars, who could cut off any investigation at any time. The Mukhtars thought of knowledge as a resource to be controlled by those in power, to be parceled out to others as a favor or in order to secure their own interests, not as an end in itself to be pursued for its own sake.

The students had been told that they were free to study whatever they liked, but Mahala knew that this was not really so. Solveig might prefer to spend all of her time on astronomy and astrophysics, but she was directing much of her effort to physics, a far more practical discipline. If Mahala were to go to her teachers here and tell them that she was unsure of what she wanted to do and wanted to explore various specialties for a time, they might conclude that she was wasting their resources and that her place here should go to someone else. At best, they might refer her to a Counselor, who would discuss her aptitudes and give her advice on what was best for her. There was no appeal from a Counselor's advice, which had almost the effect of an order; Solveig had told her to avoid going to Counselors with her problems at all costs.

After two months on Island Two, anyone looking at her record would have seen a student who had the makings of a biochemical specialist, or so she hoped. If she seemed inclined to spend more time than she might have on mathematics or ecological systems, so much the better. Her record would not reveal any sign that she might be someone so involved in her own interests that she would neglect what she owed to the Project.

Before long, she rarely thought of what Malik had said about what the Habbers might do. That was far in the future, if it ever happened at all. Only occasionally, usually if she suddenly woke in the night, would she think of their threat to abandon this system, however distant and improbable that might be, and the danger it might pose to the bit of freedom the Cytherians had won.

Xelah Barringer had started out as a physician, had pursued further studies in biochemistry while treating patients, and was now one of the teachers at the Island Two preparatory school. Unlike most of the other teachers, she made no attempt to be easily approachable. She answered any questions during lectures or seminars readily enough, but kept to herself the rest of the time, glaring angrily at any student bold enough to trouble her with queries during her free moments.

Mahala was not put off by Xelah's manner. She had seen that steely look before, in Risa's eyes, and knew what it really meant: Don't trouble me unless it's really important or interesting. She knew that Xelah often took a long walk after last light, near a small hill that overlooked a star-shaped building that housed workers and their families, and caught up with her teacher there.

"I have to ask you something," Mahala said.

"Ask, then." Xelah kept walking, opening her legs into a longer stride. She was not much taller than Mahala, but it was hard to keep up with her.

"Every person born here and on Earth is scanned while they're still in the womb, and then any genetic abnormality is corrected before birth."

Xelah's lip curled. "Tell me something I don't know, Mahala, or else stop wasting my time."

"Since we read the genome anyway and correct the abnormalities, there's no reason we couldn't engineer the DNA strands to keep on repairing themselves, so why don't we do it? That has to be something like what the Habbers do, even if it seems they use nanotechnological devices rather than—"

Xelah halted abruptly, then turned around; Mahala barely kept from bumping into her. "Every biology student has probably asked that question for the past two centuries at least. Shit, I asked it myself for the first time when I was a lot younger than you are, so you're even more foolish than I was. Why can't we have the same long lives the Habbers do? Why do we settle for only enough rejuv therapy to extend our youth for a few decades? Why do we shut down at a hundred and thirty or thereabouts when theoretically we could go on for a good deal longer?"

The teacher looked furious now; Mahala took a step backward. "Study some politics, you stupid girl," Xelah said in a low voice. "Do some work in demographics, in population control, maybe some history. The Mukhtars won't let us do what we might be able to do, and we don't have the resources, and anybody who even tried would get slapped down fast enough."

"Maybe they've already extended their own lives in secret," Mahala murmured.

"Maybe they have, although I doubt it. They have their religions to console them. They can dream of eternal life later on. And surely even a foolish girl like you has to know by now that whether it's biology or physics or anything else, we get to a certain point and then we have to stop." Xelah resumed walking. "Now leave me the fuck alone."

The teacher's words were like another door closing.

Mahala was sitting at a table, eating a meal while reviewing some material on her screen, when she heard someone call her name.

She looked up from her rice and vegetables as Chike Enu-Barnes sat down across from her. He was smiling as usual; his black eyes danced, and his dark brown face was almost glowing with good cheer.

She grinned back at him, unable to resist his cheerful countenance. She liked him, perhaps more than almost anyone else here except for her old friend Solveig; she felt calmer and even happier in his presence. Chike leaned toward her, propping his elbows on the table; she picked up her cup of tea before he could take her hand. She liked him, and that was the problem; the current of her feelings ran no stronger than that. It had become fairly obvious during the last few days that he wanted her to be more than just his friend.

"Where are you going during our break?" he asked.

"Not much for me to decide there," she replied. "My grandmother's already expecting me in Oberg, and then I'll visit my uncle in Turing."

His smile faded only slightly. "I thought there might be a chance you'd be staying here for part of the time."

Some of the other students from the settlements would be spending the time off here instead of visiting their families. They did not want to lose their momentum or miss finishing any assignment; she also suspected that several of them had other reasons for not wanting to go home. For a moment, she wished that she could have come up with an excuse for staying here, but that would only have encouraged Chike to hope.

"Too many people are expecting me," she said.

"Anyone in particular? Outside of your family, I mean."

She thought of Ragnar. His presence in Dyami's house wouldn't make her visit there any easier. He had offered to move out; Frania had said that in her last message, but Dyami and Amina had put a stop to that. They had plenty of room, especially now that Mahala was on Island Two, and Frania, being an apprentice pilot, was away more often.

"Maybe there is," she said at last. Chike averted his eyes, looking disappointed. "I mean, I have to work some things out with somebody," she continued, softening the blow. "I should get everything settled by the time I come back."

"I hope so," he murmured, and she wondered if it might have been kinder not to say anything at all.

"You needn't pack for your trip to Oberg this soon," Benzi said, "and you don't have to take so much with you."

Mahala closed her duffel, then turned to face her great-uncle. "I'm not taking any of this with me," she said. "Solveig got permission for me to move into her room in the student quarters. It'll be crowded, but not for very long. At least a few students will be asked to leave after the break or decide to leave school themselves." She took a breath, wishing suddenly that he would show some reaction—bewilderment, hurt, even relief—instead of just staring at her with his usual calm expression. "We can move to a larger room then."

"Is there any particular reason you decided to move out?" he asked. "I thought that we were getting along. You'd have more distractions in the student quarters."

That was true. Benzi was away often and unobtrusive even when he was here. It had been easy for her to retreat to her room in the pilots' quarters and concentrate on her studies.

"I'd rather stay here," she said, "but I have to move out. You're a family member, but you're also a Habber, and it probably won't do me much good in the long run to . . . "

". . . live here with me," he finished. "You don't have to say it, Mahala—I understand. You don't want a record that might seem ambiguous in certain respects."

"If it were just you, Benzi, it wouldn't matter as much, but I've got a grandfather who's a Habber, too." She looked away from him. "I wish Malik had never come back here. He should have stayed where he was. He isn't needed here."

Benzi lifted his brows. "Even as a teacher?"

"He isn't teaching anything that's important." She tried not to think of all the times she had spotted Xelah Barringer speaking to him, during one of her walks or while sitting with Malik, drinking tea in one of the garden dining areas; Xelah never looked impatient or irritated in his presence, but seemed to hang on his every word. "Students go to his lectures mostly to enhance their records a bit, so they won't seem too narrow in their interests."

"I see."

Mahala sat down on her bed. Malik had to know that she was traveling to Oberg and then to Turing, but he had said nothing about accompanying her there.

"If you change your mind," Benzi continued, "and decide that you want to move back here, just let me know."

"That's kind of you, but it's time for me to live in my own place."

He smiled. "You're probably right."

Benzi was always so reasonable. It had to be easier for Habbers to be reasonable, since they were not bound by any true obligations here. Balin had undoubtedly sounded just as reasonable while telling Dyami that he was leaving Turing.

*   *   *

Mahala was just entering the airship bay when she saw Malik at the edge of the group of passengers, with a small duffel hanging by a strap from his shoulder. He was clothed in a loose brown shirt and black trousers instead of the long robe he usually wore when giving his lectures. Most of the people getting ready to board the airship for Oberg appeared to be older students, specialists, or people in the gray garb of workers, and all of them seemed to recognize her grandfather. Two young women whispered to each other, then glanced toward him. The other students were watching him uneasily, as if trying to decide whether or not to greet him.

She turned away, then moved toward the airship with the others, ignoring Malik. She was aboard the airship and securing her duffel under her seat when he sat down next to her.

"Salaam, Mahala."

"There are plenty of other seats," she said in a low voice. "You might be more comfortable with an empty seat next to you so you can stretch out."

"I'll be comfortable enough here."

"I didn't know you were going to the settlements. I thought you'd changed your mind." She leaned back against her seat. "You didn't bother to say anything to me about your plans."

"No, I didn't. I suppose that I should have, but I thought it might be easier for you this way, not having to dread traveling with me ahead of time."

She looked at him from the sides of his eyes. He had a faint smile on his face. "Risa didn't tell me you were coming to Oberg, either," she said. "Didn't you even let her know?"

"Of course I did. I sent a message to her, and then called her, but she refused to come to the screen. Her bondmate Sef spoke to me instead and gave me her message, namely that she would be damned if she would allow me to set foot in her house and would appreciate it if I kept out of the west dome as well."

She could imagine her grandmother saying much worse than that. "You have to understand," Mahala began to say.

"Oh, I do understand." The half-smile was still on his face.

"Then why are you going to Oberg at all?"

"There are Habbers there. I can stay with them in their residence and still visit with you. And perhaps Risa will change her mind."

"She doesn't change her mind very easily."

Malik made a sound that might have been a laugh. "How well I remember the truth of that." He settled back in his seat and closed his eyes. Mahala pressed her lips together, resenting his presence.

Malik slept during most of the journey, stirring only when the howl of the wind outside the airship rose. At least Mahala assumed that he was asleep, although he might have been communing with other Habbers through his Link. He had not seemed interested in viewing the images on the forward screen, the images enhanced to show what the Venusian surface would look like if sunlight could reach the surface, the images that seemed more real than what the sensor lenses would show her because they were enhanced. The darkness that was actually out there would be only a void into which one could project one's dreams or be lost.

Her grandfather opened his eyes as the airship descended into the maw of Oberg's bay and dropped toward the metal eggshell of a cradle. Mahala hefted her duffel after the landing and followed the other passengers off the airship, with Malik just behind her. He kept at her side as they walked down the ramp and through the bay, glancing uneasily at the row of cradled airships near one wall.

He seemed apprehensive, looking around uneasily as they left the bay and entered the main dome. Unexpectedly, Mahala found herself feeling some sympathy for the grandfather who had abandoned this world so long ago.

A cart carrying only a few passengers rolled toward them along the main road, then came to a stop. Mahala turned toward her grandfather. "I'm going to walk to Risa's house," she said, "for the exercise, so if you need a ride to where you're going—" She gestured toward the cart.

"I'll walk part of the way with you," he said.

"Risa and Sef will expect me to go by the monument and the other memorials to pay my respects."

"Then I'll come with you, if you don't mind."

She did mind. She wondered if he knew about the memorials that had been erected since he had last been here. "Come along, then," she murmured.

She quickened her pace. Malik easily kept up with her. They did not have far to go to get to the clearing where the memorials stood. As usual, there was a floral tribute, a small wreath of slightly wilted flowers, at the base of the monument to her great-grandmother Iris Angharads.

Malik looked up at the sculpted faces of Iris and Amir Azad, the man who had died with her, then lowered his eyes to the Anglaic inscription. "In honor of Iris Angharads and Amir Azad," the inscription read, "the first true Cytherians, who gave their lives to save our new world. They shall not be forgotten. May their spirit live on in all those who follow them. They rest forever on the world they helped to build." Malik must have seen the monument and its inscription many times in the past, yet he continued to stare at the words as though reading them for the first time.

For my benefit? Mahala wondered. No, it went deeper.

At last he moved away from the monument and wandered toward the other memorial pillars. Mahala trailed after him, unsure of what to do. He stopped in front of a pillar covered with holo images of faces.

"Chen's there," Mahala said hastily. "Liang Chen—Risa's father." It came to her then that Malik had to be as old now as her great-grandfather Chen had been when he had died, maybe older.

Malik glanced at her. "I know. I remember Chen very well." He stepped away from that pillar and turned toward the next memorial. She saw him tense as he caught sight of the face of his daughter Chimene at the top of the pillar, set apart from the images of faces below.

He was silent for a long time, then said, "Who put up this memorial image to your mother?"

"I don't know. I know it wasn't Risa or anyone in our family. No one ever told me. I suppose some of her followers or friends must have taken care of it."

"With no one else's face anywhere near hers," Malik said. "I suppose that's appropriate." He paused. "I wasn't much of a father to your mother. I left when I had the chance, thinking that there was nothing left for me here, that even my daughter was lost to me, and yet perhaps I was responsible for what she became."

"You couldn't have known—"

"Oh, but I should have seen the signs. I could have reached out to her more instead of being grateful for the wall that rose between us, since that wall left me freer inside myself."

Mahala moved closer to him. "Is that why you left the Project, because of Chimene?"

"It was part of the reason. I could cite others, but the fact is that I left largely because I had grown tired of my life on Island Two and was fortunate enough to fall in with people plotting an escape. The truth is that I didn't much care whether I reached a Habitat or lost my life in the attempt—it was all the same to me."

"It must have taken some courage to leave," she said.

He shook his head. "Believe me, child, it took none at all. It would have been more courageous of me to stay." He adjusted the duffel strap on his shoulder. "I've kept you long enough, Mahala. Risa and her household will be waiting for you. I can find my destination by myself."

Mahala was about to walk away, then turned back. "Malik," she said, "Risa wouldn't throw you out if you came to her house with me."

"Showing up suddenly, uninvited—I won't do that to her." He moved toward another pillar, as if searching for the images of people he might once have known. She left him standing there among the faces of the dead.

Dinner was what Mahala had expected, with Kristof and Barika questioning her about her classes and friends while Grazie filled her in on recent Oberg gossip. Only her grandmother seemed unlike herself; while her housemates chattered and passed around platters of food and bottles of wine, Risa picked at her plate of vegetables and beans and said little.

Often her grandmother went to the greenhouse after dinner or discussed the first chores of the next day with Sef, but this time she got up from the table and beckoned to Mahala. "I'm going to take a walk," she said. "Maybe you'd like to come along with me."

"Of course," Mahala said. "Should I help clear the table first?"

"Go," Sef said. "It's your first night home—we'll find enough work for you to do tomorrow."

She followed Risa from the house. Overhead, the dome's light had faded into the faint glow of early evening. Risa strolled in the direction of the tunnel that led to the main dome, then abruptly turned toward a path of flat pale stones that led to the community greenhouses.

"Malik is in Oberg, isn't he," Risa said.

"Yes. He came on the airship with me."

"I knew he would come."

"I told him that if he came to your house with me, you'd probably welcome him, no matter how you felt, but he wouldn't come here knowing that you didn't want to see him."

Risa halted near a tree. "It was all so long ago," she murmured. "He was the most beautiful man I had ever seen. Maybe if he hadn't looked the way he did, and hadn't spoken to me in such poetic phrases, and hadn't been so gentle with me, I would have been able to see how wrong he was for me, and how wrong I was for him." She fell silent for a few moments. "It wasn't entirely his fault that we parted. I was to blame for much of what went wrong, although it took me a while to see that. I suppose he still looks much the same."

"He doesn't look his age," Mahala admitted.

"He must look as if he could be my son."

"Not when you look right into his face, into his eyes," Mahala said. "He seems older then."

They walked on until the main road was in sight. Others were out for a stroll; two women waved at Risa from a distance. Normally her grandmother would have waved back, perhaps gone over to talk to them. This time, she led Mahala away from the road and toward a grove of trees.

They sat down under one tree. "He would look at me now," Risa said, "and see an old woman."

"No, he wouldn't." In the faint silvery evening light, Mahala could almost envision the girl her grandmother had been. Even in daylight, Risa still had the appearance of a woman in her middle years. Rejuvenation would keep her near her physical prime, with only gradual signs of aging, until she was a decade or two past the century mark, and then her decline would come fairly rapidly. Mahala wondered if Risa envied the Habbers their extended lives, the life spans Earthfolk and Cytherians might also have had if their biologists hadn't been held back, or if she was content with her more limited span. Mahala had always supposed that she herself would make her peace with death when that time came, but perhaps that was only because her end was so distant in time that her death hardly seemed real.

"There's one reason I wouldn't mind living as long as Malik or Benzi," Risa said. "Maybe then I could live long enough to leave this dome and walk outside unprotected. I could be around to see what so many gave their lives to build. Sometimes—" Risa put her hand on Mahala's arm. "Sometimes I wonder if it was worth it. Your mother might have been different somewhere else—in a way, the dream of the Project was what killed her. I occasionally wonder if I did the right thing by bringing you up in such a place, inside these domes."

These words were so unlike her grandmother that Mahala could hardly bring herself to speak. "Grandmother," she said at last, "you've always—"

"I've always thought of my duty," Risa interrupted. "I was always a good Cytherian. Now I find myself thinking more and more of what this world did to your mother Chimene, and to Dyami, and to the other daughter I lost." Risa had never spoken of her younger daughter, who had died while still a child, during an epidemic that had killed many in the enclosed environment of the settlements, where deadly microbes could spread more rapidly. "What do you want to do, Mahala?"

"I don't know."

"At least you're honest enough to admit that. I expected you to say that you wanted to do whatever would be of most use to the Project. Well, then, what do you think you might do?"

Mahala considered how much she could admit to Risa. "I want to go to the Cytherian Institute," she replied, "and not just for the sake of the Project, but because I could visit Earth."

"And after that?"

"The Administrators and Counselors will probably decide that for me."

"That's also what you're supposed to say. I want to know what you might choose."

Mahala was silent.

"There were times," Risa continued, "when I was young, when I would imagine that I could somehow rush forward in time and see the sun shining on this planet again, the clouds gone, the plateaus and mountains green with life. But I doubt that even a Habber could live that long." She sighed. "The Project wouldn't have been possible without the Habbers. I know that, too."

"Risa—"

"Foolish of me," Risa said, "to think that my life is that different from those that people have led for ages. When did anyone ever live long enough to see if their dreams and those of their children and grandchildren would be fulfilled in the end?"

Risa got to her feet quickly, in one movement; she was still limber.

"I'll tell you what I suspect," she went on. "I think the Habbers are tiring of their efforts here. I think they're growing weary of their dealings with Earth. They have worlds of their own. What's to stop them from simply leaving?"

Mahala tensed. Either Risa's instincts were even better than she realized, or else she knew what some of the Habbers were considering; perhaps Benzi had told her.

"Not that there would be anything we could do about it if they did," Risa murmured. "We had better go back to the house. Sef will want to hear all about your studies and your new friends."

Within two days of arriving in Oberg, Mahala was impatient to be on her way to Turing and her visit with Dyami. Her former schoolmates, at sixteen and seventeen years of age, were already leading the lives of adults, choosing bondmates, deciding where to live, volunteering for Bat duty, or finishing their apprenticeships. Even though she was their contemporary, to them she was still leading a child's life, without any real responsibilities.

She busied herself during the day with household tasks and then took a walk around Oberg after last light, when she was unlikely to run into her childhood friends, who would be sharing evening meals with their families or getting some much-needed rest after a shift of work. Given the demands of the Project, perhaps her former friends had been wise to settle for their more limited lives, for the rewards of duty and work instead of trying for more. Whatever disappointments lay ahead, they could know that they were a part of something larger than themselves, something that would outlive them. She might spend several years trying to discover what it was she wanted for herself and end up leading the sort of life most of the others already did, but without their inner satisfactions.

As she passed the entrance to the tunnel and turned toward Risa's house, she thought of Ragnar and how he was trying to reconcile his dreams with the restrictions on his life.

"Mahala," a voice said from behind her.

She turned to see Malik coming toward her from the tunnel. "What are you doing here?" she asked.

"Risa asked me to come," he replied.

She turned toward the house and saw then that Risa was outside, sitting under a tree, and wondered why her grandmother had said nothing to her about this.

"Did she say why?" Mahala asked.

"No." He walked toward Risa; Mahala followed him. He stopped a few paces away from Risa, who got to her feet and gazed at him in silence.

"You look much the same," Risa said.

Malik said, "I would have known you, Risa. You haven't changed very much."

"Oh, but I have. It's why I asked if you would come now, after the dome darkens. You'd see an older face if you had come here at first light. You'd see my gray hairs."

"Is Kolya Burian still part of your household?" he asked.

"Oh, yes." Risa glanced toward Mahala. "Kolya came here with Malik from Earth," she added, although Mahala already knew that; Kolya had told her the story many times.

She lingered near her grandparents, then moved toward the house. "Don't go," Risa murmured. "What I have to say concerns you, too." She sat down again, then gestured to Malik to sit with her. "My bondmate Sef has never been a jealous man, but it will reassure him to see us all sitting out here together. He knows how much I once cared for you, how much I loved you."

Malik seated himself. Mahala hesitated, then sat down next to her grandmother. "I should have cared for you more," the Habber said. "I should have loved you more. I have often thought of what I might have done differently."

"What you might have done was not to have become my bondmate at all, but I didn't leave you much choice, telling you that I wanted your child whether or not we ever made a pledge, whether or not we were ever bondmates."

Mahala had not heard that tale before. "I could have refused," Malik said.

"It's just as well that you didn't. We wouldn't have had Mahala then." Mahala felt Risa's hand on her arm. "That's why I asked you here, Malik. I want you to look out for our granddaughter."

"There are enough people to look out for me," Mahala objected.

Risa's grip tightened. "Be quiet, Mahala," she said. "You don't know what I mean to ask Malik. You told me that you want to see Earth."

"Yes, I do."

"And why do you want to go there? Is it mostly to be able to study at the Cytherian Institute, or is it mostly so that you can see our—humankind's—home planet?"

"Those are both good reasons," Mahala said, "aren't they?"

"Of course they are, child. But you can experience any part of Earth with a mind-tour and without the trouble and inconvenience and discomfort of actually going there." Risa paused. "As for the Cytherian Institute, I think their main purpose in bringing students there from our settlements and Islands is to further the aims of the Council of Mukhtars, to build more loyalty to Earth."

"That doesn't mean they'd succeed in doing that with me." Mahala took a breath. "Just one time, I'd like to stand outside a dome, breathe open air, be on the surface of a world with nothing to protect me."

"You might not be able to endure it," Risa murmured. "Then they'd have to send you back here, troublesome and costly as it would be."

"Then I'd know for certain that I couldn't live elsewhere, that this is the environment for me, but at least I would have seen something else in my life."

Her grandmother let go of her arm. "Some say that the Habbers are looking for a way to gain more control of the Project and speed its progress, while others say that they are thinking of abandoning this solar space altogether. I have only one request to make of you, Malik. If there is a chance for Mahala to go on whatever voyage the Habbers might make, to have whatever adventure might lie ahead for her, do what you can to see that she gets it if that's what she wants. You won't be stealing my granddaughter from me. She is not to torment herself thinking that she has betrayed me or this world by making such a choice."

Mahala felt that she had to object. "I wouldn't—"

"Hush," Risa interrupted. "If you go on such a journey and there is any way to return, you'll find it. That is all I have to say to both of you. Do whatever you feel you must do."

Risa stood up and faced Malik. "I was so angry with you for running away, for going to the Habbers," she continued, "but I think it must be easier for you to be an outsider there than to live among us as one."

"You still know me fairly well," Malik said.

"I won't ask you inside. It's better if I don't. But before you leave Oberg, do call or leave a message."

"I shall," Malik said.

"Go," Risa said, dismissing him. "Mahala, come inside."

Two days after Risa had spoken to Malik, Mahala went to the airship bay to board the ship going to Turing. Malik had spoken to her only a few hours ago, saying that he had changed his mind about coming with her. Perhaps Dyami had said that he was not welcome in that settlement, although that was unlikely.

Frania had told Mahala that she had over two weeks off and would be there to meet the airship. Mahala, sitting down in one of the front seats, thought of her friend as she watched the pilots put on their bands and suddenly felt how much she missed Frania, how much she longed to be in Turing again.

Frania was waiting just outside the airship bay. She ran to Mahala, threw her arms around her, then reached for her duffel. "I should have sent you more messages than I did," Frania said, "but with this apprenticeship, about all I felt like doing at the end of the day was grabbing a meal and then going to sleep."

"You don't have to make excuses," Mahala replied. "Sometimes that was about all I could do, too." She had sent her friend only two messages.

"Feel like walking?" Frania asked.

"Sure."

"I've got a lot to tell you. I'll be taking airships up to the Islands soon. I'll be able to visit you when I get to Island Two. And—" Frania paused. "I don't know if I should tell you this. I promised I wouldn't."

"I can keep a secret," Mahala said.

"I know you can. It's just—oh, I have to tell you. It's Ragnar. He wants us to make a pledge, to be bondmates."

Mahala stopped suddenly, thinking she had misunderstood. Frania halted next to her. "What is it, Mahala?"

"Nothing." Mahala steadied herself. "I'm just surprised."

"So was I. He only asked me for a promise a couple of days ago, right after I got back here." Frania set down Mahala's bag. "How thoughtless of me, when I know you and Ragnar—" She stood there, staring at Mahala with her beautiful hazel eyes as a passenger cart rolled past them. "He told me all about it. He wanted to be honest with me. He admitted that he had asked you for a pledge and you had said no, so I was certain you'd be over him by now."

"It's all right," Mahala made herself say. "It's past. You mustn't worry about that."

"I promised him that I'd become his bondmate. I wouldn't have promised that if I thought there was any chance it would hurt you. I could have waited."

"I know that," Mahala said, still feeling numb, surprised at how affected she was by Frania's words.

"We don't know when we'll have the ceremony yet, whether we should make our pledge before I start shuttle pilot training or afterward. It probably depends on whether he can get a work assignment on the Islands."

Frania reached for the duffel. Mahala grabbed for the bag and hefted it onto her shoulder. "Let me carry it as far as the tunnel, Frani."

They walked on. Frania spoke of her training and some of the friends she had made among the other apprentice pilots. Mahala listened, thinking of Ragnar and Frania and the pledge they had promised to make. Clearly she had shown good judgment in refusing Ragnar's offer. She had given him time to realize that he did not love her so much after all, and losing her had allowed his feelings for Frania to flower. She could tell herself that, but she did not really believe it.

He had turned to Frania only to ease the hurt inside himself. With a few words to him, Mahala might even convince him that asking Frania to be his bondmate was a mistake. She hated herself for the thought.

Dyami and Amina knew just how to behave at dinner, letting Mahala talk of her studies and her fellow students and prompting her occasionally with a question, careful not to be unduly inquisitive. Frania said little, but surely her aunt and Dyami had noticed the glow in her eyes and her obvious happiness and wondered at the cause.

Tasida was staying in the south dome for a few days, seeing two patients there who were recovering from serious injuries after a wall had collapsed on them during a recent quake. Ragnar was absent, but Frania had already told Mahala that he was working late shifts with the crawler and digger workers. That was a relief; he would be sleeping during the days and working in the evenings. With any luck, she would hardly have to see him at all.

"I am surprised," Dyami said then, "that Malik didn't come here with you."

Mahala looked up from her bowl of fruit. "Didn't he send you a message?"

"No, he didn't. Risa mentioned that she had seen him briefly, and you had implied that he might come here with you. I didn't want to ask you about it before, but when you didn't say anything—"

"He sent a message just before I left Oberg saying that he decided not to come with me. I thought he might have sent you the same message."

"Well, he didn't, so I must assume that he's not coming at all." Dyami looked disappointed. Of course, Mahala thought. He must have been hoping that Malik might have a message for him from Balin.

They finished their supper. Mahala helped Frania clear the dishes. The two girls sat up for a while after Dyami and Amina had gone to sleep; Frania seemed anxious to tell Mahala about her plans. She would finish her apprenticeship as a pilot and was even hoping for a chance to train for being a torchship pilot. She would have to live on an Island if she was assigned to shuttle duty later on, but she would prefer a home in one of the settlements, and there was a good chance she would have that wish granted because most of the pilots preferred shuttle duty to airship piloting. A home in a settlement, rather than on an Island, would give her more time with Ragnar and any children they might have.

"Ragnar's a digger and crawler worker," Mahala said. "How can he live on an Island if that's where you end up? He's needed here, not there."

"There are other things he can do. The Islands need workers, too. He could train as an apprentice to a mechanic. He told me that he was already learning about homeostat repairs and life-support systems."

"He'd have to go through another apprenticeship," Mahala said.

"He's willing to do it. Besides, if we're bondmates and I have to be on the Islands, the Counselors would want to keep us together. If Ragnar needs to learn another skill or do another apprenticeship for that to be possible, I'm sure that he could get permission."

Ragnar seemed to have his life planned, or perhaps Frania was planning it for him. Mahala had no way of knowing what he thought anymore.

"I've been talking about myself ever since you got here," Frania continued. "Tell me what you've been doing."

Mahala described some of her courses and teachers, then mentioned a few of her fellow students. Her life seemed unfocused next to Frania's.

A question suddenly came to her. "Frani," she said, "this may seem a strange thing to ask, but what would you do if you had the chance to travel somewhere—well, besides Venus and Anwara and Earth?"

Frania laughed softly. "There isn't anywhere else, at least not any place we're ever likely to go, unless you want to count Mars and the Habitats."

"Would you welcome the chance to see a Hab?"

"I wouldn't mind visiting one or seeing Mars, for that matter. If I had the chance, I'd take it."

"What about leaving this system altogether?"

"Oh, Mahala. That wouldn't be like traveling to another place. People would have to leave without knowing what they would find and whether they would ever get back. I think that if human beings were going to do something like that, they would have done it a long time ago, but Earth doesn't have the means, and the Habbers seem content to stay where they are."

"Things could change."

"They won't change that much. Not for us, anyway." Frania yawned. "I was going to wait up for Ragnar, but I'm exhausted."

"Go to sleep," Mahala said. "You're supposed to rest during your time off."

"You're right." Frania walked across the room, still yawning, and rolled out one of the futons, then wandered toward the bathroom. Dyami had told Mahala that she and Frania could sleep in the common room, since Ragnar was sleeping in their former bedroom while working his darktime shift. Apparently Frania and Ragnar were not sharing a room yet, although they probably would be before much longer.

Now that she had been away from the Islands for a while, Mahala was beginning to see her student's life on Island Two as someone else might see it. She was flailing around, picking up a smattering of knowledge in different fields while getting a grounding in biology. If the student Counselors had known about her desire to study at the Cytherian Institute, they could legitimately ask whether that desire grew out of her devotion to her world or only from her longing to see new places. They might wonder why she had agreed to live with Benzi, a Habber, during her earliest days on Island Two instead of in student quarters. The Counselors could question her commitment, even whether she had any true commitment at all. If she passed a few more months following her present course, a Counselor might call her in for a discussion, even suggest that she leave school and choose an apprenticeship.

A vision came to her of what she might want to do, although her dream was formless and vague. Venus was being changed, but not rapidly enough for people alive now ever to hope to live outside the domes. Planetary engineering, she thought, could work both ways. A planet could be made habitable by human beings; people might also be transformed so that they could live on other worlds. Biological transformations could make it possible for present-day Cytherians, or their children, to venture outside the domes for periods of time, perhaps even to live entirely outside them. There was something that would be worth her dedication, that would be a true life's work.

But to accomplish that, she knew, was beyond the Project's capacities. Even if it were not, many would find the idea of adapting people to the still-alien Cytherian environment completely contrary to the Project's aims. Venus was to be a world that would not cut its inhabitants off biologically or socially from their home planet; changed people would have even less reason to feel any loyalty to Earth. She thought of what Xelah Barringer might say about her hopelessly naïve ideas, notions that many others had probably entertained.

The Habbers might be capable of such a feat of genetic engineering; rumors had circulated for some time that the Habbers had altered themselves more radically than was apparent, that there were some living in the Habs who were hardly human at all.

The ceiling lights dimmed, then went out. Mahala heard footsteps behind her and turned her head to see the shadowy form of Frania. "Aren't you coming to bed?" Frania asked.

"I'm going to sit up for a while."

"Good night, then." Frania stretched out on her futon and pulled her coverlet over herself.

Mahala felt restless. She sat there, gazing at the trees outside the house, then got to her feet, crossed to the doorway, and went outside.

She walked downhill in the direction of the lake. Usually everything was quiet at this hour, but in the distance, she heard what sounded like the song of a bird. She halted to listen, heard voices, and then more of the high-pitched musical notes. Someone was playing a flute. Mahala moved away from the sound and continued down the slope until she came to the lake.

She sat down and gazed out at the calm, almost motionless dark surface of the lake. Now that she had at least a vague notion of what she might want to accomplish, she might try to find a way to reach for it within the restrictions of her life. Specializing in biology, and genetics in particular, was clearly the first necessary step, and it was likely that she would be steered in that direction anyway. Perhaps she should not think any further ahead than that until her vision became clearer to her.

One possibility was becoming increasingly obvious, and she was certain that she was not alone in coming to this judgment. Those who had envisioned the Project had assumed that the earliest settlers, the first Cytherians, would be content to live out their lives knowing that they would never see Venus become a green and growing world. They had forgotten that people tended to become more impatient and more restive when what they wanted seemed within their grasp, however unrealistic their hopes might be.

Mahala drew up her legs and rested her arms on her knees. Maybe Malik's lectures in history were not so useless after all. She considered what she knew about her grandfather. He had come to Venus as an exile from Earth, one whose ideas had troubled Earth's governing Council of Mukhtars. She wondered how many of his unpopular ideas he still harbored.

"Greetings, Mahala," a familiar voice said.

She looked up to see Ragnar emerge from the nearby trees. "I thought you were working the darktime shift," she said to him.

"I am. I asked my team leader if I could leave early. I'll make up the time tomorrow." He sat down next to her. "I guessed I'd find you here."

"You think that you know me so well."

"I know Frani pretty well. She said that she was going to meet you. I'll bet that as soon as she saw you, she told you all about becoming my bondmate and then begged you not to tell anyone else. I didn't even tell Solveig about our plans yet or our parents."

"And when were you going to let Dyami and Amina know about your pledge?"

"After you left," Ragnar said. "I thought that might be easier on you, but since Frani's obviously already told you, there's no point in keeping it to ourselves."

"You got over me awfully fast." She had not meant to say that. "How can you do this to her?"

"What am I doing to her, Mahala?"

"You don't love her."

"How do you know?"

She was silent.

"If you had agreed to be my bondmate," he said in a lower voice, "I wouldn't have gone to Frani even if our agreement had allowed us to have other companions and bed partners, because it wouldn't have been fair to her. But you didn't, and you left, and after you were gone I started looking forward to when Frani would be back here on leave. She sent me a message every day, even if it was only a few words, and when she was here, I felt happier being around her. Maybe it isn't what I felt for you, but it's enough, it's a kind of love."

"I was right to say no to you, then," Mahala said. "You didn't care about me as much as you thought you did."

"You're wrong, Mahala. I still love you. That love would have grown if it had a chance. And if you cared about me, you'd be glad I found someone who can make me happy, someone I can care about this way, someone you care about."

"Maybe so," she said. "It's just kind of sudden, that's all."

"It seems that way to you, but it doesn't to me," Ragnar said. "I've had almost half a year of working with diggers and crawlers and trying to master sculpting and casting molds and wondering if my whole life was going to be hours of tedious tiring work in exchange for a few moments of doing what I really want to do—what I have to do." He paused. "It'll be different with Frani as a bondmate. It won't be such a lonely life."

"I see."

"No, you don't. You think I'm just turning to her because it's better than being alone, but I care about her, I trust her, and she's never done an unkind thing to me. It might last longer than any bond I could have had with you."

The words stung, but there was truth in them. She thought of what she knew about her great-grandmother Iris Angharads. Iris's bond with Mahala's great-grandfather, Liang Chen, had endured until the heroic end of Iris's life, but she knew from Benzi that there had been a long estrangement between the two during Iris's student days at the Cytherian Institute and then later, after the two had come to the Islands. Being separated physically for long periods had only increased the emotional distance between them. Ragnar might have found a way to follow her to Island Two, but following Mahala to the Cytherian Institute, if she won a chance to attend, would have been close to impossible.

That would not have been fair to Ragnar, she thought, trying not to think of the fact that, with a bondmate, especially a bondmate as solitary and unconventional and with as many black marks on his record as Ragnar, her chances of being chosen for the Cytherian Institute might have been almost nonexistent.

"I am happy for you, Ragnar," she said, trying to believe her own words. "How long a bond do you two want?"

"I said I'd promise twenty years, but Frani said that if I changed my mind after a few years, she didn't want me to get another mark on my record." He shook back his hair. "So we agreed on ten, with a provision to promise ten more if we have a child."

"That's good," she murmured. "It's better for a child to know the parents have a bond of some duration, that they'll be together at least until the child's an adult." She sounded like a Counselor.

They were silent for a time, gazing out at the quiet waters of the lake.

"How are things going with you?" he asked.

Frania had sent him daily messages; she had sent him none at all. "To be honest," she said, "I'm still trying to figure that out. I haven't even decided on what kind of specialist I might want to be."

"You can always let a Counselor decide that for you."

"If I don't start concentrating on a particular field pretty soon, somebody else will decide it for me." She sighed. "I moved in with Solveig just before I left. I don't know if she told you or not."

"No, she didn't. We don't send each other many messages." Ragnar got to his feet. "I have to get some sleep," he said. "Are you coming back to the house with me?"

"I'll stay here for a while." She did not want Frania to wake and see them come inside together; the other girl might wonder if they had done more than talk. And, she told herself, the two might want a few moments to themselves. That thought pained her.

"Good night, then."

Ragnar left her. A pang of longing filled her for the life she had once had here in Turing. She toyed for a moment with the notion of leaving school and coming back here to live. Dyami would make a place for her; there would be work in the community greenhouses, the ceramics plant, or the refinery. She could live out her life knowing that Venus would one day be a true home for humankind without dwelling on what she might do to bring that time closer.

It was a fantasy, of course, no more than a hope at recapturing her childhood; she knew, even as she imagined that kind of life for herself, that her true life waited for her on Island Two, and perhaps elsewhere.

14

Mahala returned to Island Two a day early, to find that Solveig had come back the day before that. Solveig said nothing about her visit to the surface, although Mahala knew that her friend had been staying with her parents when Ragnar had called to tell them of his pledge to Frania. Solveig had more urgent business on her mind.

There was a rumor that the Counselors were going to call in all of the first year students, and most of the older ones, for consultations. No one knew what that meant. Normally, a student was not called in for counseling until the end of each year of study, unless there were signs of a serious problem. Few looked forward to these sessions, since that was when students were either directed toward specific studies or advised to leave school altogether, advice that amounted to expulsion.

Solveig had delivered this news only a few minutes after Mahala had entered their new quarters. They had been given a space slightly larger than Solveig's former room, and Solveig had already moved Mahala's belongings there.

"And that isn't all," Solveig continued as Mahala unpacked and hung her clothes on a rod. "The Administrators have suddenly canceled Malik Haddad's next series of lectures, and no one knows why."

Mahala frowned. "Not many students were going to those lectures anyway."

"Oh, nobody will stop him from giving his talks if he insists. He just won't be given a room in which to deliver them or be able to offer them as part of our course of study. If students want to meet with him, they'll just have to arrange to do that on their own or call up the lectures he's already recorded."

That probably meant that even fewer students would go to Malik's lectures if they thought that the cancellation was a sign of official disapproval.

"He's my grandfather," Mahala said. "I can't exactly avoid him altogether, even if it does mean a black mark on my record."

"No one's going to blame you for seeing a family member, and it's not as though you see him that often anyway. It might be more of a mark against you if you ignored him. That might show a certain lack of family feeling." Solveig chuckled. "That's the problem, isn't it. Everything here is a test. We can never be sure what it is they expect of us, or want from us, outside of working hard at our studies. We can think that we're doing everything we should and still be killing our chances to advance without even knowing what our specific mistakes are."

Mahala finished hanging up a tunic and sat down on a cushion in one corner. "How did your trip go?" Solveig asked.

"Fine," Mahala replied. "Malik came to see Risa one evening. They sat outside and talked for a while, and she doesn't seem angry with him now. Dyami's household is the same as it was, but I can tell he's missing Balin." She paused. "Your brother and Frani told me about the pledge they're going to make." It was easier to say than she had expected.

"I know," Solveig said. "My parents were surprised. My mother always assumed he would eventually ask you to be his bondmate."

He did ask me, she almost said, but restrained herself. "Obviously your mother was wrong."

"Thorunn thinks they're too young to be promising each other a bond, not that Ragnar would ever consider her opinion." Solveig sat down across from Mahala. "There are other rumors going around about the Council of Mukhtars. I've heard that they've sent messages about appointing another Liaison to the Project Council here and that some on the Council may resign. Nobody seems to know why."

"Maybe that has something to do with why our Counselors want to see us," Mahala said. Most Cytherians would view any such changes with suspicion and uneasiness; changes, even changes they chose for themselves, meant more uncertainty for everyone here and in the settlements. "Maybe it's why they canceled Malik's lectures, too."

"I don't like it," Solveig said. "Sounds as though Earth wants more to say about what happens here."

Mahala got up. "I'm going to take a walk," she said. "Want to come along?"

Solveig shook her head. "I've got some work to catch up on. If the Counselors are going to be hauling us in for counseling, I want to make sure there's absolutely nothing they can hold against me."

Mahala had come to a path near the north end of Island Two before she realized why she had come here. Chike Enu-Barnes often came here after last light, usually by himself, to walk or jog near the railing at the edge of the Island before going back to his room to sleep. He was interested in her; if she took more of an interest in him, her feelings for him might grow. She would not have to think about Ragnar and Frania and their pledge.

But suddenly she knew that she could not use Chike that way. She had been about to climb the steps that led up to the platform and railing; she turned and headed back toward the center of the Island, heedless of the robed Linkers and workers in gray tunics and trousers who were walking along the stone paths, getting their evening exercise. She was near the rounded stone structure of the Habber residence before she saw a shadowy form beckon to her.

Malik was outside, sitting at a table in a clearing. A small teapot sat in front of him; he lifted his cup as she sat down in the other chair.

"Shall I pour you a cup of tea?" he asked.

"No, thank you. My roommate Solveig told me that you can't give your lectures anymore."

He nodded. "I would have told you that myself. I won't be stopped from giving talks informally, but with the withdrawal of official approval, it seems wiser for me to refrain."

"Did anybody tell you why your lectures were canceled?"

"No, but I can guess. The Administrators have been holding more meetings lately, and there are rumors that alliances among the Mukhtars are shifting once more, that Earth has been communicating more frequently with the Project Council. Obviously the Linkers here want to see if any new controlling faction on the Council of Mukhtars might be more hostile to the Habber presence here before they approve any more of my lectures."

Mahala looked down. "Solveig also heard that most of the students are going to be called in by Counselors soon. That doesn't usually happen at this point unless a student has serious problems. I haven't even gone to any of the Counselors yet." Risa had always been suspicious of Counselors and content that there were no Counselors assigned to the settlements. Dyami, who shared his mother's feelings, had felt that people needing help or advice were better off consulting a mentor or a physician who knew them, rather than going to a Counselor, who would be more mindful of the Project's interests.

"I had not heard that the students were to get counseling," Malik said, "but somehow it doesn't surprise me." He finished his tea, then set down his cup. "There seems little purpose in my staying on Island Two now."

"You're going to leave?" she asked, feeling both relief and a twinge of regret.

"I think I may wait until I find out what your Counselor has to say to you."

"I can tell you that now. Either I'll be told that my work is satisfactory and that I can continue my studies here or I'll be advised to leave this school and train for some other work." She could not see how either result could affect Malik's decision. "Don't you ever miss your Habitat and the people you know there?"

"Not especially. I can commune with anyone I know through my Link at any time."

"With any Habber at all, I suppose."

"No," Malik said. "I once thought there were no barriers among Habbers, but the more I live among them, the more I see that there is much I still don't know about them, about certain Habbers anyway." His voice trailed off; he looked away for a moment. "Have you given any thought to what you would do if you're told to leave the Islander school?"

"No." She folded her hands and rested them on the tabletop. "I refuse to think of that," she said, deluding herself with the idea that if she did not consider expulsion a possibility, it would not happen.

Mahala found a message from Counselor Aimée Lon on her screen the day before classes were to resume. The Counselor wanted to meet with her that afternoon, in one of the small seminar rooms. Mahala was advised not to make any rearrangements or adjustments in her schedule of courses and study groups until after the meeting with the Counselor.

"That sounds ominous," Solveig said after Mahala told her about the message.

"I know." Mahala pulled on a blue tunic. She had been trying on clothes for almost an hour, wondering if she should wear a more formal robe or a long, modest dress. She had finally settled on a tunic and pants; dressing up too much might make Counselor Aimée think that she was trying too hard to impress her.

Solveig sat down at her desk. "Which Counselor asked to see you?"

"Aimée Lon."

"Never heard of her." Solveig turned to her screen and murmured, "Counselor Aimée Lon, public record, written form." An image of a dark-haired woman appeared, followed by a few lines of Anglaic letters. "No wonder—she just got to the Islands two months ago. Born in Hanoi, grew up there, left the Nomarchy of the New Co-Prosperity Association to attend the University of Amman. She stayed in the New Islamic Nomarchy after graduating from the university five years ago. No bondmate. Was given her Link two years ago."

"She's a Linker?" Mahala asked.

"That's what the record says."

Mahala felt even more apprehensive. There were Linkers among the Counselors, as there were among all the specialists, but Linked Counselors were usually called in only to aid the most seriously disturbed or to advise highly placed people who might require special attention. She had never heard of a Linker advising a first-year student.

"What do you know," Solveig continued. "Linker Aimée has asked for a session with me, too. She wants to see me tomorrow." She turned away from the screen and gazed solemnly at Mahala. "She's not going to ask me to leave school. She can't. I don't know what I would do if she did."

"She won't tell you that. She couldn't—you're one of the best students here. They wouldn't use a Linker just to call students in and then tell them that they've got to leave."

"Maybe they would," Solveig said. "That's one way to convince us that we really aren't worthy of more training, having a Linker deliver that message." She turned back to the screen and bowed her blond head.

*   *   *

Counselor Aimée Lon greeted Mahala with a smile, led her to a cushion, offered her a cup of tea. Her graciousness did not put Mahala at ease.

"I have been assigned to advise you," the woman said in her pleasant voice, still smiling. Mahala forced herself to sip her tea. Counselor Aimée went on to speak of Mahala's record. She was an excellent student; her recent projects in gene splicing and the bioengineering of microbes showed real promise. She kept to herself a bit too much, but that was true of many first-year students from the settlements, who had to keep up with their work while adjusting to a new environment. Now that she was living with another student instead of in the pilots' quarters, Mahala's Counselor fully expected that she would soon become more outgoing and social.

"Is there anything in particular that you want to ask me now?" Aimée said.

"Yes, there is."

"Go on."

The Islanders among the students always said that if one had to meet with a Counselor, it was better to be honest, that Counselors had ways to tell if a person was lying or concealing something important. At the same time, they also claimed that it was unwise to volunteer information. But the question that she wanted to ask was innocuous.

"Isn't it unusual," Mahala said, "to assign a Linker as Counselor to a first-year student? Unless the student's a real problem, anyway."

Aimée said, "It is unusual, and you're certainly not a problem. But I haven't been a Linker for very long. It isn't as though you're getting a Linker with lots of years of experience to advise you."

Mahala nodded, although she felt that the woman had not really answered her question.

"Now I have a question for you," the Counselor continued. "Usually even first-year students have some idea of the specialty they would like to pursue. Your record shows an interest in biology, but you haven't yet specified any particular areas in which you might like to get more training. Have you given this matter any more thought?"

"Yes, I have," Mahala replied, and hesitated. Aimée Lon still wore her warm smile and kindly expression.

Mahala set down her cup and said, "I'm thinking of concentrating on either microbiology or genetics. Right now, I can't decide between them, but either specialty would be useful to the Project."

"That's true," Aimée said, "although we like to think that every person here, and certainly those who are given more schooling, will be of value to the Project in some way. But you're right that we are especially in need of those who are specialists in genetics or microbiology. Given all the ways in which geneticists have improved the physical health of the people here, and the varied microorganisms biologists have developed for seeding Venus's soil and atmosphere, they're likely to remain some of our most important specialists."

"And even without advanced training in those fields," Mahala said, "I could still be useful as a physician or possibly a greenhouse team supervisor."

"Well, of course. But I wonder if having less ambitious goals, or ones more easily achieved, is really the way to do one's best and achieve one's potential."

Mahala's cheeks warmed. She had wanted to impress the Counselor with her practical sense and instead had only made Aimée think that she lacked drive and ambition.

"I would rather be a specialist," she said, "because that's the best chance I'll have to make a discovery, contribute something new to my world. But if that doesn't work out, I can be satisfied doing other work."

That was not exactly a lie, but she knew that she was shading the truth. She would accept whatever work she was eventually directed to do because she would have no real choice, and she would be conscientious about it because she could not imagine being careless. Carelessness and thoughtlessness, as Risa had often told her, were often worse failings and could endanger more people than outright malice. She would do her best at whatever she ended up doing. That did not mean that she would be happy at having to limit her dreams.

It seemed a contradiction, to be part of the great centuries-long effort of terraforming a planet, a Project that had pushed human beings to their limits and beyond, and yet know that she might have to scale back her hopes in order to contribute to that long-term endeavor. She thought of Ragnar, who had deliberately set his own limits on his life so that he could do what he longed to do within those limits. Maybe that gave him more freedom than she would ever have.

"Mahala," Aimée said softly, "I want you to be completely honest about answering my next question, because otherwise I may not be able to advise you properly. What would you choose to do now if you could do as you liked? A general answer will do."

Mahala looked directly into the Counselor's tilted brown eyes. She's good, she thought; she makes me want to tell her everything. She had the feeling that Aimée already suspected what she was holding back.

"I want to travel," she said. "That's a bad way of putting it. I want to explore, see things I haven't seen."

"You might have put in for pilot training, then," Aimée said, "and yet you didn't."

"That isn't what I meant. Pilots move people from one place to another along the same routes. They don't see truly new places, only the same ones again and again. I'm not saying it can't be an interesting life—one of my best friends in Turing is an apprentice pilot. After living in the pilots' quarters here, I know a lot of them don't mind being away from their homes and their families or housemates for a while—it's a change, and most of them appreciate their homes more when they go back. It's probably a good way for the Project to keep some of the more restless people here content, allowing them to become pilots."

"You might say that," Aimée murmured.

"But that's not what I'm talking about. I'd like to see Earth, of course, and Mars if the Habbers would ever allow that, but mostly what I imagine is going to places that are completely unknown to us now."

The Counselor was silent.

"I know it's impossible," Mahala added, "or at least completely unlikely."

"Even so," Aimée said, "it tells me something about you." Mahala had expected to see doubt in the woman's eyes, maybe even concern, but the Counselor was still smiling; she almost looked relieved. "And, as it happens, you may get some of what you want."

Mahala sat up straight.

"You needn't remain here as a student during the next session. The Project Council is going to offer a very few students the opportunity to go to our space station of Anwara. You would continue with your studies there, but with screens and bands and any mentors you find there. Of course, you would still be able to form study groups if you like, and view lectures, and have conferences and discussions with your teachers over the screen."

Mahala did not know what to say.

"Well?" Aimée said, clearly expecting some kind of reaction. "You look stricken, Mahala. Are you pleased or apprehensive?"

Mahala emitted a feeble laugh. "Both. I'd really enjoy seeing Anwara—I've never been there. I could understand being sent there if I wanted to do astrophysics or engineering or life support, but—" Her voice trailed off.

"You don't see why you've been chosen for this program. Let the Project Council worry about that." Aimée folded her arms. "All I'm going to ask is that you keep this to yourself for now, until all of the students being called in have been advised by their Counselors."

She would be able to continue her studies and would not be advised to leave school; Mahala knew that she should be happy about that. But to be sent to Anwara was completely unexpected. She did not know what it meant.

"I am only advising you," Aimée said. "You have to make the choice, Mahala. If you would rather continue your studies here, you may. Such a choice won't be held against you. If your work remains at its present level, you're just about certain to win a position as a specialist in the biological sciences."

That would be the safest course, staying on Island Two. Counselors might be manipulative, but they did not lie; Aimée would not be telling her that her future as a student here was assured unless that was the case. But the Counselor had said nothing about what she might be risking if her course work suffered during her time on Anwara.

Things had to change. The Cytherians of the surface settlements would grow increasingly impatient and more resentful of the fact that some of the Habbers aiding them were much more likely to see a radically transformed Venus than were the settlers. If things got bad enough, Earth might find itself confronted with some extremely unpleasant choices. Demoralized and discouraged settlers could threaten the Project; that had happened before. Earth might have to admit that building surface settlements was premature and possibly a mistake. The Habbers might have to take on a greater role in terraforming her world.

Given all of those possibilities, for her to draw back from an unanticipated course seemed foolish. Had her ancestor Iris Angharads refused the opportunity offered to her, her line might have come to an end on the North American Plains. If Benzi had not fled to the Habitats, about which he had known almost nothing, he would by now be no more than a remembered face on a memorial pillar.

"I'll go to Anwara," Mahala said and knew as soon as she spoke that this was the choice she had to make, whatever it brought her.

During the four days after her session with Aimée Lon, Mahala saw little of her fellow students. Some returned to their quarters after meeting with their Counselors and then disappeared into their rooms, emerging only for meals or short walks around the Island; she could guess that they had been advised to continue their studies and were getting in some extra preparation. Others simply vanished, without saying farewells even to their closest friends, and Mahala assumed that they had been advised to leave school. Sean Sellars-O'Dowd held a party to announce that he was leaving school, inviting anyone among the students who wanted to come, but then Sean had grown up on Island Two; except for having to apprentice himself instead of remaining a student, little would change in his life. The three other Islanders who were dropping out with him did not seem all that disappointed with the advice they had received; it was the students from the surface settlements who abruptly disappeared, as if too embarrassed or ashamed to linger to say farewell to friends.

Solveig said nothing about what Counselor Aimée had told her, but she was clearly content with the Linker's advice. She smiled more easily, slept a bit later instead of pushing herself to wake early in order to seize every available moment for study, and made no move to pack her belongings. Mahala supposed that she should sort through her own things and decide what to give away; there would be a limit on what she could take to Anwara. But there would be time enough for that later, and she did not own that much anyway.

Five days after Mahala's meeting with her Counselor, the names of the ten students who would be going to Anwara were made public. Mahala scrolled them up on her screen while Solveig was still sleeping and saw that Solveig's name was on the list; so was Chike Enu-Barnes's. She studied the other names, trying to discern some sort of pattern. All of the students chosen to go to the satellite had different interests; two, including Chike, had grown up on the Islands, while the others had come from the settlements.

Mahala heard Solveig yawn behind her. She turned to see her

friend sit up in her bed. "I just found out," Mahala said, "that you're going to Anwara."

Solveig grinned. "I've been wanting to tell you, but I couldn't. I will miss you, but—"

"You won't miss me. I was advised to go to Anwara, too. Naturally, I said I would."

Solveig's smile broadened. "But that's wonderful."

"I am happy about that," Mahala said. "I'll see a different place. I just wish I knew what it meant."

Her screen chimed at her. She turned back to it to see the face of Jamilah al-Hussaini. The Administrator and Liaison to the Project Council wore a white scarf over her dark hair and had a grim look on her face.

"In the name of God," Jamilah began, "the Compassionate and Merciful, Whose hand guides us all."

Solveig got up, came to Mahala's side, and sat down next to her. "It doesn't sound as though she has good news," the blond girl whispered.

"I wish to announce," Jamilah continued, "that I am resigning my position as Liaison to the Project Council, effective immediately. I am giving up my post solely of my own volition and willingly, so that I may devote my time to my specialty of geology and to my family on Earth."

Her family on Earth? Mahala shook her head. Any family Jamilah had on Earth would most likely be strangers to her. The Linker had been born here; she had been to Earth only during her years of study at the Cytherian Institute.

"Much as I will miss my Island home," the Administrator said, "I am looking forward to what lies ahead. I am also pleased to tell you that Masud al-Tikriti has been appointed as Liaison in my place. Since he is already on his way to Anwara, he should, God willing, be here and ready to assume his new position within the month. I trust that he will be treated with the courtesy and kindness all Cytherians have shown to me. My thoughts and prayers will be with you always."

The image of Jamilah vanished, to be replaced by the image of another Administrator, a brown-bearded man who was one of Jamilah's aides. "That concludes the official statement of our departing Administrator and Liaison, Jamilah al-Hussaini," the man said. "We wish her well as she prepares to journey to Earth to become a member of the geology department at the University of Tashkent. The Administrator's statement will be repeated at one-hour intervals for the next eight hours."

The screen went blank. Jamilah had been the most powerful Linker and Administrator here ever since Mahala's childhood, the Administrator who dealt with the members of the Project Council on Anwara and with the Council of Mukhtars on Earth.

"The University of Tashkent," Solveig said. "If they're sending her there, she can't be in disgrace." The university was one of the most selective schools on Earth.

"It doesn't make sense," Mahala said. "She's kept everything going, new settlements are being built on schedule, and there haven't been any real disputes between the settlement Councilors and the Island Administrators. Why wouldn't they keep her here?"

"Obviously because they want her on Earth," Solveig said, "and since she's being given a position at such a prestigious university, they must want her there so that they can consult with her. It must mean they're planning for changes involving the Project."

"Administrator Masud al-Tikriti, public record, written form, in Anglaic," Mahala said. Rows of Anglaic letters appeared on the screen; Solveig moved closer to read the record. Masud al-Tikriti had been born in the New Islamic Nomarchy, in a town not far from Baghdad, had been educated at the University of Damascus, and had been a professor of physics at the Cytherian Institute before being promoted to an administrative post in his native Nomarchy. He came from a family of Linkers and numbered a few Mukhtars among his ancestors. He had been given his own Link while in his early twenties and was considered brilliant and accomplished. There appeared to be no black marks on his record. He and his bondmate, Aisha Alzubra, had one child, a son who was now a student at the University of Amman.

"Quite a record," Solveig said. "Looks as though the Mukhtars have decided that we deserve one of their best."

Mahala called up an image of the man. Masud al-Tikriti was a lean-faced man with black hair and dark penetrating eyes. "I don't know," Mahala murmured. "It could mean that the Council of Mukhtars wants tighter control over everything here." She stood up, forcing herself to ignore her apprehensions. "We'd better start thinking about what we're going to take with us to Anwara and what we're going to give away."

✻   ✻   ✻

Mahala had meant to visit Malik after sorting through her belongings and attending a party several students had hastily organized for those who would be leaving for Anwara. She left the student quarters with Solveig at last light only to find her grandfather waiting outside for her.

Solveig greeted Malik while Mahala hung back, resenting him just a little for showing up now. "We've both been chosen to go to Anwara," Solveig said.

"You look most pleased about that," Malik said.

"Of course we are," Solveig replied. "I was there before and always hoped I could go back."

"We were just on our way to a party," Mahala said pointedly.

"I will not take up much of your time, Mahala," her grandfather said, "but I must speak to you."

"Go on," Mahala murmured to Solveig. "Tell the others I'll be there soon." The other girl nodded her head in Malik's direction, then walked away. "What is it, Malik?"

"Not here," he said. "Please come with me."

She followed him, keeping at his side. "That party is being given for us," she said. "I should at least be polite enough to be there when it starts."

"This is something you should know."

He stopped abruptly, looked around, then led her toward a small grove of trees. "I'll tell you here, Mahala," he continued. There was no one near them; she could barely see his face in the shadows under the trees. "This new Liaison, this Masud al-Tikriti—he is a kinsman of mine and of yours. One of my uncles lived in the town of Tikrit. His son attached the name of the town to his own. Masud is the grandson of my uncle."

She took a breath. "Are you certain?"

"Yes. It was easy enough to find out. Had you sorted through the records, you could have discovered it for yourself, but there was no need for you to think you had any connection to him. I was curious because I knew that I once had an uncle in Tikrit, and I thought Masud might be related to people he knew."

"The Council of Mukhtars would have to know he's a relative of yours," Mahala said.

"Of course. Perhaps we should simply assume that enough time has gone by that members of my family are no longer disgraced by their connection to me, a man who left Venus for the Habitats, and that they are now free to rise again to positions of some influence. Perhaps we should not be too quick to suspect that this might mark a change in how the Project is to be conducted."

She was already wondering if this new Liaison had anything to do with sending her to Anwara. That could not be; other students would be going with her. She was too insignificant for anyone close to the Mukhtars, even a kinsman, to take an interest in her. But Earth's rulers had the power, and maybe the inclination, to manipulate people as if they were pieces in a larger game, to move them around simply to see what might come of that. Her great-grandmother was the martyred Iris Angharads, her grandmother was the respected Risa Liangharads, and her mother, Chimene Liang-Haddad, had threatened the survival of her world before acting finally to save it.

And, she thought, there was Malik. Maybe the Mukhtars did not think of her as unimportant.

"This may mean little," Malik continued, "but now I wonder if this means I should leave the Islands. The Administrators might have canceled my lectures so as not to risk offending my relative when he arrives."

"I'd miss you," she said, almost as an automatic courtesy, then realized that she meant it. Knowing that Malik was here, that he had come back at least in part to see what had become of his grandchild, had been a kind of comfort.

He smiled. "You would miss me anyway," he said, "since you'll be going to Anwara."

"But if I knew you were still nearby, I wouldn't miss you as much."

"We'll see." He rested his back against a tree. "I'll ask if there's a place for me on the Habber ship orbiting Venus. I wouldn't be so far away then."

Yes, you would be, she thought. The only time her people had any contact with those aboard that vessel was during the rare times the ship docked at Anwara. Malik would be almost as distant from her as he would be if he returned to one of the Habs.

"I should have spent more time with you when I had the chance," Mahala said.

"I understand, child. You needn't sound so apologetic. I came into your life abruptly—I am not surprised that you needed time to get used to that." He rested a hand on her shoulder. "Go to your party and look forward to your time on Anwara, and I will wait to see what the future may hold for us."

High Orbit

15

To travel to Anwara, the large space station orbiting Venus, required going to the port of the Island Platform by airship and then taking a shuttle from the Platform to the satellite. Mahala and Solveig were traveling with Chike Enu-Barnes and Stephan AnnasLeonards; the six students from the other Islands would be going to Anwara on later shuttle flights.

She and Solveig boarded their airship, stored their duffels under their seats, and were about to strap themselves in when she heard a few passengers behind her whispering to one another. "Salaam, Linker Jamilah," a man said. Mahala peered around the back of her seat and saw Jamilah al-Hussaini making her way down the aisle.

Other passengers greeted the Administrator—the former Administrator and past Liaison to the Council, Mahala reminded herself—touching their foreheads with their fingers as she passed them. Jamilah wore a plain brown tunic and pants instead of her usual formal white robe and had covered her hair with a plain white scarf; she nodded at each passenger in turn as she walked by.

"I didn't know she was leaving this soon," Solveig whispered, then touched her forehead as Jamilah came to the front of the airship. Mahala did the same, wondering if she should also get to her feet. Jamilah nodded absently at both of them.

The two pilots were already standing in the open entrance to their control cabin. "Please do go back to your stations," Jamilah murmured to the pilots, "and continue to run your checks." She turned to face the other passengers. "I should tell you now that it is my privilege, and also my great pleasure, to be among those who will welcome Masud al-Tikriti when he arrives on Anwara in a few days. I will greatly miss the friends I've made among those I have served here, but please be reassured that all Cytherians will be in Linker Masud's most capable hands and that he is most sympathetic to our interests. And perhaps, God willing, I will not be separated from you for so very long, much as I am looking forward to my new position on Earth."

Mahala studied Jamilah's face, but could read nothing in the Linker's impassive expression. However sudden her resignation had seemed, it was now obvious that her departure had been planned for some time; otherwise, her replacement would not already be on his way here from Earth.

Jamilah sat down in one of the seats in the front row. Mahala finished securing her safety harness, then leaned back. There was no point in worrying over what was going on among the Administrators and the Project Council; there would be enough to occupy her once she got to Anwara.

On the Platform, standing at the bottom of the enclosed cylinder of their dock and waiting to board the shuttlecraft with Solveig, Chike, and Stephan, Mahala discreetly studied the other passengers gathered at the base of the ship. Most of the people aboard the airship had been mechanics coming here to work on repairs and maintenance, while others had come to the port to connect with shuttles that would take them to the Bats. Except for Jamilah and the three students with Mahala, the people who were to board this shuttle had arrived at the Platform from the other Islands, and several of them wore the pins of specialists on their collars—silvery clouds for climatologists, tiny hammers for metallurgical engineers, a green leaf for a botanist, a small disk with an equation for a physicist. Two were marked as Linkers by the diamondlike gems on their foreheads.

As she had done aboard the airship, Jamilah was soon greeting her fellow shuttle passengers as though she were still Liaison to the Project Council, touching her hand to the diamond on her brow as they nodded back. The Linker stopped to gaze at Mahala and her three companions for a few moments in silence. Mahala lowered her eyes, feeling distinctly uneasy, thinking of how easily Jamilah could call up any information she wanted through her Link. The cyberminds could provide her with the public record of anyone aboard this shuttle, and perhaps some private records as well.

"These four young people with us," Jamilah continued, "are students at Island Two's secondary school. They have been chosen to go to Anwara to study."

"I heard about that," one man said. "Isn't that out of the ordinary, sending young students at that level to Anwara?"

"Students have gone there before," Jamilah replied, "but it's true that they haven't remained on Anwara for more than very short periods of time." She gestured at Solveig. "This young woman here, Solveig Einarsdottir, has traveled to Anwara before, but only for a week." Solveig's eyes widened, even though the blond girl had to know that Jamilah's Link had provided her with that small detail. "Some of us felt that it was time we exposed more of our young people to life on Anwara, where Cytherians, Earthfolk, and Habbers regularly meet to discuss the Project's needs. I myself made that recommendation to the Council, and Masud al-Tikriti apparently concurs."

First her comments aboard the airship, Mahala thought, and now this. She did not think that Jamilah was simply making idle chatter. The Linker had to know that most Cytherians were quick to pass along anything they heard from an Administrator, however innocuous. Jamilah wanted them to know that she had been consulted on whatever changes might be coming to the Project and that she still had something to say about its fate.

August 649
From: Mahala Liangharad, Anwara, Center Ring,
Room 432
To: Risa Liangharad and Sef Talis, Oberg

I've been on Anwara—inside Anwara—for three days now, and according to what others here have told me, I made the adjustment fairly well. Stephan AnnasLeonards, one of the students who traveled here with me, told me just today that he still feels slightly disoriented and dizzy. We were at zero-g at Anwara's hub, where our shuttle docked—luckily, none of us found weightlessness hard to take there or during the flight—but in the rings, we're at one-g, just a little more than the gravity on Venus or the Islands.

So theoretically we should all adjust fairly quickly, except that some people have more difficulty than others in adjusting to the spin of an orbiting space station. I can't really sense any difference. I looked up the statistics, and about half of the people who come here have minor problems like Stephan's for up to a month. A few, about ten percent, need small implants in their inner ears to compensate for their loss of balance, but the physicians won't bother with that unless you're really important and are needed here. A very few people, about two percent, end up leaving after a couple of months because they can't adjust at all, and almost all of them are people who came here directly from Earth rather than from Venus, and whether or not that means anything, I don't know. Seems peculiar; given that Venus's gravity is about eighty-five percent of Earth's, you'd think more Cytherians would have that particular problem. Maybe settlers, and the descendants of settlers, are just more adaptable to begin with. I'm curious, so I'm going to look up some research on the subject.

I should start at the beginning. I don't know how much you saw, Sef, when you first came here from Earth on your way to Venus, but Anwara looked to me like three large circular tubes turning slowly around a hub when I saw it on the screen. They keep adding new modules to the rim, and from space the modules almost look like jewels. At the hub, there are docks for shuttles, for the torchships arriving from Earth, and for Habber vessels, and one of the first things we were told is that the docks where Habber ships are berthed are off-limits and can't be entered. Earth's Mukhtars and the Project Council here supposedly insisted on those restrictions, but presumably the Habbers have their own reasons for wanting to keep us away from their ships.

At the Platform, before the shuttle took off, the pilots issued us all adhesive strips for our shoes, but they warned us to be careful moving around in weightlessness. Except for using the lavatory — and I won't even get into that — most of us stayed in our seats during the flight, floating up against our harnesses. We were in zero-g at the hub, after our ship docked, but we weren't there that long before a woman came to show us to our quarters. Her name is Orenda Tineka, and even though she trained in environmental systems, she seems more like a psychologist or a Counselor. Apparently her job is to advise the students, answer our questions, and help us get used to Anwara.

Solveig and I were assigned to the same room, number 432 in the center ring. I haven't seen much of the other two rings yet, but they look about the same as this one. The passageways are always lighted, and I'm getting used to that, but Chike Enu-Barnes says it starts to bother him if he has to be in the corridors for more than half an hour. I know what he means. I had a long walk back from Orenda's room to mine last night — yesterday — and it seemed endless, just walking through this gently curving corridor past door after door, peering at the numbers or images on the doors, hearing people's voices and then seeing tiny figures emerge in the distance from around the curve — well, it isn't anything like Oberg or the Islands.

As for my quarters, this room is about half the size of the room I used to have in your house, and I've got to share it with Solveig. It isn't so bad when our beds are in the walls, but when we open them up, there isn't room to do anything except lie down and study with a pocket screen or sleep. Maybe that won't matter all that much, since it looks as though we'll have a more rigid schedule here than we did on Island Two. The students go to meals together, take our exercise and recreation together, and attend discussion groups together. So far, Orenda is the only person who has led us in discussions, but it looks as though we'll be meeting in one group with most of our teachers, too. It's almost as if one of the things they want us to learn here is how to get along with everyone in the group. That's probably necessary here. In Turing, I could wander in the woods, and even on Island Two, there are the gardens. Being alone on Anwara, unless you're in your room by yourself, is almost impossible.

Mahala paused in her recitation and leaned back from the screen. She was alone now; Solveig was in the outer ring, visiting with the astronomers and studying images picked up by Anwara's telescope. According to her, the astronomers and astrophysicists on Anwara felt much neglected by the Project, even though they had a little more support than their few counterparts on the Islands did. There were only four of them, because their discipline was not considered all that essential. Their equipment was little better than that of astronomers centuries ago, and their knowledge of stellar evolution had not advanced much past what those early colleagues had discovered. The engineers who had always controlled the Project did not see, or else refused to see, that astrophysics was of any practical use to them.

The Habbers would not have taken such a view. Mahala had overheard enough of Balin's conversations with Dyami to know that Habbers encouraged people to master whatever intellectual disciplines appealed to them. They had telescopes that had yielded data about Alpha Centauri, Tau Ceti, and other star systems, where it had long been known that there were planets. They probably knew much more about the universe beyond the solar system than the meagerly supported astronomical team of Anwara did.

Why had the Habbers never sent out an expedition to explore space beyond this system? But perhaps they already had. They might have sent out crews of people aboard exploratory vessels without anyone on Earth knowing about it or being able to stop them; the Mukhtars would have little interest in making such expeditions public knowledge. But the Habbers would not have had to go on such voyages themselves, and she knew from Benzi that the Habbers had sent out probes. Some of those probes had been what he called "listeners," sent out to scan the heavens for anomalous phenomena that might be signals from an alien civilization.

There had not yet been any communications from their probes, as far as she knew, but Habbers might be content to wait for decades or even centuries for them to transmit any data. Their long lives would also be an advantage in interstellar exploration, where the duration of even a round-trip to a near star might take decades. She thought of what Balin had said to Solveig once, when she had given up trying to worm information from him about what the interstellar probes might have discovered and had then asked him why the Habbers had never, even under extreme provocation, severed all their ties with Earth and the Venus Project.

"We are trying to hold on to our humanity," Balin had replied. "We fear diverging too greatly from the rest of our kind, and yet I wonder if some Habbers haven't done so already." This might also have held them back from traveling outside this system.

Mahala pushed those thoughts aside, then realized for the first time how automatically she had done so, how instinctively she allowed herself to get to a certain point and no further. It was almost as though she had been trained not to speculate on what the Habbers might be doing that might be unknown even in the highest circles of the Council of Mukhtars. To dwell on the Habbers and their possible accomplishments was to risk viewing both Earth and Venus as backward places, growing ever more dependent on the Habbers while refusing to admit it, clinging to the Project as a demonstration of their technical prowess while never acknowledging that even there, the aid of the Habbers had been necessary. To think too much about the Habbers and their ways could even bring one to doubt the purpose of the Project.

She forced herself to concentrate on the message to her grandparents:

Whatever problems we have in getting used to life here, Orenda tells me that adjusting psychologically should be easier for us than for people who come here directly from Earth. Since we all grew up in domed settlements or on the Islands, we're used to a more enclosed environment. Earthfolk can find a place like Anwara claustrophobic.

Mahala fell silent again. She had been about to say that one aspect of life on Anwara did disturb her, but she had not yet mentioned it to anyone else, not even Solveig. She suspected that others shared her apprehension, but maybe it was better for her to ignore her fear instead of allowing it to blossom into a phobia. Speaking of one's fears, as Risa had often told her, could sometimes dispel them, but could also feed those fears and make them grow larger and more real. That was probably especially true on Anwara, where phobias and unspoken fears could so easily spread among people thrown so close together.

Her unvoiced fear was that Anwara was too vulnerable and unprotected in its high orbit, its walls too readily able to be breached by tiny meteorites and other debris. Because of Anwara's orbital path, Venus and its Parasol were always between the space station and the sun, so Anwara's inhabitants did not have to fear the effects of solar radiation, and the rings were heavily shielded in any case. During the few times micrometeorites had threatened the satellite in the past, the alarms had sounded in time for people to evacuate the endangered areas and seek safety; there had been breaches in the outer walls only three times, and those small openings had been quickly repaired. She knew this, and yet felt far more vulnerable here than behind the transparent dome of a settlement or an Island afloat in Venus's atmosphere.

Perhaps that was only because, unless Mahala was standing in a place where she could see through a dome, she could forget that the dome was there to shield her from the dangers outside. Maybe she was simply more used to domed Islands and settlements. Maybe she had more faith in the Habber technology that had created the ceramic-metallic alloy of the dome material than she did in the engineers from Earth who had designed and built Anwara.

That was also not a thought to dwell on for long.

She continued:

You might be interested to know that Jamilah al-Hussaini traveled with us on the airship to the Platform and on the shuttle to Anwara. She's still here, staying with members of the Project Council in their quarters, waiting to meet Masud al-Tikriti when he arrives. She spoke to all of us on the airship and sounded as though she has a lot of respect for the new Administrator.

And that, Mahala thought, was probably all she should say on an open channel about Jamilah and Masud.

She concluded:

Please give my regards to everyone in the household—I don't mind if you show them this message. I would tell you when I might be visiting, except that we haven't been told anything about when we might get some time off, and right now it's too soon to ask.

October 649
From: Mahala Liangharad, Anwara, Center Ring, Room 432
To: Frania Astarte Milus, Turing

I owe you an apology, Frani. I should have sent you a message a long time ago. You didn't say how much longer you would be at Dyami's house, but if you've left already, I hope you pick this up soon so you don't think I'm ignoring you.

You didn't say anything about why you and Ragnar decided to wait a little while longer before making your pledge. Is it because you might be spending more time on the Islands for your training? Not that I mean to pry—you don't have to answer that.

As for how I'm doing here, I've been working with the physicians and learning about what therapeutic implants are useful in treating people who have problems adjusting to Anwara. That may sound like the kind of work a paramedic in training might be doing, but it's been giving me some ideas about—well, maybe I'll go into that another time.

If you're still at Dyami's, show him and Amina this message and tell them that I'll be sure to send them one in the next day or so. I am getting behind in all of my messages.

October 649
From: Mahala Liangharad, Anwara
To: Dyami Liang-Talis, Turing

I've been here for over two months now, and I'm still not sure why I'm here. Neither are any of the other students. I'm doing some of the work of a paramedic and Chike Enu-Barnes spends some of his time learning about the life-support systems here and the rest of his time in the chemistry labs. It's pretty much like that with all of us. Solveig's spending a lot of her time with the astronomers and astrophysicists, which is what she wants, but even she admits that she would probably be making more progress with her studies—with physics, which is still allegedly her specialization—if she were back on Island Two.

It's not that we mind the work. Given what has to be done simply to maintain life support here, we've all ended up appreciating the Islands and the settlements more than we did; Anwara is potentially more unstable as an environment and more dependent—almost completely dependent—on the outside. Our main problem as students is that we're keeping up with our studies mostly through readings and with our bands and screens. We hear lectures, but there isn't much discussion with the specialists here. About the only person who spends much time discussing our studies with us is Orenda, our adviser, and she isn't equipped to go that deeply into most of our courses.

I could ask her what the purpose was in bringing us here, but since we haven't been here for very long, she might think I'm being impatient. Or maybe we're supposed to have figured it out by now.

Solveig led Mahala and Chike past the entrance to the observatory and into a small meeting room. Except for a low table with screens and a few cushions, the room was empty.

"We can talk here," Solveig said. "The astronomers come in here for meetings, and they basically hinted to me that they scan the place periodically for any listening devices the Project Council might have planted."

The blond girl sat down on a cushion. Mahala and Chike seated themselves across from her. "You're sounding awfully conspiratorial," Mahala said.

"This is important, but it isn't exactly a secret," Solveig said. "At least it won't be. You know where the Habitats have been for some years now."

"Of course we do," Chike muttered. One followed Earth's orbit, but kept on the other side of the sun; Mahala had always assumed that this was the Habitat in which Malik and Benzi lived when they were not on Venus and that it was also the home of the other Habbers who were staying among the Cytherians, since it was closer to Venus than any of the other Habs. Two Habs were inside the Martian satellites Phobos and Deimos, three were in high orbits around Mars, five were in the asteroid belt, and three had begun to move toward Jupiter two decades ago and were following the gas giant's orbit around the sun at a distance.

Solveig took a breath. "Two of the nearer Habitats orbiting Mars have left orbit," Solveig said, "and they're following a path that will take them closer to Earth. My astronomer friends here made the observations and confirmed them."

"Does the Project Council know?" Mahala asked.

"Of course they do," Solveig replied. "They have to know. You don't think anyone's going to keep that a secret, do you? They couldn't hide it anyway—I'm sure Earth's orbiting observatories and Lunar telescopes have made the same observations. They'll have to say something publicly about this soon."

"What can it mean?" Mahala said.

Chike glanced at her. "Seems to me that it can mean only one of two things. Maybe the Mukhtars and the Habbers have come to some sort of agreement allowing the Habbers to move into this part of our system for whatever reason—more aid for Earth, more assistance for the Project. Or else the Habbers are simply doing this on their own to see how Earth will react."

"Why would they want to provoke Earth?" Mahala asked. "There's no point."

"Don't assume you'd know what they'd do," Chike said, "just because you've got a couple of kinsmen with them." Mahala grimaced, but he had said the words gently, clearly not meaning to offend her.

"I still don't think they'd be doing that unless they were sure the Mukhtars had no objection," Mahala said.

Chike shook his head in disagreement. "Maybe the Habbers want to see what the Guardian forces will do."

Solveig had a strange smile on her face as she turned toward Chike. "The Habbers don't have to test the Guardians," she murmured. "They don't have to worry about the Guardians at all, because the Habbers are probably the only reason the Nomarchies still exist, that any of us are alive, that millions and maybe even billions didn't die on Earth long ago."

"What do you mean?" Chike asked.

"If you knew more astronomy and astrophysics, you'd see," Solveig replied, "and you should be able to figure it out even with what you do know. Think of all those asteroids that have been mined and brought in closer to Earth. They aren't there just because Earth needs the resources or because the Habbers like throwing Earth a few small gifts once in a while. I've looked at the records the astronomers here can call up. One of the first asteroids the Habbers sent toward Earth was previously on a course that would have resulted in a direct strike on the home world. It seems that the Habbers altered its course so that it ended up in orbit instead, harmless and ready to be mined, which means that the Habbers are responsible for the fact that Earth isn't a dead planet by now."

"That can't be true," Mahala said. "One of the responsibilities of the Guardians is to deflect any objects that might threaten Earth."

"And have you ever heard of them doing that? Think, Mahala—the closer any such object is to Earth, the more power it would take to deflect it from its course. The Guardians might have the capacity to do it, but it would be costly, and as it is, they've never had to perform such a mission, because the Habbers can probably do it for them much sooner and with much less energy."

Chike leaned forward. "How could anybody keep something like that a secret all this time?"

"It wouldn't be that hard," Solveig said. "How many people on

Earth get to learn much of anything at all? Even on Venus, advanced schooling and university training is parceled out. Given how few among us have any training in even basic astronomy and astrophysics, there are probably specialists and even Linkers who would have a hard time finding out anything about past movements of asteroids and other bodies, and others wouldn't be interested enough to bother doing a search for it."

Chike scowled. "And you've found out something that many Linkers don't know. That's hard to swallow, Solveig."

"I didn't figure it out. The astronomers here did, and I'm sure others have to know. Every astronomer and astrophysicist certainly knows, and probably a good many other specialists. But it's not something to talk about carelessly with just anybody, or to publish a study about, unless you really want trouble."

Solveig could be wrong, Mahala thought; her mentors could be making guesses with insufficient evidence. If there was any truth in what her friend had said, the Linkers would have set up blocks long ago that would keep anyone from gathering any confirming data on such a sensitive subject.

Chike's dark eyes darted from Mahala to Solveig. She could read his expressions more easily since they had come to Anwara. She saw him struggling with himself, almost believing Solveig and yet trying to remain skeptical.

"I'm thinking," Chike said, "of one of your grandfather's lectures." He was gazing steadily at Mahala now.

"I didn't know that you were that interested in history," she said.

"There's no point in being overly interested in history," he said, "if you're a Cytherian. After all, it's not that useful a subject for those who are creating a new world free of the past." He paused. "In one of his lectures, Malik mentioned the Resource Wars briefly and said that the first one came at a time when most people on Earth had access to a flood of information. He hinted that this might have been a factor contributing to the crisis. We think that those wars were fought mostly over control of fossil fuels or scarce arable land and other natural resources, but Malik hinted that having larger and larger numbers of people able to collect data on all sorts of subjects might have been one cause of the conflict."

"I don't see why," Solveig murmured.

"Just because people could investigate all kinds of things," Chike said, "doesn't mean they knew how to assess what they found out or how reliable their information was. A lot of them, maybe even most of them, probably didn't know how to figure out what was the truth and what might have been mistaken conclusions—or even something meant to be deliberately misleading. Think of how much time we've already spent in school learning how to think about things and how to reason about them. Think of how Linkers have to be trained so that they can call up exactly what they need to know without being flooded with too many irrelevant facts. Too much information with no way of sorting it can be almost as bad as none at all."

"Are you saying that people might have drawn the wrong conclusions from all the information they had?" Mahala asked. "And that helped to bring the Resource Wars about?"

Chike nodded. "That's exactly what I'm saying. And the survivors realized afterward that information was another resource they would have to control unless they wanted to risk an even more destructive conflict. Control of information is what gives the Mukhtars their power."

Solveig frowned and said nothing. Mahala found herself recalling a brief conversation that she had overheard between Dyami and Balin. She had been in the kitchen, helping Frania clean up after supper, and had wandered into the common room to see if there were any dishes left on the table.

"Do your people expect gratitude?" Dyami had asked Balin. "Is that what it's about?"

"No," the Habber had replied. "Gratitude? Some appreciation for our good deeds? We certainly never expected gratitude—only hurt pride and resentment."

"Which is exactly what you got," Dyami murmured in the same slightly mocking tone.

"And maybe we'll finally realize that resentment and rancor is all we'll ever have for whatever aid we manage to give, and—"

"Mahala," Dyami said when he had spotted her in the doorway. Balin had glanced at her and then fallen silent.

What had Balin been about to say? That the Habbers might tire of the present situation and demand some recompense from Earth? But what could Earth possibly offer them? The Habbers had a superior technology, greatly extended lives, the demeanor of people who were largely satisfied, content, and untroubled by many of the more disagreeable human emotions. Perhaps now they finally wanted to be entirely free of Earth and its needs.

She thought then of what Benzi had told her, that Habbers were contemplating leaving this system altogether. There was nothing to stop them from doing so, nothing except whatever sentimental feelings they might have for their ancestral world or emotional ties they might have to individual Cytherians. Perhaps they had lost any fear they might have of diverging from the rest of humankind. She could not guess at most of the consequences of such an exodus, except for one: Earth would surely tighten its grip on Venus, since there would be nothing to prevent that.

She considered Balin. He loved Dyami; she was certain of that, despite his decision to leave Turing. Benzi could not be completely indifferent to the fate of the Cytherians. Malik would not have come back to the Islands if he cared nothing for the people he had left behind.

But other Habbers might not be like any of those people. Many, perhaps most, might feel that events on Earth and Venus had nothing to do with them and that the future of those worlds was no longer their concern. Would they leave? Were they preparing to tell Earth that they might leave? Such a threat might get them concessions of some sort, but what could Earth grant them?

"You two are being unusually quiet," Chike said at last.

"No wonder the Mukhtars have to keep such tight control of information," Mahala said. "If most of Earth even suspected that only the Habbers stood between them and total disaster, they might begin to wonder why they needed to be governed by Mukhtars and Linkers at all."

"It isn't just Earthfolk who would feel that way, either," Solveig said. "What about our world? We need the Habbers as much as Earth does—maybe more, when you consider how much more difficult the Project would be and how much longer it would have taken even to get to where we are without the technology the Habbers offered. What happened during the Revolt would be nothing compared to what might happen if the Habbers abandoned us."

Chike rested his back against the wall. "Linker Jamilah was here for almost a month, going to private meetings with the Project Council before she left for Earth. Now Masud al-Tikriti is meeting with Habbers a lot more often than any of his predecessors did."

Mahala tensed in surprise. "What are you talking about? How would you know, anyway?"

Chike averted his eyes for a moment, then focused on her again. "I thought maybe you already knew that."

"I didn't."

"My brother Kesse told me." Chike rested his hands on his knees. "Oh, he didn't tell me outright, but I know what he's saying in his messages even when he doesn't come right out with it. Administrator Masud has been meeting with your kinsman Benzi, as a matter of fact. He sees him at least twice a week."

Chike's brother, Mahala recalled, was an organic chemist who was also an aide to one of the Administrators; he would be in a position to know who went to meet with Masud. She suddenly resented that she had not known any of this, had not even suspected, that Benzi had never sent her a message even hinting at his meetings with Masud.

Benzi might, of course, simply be trying to protect his Cytherian relatives, especially if the meetings concerned sensitive matters. He might be thinking that there was no reason for Mahala to know that Masud al-Tikriti was conferring with him, that she would only worry or grow too curious about matters that did not concern her.

"We shouldn't even be talking about any of this," she said in a whisper.

"I told you," Solveig said. "Nobody's going to hear anything we say in this room."

"That isn't what I meant." Mahala kept her eyes on her friend. "I meant that there's nothing any of us can do about it."

"Everything's changing," Chike said. "I can feel it. Something's going on, and sooner or later—" His voice had risen a little; he cleared his throat, then stood up. "We'd better get to supper now before the others start wondering where we are."

Orenda Tineka had left a message requesting that all of the students from the Islands come to one of the meeting rooms immediately after breakfast. That was unusual, Mahala thought as she left the narrow lavatory cubicle she and Solveig shared with four other students. Normally the hour after their first meal was set aside for study, to be followed by an hour of discusssion or a lecture, and the students had been told that a member of the Project Council would be speaking to them about future refinements on Anwara and asking them for their predictions of future problems.

Now that exercise in troubleshooting had apparently been canceled. Mahala pulled a shirt on over her head, then put on a pair of drawstring pants. Solveig sat on a cushion, already clothed in a loose blue coverall, her head bent over her pocket screen.

"I wonder what's going on," Mahala said.

Solveig looked up. "I couldn't begin to guess." She got to her feet; Mahala followed her out of the room and down the bright corridor. She had grown used to the light, to the occasional unsteadiness the spin of Anwara induced in her, an unsteadiness that quickly passed. Only a few hours ago, just before falling asleep, she had realized that she was looking forward to her remaining time on Anwara. She had decided not to think about her secretive talk with Solveig and Chike only two days before. They had all, she concluded, probably drawn the wrong conclusions from their easily roused suspicions.

Now, as she followed Solveig into the small meeting room where Orenda was waiting for them, she suddenly had the feeling that Chike's instincts were sound and that she had been trying too hard to ignore her own misgivings.

She and her roommate were the last to arrive. Mahala made her way among the eight seated students and sat down on a cushion near the back, next to Chike. His mouth curved in a half-smile, as if he were about to say: I was right. Solveig sat down in front of them. Mahala waited for Orenda to sit down and say whatever it was she had to tell them, but the tall slender woman was still standing and staring down at the floor.

"I have some news for all of you," Orenda said, "and I hope that you will regard it as welcome news." She smiled in the mechanical way that Administrators often did before making public announcements. "It's been decided that you are all to go back to your Island schools. You will continue with your studies there, and given that you haven't been here that long, and that all of you are fine students, it shouldn't take much time to catch up with whatever work you might have missed."

"This is kind of sudden," Wendine Hu said in her gentle voice. "We were expecting to be here for at least one term, possibly longer."

"Yes, I know," Orenda replied, still wearing her impersonal smile.

"So is this going to count against us?" Stephan AnnasLeonards asked, his narrow face looking even more solemn than usual.

"Of course not. I wish to emphasize that. The decision to send you back to the Islands has nothing to do with the quality of your work. All of the personnel who have spoken to you, worked with you, and been mentors to you have commended your intelligence and your character. This isn't a black mark on your records. On the contrary, we hope that you've gained something from your time here and—"

"Will we be allowed to return later on?" Solveig asked.

Mahala stared at the blond braids that hung down Solveig's back, surprised that her friend had interrupted Orenda. The older woman folded her arms and frowned, but did not reply.

"Will we be able to come back," Solveig continued, "or is this it for us?"

Orenda's mouth twitched. "I can hardly answer that now, Solveig. Maybe you'll be assigned here later, maybe you won't. Maybe more students will be coming here another time. All I can tell you is that, at the moment, the Project Council has decided that you should return to the Islands."

Solveig said, "Does this have anything to do with the fact that two Habs are now on a course that will bring them close to Earth if they continue on their current trajectory?"

Mahala held her breath. The other young people in the room were all looking at Solveig now. Orenda's smile had disappeared completely.

"Well?" Solveig said. "I think it's a reasonable question."

Orenda can't deny it, Mahala thought. It came to her then that Solveig would be losing more than any of the rest of them when she went back to Island Two. She would lose her sessions with the astronomers here; she would be losing the stars.

"I'm wondering the same thing," Mahala said. Chike poked her in the side; she ignored him. She was not about to let Solveig be the only one pressing Orenda for an answer.

Orenda was silent for a while, as if trying to decide what to tell them. Then she said, "The fact that two Habitats have departed from their usual orbital paths would have become known within a few days." The woman showed her teeth. "And we have no reason to assume that their movements are of any concern to us."

Their adviser, Mahala thought, had waited too long before giving that response. That she had known about the two Habs was no surprise; the astronomers would not have kept that information to themselves for long. All of the Linkers and most of the specialists on Anwara had probably already been informed. If there was no reason to worry about the two Habs, Orenda would have admitted that right away. Either she was completely ignorant of what the Habitats' altered paths might mean or she was worrying about it herself.

"And none of that," Orenda continued, "has anything to do with your having to return to the Islands."

"Then it certainly is a striking coincidence," Mahala said.

"It's nothing of the sort." Orenda folded her arms. "You place a very high value on your importance, thinking that such things have anything to do with you."

Mahala put up a hand, then gave Orenda what she hoped was a sheepish enough look. "Sorry, Orenda. I didn't mean it that way."

She had pushed this far enough, but suspected that the movements of the two Habs had everything to do with the departure of the students from Anwara. If the Project Council and Earth were worrying about Habber intentions, they would soon be asking to meet with them, and Anwara was the place where any such meetings were likely to be held. The last people the Project Council would need here were a group of inquisitive students.

October 649
From: Mahala Liangharad, Anwara
To: Dyami Liang-Talis, Turing

I'm sending this message to you, Dyami, because maybe you can help me sort some things out when I come back. If you think I'm being overly cautious by sending this on a closed channel, all I can say is that I feel like being cautious. I know that nobody's likely to call up a personal message on an open channel, and I know that any experienced Linker who's interested can probably get hold of this even on a closed channel. I'm not telling you anything that won't be public knowledge soon—if it isn't already—and this isn't anything embarrassing or disgraceful about myself. It's just—

I'll get to the point. I'm going back to Island Two tomorrow. So are all of the students who came to Anwara with me. Orenda Tineka, the specialist who was advising us, assured us all that it's just an unexpected change in plans, that it has nothing to do with our abilities. Just to check on that, I called up my public record today and found a commendation for, and I quote, my "ability to think, reason, cooperate with others, and adapt to the environment of Anwara." Solveig had exactly the same commendation in her record, and my guess is that all of the other students do, too.

So we're to go back to the Islands and go on with our studies there, which means all the trouble and expense of bringing us to Anwara in the first place is largely wasted. The Project

Council wouldn't have made such a decision unless they were sure the Mukhtars wouldn't object, and it seems out of character for them to decide on this so quickly. Normally, you'd expect them to keep us here for the eight months they'd promised us, and then decide later that bringing students here wasn't worth the trouble.

So I think that something must have happened suddenly to bring the Project Council to this decision. And it just so happens that two Habitats are no longer orbiting Mars and are moving in Earth's direction. You may know that already, but even if you don't, you probably will soon enough. Orenda confirmed the observations, but Solveig also found out from the astronomers here that those two Habs had changed course. Nobody's keeping this a secret, and Orenda insists it doesn't mean anything, but I wonder. Maybe those two Habs have something to do with why they're sending us back to the Islands.

I wish we could stay here. During the first month, I was wondering if I'd ever get used to Anwara, and now I'm really sorry that we're going.

Tell Frani — no, don't tell her anything, except that I'm going back to Island Two. I'll send her a message when I get there.

16

Solveig took off her band and turned away from the wall screen toward Mahala. "No change," she said.

Mahala knew what she meant. After fifty days, the two Habitats that had left their orbits around Mars were still following a course that would bring them within half a million kilometers of Earth.

A few days after the students had returned to the Islands, rumors were already circulating among the Islanders about the two Habitats and what their movements might mean. By then, stories that more Guardians were being sent to Anwara were also part of the talk. At last the Project Council, through the Administrator and Liaison Masud al-Tikriti, had issued an announcement.

The Habitat-dwellers had changed course only to run certain tests on newly installed drives that powered the two Habs. Although Earth's Guardians would maintain their readiness, the Council of Mukhtars and the Project Council had been assured that the Habs had no intention of provoking Earth's forces into a confrontation. In the meantime, the Project Council was holding more meetings with some of the Habbers who were living among the Cytherians, but only to discuss possible ways to speed up the progress of their terraforming efforts.

All of which left Mahala wondering why the Habbers might have needed to install new drives.

"You look worried," Solveig said as she began to unbraid her long blond hair.

Mahala shook her head, not wanting to give voice to her suspicions.

Since coming back to Island Two nearly a month ago, she had sent two innocuous messages to Benzi. He had replied cordially but briefly. He had not asked to see her, which might mean that he had nothing to tell her that was any more illuminating than what the Project Council had already announced.

Or, she thought, he had nothing to say to her because he preferred to keep her in the dark about whatever was going on.

Mahala stood up and moved toward the door. "Where are you going?" Solveig asked.

"I promised I'd meet Chike."

"Oh." Solveig arched her brows. Mahala left the room and hurried down the hall. Solveig seemed intent on believing that Mahala was becoming more serious about Chike. Maybe that was because Solveig had apparently never been in love, or even infatuated, with anyone, preferring to amuse herself with speculating about the various emotional attachments of her friends. She had admitted to having slept with one of her fellow students shortly after arriving on Island Two, but more out of curiosity than because of affection or infatuation. Having had that particular experience, Solveig now seemed content to ignore the sexual aspect of life while she concentrated on her studies. Delaying the onset of puberty hormonally, as some children of prominent Earth families did in order not to be distracted from their studies, would have been unnecessary in Solveig's case.

Mahala had grown closer to Chike since their return from Anwara, drawn to him by his steadiness and his kindness. She had made love with him and had stayed with him in his room when his roommate was absent from their quarters. He had grown close enough to her to admit that he wanted to study at the Cytherian Institute largely so that he would be able to visit Earth, and she had confessed that she felt the same way. She felt at ease with him, could talk to him readily, and looked forward to their moments together. Now she wondered why she could not feel more passion for him.

Because of Ragnar, she thought. There was nothing she could share with Ragnar now except for friendship; he would become Frania's bondmate soon. Frania had decided that they would make their formal pledge during the term break three months from now, so that Mahala and Solveig could attend the ceremony. She wished now that Frania had not been so considerate.

She came out of the building and into the Island evening of dim silvery light and dark shadows. Chike was standing under a tree. She was suddenly annoyed with him for being early, for waiting there for her, for caring as much about her as he did.

He came toward her, but did not smile. He took her arm, saying nothing, and she felt his grasp tighten. They walked until they came to the rise that overlooked the sprawling star-shaped workers' residence. Except for a few people sitting on the grass outside one of the entrances, no one seemed to be out tonight.

Chike sat down. She seated herself next to him. It was uncharacteristic of him to be so tense, not to smile at her at all. "What's the matter?" she asked. He did not reply. "Something's bothering you, I can feel it."

"My Counselor wants to see me tomorrow," he said.

She glanced at him. "It's probably nothing."

"Counselors don't call you in for sessions just to pass the time." He sighed. "Maybe he's going to advise me to leave school."

"There's no reason for him to do that."

"Maybe not, but there's a rumor that the Administrators here are being pressured to get rid of more students so that some of our teachers can be given other work to do."

"I've heard that rumor, too," Mahala said, "but there are always rumors like that, stories that more students will have to leave or be advised to change their specializations or—"

"I didn't just hear this from other students, Mahala. I heard it from my brother Kesse. He told me just a couple of hours ago, and he didn't send a message, he came over to my building and told me in person. Something's going on with the Administrators here, something involving the Habbers and the Project Council."

"Does he have any idea of what it could be?" Mahala asked.

"Only that it's something they don't want everybody to know about, at least not yet. There's nothing on any public channels. Kesse did a little probing, but there are more blocks on certain channels than usual, so he didn't push it. But he did find out that some students are going to have to leave their schools."

Mahala reached for his hand. "They won't tell us to leave," she said. "They can't. We've been doing well, and . . . " Her voice trailed off. There might be no justification for advising her or Chike to leave school, but she knew that the Administrators, in the end, would do whatever they felt they had to do for their own reasons.

She thought then of something Risa had once said years ago. "We're pawns," her grandmother had murmured, "in some game that the Linkers have been playing for ages now. I don't think they really consider what might be best for one person. I think they look at how they can make use of that person to score points in the game."

They sat in silence for a while. At last Chike said, "I was going to ask if you wanted to have a late supper with me, but right now I don't feel that hungry."

She leaned against him. "I'll come to your room if you want."

"You can't. Jiro's there, and he's already asleep—wore himself out on a chemistry lab report earlier."

She said, "Promise me you'll send me a message right after your session."

"I will." He stood up and helped her to her feet. "Good night, Mahala."

"I'll walk back with you," she said.

Chike shook his head. "I think I'd rather be alone right now." He turned around quickly and walked away.

Mahala followed the path of flat stones that led to her residence. Maybe she should send another message to Benzi, who might be too busy to see her, but who also might be avoiding her. She could press him, make him feel that she needed to see him. She thought of what Risa had often said about all of them being pawns in some game. Maybe the Habbers saw them that way, too.

She was halfway up the narrower path that led to her building's side entrance before she noticed that Solveig was sitting outside the doorway. Solveig got up as Mahala hurried toward her.

"What is it?" Mahala asked, already suspecting what her friend was about to say.

"Aimée Lon has asked to see me tomorrow at eight hours." Solveig folded her arms. "The message came in right after you left. There was a message for you, too. I didn't look at it, but since it's from Counselor Aimée, I'm assuming that she wants to see you as well."

Mahala sighed. "Somehow, I'm not surprised."

"I am." Solveig bowed her head. "If they tell me to leave, I don't know what I'll do. I could put up with anything as long as there might be a chance to do some astronomy and astrophysics later. But that'll never happen if I have to go back to the surface." She looked up. "You'd better go and see what your message says."

Mahala went inside and strode down the hallway. A few students were sitting in front of an open doorway, talking, but most of the doors were closed. Two of the students greeted her; Mahala ignored them. She came to her own room and pressed her palm against the door; as it slid open, she hurried inside.

She went to her wall screen and called up the message. Pale letters appeared; Aimée Lon wanted to see her at nine hours tomorrow in the Counselor's quarters. Mahala sank onto a cushion and stared at the screen, not bothering to erase the message.

"Greetings, Mahala," Aimée Lon murmured as Mahala entered the small room.

"Salaam, Linker Aimée." The Counselor lived in a building inhabited by specialists and Linkers, but her unadorned room, with a wall screen showing a scene of snow-capped mountains in order to give an illusion of more space, was even smaller than the one Mahala and Solveig shared.

Aimée was standing; she gestured at a cushion, waited for Mahala to seat herself, then sat down across from her. The Counselor looked distinctly uneasy, glancing around the room as if afraid to meet Mahala's gaze.

Mahala said, "I think you're about to tell me something that you don't want to say."

Aimée nodded. "There's no reason to drag this out, Mahala. I am to advise you to leave school. You'll be offered certain choices—for instance, you're free to return to Turing, or to live with your grandmother's household in Oberg if you prefer, and of course you could see what kinds of apprenticeships might be possible in the other settlements if you'd rather live on your own. Naturally, you are strongly encouraged to continue with your studies however you can, insofar as—"

"I don't know why I'm being asked to leave." Mahala kept her voice steady, trying to absorb this news. Even though she had been expecting Linker Aimée to tell her that she might have to leave school, hearing the Counselor offer that advice had still come as a shock. "There's nothing wrong with my work."

"You're right. There's nothing wrong with your work. In fact, you show every sign of being a superior student. You may lack the brilliance of some students, but you've made up for that with persistence. You're the kind of person who will probably come into her own later on, and—"

"Then I don't see why I have to leave," Mahala said, interrupting the Counselor again.

Aimée lifted her head. She stared at Mahala for a few moments in silence, and then something in her expression changed.

The Counselor's eyes narrowed as she said, "I've closed my Link for a moment. I didn't want to give you this advice, Mahala. I didn't want to tell you to leave. I went to the Administrator who is the head of our team of Counselors and told him that I thought we were making a mistake, that we might be getting rid of some of our most promising students. He told me that it wasn't his doing, either, that he had no choice. The directive came from the Project Council, and he's not even sure if it was entirely their decision. Certain students are being asked to leave their schools, and no one seems to know exactly why. It's not because they've failed in any way or because we have any doubts about their commitment to their studies, which is what makes their expulsion so peculiar. I think you have the right to know that."

Mahala pressed the palms of her hands together, not knowing what to say. The Counselor's eyes widened slightly, and Mahala had the feeling that Aimée had opened her Link again.

"As I said," Aimée continued, "you'll have a choice as to where you'd like to live. You may even stay on one of the Islands if you can find work here or someone willing to take you on as an apprentice. But my feeling is that it might be easier for you in a surface settlement. With your training in biology, I know you'll find useful and interesting work, and as I said, there's no reason you can't continue to study in your spare time. I hope that you will. It would be a shame if you didn't."

"Then what's the point?" Mahala asked. "Why aren't you advising me to stay here? There probably isn't any kind of work I can do in a settlement that couldn't be done just as well by somebody else."

"True," Aimée said, "but that doesn't mean you can't be useful."

"I'd be more useful to the Project in the long run with more schooling."

"Perhaps."

"I could understand if I hadn't been trying or if I just couldn't measure up."

The Counselor sighed. "I wish there were more I could say, but I know very little more than you do." The woman leaned forward. "Look, that may be a good sign, if you think about it. You aren't being told to leave because of any failure on your part. That means it won't count against you later on."

"You mean that there won't be any black mark on my record."

"Of course not," Aimée said. "It's just the Project Council rearranging things, so to speak. It has nothing to do with you or any mistakes you might have made."

Mahala supposed that should be some consolation. Instead, it made her feel worse, as though her work and effort had made no difference in deciding her fate.

"You needn't feel any embarrassment in front of others when you leave school," Aimée went on.

Mahala glared at her. "I wouldn't feel embarrassed anyway. I don't feel ashamed, Aimée—I'm angry. It isn't likely that I'll get a chance to study at the Cytherian Institute now."

"No, I don't suppose you will."

"Then there's nothing more you have to tell me," Mahala said.

"If you need someone to talk to—"

"That isn't going to change anything." Mahala stood up. "I assume that I should make arrangements to leave as soon as possible."

Aimée lifted her head to look up at her. "This term will be over in a little less than a month. You'll have time to make any arrangements."

Mahala turned and left the room.

She walked, still feeling stunned, her mind racing as she considered what to do now. Going to live with Risa and Sef would mean getting drawn into the life of their household; there would be little quiet and solitude for any studying. She could stay with Dyami, but did not know if Frania and Ragnar planned to live there after becoming bondmates. They probably would, at least for a while. She wondered if she would be able to live with that.

She was nearly at the triangular building that housed the pilots before she realized that she was looking for Benzi. Mahala sighed; Benzi, she recalled, was not living there now. He had moved to the Habber residence on Island Two a while ago, while she was on Anwara.

She turned onto a path that would lead her to the Habber residence. As she came toward the stone building, the entrance opened and a bearded dark-haired man in a dark tunic and pants stepped outside.

Administrator Masud, she thought, recognizing the man immediately before he averted his face; almost automatically, she stepped behind a tree. There was no reason to conceal herself; even if Masud al-Tikriti took the trouble to identify her through his Link, he would not find it odd that she should come here looking for her great-uncle. But she suddenly did not want him to see her.

Masud hurried past her along the path. Had he looked up, he would have seen her standing there behind the slender tree trunk. But the frowning Administrator seemed preoccupied with his own thoughts. His head was down and he was moving swiftly, almost as though he wanted to make certain that no one would see him near the Habber residence.

Why had he come here, she wondered, instead of summoning any Habbers he wished to see to the ziggurat where the Administrators were housed? That was the usual protocol. What could have brought him here, in plain clothes instead of his formal white robe and headdress, without any of the aides who would normally be at his side during any official meeting?

Not that any of this had anything to do with her, she reminded herself. She would have to leave this place. Aimée's words came back to her; the sick, stunned feeling filled her again, along with helplessness and despair. That would pass, she told herself. By the time she left this Island, she would have to accept what her Counselor and the Project Council had decreed for her, and then thinking about what lay ahead of her would not seem so painful. She had no marks against her; she had family members who would welcome her and do what they could to get her settled. She could find work that would be both interesting and useful, and if she continued her studies on her own, a school might accept her again in the future. She had to look at things that way. As time went on, she might even find contentment and be grateful that the Project Council had dealt with her as it had.

She had come here to see Benzi, but what could she expect from him? Sympathetic, soothing words? A promise to do what he could to help her stay on Island Two? She should not have come here; Benzi could do nothing for her.

She glanced down the path, made sure that Administrator Masud was out of sight, then hurried to the entrance and pressed her hand against it. The door remained closed. She put her palm against it once more; the entrance opened suddenly.

The large room inside was empty, the only light the softly glowing ceiling. A slender woman with long reddish hair and wearing a long blue robe stood in the center of the room. "Mahala," the woman said.

"Tesia," Mahala replied, recognizing the Habber then, even though she had not seen Tesia for some time. "I came here to see Benzi."

"He cannot see you now."

"He isn't here?"

"He is here, but he cannot see you at the moment."

Mahala could not read the expression on the woman's face. "Then I'll come back later."

"He will not be able to see you then, either."

Mahala took a breath. "I've just come from a meeting with my Counselor. She told me that I'll have to leave the school here. She advised me to go to a surface settlement, since I have family there. I know Benzi can't do anything about any of that, but I thought he might at least see me."

Tesia said, "He can't see you now. When he's free, he'll try to send you a message—"

"Tesia!" Mahala cried out and took a step forward; Tesia backed away from her. "First we're brought back from Anwara sooner than expected, and now I'm told to leave here, and—" She struggled to control herself. "I could use a kind word right now."

Tesia's angular face softened. "Of course you could, child. I am sorry for your disappointment, but I think you have the capacity not to let this affect you adversely."

That was the kind of comment that she could expect from a Habber. Benzi probably would have told her the same thing. "I saw Administrator Masud al-Tikriti leaving here before," she said quickly. "He didn't notice me."

Something almost imperceptible changed in Tesia's expression; Mahala could almost believe that she had surprised the Habber with her statement.

"Yes," Tesia said. "He has consulted with us more often lately— with Benzi and with others." She fell silent, and Mahala sensed that Tesia would say nothing more about the Administrator.

"Well." Mahala looked down. "Please tell Benzi I came by to see him."

"He knows that now."

"I see," Mahala said bitterly. "He'll eavesdrop on our talk through your Links, but he won't bother to come out and talk to me himself."

"You are mistaken," Tesia said. "He has this to say to you. He says to you, 'I understand how disappointed and hurt you must feel now.' " Tesia's voice had changed, dropping in tone, taking on what Mahala recognized as Benzi's inflections. " 'Do what you have to do, Mahala, and make a life for yourself. More may lie ahead of you than you realize. That is all I can say to you at this time.' "

"Platitudes," Mahala muttered.

" 'It's the only advice I can give you,' " the Habber woman said, still sounding a bit like Benzi. " 'Do you know where you're going to go?' "

"Probably back to Turing, at least at first," Mahala replied. "I was going to go there anyway, to see Frani Milus and Ragnar Einarsson make their pledge." She swallowed hard, thinking that she might at least have had a bondmate to return to now if she had accepted Ragnar's proposal. No, she thought, that was over long ago, and realized with some surprise that it was not quite as painful for her to think about Ragnar and Frania living together.

"Benzi probably won't be able to see you before you leave," Tesia said in her own voice, "but as I said, he'll try to send you a message. You should go now, Mahala. There are probably other things you have to do."

She was due at a seminar in molecular biology in a few minutes. For a moment, she thought of neglecting all her appointments, the seminars and lectures and the computer models of possible new strains of bacteria, but that would accomplish nothing except to give her more time to brood over her situation. Better, she thought, to finish what work she could while she was here.

"Tell Benzi—" Mahala paused. "Tell him that I'll try to make the best of things."

"He is happy to hear that. Farewell, Mahala."

She moved toward the entrance and left the residence. As the door slid shut behind her, it came to her that she had not even thought of

Chike and what his Counselor might have told him, and felt a pang of guilt. Maybe he had been advised to stay on; she hoped that was so, knowing how unhappy he would be to have to leave school. She realized then how much she would miss him if they were parted.

Solveig stared at the pocket screen in her palm. "There's the list," she said to Mahala and Chike, who were sitting across the table from her. "All the names of the students who are leaving school are now public, and every single student who came to Anwara with us is listed."

"Kind of a coincidence, isn't it," Chike muttered.

"There are some other names, too," Solveig said, "but it does seem strange that all of the students who were on Anwara have to leave." She frowned. "I want to check something else now."

Solveig said a name under her breath, then another. Mahala finished her glass of fruit juice. The table at which they sat was near the wide stone path that led to the Administrators' ziggurat. She wondered if she should feel relieved by the notion that the Project Council might have hidden reasons for expelling them all from school or if she should start worrying about why such powerful people might pay that much attention to her.

"So you're definitely going to Turing," Chike said at last.

"Solveig and I were going to go there anyway during the break, and my uncle's housemates Amina and Tasida hinted that they might have found some work for me."

"I was going to stay here," Chike said. "Either my parents or my brother can find room for me for a while. But I might also be able to get a lab technician apprenticeship in a settlement, maybe in a refining and recycling plant."

"Maybe there's an opening in Turing," Mahala said, "and if there isn't one in the refinery, they might be able to use someone in the ceramics plant. I'll ask around when I get there."

"Thanks, Mahala. It might help if somebody there puts in a word for me."

"You'd be better off here," she said. His brother, as an aide to an Administrator, might be able to find a better position for Chike than that of a lab technician.

"Probably, but maybe it's time for me to be on my own." He

reached out and touched her hand. He would not say it, but it was likely that he also wanted to have a chance to be closer to her. That thought made her smile.

"Well, here's more strangeness," Solveig said, still gazing at her screen. "Three students leaving the Island schools are being expelled—excuse me, advised to leave—because they haven't been applying themselves to their studies. Three more are getting black marks for being disruptive, and one for having cheated on an independent study project. But everybody who was on Anwara with us has the same notation on their record all of us got." She leaned back. " 'This student has earned a commendation for scholarship, discipline, and adaptability,' " she recited, " 'and has been advised to leave school only because it is felt that her particular gifts might be better utilized elsewhere.' " She looked up. "It's exactly the same for all of us."

"Small consolation," Chike said.

Mahala studied her friend's face. Solveig had not betrayed any emotion when she had first told Mahala that she would have to leave the school. In the week since then, she had applied herself to her studies as methodically as always and had mentioned in passing that she was considering a position as a teacher's aide. She was burying her disappointment deeply.

"It'd be easier," Chike said, "if I just knew why we had to leave, but even my brother can't find anything out."

Benzi had sent only one message, telling Mahala that he wished her well and that he and other Habbers would remain on Island Two for some time to come. She had a feeling that this was all that she would hear from him before she left.

Solveig stood up. "I have just enough time to get to a study group meeting," she said.

Mahala and Chike got to their feet. "And I've got a seminar," Mahala said. She could forget for a while that she would be leaving Island Two in less than a month.

17

Aboard the airship to Turing, Mahala found herself watching the images of Venus on the large screen in the front of the cabin with new interest. The airship had descended below the fierce winds that swept around the planet. A light but steady yellowish and orange sulfuric rain fell into the darkness below. To the northwest, barely visible on the rust-colored plateau surrounded by the rocky black walls of the Freyja Mountains, the four tiny glowing blisters of Turing's domes were barely visible.

These screen images were more detailed than those she had seen on other screens; perhaps this ship had more sensors gathering information for its computer to use in creating the images. The temperature of the lower atmosphere had dropped to a comparatively mild seventy degrees Centigrade, while precipitation had brought the atmospheric pressure down to less than twenty times that of Earth, far below what it had been in her great-grandmother's time. If the airship in which Mahala was traveling should run into trouble and get trapped on the surface, the passengers could survive for the ten to twenty hours that it might take for a rescue vehicle, one of the scooper ships that carried compressed oxygen up to the Bats, to reach them, open its maw to receive the airship cabin, and ferry them to safety.

The shallow and sterile ocean had flooded more of the Cytherian surface around the landmasses of Ishtar Terra, Aphrodite Terra, and the volcanoes and high places that would eventually become islands. Venus had become much less hellish and deadly since the beginnings of the Project, something for people to keep in mind whenever they were discouraged by the scope of what remained to be done. The domes of the settlements, built to withstand much more lethal conditions, would continue to protect those who lived inside them.

Mahala thought of one of the last discussions she had attended with her fellow students and three of their professors. The subject of the Project's next stage had come up: Hydrogen had been imported to Venus long ago, to aid in the process of precipitation, and oxygen continued to be removed, but there was increasing evidence that importation of large quantities of calcium and magnesium might be needed to help in reducing the atmosphere of carbon dioxide to carbon and oxides. One of the professors, a geochemist, had written out the formulas for the reactions and had implied that some on the Project Council were already seriously considering such a plan. Mining Mercury and bringing the necessary quantities of magnesium and calcium to Venus would require a large-scale, robotic mining operation, with mass drivers to carry the mined minerals Venusward.

The idea had generated a lot of discussion among the students, who were soon busy on preliminary computer models of ways to accomplish the job, methods that might be feasible but were also certain to be costly in labor, resources, and technology. What had been left unsaid was that the Project could not support such an effort now, that Earth's material and intellectual resources would be strained to the limit by such an enterprise, and that the aid of the Habbers would almost certainly be required for the operation.

The Project, in other words, was stalled for the time being—and maybe for a long time to come, whether anybody would openly admit it or not. Maybe that had something to do with the Counselors advising more students to leave school. Perhaps the Project did not need so many specialists, given that educating more young people was not likely to advance the Project at the moment and might only sow more discontent.

Solveig slept on in the seat next to her. Mahala concentrated on the screen images. Better, she thought, to think of how far the Project had come instead of dwelling on how many centuries, even millennia, were likely to pass before Venus was truly habitable. Better to think of what terraforming had accomplished and not to muse on the fact that no one alive now would ever see the green thriving world that their efforts would bring into being. Her expulsion from the Island Two school had not changed the ultimate direction of her life all that much. She had always known that she would have to live working toward an end that she would never behold.

"That's my offer," Tasida Getran said. "I think you'll find the work interesting, and I'll be getting a good assistant just when I need more help."

Mahala sat with Tasida near the creek that ran down to the lake. "I'm flattered that you think that much of me," Mahala replied. The physician had recently finished setting up an office and examination room near the tunnel that led into the south dome. Patients could get to the small building easily from almost everywhere in Turing, and the extra space would be useful if anyone needed to remain there for observation.

"It isn't flattery," Tasida said. "I looked at your record. You still have a few things to learn, but you'll do just fine as a paramedic, and you'll be learning something that'll be useful no matter what you do later on. Don't think I'll make it easy for you, either." A smile crossed Tasida's freckled face. "But you'll have some time to pursue more lessons, if that's what you want."

"It is what I want." Mahala wondered if, in spite of Tasida's promise, she would have much time for additional study. There would be emergencies that required immediate attention as well as people who relied on physicians and paramedics to fill the function of Counselors. "There's no reason I have to give up my studies just because I'm no longer a student."

"I'll give you medical works to look at, but your background in biology is better than that of most paramedics, and you'll learn a lot through experience." Tasida paused. "You're taking this turn of events very well."

Mahala shrugged. She would not admit it aloud, but one reason for trying to make the best of things now was her hope that the Project Council might change their minds again and decide to readmit some of the students who had been expelled. They had unexpectedly sent her to Anwara, had sent her back to Island Two as precipitously, and had asked her to leave school without warning; the Council and Administrators might act just as suddenly to readmit her to a school in the future. It was a faint hope, but a plausible one.

"I don't think Solveig is taking her disappointment nearly as well," Tasida added.

"What makes you say that?" Mahala asked.

"I've dealt with a lot of patients. Often I can sense when something might be bothering them that they don't want to discuss. I think she's holding it all in."

"Solveig's the kind of person who keeps things to herself," Mahala said. "I used to think that was because she was just a more even-tempered person. Almost every student I know resorted to moods or implants at some point, to stay awake to finish a project or to stay calm during examinations or discussions with advisers, but Solveig never did."

"Did you?" Tasida asked, looking amused.

"A few times. It was usually the university-level students who were specializing in medicine who supplied the rest of us with the stuff."

"That doesn't surprise me," Tasida said. "It isn't really cheating—moods and implants and memory enhancers aren't going to make up for not knowing the material. They'll help somebody perform at top capacity, but they won't increase ability. And you'd have to be really excessive in your use of such things before they'd do you too much harm." Tasida paused. "Anyway, I always thought that any medical students dealing in those aids were getting some useful lessons in how to prescribe treatments responsibly for their patients, especially since the stupid and the careless and the greedy dealers were likely to get caught sooner or later. And I don't see what's so wrong about trying to enhance and improve your basic physiological equipment. The Habbers certainly don't worry about such changes."

Mahala wrapped her arms around her legs, a bit surprised at Tasida's frankness. "You're being awfully open with me."

"I had better be open with you. You'll have to back me up, and I'll have to rely on you, possibly in the middle of a life-threatening emergency. I have to be completely honest with you, as you'll have to be with me."

"Then I might as well admit," Mahala said, "that I used to think that we might eventually have to change ourselves in a lot of ways, genetically or somatically, if we're ever to be able to live outside the domes, even after Venus is completely terraformed."

"That's not exactly an original thought. I've entertained such notions myself, as have many other people. But they aren't the kinds of thoughts I share with most of my patients. People may be the products of generations of genetic scans and analysis and in vitro somatic changes and gene surgery, and a small number of them were removed from an ectogenetic chamber at birth instead of getting pushed out of a mother's womb, but many of them are very quick to tell me that they don't want any treatment that's unnatural."

"I can imagine," Mahala said.

"Now I find myself wondering if Solveig Einarsdottir avoided implants and mood alterers not because she didn't need them, but because she was afraid of them, afraid that they might open up too much inside her that she'd rather not confront."

Mahala shook her head. "Not long ago, she told me that she wouldn't know what to do if she thought there was no chance of being a specialist in astronomy and astrophysics. Oh, she can still keep up with her studies, but the things she really loves are fields the Project doesn't seem to find particularly useful right now. So she's lost the only work she ever really wanted to do."

"Yes, I suppose she has," Tasida said, "and her brother Ragnar is finding it increasingly hard to do what he wants to do, too." She stood up. "Get yourself settled, attend Frani's bondmate ceremony, even take a few days to visit your grandparents in Oberg. As you know, my equipment isn't quite as good as what you'd find on Anwara or the Islands, but I'll expect you at my office in exactly fourteen days at five hours, just before first light."

"I'll be there," Mahala said as she got to her feet.

Two days after Mahala had returned to Turing, Solveig's parents arrived, came to Dyami's house, and announced that they would be staying with their son in the house he was building until the ceremony. Dyami had offered to have the couple make their pledge in his home; Frania and Ragnar had decided on a small ceremony, but the simple plan had grown more complicated. Einar and Thorunn had decided to come to Turing to see their son make his pledge instead of only sending Ragnar their congratulations, a few of Frania's fellow pilots had invited themselves, and now Dyami was preparing for at least fifty people to show up in his common room.

Mahala and Solveig spent the four days after their arrival in Turing preparing small pastries and dumplings and arranging plates of vegetables and fruits for the expected guests. Two airship pilots had come to the house carting a gift from Risa's household: several bottles of Oberg's most famous libation, Dinel's Cytherian Whiskey. By the evening before the ceremony, Mahala had been too busy even to have a real conversation with Frania, but the pensive look she often saw on her friend's face made her wonder if Frania was having doubts about her pledge. Ragnar had not come to Dyami's house during the days before the ceremony, apparently because he was either working his shifts or finishing another room of his house, which he had decided to build in Turing's west dome instead of in the more recently completed east dome. He had perfectly good excuses for staying away, but perhaps he was also having his doubts about his commitment.

Solveig, having stored the last tray of pastries in the kitchen, had gone to bed early in the room she was sharing with Mahala and Frania. Dyami and Amina were arranging the cushions and tables they had borrowed from other households against the walls, while Tasida set out a few vases of the flowers one of her patients raised to trade for credit or services. Mahala was about to prepare for sleep when she saw Frania leave the bathroom, cross the common room, and go outside.

Mahala hesitated for a moment, then followed her. As the door closed behind her, Mahala watched Frania walk down the slope toward the lake.

She's only sixteen, Mahala thought, and Ragnar's barely eighteen; they don't know what they're doing. Older people could say all they wanted to about the virtues of finding a bondmate early, when one's feelings were most intense, before experience and disappointment in love made it harder to form strong attachments, but such promises also meant closing off other possibilities in life, or so it seemed to her. Early attachments, the challenges and rewards of rearing children, working at tasks that might have been handled largely by robots so that people could feel that they had a real part in the Project—all of it seemed a way of keeping people here from dwelling too much on whether their lives on Venus had any real purpose apart from propagating their genes and their species. A population had to be maintained, against that far off day when its descendants would leave the domes and live under an open sky.

Mahala descended the hill, keeping behind Frania until her friend halted and looked up at her.

"Mahala," Frania called out.

"Frani." She hesitated; maybe Frania wanted to be alone.

"Come on, Mahala—I could use some company right now."

Mahala came down the slope. The two walked toward the lake, then seated themselves under the trees overlooking the shore.

"This whole ceremony is getting away from me," Frania said. "First Ragnar and I were going to make our promises at his house with Dyami and Amina as witnesses. Then Dyami offered to let us have a ceremony at his house, and then Amina thought you and Solveig might want to come, and then Ragnar predicted that his parents would decide they just couldn't miss this, and the whole thing kept growing and growing after that."

"You'll have something to look back on," Mahala said.

"I hope I'm not making a mistake," Frania said more softly. "First Ragnar insisted on a pledge, and then he wanted to put it off, and then he changed his mind and asked me if we could have the ceremony as soon as possible. And after that, I kept thinking that maybe we should call it off and wait a while longer."

"Have you told him?"

Frania shook her head. "I couldn't do that now."

"Look," Mahala said, "maybe it's normal to feel this way. You're making a pledge to share your life with someone else."

"Ten years of my life, anyway."

"You'll probably renew your bond after that, the way most people do. Letting a pledge lapse isn't that easy when you have children and other members of a household involved, along with dividing up belongings and deciding where one of the partners is going to live, so—"

"I thought of telling Ragnar we should wait," Frania said, "and maybe I should have right away. But if I do it now, with all of these guests coming and his parents staying with him and Solveig being here—it would humiliate him. He'd never forgive me."

"But it might be worse if you go into this thinking it's a mistake. Going through a hearing to break your bond would be a lot more trouble than calling everything off now." Mahala put a hand on her friend's arm. "What is it, Frani? Are you thinking you might not love him enough for this?"

"Oh, no. I can't imagine not caring for him. It's Ragnar I'm worrying about, not my own feelings. He's so unhappy—I can see it even when he tries to hide it. He does his work with the diggers and crawlers, but he resents every bit of time it takes away from his drawing and designing and sculpting. And he can't earn any credit with his artwork that he could use later, so he could take longer breaks from his shifts."

Mahala frowned. "I would have thought he could make a lot of credit with his pastime."

"There are some people who asked him to make things for them," Frania said. "Two months ago, Li Po—one of the workers on his team—asked Ragnar if he would make a small metal sculpture of his two children. He told Ragnar he would give him holo images to look at and that he could come over to his home anytime if he needed to have his boy and girl model for the sculpture. Ragnar did some sketches and cast the molds over at the refinery, but he never finished it."

"Why not?" Mahala asked.

"He lost interest. Of course Li Po had given him some credit to buy materials and for his time, and the children were complaining about all the time they'd had to sit still modeling. Ragnar paid him back, but Li Po won't ask him for anything again. And there are others who had similar things happen when they asked Ragnar to make things for them."

"I see," Mahala said. She suddenly felt a rush of pity for Ragnar, along with tinges of her old feelings for him, but pushed those feelings aside. "Maybe what he should do is make whatever objects he likes and then make sure that others happen to see them sitting around in his house. That way he could sell or trade finished items to people later on."

"That might work," Frania said, a note of hope in her voice. "I could tell him—" She sighed. "I wonder if he would even listen to me. Sometimes I think he's making this pledge just to get it over with. He knows that I'll be gone for stretches of time—pilots always are. He can have a bondmate and have all of that settled without having to actually live with me all the time. He can go to his shifts and spend the rest of his time on his art. I should be grateful for that, knowing that he probably won't miss me that much while I'm away."

"Can you live like that?" Mahala asked.

"Yes." Frania's voice was low, but determined. "I'll have to. After a while, I'll get used to it, and so will he." She stood up. "We'd better get to sleep. We have a lot to do tomorrow."

*   *   *

Frania and Ragnar held hands while reciting their pledge to be bond-mates. The custom was for the couple to memorize the clauses of their pledges and then recite them in front of witnesses. As was also the custom, someone who could read always stood by with the text of the promises on a pocket screen, in order to prompt the couple should they forget any of the agreed-upon clauses. Frania had asked Amina to take on that role, but she and Ragnar rattled off their pledges without a single lapse.

Frania, clothed in a long blue silk tunic over dark blue trousers, was as beautiful as Mahala had expected her to look. Ragnar's long blond hair was pulled back in a long plait that fell halfway down his back, and he wore a bright red tunic with black pants. He had arrived with his parents at Dyami's house only moments before the time set aside for the ceremony. The assembled guests were growing restless by then, and Mahala had spied a few surreptitiously helping themselves to dumplings and pastries before Ragnar took his place next to Frania.

Maybe he had been thinking of postponing this ceremony. That would be ironic, Mahala thought, if that was what they both wanted and neither had been able to admit it to the other. She watched as people lined up and congratulated the couple, then filed past Amina to have her enter their names as witnesses. They could hardly back out of their bond now, with all of these witnesses and their pledge now part of the public record.

Mahala lingered at the edge of the crowd. Solveig, with her long braids pinned up on her head in a crown and wearing a dark green tunic and white pants, was over by one of the tables, pouring glasses of fermented juice or whiskey for a few of the guests. Mahala went to her friend. Solveig set down the bottle from which she was pouring and moved toward the kitchen; Mahala followed her.

"I spoke to my parents before," Solveig said as the door closed. "My mother said that they'd wait about two or three hours and then announce that they're going to walk with their son and his new bondmate to their home. Thorunn figures that most of the guests will decide to join them for the walk, and presumably the ones who don't will take the hint and leave. Otherwise, Dyami might be stuck with some of these people until first light tomorrow."

Mahala smiled. "You're exaggerating."

"Never underestimate how much advantage people will take of

food and drink paid for by someone's else's credit." There was a bitter edge to Solveig's voice.

"We'd better go and have Amina record our names as witnesses."

"I hope this makes Ragnar happy," Solveig said in a whisper. "Our parents are pleased—the way they look at it, he's settling down and doing his work and they won't have to worry about him. I'm the one they're worrying about now."

"Why should they worry about you?" Mahala asked.

"They don't believe that it wasn't my fault somehow, having to leave Island Two. Einar thinks that maybe the Counselors and Administrators were being a bit too lenient by not putting a mark on my record. I went to see them yesterday, over at Ragnar's house, after I met with a couple of teachers at the primary school."

"Were you asking about work there?" Mahala asked, surprised that Solveig had said nothing to her about it.

"They said that they needed two aides. They told me that with my record of studies, I could probably become a teacher within a year if I do well in the classroom and master some teaching methods. So if I want to stay here in Turing, I can, assuming I can find a place to live."

"You can stay here," Mahala said. "With Frani gone, Dyami would have room."

"I don't know if I want to stay." Solveig leaned against a counter. "Of course Einar and Thorunn think I'm mad to turn down an opportunity to become a teacher. But I could put in for Bat duty instead, which would help me build up a fair amount of credit before I decide on what to do next."

"You can't." Mahala stepped toward Solveig. "You couldn't."

"Why not? Because it's dangerous?"

"Because you're of much more use to the Project elsewhere. Because that would be a real waste of what you've learned."

Solveig said, "Ragnar's putting in for Bat duty. He told me that yesterday. He hasn't told our parents yet, but they'll find out soon enough."

Mahala gaped at her friend. "Bat duty?" She took a breath. "Has he told Frani?"

"I don't know. I didn't ask. But Frani won't try to stop him—she'll go along with whatever he wants."

"But why?" Mahala asked.

"Because it'll give him extra credit. He'll have more status, too. He won't be just a worker who wastes his time making trinkets and little sculptures and junk no one wants—he'll be somebody who was brave enough to put in shifts on the Bat. Maybe then, he can win himself more time to do what he wants to do, and maybe others will be more willing to let him."

"Frani won't accept that," Mahala said. "She'll try to talk him out of it."

"Maybe, but she won't get anywhere. He'll just point out that she's training on shuttles and that piloting isn't without its dangers and that she might be ferrying workers to and from the Bats and so they could see each other more often if he's working there."

Mahala shook her head. "He can't. And you—"

"I haven't decided anything," Solveig said. "I'm just thinking about it. I can't do the only kind of thing I really want to do, and now I have to decide—" She gave Mahala a look of despair, then moved toward the convection oven. "We'd better warm up some more dumplings for our guests."

In spite of Solveig's prediction, Einar and Thorunn did not begin to extricate themselves from the celebration until a few hours later. By then, some of the guests had already taken their leave, and a few others were noticeably intoxicated.

"We are going to leave you now," Einar called out to the assemblage, "and accompany our son and his bondmate to their new home."

"You are all welcome to walk there with us," Thorunn added, her arm around Frania.

People milled around, finishing the last of the food. Mahala glared at a man who was about to make off with an unopened bottle of whiskey; at last he put the bottle back on the table and wandered away. There were some people here whom no one seemed to know well; she wondered how many had been invited and how many had simply decided to come to the party with friends.

Small groups of people drifted outside. Mahala looked around for Solveig, saw her with Ragnar and Frania, then moved toward the door. More people had gathered near the footbridge that led over the creek; this bondmate ceremony seemed to be Turing's major social event of the month. Risa would have said that this was what came of taking occasions that called only for simple and private ceremonies and turning them into public spectacles, as more and more Cytherians were doing. "If you insist upon making a display of yourself," Risa would mutter, "even strangers will want to come and see the show."

But Mahala understood why people were increasingly going in for more elaborate rites, now that her own life seemed marked out for her. The only truly significant events of her life were likely to be such occasions as taking a bondmate, giving birth to a child, marking the deaths of people close to her. She would want to mark those times with some ceremony. Even Risa, whatever her feelings, had sent a lavish gift of whiskey for these festivities.

People threw flower petals at Ragnar and Frania as they left the house. Thorunn and Einar followed, with Solveig trailing them. Tasida made her farewells and hurried off; she had promised to check up on a patient.

Mahala hurried to Solveig's side. One of her friend's blond braids had come loose and hung over her shoulder. "How are you doing?" she whispered to her friend.

"Fine," Solveig said softly. "I'm fine, Mahala. It's a long walk, though."

"I need the exercise after all that food."

"I need it after all that whiskey." Solveig's words were slurred; she giggled. By the time they came to the footbridge, a procession was following them. Mahala looked around, but did not see Dyami or Amina; perhaps they had decided to stay and clean up after all of the guests were gone.

She slowed her pace, thinking of her uncle and Amina and Tasida and the effort they had put into this occasion, a rite they would probably never be able to celebrate themselves with those whom they loved. Some people in Turing might not see anything amiss if Amina and Tasida decided to pledge themselves as bondmates, but others would be appalled, and many of the Cytherians in other settlements would think it scandalous. People from Earth's more rustic regions, people without much learning or many pretensions, probably made better settlers and harder workers for the Project, but such people had brought many of their prejudices with them to the new world.

The long line of celebrants wound its way through the western side of Turing's north dome, past houses and the glassy square of the dome's recycling center, then through the wooded region that bordered the small Buddhist shrine, which had a pale green roof and graceful dark columns that made it seem a part of the forest. People left their houses to walk with the procession; a few young people joined them, playing flutes and beating on small drums. By the time they came to the simple stone walls of the mosque, the evening call to prayer was sounding. A few of the older men dropped out of the line to unroll small prayer rugs and say their prayers, but most of the people continued to follow Frania and Ragnar toward the tunnel that led to the west dome.

People began to sing. As they moved along the gently sloping ramp that led under the north dome's wall and into the lighted tunnel, people walking in the other direction moved aside to let them pass. The sounds of singing and flutes and drums echoed in the tunnel until Mahala seemed to feel the drumbeats throbbing inside herself. Others pressed around her; she realized suddenly that she had lost Solveig.

The crowd surged up the ramp and into the west dome. Mahala moved to one side, waiting for others to pass her. Ragnar and Frania had turned south, leading everyone toward a hill that was higher than any she had yet seen in the largely flat land that lay under the domes of Turing. The top of the hill had been planted with slender young trees, saplings that would grow quickly into an altered species of maple.

At first, in the fading light of evening, Mahala could not see the house. Then she glimpsed a glassy wall through the trees. She hurried toward the hill and followed the others toward the structure of wood and glass. Like Dyami, Ragnar had used a reflective material for one wall, so that he could look out but others could not look in. At the side of the house, surrounded by trees, was a triangular wing with a roof and a floor of green tiles on which a table and several low wooden chairs sat, but no walls. For a moment Mahala thought that Ragnar might not have finished building that part of the house yet, and then she realized that he had intended it to be an open space; the trees, when their trunks were thicker, would serve as a wall. The entrance to the house was under the open triangular wing.

People milled around under the wing's roof, then began to drift away, calling out congratulations and farewells.

"What a strange dwelling," a woman muttered at Mahala's right. "I've never seen a house like that. Who ever heard of a room with no walls right in front of a doorway? It's like inviting anybody who happens to wander by to sit down there."

"Who's going to wander by?" a gray-haired man near the woman said. "Being well away from any walkways, on this hill, with all those trees surrounding the place—I don't get the feeling that young couple care to have many visitors."

Mahala said, "I think it's beautiful." Seeing the house he had designed and built made her think that she was seeing a part of him. She suddenly felt a pang of regret that she would not be sharing this with Ragnar.

Frania and Ragnar lingered by the entrance as Einar and Thorunn hovered nearby. Mahala searched for Solveig again, then gave up and walked toward the couple. She had not had a chance to say anything to them after the ceremony besides a hasty "congratulations."

She went to Frania, hugged her, then nodded at Ragnar. "I'm happy for you both," she said, and part of her meant it.

Frania glanced at her bondmate. Mahala could not read the expression in Ragnar's face. "I heard that you're going to stay in Turing," he said.

"Yes, I am."

"Doing what?" he asked.

"Working with Tasida as a paramedic. She can use an assistant. She's even thinking of adding another room to her offices, so we'll have another infirmary—she doesn't think the one near the refinery is enough, with more people living in Turing now."

"Well, then. If I grow too discontented, you can always prescribe an implant or a metabolic adjustment or something else for me." Mahala could not tell if he was joking or not.

"By the way," Einar asked, "where is our daughter?"

"I don't know," Mahala said. "She was with me, and then I lost her. She probably went back to Dyami's house."

"Then you can tell her that we're heading back to Hypatia tonight," Einar said. "One of the pilots at the party told us there was room for more passengers on his airship, and better to leave this young couple by themselves on their first night in their new home."

"They could use a few more teachers in Hypatia," Thorunn added. "You might tell Solveig that, too."

"I will," Mahala said. "Farewell."

"And thank Dyami and his housemates for us," Einar said. "We reimbursed Amina for our share of the refreshments, but there aren't too many houses that would have had room for all those people."

"They were happy to do it," Mahala said. "Farewell."

Most of the guests had already left. Mahala went down the hill and back the way she had come, wondering if Solveig had gone back to Dyami's house. She recalled what her friend had said in the kitchen, how unhappy and despairing she had looked, and suddenly feared for her.

She decided to take the long way back to Dyami's house, along a pathway that led to the western side of the lake. From there, she could walk along the shore and then up the western side of the creek until she came to the footbridge. If Solveig was back at the house, there was nothing to worry about, and if she needed time to herself, she had probably gone to the lake, where few people were likely to be at this hour.

The dome's light had faded into the dim light of night by the time she was near the western end of the lake. A wooded area separated the houses near the pathway from the shore. Mahala made her way through the grove, heading toward the silvery water that was barely visible through the trees. As she emerged from the wooded land, she saw what looked like a body lying on the shore to the north.

She hurried in that direction, picking up her pace until she was moving at a run. As she came closer, she saw that the body was prone, with long pale hair plaited in two braids. Solveig, she thought, recognizing her friend, suddenly afraid of what might have happened to her.

"Solveig," she whispered as she came up to her friend's side. Solveig's green tunic was wet, her white pants covered with mudstains. Mahala knelt and saw that Solveig was breathing; one of her hands clutched a bottle. She was reaching toward the other girl when she heard a moan.

"Solveig," Mahala whispered again. "Are you all right?" She took Solveig gently by the shoulders and eased her onto her back. "What happened?"

Solveig groaned and clutched at her belly. "I feel awful."

"You look awful." Mahala took the bottle from her; it was empty. Dinel's Cytherian Whiskey: she wanted to hurl the bottle into the lake. "What did you do to yourself?"

"Left the rest of you when you got to the tunnel," Solveig muttered. "I went back to Dyami's, and he and Amina were in the kitchen, and I took the bottle and came out here."

"So you decided to get completely drunk," Mahala said, disgusted.

"That isn't it." Solveig was silent for a long time. "I didn't come out here just to drink. I was thinking about my situation, turning it over in my mind, wishing they'd never picked me for that school and then maybe I wouldn't ever have found out what I really wanted to do, and how I'll never be able to do it now, and the more I thought about it, the more it seemed that my life was over. And then I thought, If it's over, then it doesn't matter what I do now, I could just walk into the water and just float out until I couldn't get back. Everybody would think it was an accident, and they'd be sorry for a while but they'd go on, you and Ragnar and Frani and everybody else."

"Solveig," Mahala said, angry that Solveig could have considered such an action and yet also pitying her for having such dark despairing thoughts.

The other girl was struggling to sit up. Mahala slipped her arm around Solveig and helped her up, then sat with her, letting her friend lean against her.

"I got here," Solveig said, coughing a little, "and finished the whiskey, and by then I was so drunk I could hardly stand. I waded into the water, figuring I'd pass out, and floated for a while, and the water must have revived me. Found out I actually could swim a little. All I remember after that is stumbling out of the water, so I must have passed out after that."

Mahala did not know what to say. Solveig might have died here. Frania and Ragnar would never have been able to remember their ceremony without thinking of Solveig; Mahala would not have been able to walk by this lake without recalling her lost friend. She wondered if Solveig had thought of any of that.

"When it comes right down to it," Solveig continued, "I guess I wanted to live after all. I was thinking that before everything went black. I'm sorry—it was a horrible thing to do."

They sat there for a while, gazing out at the water. "You're lucky other people didn't come out here while you were in the water," Mahala said. "They might have pulled you out and sent somebody for help, and then you would have had a real mess on your hands. The school probably wouldn't have taken you on as a teacher's aide, since your actions wouldn't have set a good example. I don't know if they would have had a hearing or not—probably not, because you could always argue that too much whiskey marred your judgment. But the Turing Council certainly would have sent you to a physician, maybe even called in a Counselor for you."

"I would have had a black mark on my record."

"Maybe, maybe not. It wouldn't have made much difference one way or the other. Anyone who knew for sure what had happened might have tried to keep quiet about it, but you know how gossip can spread." Mahala tightened her arm around her friend. "You could have died. I would have been furious with you then, and I would have been mourning you for a very long time."

"What are you going to do?" Solveig asked.

"I don't know. If I do nothing, and you try something like this again, I'll always wonder if I could have prevented it."

"I won't do anything like this again."

"Now I know why you wanted to volunteer for Bat duty," Mahala said. "Putting yourself in the way of danger would have been another way to settle things once and for all."

"I couldn't do that." Solveig sagged against her. "I was thinking that I couldn't go on Bat duty while I was wading into the water. Not caring what happened to me, not thinking about whether I lived or died—I would have been a danger to any worker near me. Doing away with myself here seemed to make more sense—at least it would just be me and nobody else."

"Idiot."

"It made sense at the time," Solveig said. "Mahala, what are you going to do?"

"Get you back to Dyami's house. Get you cleaned up and into bed. Dyami and Amina are probably asleep by now, but if they see us come in, we can always let them think you were just celebrating too much." Mahala paused. "I won't say anything as long as you promise me you'll go to Tasida and tell her what you tried to do. As long as you let her help you, she'll have to keep whatever you tell her in confidence. She must have had people come to her with similar problems, and if it's something that needs a specialist, she'll send you to some-body else."

"A specialist?" Solveig asked, sounding apprehensive.

"In case there's some underlying physiological or metabolic prob-lem that might have contributed to your mood."

Solveig let out a sound that might have been a laugh. "It wasn't my metabolism—it was that damned whiskey." She picked up the empty bottle.

"Do you think you can walk now?"

"I can walk."

Mahala helped Solveig to her feet, but kept hold of her by the arm as they started along the shore of the still and silent lake. "I'm glad you came to your senses, Solveig. I would have missed you terribly. Just thinking of it makes me ache inside."

"Look at this. I've ruined my best tunic, my shoes are full of water, and I've got the worst headache of my life."

"Serves you right," Mahala said, looking out over the black water. "It's better than being dead."

Solveig let the door close behind her, then said, "It's settled. I start as a teacher's aide two days from now."

Mahala, seated at a low table, looked up from her small screen. "Who are you working with?" she asked.

"Virida Wynnet," Solveig replied. "She's good. Her students always give her good ratings, and she has training in both pediatrics and child psychology. I asked her about giving our students more exposure to as-trophysics and astronomy, and she heartily approves of the idea—she asked me to design a program."

"Wonderful," Mahala said. She would be starting early tomorrow with Tasida, who had one patient due to deliver a child at almost any moment. There was a chance that she might be up well before first light if the woman went into labor this evening. She studied Solveig; her friend seemed her usual calm, placid self. Solveig, she knew, had consulted Tasida, but Mahala had not asked what the physician had advised or if she had prescribed any sort of treatment.

"What are you looking at?" Solveig asked.

"I've been reviewing a couple of studies on a new strain of sulfide-oxidizing bacteria. A team of microbiologists on Island Seven has proposed seeding our oceans with this particular strain soon. Their computer models indicate that they should thrive in the deepest areas of the oceans." She sighed. "I should be reviewing obstetrical studies instead."

"I went to see Ragnar after speaking to Virida," Solveig said. "I told him that he was mad if he signed up for Bat duty. He said he'd think it over. Frani's pulled duty piloting airships on the runs between Turing and the other settlements, so she'll be back here every two or three days. That's good. It means Ragnar won't be alone for too long."

Mahala said, "You're worrying about him."

"Yes, I am."

Mahala was about to blank her screen when a tiny light winked on along the border. "There's going to be a public announcement now," she said.

"The Turing Council?" Solveig asked.

Mahala shook her head as an image of Masud al-Tikriti appeared. "No—this is from Administrator Masud." Masud's image vanished, to be replaced by that of a bearded man in a formal headdress whom she did not recognize. "Administrator Masud and someone else," Mahala added. "This may be important."

She got up, went to the small console in the back of the room, and turned on the wall screen. An alto voice murmured, "Mukhtar Tabib al-Tahir and Administrator Masud al-Tikriti have concluded their series of meetings on Anwara and are now ready to issue a statement. This statement will be given by Administrator Masud, and it will be repeated on a public channel every hour for the next two days. Those who wish to do so may call up the statement in written form an hour from now."

"It is important," Solveig said as Mahala sat down in front of the screen. "They wouldn't be repeating it so often if it weren't."

A split screen was now showing the face of Mukhtar Tabib on the left and that of Administrator Masud on the right. "I never heard of Mukhtar Tabib al-Tahir before," Mahala said.

"Neither have I," Solveig said. Neither of them had paid that much attention to Earth's politics, but it seemed to Mahala that she should have known something about Tabib al-Tahir before now if he was important enough, and trusted enough, to have been sent to Anwara in secret to discuss matters involving the Project.

"I can tell you a little about him," Dyami said from behind them. Mahala turned; she had not heard her uncle come inside. "Mukhtar

Tabib became part of the Council of Mukhtars less than two years ago. He allegedly spent his first year persuading his enemies to retire, which they were apparently only too willing to do since Tabib's cousin, to whom he is supposedly as close as a brother, became Commander of all the Guardian forces at about that time. Tabib spent a few months of his second year as Mukhtar getting several of his allies onto the Council of Mukhtars and securing Masud al-Tikriti's position as Liaison to the Project Council."

"Were you looking at his record?" Mahala asked before realizing that much of what her uncle had found out could not have been deduced from any public record.

"No—Benzi sent me a brief message this morning, telling me those few facts about the Mukhtar and saying that we can now regard Mukhtar Tabib as the most powerful person on Earth. Benzi himself has been at most of the meetings on Anwara either in person or through a private channel."

"Benzi?" Mahala felt even more confused. "Is this something involving the Habbers?"

"Yes, and the Project and our future relations with Earth as well." Dyami came toward them and sat down in front of the screen. "Amina's staying over at Tasida's office tonight. I sent a message to Ragnar and Frani telling them to stay in their house for now, and I sent Risa and Sef a message offering the same advice to them and their household. And I was relieved to find you two here at home."

Solveig gaped at him. "Is it that bad?"

"I don't know. Benzi seemed hopeful, even excited, but he also said that what happens now is going to depend largely on how people here react to this announcement."

Mahala kept her eyes on the screen. The Administrator was taking a while to begin his statement, as if wanting to make sure that he had the attention of as many people as possible before he began. The screen went blank for a moment, and then the face of Masud al-Tikriti appeared.

"Fellow Cytherians," he began, "and I address you as such, because even though I have been among you for only a short time, I consider myself one of you. I have known for some time that it was God's will that I should make your world my own."

Solveig sighed. Mahala leaned forward.

"Transforming this world was Earth's dream," Masud continued, "and yet that dream brought doubt and distrust. Our home world hoped to create a new world here, a place where something new would grow, and yet many Earthfolk feared that we might turn against the old world and break our ties with her. But that was never our dream."

His dark eyes gazed out from the screen. "Freeing themselves of Earth's bonds," he said, "and of the bonds of planets altogether, was the dream of the Habitat-dwellers, and yet they have found themselves drawn back into involvement with the people of the worlds they once sought to escape. And we who dream of making a new world for our descendants must live knowing that many generations still have to pass before that dream is realized. This is nothing new in human affairs, for people of the distant past also knew that they were sacrificing much for those who would follow and would not live to see whatever they made, but never before has the realization of a dream lain so far in the future."

The Administrator paused for a moment. "Terraforming Venus was Earth's dream, but the Mukhtars knew from the start that they would need the help of the Habitat-dwellers, the aid of their technology, to make that dream a reality. The Habitat-dwellers could test their tools and learn much by aiding the Project, and yet the Project seemed to contradict the basis of their society—that human beings should not be bound by the limits of a planet, that humankind should find a home in space. Still, they set that aside and gained by helping us, as we have gained from them. We have drawn closer, all of us, and by doing so have achieved what none of us could have won alone. Now it is time for us to draw closer still, in pursuit of a new dream and a new promise."

Mahala heard Solveig let out her breath. Here it comes, Mahala thought, unable to guess at what Masud al-Tikriti would say.

"Our first announcement," the Administrator said, "is to assure you that the Habitat-dwellers will assist us in the construction of four new domed settlements in the Akna Mountains to the west of the Maxwell Mountains and the Lakshmi Plateau. Even though our engineers no longer consider it necessary, given the slow but steady decrease in the atmospheric pressure of Venus, these domes and their installations will be built to the same specifications as those already on the surface."

That was no surprise, Mahala thought. An announcement of that sort had been expected before much longer, and making it clear that the new domes would be exactly like the others was a concession to those who might otherwise assume that the Project was skimping on safety measures.

"Our next announcement," Administrator Masud went on, "is that the Habbers have agreed to assist us in a new procedure that promises to speed up the rate at which the Cytherian atmosphere will precipitate into surface solids—in other words, will provide the means to turn more of the carbon dioxide present in the atmosphere into surface minerals."

"That's a simplified way of putting it," Solveig whispered.

"The Habbers propose to attempt this," Masud said, "by setting up a mining operation on Mercury, since that planet has the minerals required for the production of the needed quantities of calcium and magnesium." Mahala tensed, thinking of her last days on Island Two, when she and other students had discussed such a process. "They will do this with the aid of their cyberminds and machine replicating systems—no human miners or workers will be needed on the surface of Mercury or even near that planet. The magnesium and calcium ingots produced on Mercury will be hurled toward Venus from electromagnetic mass drivers. Even with all of the resources of the Project Council and Earth, it is unlikely that we could have undertaken an operation on that scale in the near future by ourselves."

Mahala glanced at Solveig and Dyami. Masud al-Tikriti had been unusually frank about their dependence on assistance from the Habbers, but had still not said anything that should cause any unrest among Cytherians, as her uncle had feared. There had to be more to his announcement.

"This new stage of the Project," the Administrator said, "impressive as it is, will be only one effort to mark a new era of cooperation among the peoples of Earth, Venus, and the Habitats." He was silent for a few moments, as if to be certain that he had the full attention of all of those listening to him. "Another venture lies ahead, perhaps the most important task our species has yet had to undertake, one in which all of us will have a part to play, however small, a venture that a few of you, God willing, may live to see through to its hoped-for end."

Mahala held her breath, unable to imagine what he might say now.

"For some time now, the Habbers have not only ventured into the more distant reaches of our solar system but have also turned their sights to what lies beyond its bounds. In their Habitats, they have traveled only as far as Saturn's orbital path, but their probes have traveled to the Oort Cloud of comets that lies in the outermost regions of our system." Masud leaned forward and an expression crossed his face that might have been either hope or fear. "We have known that much for some time. What we did not know is that we are not alone in the universe. Another civilization has raised a beacon, another race has called out to us across the light-years."

The Administrator went on to speak of the signal that had come from six hundred light-years away, to be picked up by a Habber observatory. When the Habbers had concluded that it was indeed a signal from another intelligence, they had debated among themselves about what to do, but had decided that they would have to share this news with the rest of humankind as soon as possible.

Mahala listened, feeling the dilemmas and difficulties of her life suddenly contracting into an insignificant point as her mind raced toward something much greater.

"The Habbers are asking that both Earthfolk and Cytherians now join them in the exploration of space," Masud continued. "They propose to build a Habitat that will be not only a community but a voyager, a Habitat that will move across the vast interstellar distance to this alien beacon. The Habbers might have undertaken such a great voyage by themselves, but it is their wish that we join them, that people from both Earth and Venus accompany them on this journey. We have, all of us, been looking inside ourselves for too long. It is time, and long past time, that we look outward again."

Fingers closed around Mahala's arm. "I can't believe it," Solveig said, tightening her grip. "I didn't dare imagine that anything like this could happen."

Masud al-Tikriti fell silent for so long that Mahala wondered if he might be listening to some prompting from his Link. "Let me be clear about this," he said in a lower voice, "so that there will be no misunderstanding. The time of animosity and mistrust among the inhabitants of this solar system is now past. The Council of Mukhtars, the Project Council, the Administrators of the Islands and the Councilors in the settlements, and the Habbers who speak for their people—all of us must become the representatives of a united humankind."

Mahala waited, expecting him to say more, even though there was little more he could say that would add anything to what he had already said.

"More details will be forthcoming later on," Masud said, "about the plans for mining and refining operations on Mercury and for the proposed space vessel, but for now, I urge all of you to ponder what you have heard and to look forward to a new era in our history. My thoughts and prayers are with us all."

The image of Masud vanished; the screen winked out.

"Six hundred light-years," Solveig said. "Do the Habbers actually think it's possible for us to go that far in any reasonable time?"

"Obviously they do," Dyami said. He wore the same mixture of expressions Mahala had seen on Masud al-Tikriti's face: the joy and the hope and the fear and uncertainty. "They were able to increase the rotation of Venus with gravitational pulses almost a century ago. I think they're capable of designing a drive that can carry a vessel across interstellar space."

"Maybe they've already done so," Solveig said.

"Maybe," Dyami murmured.

Everything would change, Mahala thought; everything was going to be different. Hope flared within her before doubts assailed her again. Would this mean a new era of cooperation and peace, or would these new developments only fuel suspicion and distrust? Plans for an ambitious interstellar voyage might rouse people to greater efforts at cooperation, but they might also distract people from the problems of the discontented on Earth, and from the efforts that were still needed to transform Venus.

Now she understood why Dyami had been so worried about how their fellow Cytherians might react to this great change. Administrator Masud had emphasized that the Project would go on, that the effort to terraform Venus would not be neglected. But many would now be wondering if their dream might yet be abandoned and that this new project, intentionally or not, might lead them to that abandonment.

18

Two days after Masud al-Tikriti's announcement, Mukhtar Tabib al-Tahir gave a brief speech on all of the public channels. The few Guardians remaining on the Islands would be reassigned to duty on Anwara. Those who wished to remain as settlers on the surface of Venus would be allowed to resign from the Guardian forces and travel to the domes to stay, subject to the approval of each settlement's Council.

This was yet another sign that a new era of cooperation was at hand, according to the Mukhtar. But to Mahala it seemed that Mukhtar Tabib was also trying to call people back to more immediate concerns. The preparations for a voyage to a distant star where an alien civilization would reveal itself would inspire all of humankind and lead to even greater accomplishments. Yet the realization of that hope lay far in the future, seeming to be as far away as the transformation of Venus into a green and growing world.

To travel to a star system six hundred light-years away, as Solveig had explained to the excited and curious children whom she was now teaching, meant going to a place from where it took light six hundred years to reach the solar system. "After making that elementary point," Solveig continued, "I decided that an educational mind-tour would do better at presenting the paradoxes of time dilation at relativistic speeds than I could. After that, they really got excited. You mean time will slow down for the people if they're traveling at close to the speed of light? You mean only a few years will go by for them while a whole lot of years pass here? That was our lesson for the day—they weren't interested in anything else."

Mahala was silent as she walked with her friend, thinking of the challenges the journey would present. To get to the nearer stars would have been difficult enough, but to aim for a star system six hundred light-years away—it was enough to make her wonder if they were over-reaching themselves. But the effort, whatever it took, would help to bring about the new era Mukhtar Tabib had evoked, an era of change and renewal for all of humankind. There was also the promise of what awaited them in that distant star system: contact with a nonhuman culture, an alien intelligence. In the meantime, they possessed the precious and certain knowledge that they were not alone in the universe.

"I've had time to think," Solveig said, "and I still can't get over my astonishment. Even so, Mukhtar Tabib almost made me wonder if some people are having doubts about the Venus Project. It's as if he's trying to say that even if we fail here, we might succeed somewhere else eventually."

"It's much too soon to assume that the Project might fail," Mahala said.

"It still won't hurt to have something else to inspire us," Solveig murmured, "and keep us under control—another great venture to keep us occupied."

"You're sounding more cynical."

"That's not what I meant, Mahala. I do feel more inspired. There's finally something more for me to look forward to than making the best of my life here. Now I can hope that maybe I'll actually have a chance to be chosen as one of the spacefarers. It's a slim chance, but better than no chance at all."

"Yes," Mahala said, knowing that the same ambition was growing inside her.

"Of course that'll just make it even harder later on if I'm not chosen."

Maybe Solveig was thinking that someone who was subject to her dark moods would not be considered suitable for such a voyage. "I wouldn't worry about that now," Mahala said. "We don't know anything about what sorts of people might be chosen, only that they'll come from Earth, Venus, and the Habitats."

"And more specialists in astronomy and astrophysics will be needed now. Maybe I'll be able to go back to the Islands and finish my studies."

They had followed the creek to the lake. More people were out, walking near the wooded slopes or sitting in groups on the shore. The day after Administrator Masud's announcement, Mahala had reported to Tasida as scheduled, and the two had gone to the house of Tasida's pregnant patient, who had gone into labor at first light. Mahala had noticed how few people were out, how many seemed to be keeping close to their homes.

During the past days, people had resumed their usual activities. On the surface, life in Turing, and presumably in the other settlements, was going on as it had. Work in the external operations centers and maintaining life support were not tasks that could be postponed, while crops in the greenhouses still had to be tended and harvested and airships checked and repaired. The night after Masud's announcement, it was rumored that one group of people had gathered in Turing's Buddhist temple and another group at the mosque to discuss the Administrator's statement and all of its implications, and Risa had called with a tale of people in Oberg demanding a meeting with their elected Councilors.

But there had been no disturbances, nothing that indicated that any of the Cytherians were overly nervous or fearful of what might happen now. Surely the Guardians would not be leaving the Islands if the Administrative Council had expected any serious trouble.

Even so, it seemed to Mahala that the people around her were only going through the motions of normality, that their usual routines might only be a way of keeping their new concerns at bay. She suspected that most of them were also gathering to talk to friends or engaging in long discussions over all available channels with people they knew in other settlements. Risa had called three times already in the past couple of days to tell Dyami and Mahala the latest speculations among the members of her household, while Einar and Thorunn had followed an hour-long call to Solveig with several messages.

Benzi, however, had remained silent. He had been involved in the meetings that had led up to Masud's announcement; that much she knew. She did not know exactly when he had found out about the alien signal, but suspected that he had learned of it at least two years ago, when the Habbers had finally determined that it was the product of another intelligence. Now she wondered how great a role he might have played in recent events.

Mahala gazed out at the lake. "I got a message from Ragnar before," Solveig said. "He says that Frani's going to be back on pilot duty in three days. He's working darktime shifts and spending his free time on a sculpture of her."

"Didn't he say anything about everything else that's going on?"

"No. He's got his bondmate and his work and his art, and he doesn't pay much attention to anything else. If I didn't know better, I'd almost think he hadn't even heard the announcement."

"Mahala!" Someone was calling from farther up the hill. "Mahala!"

She knew the voice. Mahala turned around and looked up. Chike Enu-Barnes was making his way down the slope, his smile visible even from a distance.

"What are you doing here?" she called out.

"You must have given me a good recommendation," he said as he came up to her. "A chemical engineer at the ceramics plant said he'd looked at my record and that I could have a job here if I wanted it."

She had forgotten that she had mentioned Chike to Dyami; her uncle must have recommended him to the engineer. She clasped one of Chike's hands in greeting, suddenly overjoyed to see him, pleased to know that he would be here in Turing.

"My airship got here four hours ago," Chike continued. "I met some of the workers at the plant, and they told me I could pitch a tent on the grounds near there until I found somewhere else to live. I asked where you and your uncle lived, and they told me, so I left my things there and came here. A blond woman at his house pointed me this way."

"Amina," Mahala said as she released his hand.

"That's what she said her name was."

"You should have told us you were coming," Mahala said.

"I wanted to surprise you."

"I'm glad you're here," Mahala murmured.

"I am, too, especially now." He linked his arm through hers, then offered his other arm to Solveig. "I wanted to be here, with everything that's going on." He glanced at Mahala. "I wanted to be with you."

"Sounds as though you're worried," Solveig said.

"I am worried," Chike replied. "My brother Kesse hasn't found out much, but he suspects that much of what's going on is still being sorted out. There's a rumor on Island Two that Administrator Masud made that speech when he did because the Mukhtars pushed him into it. Supposedly Masud wanted to wait a while, until he could be more specific about future plans, but the Mukhtars wanted to lay everything out in the open to see what the reaction would be, and the Habbers agreed with them. If everything works out, we'll have this wonderful new era to look forward to, but if it doesn't, Masud al-Tikriti and Mukhtar Tabib might make very convenient scapegoats."

"They can't take back what they've said," Solveig said softly. "That would only cause even more trouble."

"They wouldn't have to take it back," Chike said. "If the plans for the Mercury operation and for an interstellar vessel and space exploration lead to unexpected problems and delays, or everything turns out to be much more costly than they anticipated, that would be enough to bring the new era to a halt. And there wouldn't be much then to keep the Habbers from launching a space expedition by themselves." He slowed his pace. "It's only rumors. I'm probably being too pessimistic—don't pay attention to me."

"I won't," Mahala said, not wanting this new dream to die so quickly.

The Garden

19

Cutting off sunlight to Venus with the Parasol had enabled the Cytherian atmosphere to precipitate into carbon dioxide, to allow sterile oceans to form without boiling away in extreme heat, and had greatly cooled the planet. Without construction of the Parasol, getting to this stage in terraforming Venus would have taken many millennia, might even have eventually proven to be impossible. Even so, the successive members of the Project Council had always known that their progress would be slow and incremental, to be measured in stages, with each completed step likely to present a new problem to be solved.

Shading Venus had cooled the surface, but had required the development of a new and hardy strain of algae, one that could survive in darkness, without photosynthesis, and feed on the planet's sulfuric acid. Extracting hydrogen from Saturn, an operation undertaken by the Habbers three centuries earlier, then sending the hydrogen sunward in massive tanks and hurling it into the Venusian atmosphere, had been necessary to create water, while the traces of ammonia in the Saturnian elements were needed to produce nitrogen.

But even massive quantities of imported hydrogen were not enough to combine with all of the free oxygen produced by the changes in the Venusian ecosphere. To remove more of the oxygen had required the construction of thick-walled robotic factories at the poles to separate the oxygen from the atmosphere, compress it, and then carry it on robot-piloted shuttles and scooper ships to the Bats, where the oxygen could either be used for other operations or flung into space. The surface operations had always been automatic, but to have cyberminds run the rest of the oxygen disposal process on the Bats would have been too costly for the Project, much more costly than training workers for duty on the two satellites. Bat duty had soon evolved into one of the Cytherian rites of passage, a way for Cytherians to earn some respect and to feel that they had important roles to play in the Project, but the cost of that duty was paid in lives.

Within a few months after the announcement of the new era and the new phase of the Project, machines that resembled diggers and crawlers, with drills and claws and shovels as attachments, were at work mining the surface of Mercury. These machines were built by Habber technology, and soon after the first machines had been sent on their journey sunward to Mercury from the Habitat nearest Venus, the mechanical miners were making new replicas of themselves from Mercury's resources and adding new attachments to their arsenal of tools. Viewing sensor images of the machines at work often produced a feeling in Mahala that the machines were more than mechanical constructions and more than mindless servants of the Project; that they were in fact a community of intelligent robots doing their work, breeding their young, and making a home for themselves on that barren and hostile surface. The electromagnetic mass drivers that the Habber robots were building were not, it seemed, there only to fling ingots of calcium and magnesium to Venus, but also to serve as a monument to this cybernetic offshoot of human civilization.

Such speculations flickered through Mahala's mind whenever she thought about the latest Habber accomplishment. Clearly such machines could have done even more of the work of terraforming on Venus herself. Fewer people, and perhaps none at all, might have had to endure shifts of largely tedious work in the external operations centers of the domes; surely similar machines might have been used to run all operations on the Bats, making it unnecessary to endanger the lives of any workers there.

But it was useless to waste even a moment brooding on such matters. Earth could more easily afford to lose people than other resources, resources harder to come by and more costly than human workers. Those laboring for the Project had also been given a purpose in life through their labors.

During the year after Administrator Masud's declaration of a new era, Mahala turned more of her attention to the Project's past. When she was not with a patient, being tested on her medical knowledge by

Tasida, analyzing medical scans, examining patients, treating injuries, administering rejuvenation therapy, or studying medical procedures, she was often reading print accounts of the Venus Project's history or calling up visual records.

Perhaps there was more of her historian grandfather Malik in her than she realized. Maybe the prospect of a new era with new challenges to be met had awakened her interest in the events that had led humankind to this juncture. Seeing how people had met and overcome the early obstacles to the Venus Project gave her more hope for the future.

What she had not expected was that the more she discovered about the Project's past difficulties, the more uncertain its present seemed to become. The people of the past, or their children and grandchildren, could expect to live to see the conclusions of various important and distinct stages of the Project—the completion of the Parasol, the construction of the Islands, and then the movement of people to the domed surface settlements. No one alive now, and no descendants who were likely even to remember present-day Cytherians, would live to see the next stages of the Project: an ocean burgeoning with life, a profusion of plants covering the land outside the domes, people able to leave the domes wearing only protective suits and masks. No one with any memory of Mahala's time and of the generations that would follow would ever walk unprotected on the surface of Venus, to breathe its air and look up at a sun only partly eclipsed by whatever remained of the Parasol.

The people who had come here had dreamed of making a new world for their children. Instead, they might only have imprisoned them, yoked them to an end that they would never see and that might never be achieved. And now there was another dream calling to them from the stars, another dream whose realization they would not live to see.

A year and a half after the dawn of the new era, Mahala grew increasingly aware that others shared many of her thoughts and her doubts.

"It's only a few people," Chike said to Mahala as they made their way along a path through the woods. He had brought a light wand with him. She was beginning to feel foolish, slipping away with him in the dark to a mysterious gathering. "I've only gone to a couple of these discussions, but this isn't the only group that gets together. There are others."

"You make it sound like some sort of conspiracy," she said.

"It's not a conspiracy, Mahala. We're just people trying to sort things out and discuss them freely, but privately."

"Did you tell Solveig about any of this?" Mahala asked.

"No, and you probably shouldn't, either. It isn't that I can't trust her, but she might inadvertently say something to Ragnar."

And you can't trust him, Mahala thought. She had known Ragnar much longer than had Chike, but now felt that she barely knew Ragnar at all. During the few times Frania had invited her and Chike and Solveig to her home, Ragnar had sat with them saying almost nothing, as if simply marking the time until they left, or else he had quickly retreated to the open area outside the house's entrance to make sketches on a screen. Occasionally he visited Dyami's house, but only to show her uncle a few of his sketches or carvings. Frania had sold a few of his carvings and sculptures to her fellow pilots and had even secured credit for a sculpture of their two cats from a Linker on Island Seven. That was as much as Mahala knew of Ragnar's life now: that he went to his shifts and worked on his art and spent much of his time by himself. He was so closed to her that she could not even tell if he was unhappy or had finally found contentment.

She and Chike came to a clearing. More of the wooded land bordering the lake had been cleared for dwellings, and two small houses now stood on the slope overlooking the lake. "Isn't that Gino's house?" she asked, recalling that her former schoolmate Gino Hislop-Carnera had moved there not long before.

"Yes. He's the one who started this group." Chike paused. "That makes this all sound more organized than it is. About two months ago, Gino and I got to talking after our shift, about the Project and what might happen now. A couple of nights later, he invited me over, and a few other people were there, and soon we were all talking about how our lives might just drag on here while the new era proceeded without us. It isn't enough, Mahala, living this way, not now. People are getting impatient."

She had entertained the same thought too many times to object. "I know," she said.

They walked toward Gino's house, which was little more than a plain square structure of prefabricated walls and two wide windows facing the lake. The entrance opened as they approached. Gino stood in the door; he motioned them inside.

They came into a small common room furnished with cushions and a small table. There was Josef Feldshuh, another one of her former schoolmates; he was the head of his team at the ceramics plant and had just been elected to Turing's Council. Seated next to him was Dianna Su, a geologist who had moved to Turing to work at its refinery not long after Chike's arrival, but the presence of the man sitting next to Dianna surprised her.

"Suleiman," she murmured as she sat down next to Dyami's old friend. Suleiman Khan still came by at least once every month or so, to share a meal with Dyami and to ask after the rest of his household. They had both been prisoners during the uprising; together, they had lived through the violence and death neither of them had ever discussed in front of her.

"This is it," Gino said as he seated himself.

"This is the group?" Mahala asked, glancing at Chike.

"Everybody who's likely to show up," Gino said. "This isn't an organization, Mahala, or a cabal, just a few friends who like to get together and talk. A couple of people who met with us before told me they wouldn't be here tonight. That may mean they don't have much to contribute to the discussion right now, or else they may be somewhere else talking with another group."

"Another group?"

"Another informal group of friends," Suleiman said. "We aren't sitting around hatching schemes or constructing plots. We're just people who share a dissatisfaction with our present situation and who now have some reason to hope for change."

The younger people were all looking at him now. "When my parents came to Venus," Suleiman continued, "it was enough for them to leave Earth and to know that they had come to a place where their children might be freer and able to have more education and to feel that they were part of a great enterprise. When the first settlers came to the domes, it was enough for them to have the work of creating new communities and to see them grow and develop. And for people like me, who were the first to be born and grow up on the surface of Venus and who lived through a time when everything we had created here might have been destroyed, it was enough to win a small measure of freedom and to know that the Project would continue. But that isn't enough for you, and perhaps it shouldn't be."

"Maybe we're just not properly grateful for what we have," Dianna Su said. "The Habbers are doing as much as they've ever done to aid the Project, even with their hopes for the interstellar expedition. We have the Mukhtars and the Project Council cooperating instead of being used by their members for various political ends. According to the statistics I've seen, our settlements are as peaceful and nearly as free of social problems and disorders as they've ever been."

"So the best we can hope for," Josef Feldshuh muttered, "is to go on the way we are, doing our work and bringing up our children and living out our lives. Is that what you're saying?"

Dianna shook her head. "Of course not. There is the alien signal. We can hope to be part of that. People who are courageous, cooperative, intelligent, and adaptable—those are the qualities they'll need."

"Along with something else," Mahala said. "They'll have to be people who are willing to leave this system knowing that they may be leaving everything they know for good, that even when they come back, everyone they remember will be long gone. The kind of people—the kind of civilization—that they return to, assuming they even want to come back, may be completely unrecognizable."

Suleiman leaned forward. "They'd come back to share whatever they discover—that's one of the expedition's purposes."

"But they could send back smaller vessels, even probes and cyberminds with records of what they've found," Mahala said. "They wouldn't have to come back themselves. Maybe, after a while, they won't want to come back, and the longer they continue on their voyage, the fewer reasons they'll have for ever returning."

"Maybe the Habbers aren't being honest about what they're really after," Gino said. "Maybe they intend for it to be a one-way trip. We don't know what they want—can we really trust them? They all got away from Venus as fast as they could during the uprising, didn't they?"

"Gino could be right," Chike said. "Whatever the people planning this voyage hope for now, their goals could change later on. The spacefarers might decide not to return after they're light-years away from this system."

"In other words," Gino added, "what's in this space voyage for us?"

"The opportunity to contact another civilization," Suleiman said. "The chance to see our species embark on a new stage in its history, to gain more knowledge about the universe, knowledge we might have had long before now if Earth hadn't had to rebuild and reclaim all that was lost centuries ago. But maybe I should be more specific than that. Maybe having the chance, however small, to become a spacefarer will be enough for some of you. Maybe that's what you must look forward to now, as those who came before you looked toward settling this world and making homes here. And those of you who are left behind can still look forward to the messages those spacefarers might send back about the alien intelligence we know is out there, to knowledge that will enlarge our view of the universe. And there's something else."

Suleiman looked around, as if wanting to make certain that he had everyone's attention. "When the voyagers do return, and I believe that they'll hold to that purpose, Cytherians who are alive today can know that their children might actually return to see the Project's fulfillment—their own children and grandchildren, not distant descendants. People alive now can hope that people who remember them, instead of unknowable descendants who may be nothing at all like us, may come back here to stand on the surface of a terraformed Venus." His thin lips curved into a smile. "That's something else to inspire us all, isn't it?"

By the time Mahala left Gino's house with Chike, the discussion of the inspirational value of the space expedition had degenerated into a venting of personal discontents. Gino was finding his work as a maintenance worker in the ceramics plant increasingly tedious and was thinking of volunteering for Bat duty for no better reason than to have a change in his routine and to earn more credit. Josef's brief time as a member of the Turing Council was already making him exasperated with the petty complaints people brought to his attention. Mahala had nodded and listened and remained largely silent, as had Chike.

She held Chike's hand as they walked. He had become her closest friend while living in Turing, as close to her as Frania had once been, as Solveig was now, perhaps even closer. He was living in a small dormitory in the east dome with a few other young men who were waiting until they found bondmates before erecting their own homes.

Chike had never even hinted that he might ask for a pledge from her, although the people closest to both of them seemed to assume that they would become bondmates in time. She did not know if she loved him, but mulling over whether she truly did or not seemed pointless. He was kind; he challenged her intellectually; she cared deeply about his welfare and his happiness. He saw her as an intelligent, responsible, and decent person, so she tried to live up to his impression of her and that probably made her a better person than she might have been otherwise. Maybe that was what love was.

"What did you think?" Chike said as they climbed the hill to Dyami's house.

"I don't know," she replied. "Sitting around and talking doesn't do any harm, but it doesn't do much good, either."

"Everybody there wants a chance to be a spacefarer," Chike said, "whatever complaints they may have otherwise."

Mahala shook her head. "The interstellar expedition will need specialists, astronomers and physicists, people with Solveig's interests, people with a lot of training and education."

"They'll need all kinds of people. You're not talking about a crew on a smaller vessel like a torchship—these spacefarers will have to become a community. We don't know how they'll be selected or what the criteria might be."

"We don't even know who's doing the selecting," she said. "The Habbers? I don't think the Mukhtars and the Project Council would settle for that. And they've been conspicuously silent about their plans ever since that first announcement."

"They're probably just waiting until they have more to say."

"And you think there's something to accomplish in the meantime by sitting around talking about it."

"All I know is that I want to be one of those spacefarers, Mahala, and so do you. Maybe exchanging ideas with people who have the same ambition will help us think of ways to achieve it."

They had come to Dyami's house. Chike sometimes stayed over with her, since Solveig did not mind sleeping in the common room when they wanted to be together. But Solveig would already be asleep, and Mahala had to be up in a few hours to see patients.

"I wonder how many of the people we know would actually go if given the chance," she said.

"Some of them wouldn't. Most of them might even turn down the chance in the end. But they'd still know that others were going."

The ship, or worldlet, would be a Habber vessel. Ever since the announcement, she had pondered the probable duration of the journey. The spacefarers would be a kind of community, as Chike had said. Some assumed that this meant that children, and perhaps more than one generation, would grow up inside the voyager and come to consider it their home.

But there were other possibilities that might not be openly acknowledged but which had been in her mind for some time. Habbers would be among the voyagers; they might even constitute most of the spacefarers. In any case, whatever their numbers, they could hardly expect to have a stable, functioning community aboard their vessel while living out their greatly extended lives in the midst of much shorter-lived companions. Those who became spacefarers would not only be gaining a chance to explore the universe; they were also likely to gain a life span that might be measured in centuries.

If a new era was truly coming for her world, for Earth, and for the Habbers, how much longer would Earthfolk and Cytherians remain content with their shorter lives?

"I don't think many would refuse to go," Mahala said, "not with a chance at a lifetime of hundreds of years. That's also what's at stake here. Longer life spans for all the voyagers are almost a necessity for such a mission to succeed."

"I know. It's easier to tell yourself that you don't mind having a reasonably good century and a quarter or so if you know that's all there's going to be. I don't know how many people would settle for that if they had a real chance for more."

She thought of the patients whom she scanned and treated and advised on their habits and occasionally counseled. The work had its satisfactions. Relieving chronic pain, replacing prematurely worn out or damaged organs, doing gene therapy on an afflicted fetus or infant, ridding people of infections and taking precautions so that contagious infections would not spread—everything she did, however frustrating and exhausting it might be sometimes, made life better for those around her. But there were times when it seemed that she and Tasida were only practicing an imperfect, stunted art, a medicine that a Habber might view as barely superior to the chants and spells of a shaman.

"When you think about it," she said, "you have to wonder why the Habbers decided that this interstellar mission should be a unified undertaking, why they didn't just decide to go by themselves."

"It could be simply that they're as naïve as they seem," Chike said, "and thought this was the best way to do it. Maybe it's what you claimed once, that they fear becoming too different from the rest of the species and need other people among them now. Mahala—" He paused. "You might as well know. Gino asked me if your Habber relatives had told you anything, if you might know something we don't. I told him you didn't know anything, that they hadn't contacted you in a while, so now he knows that you don't have any influence with them. I thought you ought to know that."

"It's all right. You can tell them that Benzi hasn't had a message from me in almost a year, since he never bothered to reply to the ones I sent." She did not even know if Malik was still aboard the Habber ship orbiting Venus or had returned to his Hab. "Nothing I do can possibly improve Gino's chances at being chosen to be a spacefarer. Strange how things turn out. Once I got trouble from others for my Habber connections, and now they may actually improve my social status."

He laughed, then kissed her.

The announcement came over a public channel, just as Mahala was preparing to leave for Oberg. The statement was delivered by one of Masud al-Tikriti's aides. The two domes of Sagan, one of the new settlements in the Akna Mountains, were ready to receive their first settlers. Prefabricated dormitories had been set up as temporary living quarters, and workers and specialists of all kinds were needed. Cytherians between the ages of twenty and fifty were preferred, but all settlers looking for more space and a role in establishing a new community were encouraged to apply. Fifty Habbers were also planning to join the settlers, and other Habbers would soon be joining them to assist in the landscaping of the dome environments and in subsequent tasks.

Dyami blanked the wall screen. "Nothing unusual about that," he said, "except the number of Habbers. There won't be more than a thousand settlers in the domes during the first year. One Habber or more for each twenty settlers is a higher percentage than usual."

Mahala stood up. She was twenty now; maybe it was time for her to move out of Dyami's house. He had welcomed Amina and then Tasida; he had made a home for her, for Frania, and had given Ragnar and then Solveig a place to stay. He had originally built his house as a refuge for himself and then had willingly opened up that refuge to others. He deserved some of the solitude he had once sought.

"Maybe I should apply for a place in Sagan," Mahala said. "Haroun Delassi is almost through with his apprenticeship to Tasida, so he might be willing to take my place as her assistant."

Dyami looked up at her from his cushion. "Tasida tells me that you could be a fine physician yourself. Maybe it's time you took the test and became a specialist."

"I should try for that. I'd still rather work with an older physician for a while, though."

"It might be interesting for you," Dyami said, "being in the new settlement. With the number of Habbers that will be there, it sounds a bit like Turing used to be when I first came here. There were two hundred Cytherians, and about fifty Habbers, and we lived in the simplest of prefab shacks and dormitories, and whenever we weren't working, we sat around with the Habbers and discussed all manner of subjects. I suppose you could call those talks seminars, in a way. I always felt that I had learned more by going to Turing than to the Island school that had accepted me, and when I think back on those early days now, it seems the happiest time of my life."

That had been before the followers of Ishtar, before her mother and those around her, had turned Turing into a prison. Her uncle had never spoken so openly about that time to her, about what had been taken away from him.

"Balin taught me some mathematics," he continued, "and I used him as one of my models when I began to sculpt. Sometimes he came to the refinery when I was casting molds after my shift, and we'd talk until—" His voice trailed off, and she heard in it how much he missed Balin.

"Solveig might want to move to Sagan, too," Mahala said.

"She wouldn't have any young students to teach. There won't be any children there until the settlement's further along."

"If she wants to go there badly enough, she probably wouldn't mind doing any kind of work they choose to give her."

"You should think about it while you're visiting Risa and Sef," Dyami said. "It might be very rewarding for you. I could almost wish I was going to Sagan myself."

"You could apply," Mahala said. "You're only forty-four, and—"

"I'd only be trying to recapture something that's past, Mahala. I've made a life for myself here."

She went to him and hugged him. At last he let her go and got to his feet. "Come on," he said, "you're going to be late for your airship, and it's almost time for my shift at the refinery. I'll walk with you that far."

Three airships were cradled in Turing's bay. Mahala walked into the bay, then set down her duffel just inside the open entrance. At her left, a tall brown-haired woman was engaged in a spirited discussion with Wendolyn Marliss, the paramedic on duty. Mahala nodded sympathetically at Wendolyn, remembering her own experiences during her times on duty in the bay. Bay medical duty was usually easy work, often requiring no more than a quick look at medscan results and verifying that a passenger was cleared for travel, but occasionally someone arrived who was incubating a virus or bacterium that, at least theoretically, might prove virulent and spread among people in other domes who had not been exposed to it before.

"But I have to get to Lyata," the woman was saying to the paramedic. "My sister is expecting me. She's probably in the middle of giving birth to my nephew right now."

"All the more reason to make sure you don't pass anything on to him that could be dangerous," Wendolyn murmured soothingly. "The cybermind tells me that this is a new virus, so it'll take a couple of hours to make a specific antidote, but we should have you cleared and ready to leave no more than twelve hours from now."

"I'll lose almost one whole day off. I only have five."

"I'm sorry. You'll have to stay here, too." Wendolyn gestured toward a waiting area of chairs, cushions, and three cots near the lavatory door. The whole problem could have been avoided had the passenger gone to a physician or paramedic for a scan earlier, as all travelers were advised to do; she would have been treated then and have been cleared by now. But there were always a few people who did not bother to get scanned until they came to the bay.

Wendolyn glanced at the results of Mahala's scan on her small screen, then waved her ahead, as Mahala had expected; Tasida had scanned her in their examination room. She hurried toward a group of people standing near one airship cradle. The airship cabin, looking small under the vast metallic bullet-shaped balloon of helium cells that fueled the dirigible, was nested in the cradle.

No one had yet opened the doors or lowered the ramps for passengers to board.

"Oberg?" Mahala asked.

A gray-haired man nodded at her. "Yes, but this gasbag isn't leaving for another hour at least. The pilots say a failed component needs to be replaced."

Across the cavernous bay, a few more people stood near another cradle holding an airship. Several tall crates of cargo formed a wall partly blocking her view, and then a tall figure with a long blond braid moved out from behind a crate.

"Ragnar," Mahala whispered. He had seen her; he stood still and waited as she walked toward him. The five people with him were all young, and one of them was Ouray Chang, whom Mahala had examined only yesterday, to make certain that he was fit for Bat duty. She suddenly knew why Ragnar was here.

"Greetings, Mahala," Ouray said.

She ignored him. "You volunteered," she said to Ragnar. "You're going to one of the Bats, aren't you."

He gazed at her steadily. She wanted to lash out at him, but could not tell him that he was taking a risk he did not have to take in front of others who had made the same choice. She could not consider his life more precious than theirs, or their lives more expendable.

Ouray's eyes shifted from Mahala to Ragnar, and then he drifted discreetly away, followed by the others. "Yes," Ragnar said, "I volunteered."

"When did this happen?" She kept her voice low.

"Five days ago. They gave me a job monitoring the automatic ship operations, so I'll be in a control room or a lock most of the time. I won't be suited up and out on the docks."

"Unless they suddenly need a few extra people to replace failed components."

Ragnar's mouth twisted. "There's always that chance, but the odds are I'll be relatively safe. Frani'll be at the Platform when our airship gets there, so we'll have a few hours together before my shuttle leaves for the southern Bat."

"So you told her what you were going to do."

"Of course I told her. She's my bondmate. She didn't want me to go, but it didn't exactly come as a surprise to her, and I had to arrange things with my team leader at work. I gave our cats to a household in the east dome—they're having more trouble with vermin there, so they can use them. And I sent a message to the Turing Council today saying that any new arrivals who need a place to stay temporarily could use the house." He looked away for a moment. "That's unless you and Solveig want to move there for a while."

She tried to imagine it, living in his house, thinking of the life she might have had there with him.

"Did you even tell Solveig?" she asked.

"I sent her a message just before coming here."

"Because you knew she'd be with her students and wouldn't listen to your message until later. You knew she'd try to talk you out of this if you told her any sooner."

"Maybe she wouldn't have," Ragnar said. "Maybe she would have figured this was my business."

"You don't have to do this," she said. "You can tell them you've changed your mind."

"And get a black mark for not honoring a commitment I made freely? I have enough marks on my record already. And I don't know why you're so concerned."

She could not explain it to him. There were people she knew whom she would have argued with if they had volunteered, but in the end, she would have accepted their decisions. If Chike had come to her and told her that he was going to work on a Bat, she would have pleaded with him not to go and worried about his safety, but she would not have had feelings of fear and panic, because she could trust Chike's judgment. Others volunteered for Bat duty out of a sense of obligation, to make extra credit, to win some status for themselves, and all of them intended to finish their work there somewhat better off than when they started. They all expected to live. Ragnar might have some of their reasons for volunteering, but there were others— to prove himself, maybe even to risk a life he did not seem to value all that much.

"They're looking for settlers to move to Sagan now," Mahala said. "You might have tried for that instead."

"I heard the announcement."

That's where you belong, she thought, not on a Bat. You should be in a place where you won't be alone so much and where you're relatively safe and where you can pursue your art among people who might appreciate it. The Habbers might have offered him a sympathy and an understanding that he had been unable to find among Cytherians. She was not sure why she was so certain of that; maybe it was because of what Dyami had said about his early days in Turing being so happy. The Habbers working in Sagan might have found a way to reach out to Ragnar.

"Well," she said.

"Well, Mahala. You had your chance to worry about what I did with my life and to be involved with me. You turned it down. So don't start telling me what to do now." He turned around and walked away from her.

Risa and Sef's household was as full of people as ever, and all of their housemates were there to welcome Mahala. Kyril Anders, the son of Barika Maitana and Kristof Anders, was now thirteen and hoping for a chance to study geology at an Island school; his sister Liesel Maitana, born five years ago, had grown into a sturdy child with her mother's black hair and warm brown eyes. Akilah Ching, the daughter of Risa's housemates Hoa Ching and Jamil Owens, was eleven, already strikingly beautiful, and intensely curious about Mahala's work as a paramedic. Also crowded around the table were Paul Bettinas and Grazie Lauro, along with Kolya Burian and Noella Sanger, who divided their time between this house and that of Noella's children.

Risa had lived her life among others, welcoming people into her household, concerning herself with the public affairs of Oberg and the other settlements. She was eighty-three now, her black hair showing more gray streaks, the lines around her brown eyes a bit more sharply etched; she had lived out most of her life, but could expect to go on for at least three or four more decades. She still worked her shifts at the External Operations Center and the community greenhouses, although with more time off than when she was younger. None of the brief messages she had sent to Mahala during the past two years, messages filled with news of Oberg, had given any indication of how Risa felt about the changes that might come to her world. Mahala thought of her visit here four years ago, when Risa had spoken of her regrets and of her feeling that the Habbers might abandon this system.

The people sitting around the long low table talked, asked about

Dyami, then left it to Grazie to relate recent Oberg gossip while they dined on fish Kolya had caught, bread Sef had baked, and fruits and vegetables from the household's greenhouse. Mahala felt easier with the household than she had during past visits, maybe because she had stayed away long enough to miss them and to imagine the life she might have had if she had stayed here with her grandmother. She might have become Paul's medical apprentice and lived on in this house. Her bonds to these people and this community would have been so strong by now that it might have been almost impossible for her to break them, even for a chance at becoming part of the interstellar mission.

They ended the supper with some tea and a new concoction Andrew Dinel was now distilling and selling, a pale sweet alcoholic beverage its creator had ostentatiously dubbed Dinel's Cytherian Nectar. As Mahala had expected, Risa wanted to take a walk with her after supper, as she had so often during earlier visits.

"Going to see Yakov?" Sef asked. Yakov Serba was still on the Oberg Council and still often consulted with Risa.

"No," Risa replied, "just a walk. We might stop by to see Ah Lin Bergen."

"Risa's trying to talk your old schoolmate into running for the Council," Grazie said, "now that a seat's opened up. Have you convinced her yet?"

"No," Risa said, leading Mahala to the doorway.

"She is a bit young to think of running," Grazie said.

"Maybe we need some younger people on the Council," Barika said as she picked up an empty platter.

The door closed behind Mahala and her grandmother. "If you'd stayed here," Risa murmured, "maybe I would have been trying to convince you to run for the Council." She said it gently, as though she was only ruminating on a possibility rather than regretting a lost opportunity. "Ah Lin would like to see you while you're here. She's sorry she hasn't sent you more messages."

"I haven't sent her any for a while, either, so there's no reason for her to apologize." Mahala paused. "So you think she'd make a good Councilor."

"I think she'd be a good Councilor for Oberg. Whether that would be the best thing for her to do with her life right now is another matter." Risa was walking along the path in the direction of the west dome's lake. "Have you heard anything from Benzi or from Malik?"

"No, I haven't."

"I didn't think so. I had a message from Benzi a few days ago. He didn't say much more than that he had been spending a lot of his time with the Administrative Council and that Malik would be returning to the Islands soon, after the orbiting Habber ship docks at Anwara. Apparently the Habbers don't feel it necessary to keep a crew of observers in Venus orbit anymore."

"Benzi didn't tell you much then."

"I think he just wanted us to know that he and Malik hadn't completely forgotten about us." Risa turned from the main road onto a dirt path, then halted. "Here we are."

Her grandmother had stopped in front of a walled enclosure that adjoined a small house. Mahala had not seen this house before. "Is this where Ah Lin lives now?"

"She and two friends put it up about a year ago and moved in." Risa gazed at the scanner lens embedded in the entrance, then pressed her hand against the door.

The door opened. Mahala followed Risa into a small grassy courtyard, where five people sat on blankets. Ah Lin Bergen was among them; the young woman got to her feet.

"Risa," Ah Lin said, and then she clasped Mahala's hands. "Mahala, I'm glad she brought you."

Risa seated herself; Mahala sat down next to her. Ah Lin passed them cups of tea. Eugenio Tokugawa was here, along with Mahala's former schoolmates Devaki Patel and Ellie Ruiz. The young man sitting next to Ellie was a stranger.

"You know everyone here, except for Tomas." Ah Lin gestured at the young man, who had broad shoulders, a dark drooping mustache, and wore a pin with a chemist's beaker on his collar. "Tomas Sechen. He moved to Oberg a few months ago. This is Mahala Liangharad—she's Risa's granddaughter. Mahala went to an Island school, too."

Tomas Sechen gazed at her impassively. "I was on Island Seven," he said in a low-pitched voice, "but I grew up in the Galileo settlement."

"Tomas is working in the main dome's labs," Devaki Patel said.

"For a year," Tomas added, "and then I'll have to find something else, preferably in another settlement. There isn't room for many more new arrivals in Oberg."

"New settlers are needed in Sagan," Ah Lin said. "I wish I could go there myself, but they're not going to need teachers for a while."

"Put your name in now, Ah Lin," Risa said, "and when they do need teachers, you'll have a better chance of getting permission to move there later."

Mahala turned toward her grandmother, surprised. Apparently Risa was not here to pressure Ah Lin into running for the Council.

"I may try for a place in Sagan," Tomas said.

"If I were younger," Risa said, "I'd ask to go myself." She finished her tea and set down her cup. "And it wouldn't be just so that I could recapture my childhood, when there wasn't much in Oberg except for grass and young trees and tents for us to live in until we could put up some houses."

"Maybe we should tell Mahala why we're here," Ah Lin said.

"I'll tell her." Risa leaned back against the wall. "We're here to talk. We're here to consider what might happen to the Project now. I'm older than all of you—I can look back and feel that I've contributed in my own way to getting us this far, and there's some satisfaction in that. But some of you younger people have the opportunity for another kind of accomplishment."

"We've been having these meetings for a few months now," Ah Lin said, "sometimes here, sometimes with other people elsewhere. Tomas says that a few people he knows in Galileo were getting together to talk."

"In Turing, too," Mahala said. "I've gone to three such meetings already. We sit around and talk about what might happen and what we'd like to see happen and whether or not any of us has a chance at becoming a spacefarer and even whether or not that expedition will ever become a reality."

"Habbers are long-lived," Ellie murmured. "We don't even know exactly how long-lived. They're probably used to thinking in the long term, so maybe there's no real reason to expect any interstellar expedition to become a reality during our lifetimes."

"Then why did they ever reveal their hopes to us?" Tomas asked. "Why didn't they just keep quiet about the alien signal until their plans were further along?"

Devaki let out her breath. "We sit here and talk, but others will decide things, and we'll have almost nothing to say about it."

"You may believe that if you like," Risa said. "It isn't the way I've led my life. Whatever mistakes I made, I didn't let others decide my life for me." She kept her gaze on Devaki for a few moments, then looked away.

"Now I'll tell you young people what I came here to say," Risa continued. "Some years ago, when he was about your age, my son Dyami went to live in Turing as one of its first settlers. There were a fair number of Habbers there to aid those early settlers, and for a short time, before the followers of Ishtar started making the lives of anyone who objected to their cursed cult miserable, those Habbers and Cytherians were able to bridge the distance between their people and ours. They were able to become friends and to form strong bonds. They saw themselves as comrades—so Dyami has told me, and I have heard the same from a few who shared those times with him. I think those Habbers in Turing a couple of decades ago were already dreaming of the new era that we are supposed to be entering now. I think that they were hoping to learn more from us and to teach us. Those settlers in Turing and the Habbers with them might have been early signs of a new era. But Ishtar put a stop to that."

"You think that Sagan may become what Turing was supposed to be," Mahala said.

Risa smiled. "You understand what I'm getting at."

"Dyami mentioned his early times in Turing before I left," Mahala said. "He said they were the happiest times of his life."

"Maybe Sagan will be a place like that," Risa said, "in which case anybody applying to go there now might have a chance at something different, a chance to learn from the Habbers. I often wish that I'd valued learning more when I was younger. And there would also be the work of establishing a new settlement. That's something to look back on and to take pride in when you get to be my age."

Ah Lin nodded. "You've given me something to think about, Risa. Everybody says that you always seemed to have a sense about what was going on that might not be obvious to other people and that you knew how to take advantage of it."

Risa shook her head. "Those stories are exaggerated."

"You're one of the most influential people in Oberg," Ellie said.

"That's also an exaggeration. I've simply lived here longer than most people. When you're around long enough, people often assign you more importance than you actually have." Risa rested a hand on Mahala's shoulder as she got to her feet. "I've said what I have to say. It's time for me to go home."

Mahala looked up. "Should I—"

"Stay here, child," her grandmother interrupted, "and visit with your friends."

June 653
From: Mahala Liangharad, Oberg
To: Chike Enu-Barnes, Turing

I've already sent a message to Solveig, but I wanted to tell you, too, before we talk about this.

I've decided to apply to be one of the first to settle in Sagan. I have a feeling you're thinking of doing the same thing. Part of it is that I've been living with my uncle long enough, and it's time for me to start making my own life. Being here, seeing what's happened to some of my childhood friends—there are a few, like Ah Lin Bergen, who decided to set up their own households or live with friends, but several of them are still members of their family's households, and the ones who aren't have bondmates and homes in Oberg. They're doing just what they expected to do, and you get the feeling their children may do the same. A few have moved to settlements where there's more space, but after a while, many of them may end up living in the same way they would have here, with their bondmates and their households and . . .

Not that I'm holding myself above them. The fact is that I can understand it, staying with people who care about you and living that way, settling into the kind of life most people have here. That would be easier than wanting something else and not even being that sure of what it is that you want, the way it is with both of us.

Anyway, I'll be very surprised if Solveig doesn't try to get on the first list for Sagan. They won't need teachers yet, but she could do other kinds of work. Dyami and Amina and Tasida would miss us, but they would understand, especially since they did the same thing themselves when they were our age. Dyami was even encouraging me to consider moving to Sagan before I left to come here.

What really surprised me is that my grandmother is suggesting that I do the same thing. Here I was, thinking that once I got here, Risa would start hinting that this was my home once and that living with Dyami was all very well but that maybe I should consider coming back to Oberg and she could always add another room if she had to, and instead she's saying that Sagan may offer us a chance to learn and provide opportunities we might not otherwise have.

I had just about made up my mind to try for the new settlement anyway, but having her encouragement along with Dyami's doesn't hurt.

You'll want to go there, too, I'm sure of it. You'd want to go even if I didn't. I think I know you well enough to predict that. But I'll tell you this now anyway.

My grandmother sent a message to Benzi. She mentioned it to me. She told him that the old might be content to look back, but that young people should look forward, and that the young people here were meeting and talking and wondering if anything was going to come of this new era. I don't think she expected a message, but she got one, and here it is in its entirety:

Tell them that their patience will be rewarded, and that the stars will soon be within our reach.

20

The passenger cart carrying Mahala and Solveig emerged from the lighted tunnel that connected Turing's north and south domes and continued along the wide main road. Mahala glanced at the forested area on her right. The trees were still thick, but more houses stood on the land that had been cleared near the woods; a wide roadway for passenger carts now ran through the forest. Turing was getting more crowded.

Mahala had passed both her written and medical simulation tests and had won her physician's pin four months ago, just after returning from her visit to Oberg. She had been correct in thinking that this would give her a better chance at getting on the list for Sagan; the new settlement needed physicians, since not many had applied to go there.

Solveig, happily, would be going to Sagan with her. There would be work for her in the greenhouses and with the diggers and crawlers, on which she was already training. Chike would also be going. He had sent a message only a few hours ago informing her of that, followed by another saying that he had heard from their former schoolmate Stephan AnnasLeonards, and that Stephan would be meeting them in Sagan. Mahala, intrigued, had called up more records and had found out that all of the students who had been with her on Anwara had also been chosen for the settlement.

"What are you brooding about?" Solveig asked.

"Just that it seems quite a coincidence that everybody who came to Anwara with us is also going to Sagan."

"I thought so, too, but maybe it isn't so strange. The Administrators would see that we were able to adapt to Anwara, so they might assume that all of us could adapt even more easily to living in a new settlement."

Mahala wondered if the Administrators had actually made the final decisions about who would go to Sagan. Their cyberminds would have eliminated the obviously unsuitable from the list, and the Administrators would also have conferred with Councilors in each of the surface settlements, but there had been rumors for some time that Habbers had also been consulted, perhaps as a bow to the announced new era of cooperation and friendship.

The cart came to a stop; the four people sitting in front of them in the vehicle got out and walked toward the long metal wall of the refinery. On Mahala's left, across from the refinery on the other side of the wide main road, a few people were taking an exercise break outside the large glassy dome of the ceramics plant. The cart rolled on toward the airship bay at the end of the road.

A new wing had been added to the dormitory that housed the pilots who had to stay over in Turing. Mahala and Solveig had thought of sending Frania a message, but then had decided to come here to tell her their news. Frania, who had arrived in Turing after last light, had claimed in her message that she did not want to stay in her own house, since Ragnar would not be there and she did not want to disturb anyone using it as a temporary residence; it was easier for her to stay with the other pilots, since she would be leaving in two days anyway.

The cart stopped near the entrance to the airship bay. Mahala followed Solveig out of the cart and toward the dormitory. The entrance opened as they approached; two young men in the blue coveralls of pilots came outside.

"Looking for somebody?" the dark-haired young man asked.

"Frania Milus," Mahala replied.

"I was Frani's copilot on this run." The man slapped his palm against the door, opening it for them.

In the common room, several pilots in blue coveralls sat on the floor around one of the low tables, drinking tea or beer as they talked. Frania was there, murmuring to the female pilot next to her; everyone at the table suddenly laughed. Frania had cut her hair short since Mahala had last seen her; she sat on a cushion, legs folded, looking happier and more confident than she ever had before.

She looked up; her smile widened. "Mahala," she said. "Solveig. I didn't expect you to come all the way over here just to walk me to the house for dinner." Before Mahala could reply, Frania was asking them to sit down and introducing the other pilots at the table. She seemed more at ease with these people than she ever had in Ragnar's presence.

"We have some good news," Mahala said at last. "Solveig and I are going to be moving to Sagan."

"That's wonderful," Frania said. Her companions were soon talking about the new settlement. One young woman whose name Mahala had already forgotten told them that she was scheduled to ferry a few people to Sagan from the Islands; a brown-haired young man, flirting with Solveig, went to fetch her and Mahala two glasses of ale.

The pilots talked of their recent runs and the plans they had made for their brief time off in Turing. Mahala drank her ale, content to listen to them. Frania, usually so quiet, had as much to say as any of her companions.

After a while, the others drifted outside or off to rooms to rest. "We should probably go," Frania said.

"It's early yet," Solveig replied.

"I know, but we might as well take our time."

"We can take the long way around through the west dome and stop at your house," Mahala added.

Frania's smile faded. "Other people are living there now," she said.

"They wouldn't mind if you stopped by. After all, it's still your house."

Something flickered in Frania's eyes. "It's Ragnar's house," she said softly. "That's how I've always thought of it, as Ragnar's house." She got to her feet in one swift movement. "Let's go."

They left the dormitory. Frania was silent until they came to the main road. They kept to the side of the road, moving at a slow but steady pace.

"I am happy about your news," Frania said at last. "I may see you in Sagan before long. I've asked for duty ferrying people and supplies there."

"I thought you were scheduled for more of the shuttle routes," Solveig said. Piloting shuttles meant more opportunities to be with Ragnar on the southern Bat, even for brief visits.

"I was. I can ask for a change. Most of the younger pilots prefer shuttle duty. It keeps our skills honed, and it means more time on the Islands between trips. They won't have any problem finding someone to replace me." Frania's voice sounded brittle. "I might even decide to move to Sagan myself if they'll let me."

"Is Ragnar thinking of living there?" Solveig asked.

"Ragnar has another year on Bat duty," Frania said, "and then he gets some time off, and then he can either go back to the work he had before or sign up for another tour on a Bat."

"He wouldn't do that again," Solveig said. "He couldn't."

"You haven't talked to him lately," Frania said. "You see, he has this idea. If he can earn enough credit to fulfill more of his responsibility to the Project, he can take longer periods of time off, and that means he'll have more time for his designs and his sculptures. He can do a little work, greenhouse duty and whatever else, just so everyone will know he's still a functioning member of the community, but most of the time, he wants to do as he likes. He's not talking about a month or two off—he's thinking of years."

"He can't," Solveig said.

"That's what I told him. I didn't want him going to a Bat in the first place. I did everything I could to talk him out of it—I even threatened to go to the Turing Council and ask for permission to break our bond early."

"That's a pretty strong threat," Mahala said. It was not unknown for bondmates to ask to have their bond severed officially, but the usual practice was to make any necessary arrangements privately and then live apart, as if only temporarily separating. Anyone who could not keep a pledge was considered untrustworthy by others, and perhaps less likely to keep other promises.

"It was also a pointless threat." Frania picked up her pace, as if suddenly wanting to get to their destination as quickly as possible. "Ragnar pointed out that if I had wanted to put a clause in our agreement about not volunteering for Bat duty for the duration of our bond, I should have said so before we made our pledge."

"But that's ridiculous," Mahala said. "Nobody's going to ask for a promise that might keep a partner from—"

"I know. I did what anybody else would have done. What I didn't expect is that he'd come up with the idea of volunteering again and putting in even more—"

Frania stopped suddenly. Mahala and Solveig stood with her at the side of the road as a passenger cart rolled past them.

"It isn't working," Frania continued. "It isn't working out at all." Her head was bowed, her shoulders slumped. The confidence she had shown among her fellow pilots was gone; she was again the shy, uncertain child she once had been. "I thought that I could live like this, but I can't."

"Ragnar must love you," Solveig said. It was the kind of remark

Mahala would expect Solveig to make about her brother, useless and possibly untruthful as it was.

Frania's eyes narrowed. "I don't know if he loves me or not. That isn't why he wanted a bond anyway. He wanted someone to hang on to, somebody to keep him from being completely alone, but he still made sure he picked somebody who would have to go off and leave him by himself most of the time."

Mahala felt sympathy for Frania, but her pity for Ragnar was mixed with fury at him for causing her friend pain. "How can he treat you this way?" she asked.

"Oh, Mahala—I knew what he was like. I saw what our life together was probably going to be like, and then I told myself that maybe I was wrong, that maybe he would change."

"So what are you going to do?" Solveig asked. "Break your bond? That might be easier to do here than in some of the other settlements—people here are a little more understanding of such things."

"No," Frania said, "I won't do that."

They continued along the road, Mahala and Solveig on either side of Frania. "What's the point of an open break anyway?" Frania went on. "That would only make things worse for him, for both of us. We don't see each other that much, and whether I spend my time off here or in a new settlement doesn't really matter. If he wants to be alone, he can come back here, but maybe he'll want to stay with me in Sagan if I'm there. And maybe he'll decide later that being in Sagan is more interesting than signing up for another stretch on a Bat." Frania put a hand on Mahala's arm. "It'll be different there, won't it? A new start for the new era—that's what some are calling it. Maybe that's what Ragnar needs."

Frania left long after last light, in better spirits and with some of the assurance that she had displayed among her fellow pilots restored. She would come back tomorrow, to share another meal and to have more time with her aunt Amina.

"You needn't come in early tomorrow," Tasida said to Mahala after Frania was gone. "We don't have anything scheduled after first light except analyzing medscans."

"That's why I should be there," Mahala said. "We should discuss who's going to replace me."

Tasida shrugged. "We'll have plenty of time for that. It'll probably be Haroun—he'll be expecting me to take him on, now that you're leaving, and he did very well as an apprentice."

Chike had sent a message, saying that he would be working a late shift tonight. "I'll go meet Chike at first light," Mahala said, "and then join you after that."

Tasida glanced at Amina. "It's good that you'll both be going to Sagan," the physician said. Tasida and Amina would not say so outright, but they obviously expected her and Chike to make a pledge before too much longer.

Solveig yawned. Dyami stood up. "Time to get some sleep," he said, and then his eyes narrowed. "It seems we have visitors."

Mahala turned toward the glassy walls at the front of the common room. The soft glow of a light wand held by a slender shadowy form moved through the darkness, trailed by another indistinct shadow. "Frani's back," Mahala said, recognizing the blue of a pilot's coverall in the light, "and somebody's with her."

Dyami went to the door as it opened. Frania came inside, saying, "We met each other a little way from the bridge, so I thought I might as well walk back with him, and—"

"Balin," Dyami said as the Habber emerged from the darkness.

"I should have sent a message," Balin said, "but I've only been on Island Two for three days, and I didn't want to tell you anything until—"

"—and maybe you simply wanted to surprise me," Dyami said softly.

"That, too."

The two men gazed at each other in silence, and then their arms were around each other. Amina glanced at Tasida, then beckoned to Mahala and Solveig.

"Come on," Amina whispered as she led them all to the door; Frania followed them outside.

"Frani," Amina said then, "I'll walk back to the dormitory with you and ask if your comrades can spare me a bed. I've got a day-long shift at the refinery, starting early, so I won't be there long." She turned toward Mahala. "And maybe you two won't mind sleeping at the office with Tasida tonight."

"Of course not," Mahala said.

"Let them have at least a bit of time to themselves." Amina looked back at the house. "Dyami's missed him so much. He got past the worst of it, but I wondered if he would ever get completely past it, and now—" She sighed. "I hope it isn't just for a little while, before Balin leaves again."

"Now that I know I'll be leaving in a month," Mahala said, "I'm beginning to miss Turing already."

"You're not sorry you agreed to go to Sagan," Chike said.

"No, I'm not."

She sat with him on a slope overlooking the north dome's lake. Frania had left Turing; she had not wanted to visit her house herself, but had asked Mahala and Chike to check on it for her. The three young women living there were keeping the place neat and had acquired three cats of their own, who kept the house free of mice and the other small creatures that had established small colonies in all of the settlements despite the best efforts of the settlers. Two of them had asked about the figurines Ragnar had carved in wood or cast in metal that sat on the shelves of one common room wall, wanting to know if they were for sale. Mahala would send a message to Frania about that and let her handle any arrangements.

She thought about one carving she had seen, of her own face, and wondered when Ragnar had carved it and why he had given her an expression that seemed both pensive and implacable.

"I was thinking," Chike said, "of asking you something before we leave Turing. Maybe this is the time to ask you—" He paused. "To ask you if you would consider becoming my bondmate."

"Chike—"

"Let me finish, Mahala." He reached for her hand. "The reason I haven't asked before is that I was almost certain you'd say no, not because you don't care for me but because you've decided that we have a bond already." He shook his head. "That isn't what I meant to say. I meant that whether we have a bond or not, we'll be together, that there will always be something between us."

Mahala said, "That's exactly how I feel. You didn't have to say it."

"It was time to say it."

"I love you," she said, "and I always will love you in some way, and that's enough right now."

"That's just the way I feel."

Mahala thought of Dyami and Balin. Balin had said little to her uncle's housemates except that he would be staying at Turing's Habber residence while setting up some new educational programs for Turing's children and young people. Balin had hinted that he might seek Dyami's advice and that the new programs would be a more radical departure from the standard primary curriculum. Presumably Balin's efforts were a part of the new era, and she hoped that the work would keep him here for a while.

"Maybe I need you more now," Chike said, "because everything's going to change. A few years ago, I could look ahead and the alternatives were fairly clear. I'd finish my schooling and become a specialist in chemistry, or I would be advised to leave and apprentice myself, probably as a lab assistant, and I'd live on an Island or maybe in a settlement and bring up however many children my bondmate and I could get permission to have and live out my life in service to the Project. Now I can't be sure of anything."

"You don't regret that," Mahala said.

"Not at all. You know that. But it does make me feel that I need just one thing that is certain, that you'll be there for me."

"I'll be there." She leaned against him, suddenly grateful for his love.

21

May 655
From: Harriett Teresas, Commune of Teresa Marias,
Lincoln, Nomarchy of the Plains Communes
To: Mahala Liangharad, East Dome,
Cytherian Settlement of Sagan

Greetings from Earth!

If you don't know who I am and haven't checked any records yet, I'm a kinswoman, a cousin of yours, Harriett Teresas. In case you haven't looked at a genealogical chart or called up a recitation of our list of ancestors, I am a descendant of your great-great-grandmother Angharad's first cousin Elisabeth, who had a daughter, Lilia. Lilia's daughter was Sylvie, who took over this farm back in 593. Sylvie merged our farm and household with—well, a Plainswoman can spend hours going through her line of ancestors, so I won't go into all of that.

Sylvie had a son, Gregor, who left Lincoln, and then much later in life a daughter, Maria, who's my grandmother. Maria's still alive, but she's well into her middle years, since she didn't give birth to my mother Teresa until she was in her late twenties, but a fair number of Plainswomen are becoming mothers later in life these days, instead of following old custom and having their children in their teens. And my name is Harriett Teresas, and as I said, I am your cousin, but it must seem like a very distant relationship to you.

If you'd like to view a mind-tour of Lincoln, please feel free to call one up, and bill it to my account; I already gave permission for that. In the meantime, I can tell you that this town has changed quite a bit since your great-grandmother Iris Angharads left for Venus over a century ago.

For one thing, it's smaller, and Lincoln wasn't any too populated to begin with; over three thousand people live here now, which is actually more residents than we had here a few years ago—but I'll get to that.

My mother, Teresa Marias, who was elected as mayor of Lincoln a couple of years ago, is head of this household and in charge of our farm, and we still live in the same house—with some improvements, needless to say—where your great-grandmother Iris grew up. We've probably got more room than she and her housemates had, though, because there aren't as many of us. Our regional Counselors are stingy about granting permissions to have children, and the fact is that the Nomarchies don't need as many of us to run our farms. In the old days, many women could get permission for at least two children, a girl to run the farm and continue the line and a boy to wander off to other places to work and spread the line's genes around, but I can think of only a few women who ever got permission for more than one child, and some who never get permission at all, and if you're told to have a boy, you just have to leave it to a sister or a female cousin to carry on your line.

I'm going to tell you about myself now and a little more about Lincoln, and then you'll understand why I'm sending you this message. I'm twenty years old, and I grew up in Lincoln. By the time I was six, I had learned how to read and was spending a good deal of my credit on screen lessons. You probably know how unusual that is here, since farmers don't need lessons except for subjects that are related to agriculture or running a farm, but my mother actually encouraged me in my studies.

One reason was her pride in knowing that Iris Angharads was part of our line. I grew up hearing stories about how Iris learned to read in secret, even when her friends made fun of her, and how she was chosen for the Cytherian Institute and later gave up her life for the Venus Project. Our line may not have as many branches as it once did, but at least we know we have one branch on Venus, and we are very proud of that. But Teresa also encouraged my lessons because she saw that a time might come when I'd have to know more than how to run a farm. "Things can change," she always said. "They've been the same for a long time now, maybe for too long." And as it turned out, she was right. But I'm getting ahead of myself.

About seven years ago, our regional Counselor, Torie Crawfordsville, called us all to a meeting in the town hall. Everybody in Lincoln—farmers, shopkeepers, the older boys and any men who happened to be passing through, and all of the children who were old enough to behave properly and understand what was being said—went to the meeting, because Torie had said that it was going to be really important. That was when she told us that the Administrative Committee for our Nomarchy had been directed by the Council of Mukhtars to open a primary and secondary school in Lincoln. Some of the older students would come here from other Plains towns and live in houses with some of the teachers while the school was in session, but any child in Lincoln who had the aptitude and was willing to do the work would also be admitted to the school. And they really did mean anyone—boy or girl, the child of a shopkeeper or a farmer—everybody would have a chance at an education.

After Torie Crawfordsville made that announcement, there wasn't a sound in the room. People were stunned; I was wondering if some of the old women might even drop dead from the shock. Torie went on to speak about the curriculum and the teachers and how some of the young people in Lincoln might go on to become teachers to another generation of children, and I was thinking: I'll be able to go to school, they'll have to let me in, and I'll be prepared because of all those screen lessons I took. It won't be just teaching images giving me lessons anymore, it'll be real teachers and people from other places and students like me who want to learn new things and are curious about the world and who won't make fun of me because I know how to read and want to get something more from a mind-tour than a mindless adventure and want to grow up to be more than a farmer and Plainswoman who sits around gossiping, drinking whiskey, and bedding any attractive man who comes through Lincoln and is willing.

It didn't turn out quite that way, and most of the children from Lincoln who entered school with me either dropped out or were asked to leave after a year or so, but the ones who came after us did better at their lessons. I was able to go to school and get more training, and now I'm instructing some of the youngest children in reading and mathematics and also showing them how to locate and call up educational mind-tours they might not have found out about by themselves. And next autumn, I'll be going to a university, something I thought could never happen to me. There are still people here who think too much schooling is a waste of time and will only addle your brain, but there aren't as many of them as there used to be, and the children entering now are more prepared for school than we were.

That was the first shock for everybody in Lincoln, having a school set up here. The second, of course, was the announcement by Mukhtar Tabib al-Takir that a new era of cooperation among the peoples of Earth, Venus, and the Habitats was at hand and that the Habbers would be providing more aid to the Cytherians and the Venus Project and that an alien race had sent a signal from the stars. That nearly sent some people over the edge. But all of that would have come to us as an even bigger shock without the school; it was almost as though the Lincoln Academy were deliberately set up to prepare us for more changes later on.

So now we have students who come here from other towns to attend our Lincoln Academy, and we have teachers, and even the old women who still shake their heads and cluck disapprovingly about it all admit that Lincoln is a lot more interesting than it used to be. At mass in our Marian Catholic Church—that's where most of our household goes, although there are a lot of Muslims and Spiritists in town, too—we actually fill all the pews now, and the mosque draws more people, and the Spiritists had to move out of their building next to the town hall into a larger structure. That's partly because there are more people living here now, but I think it's also because more of us are trying to hang on to some of our old customs in the middle of all this change. There's a kind of comfort in going to mass and lighting candles for Mary and Her Son and knowing that some things won't change, even when you aren't really sure you believe in any of that.

I don't know how much you Cytherians keep up with what happens on Earth. Most people here know little more about your lives than what they might hear about in progress reports about the Project, and of course we know about the major political events, such as your uprising and how Mukhtar Kaseko Wugabe so cleverly allowed the oppressors among your own people to think that he was willing to deal with them when he was actually just waiting for the Cytherians to rise up and overthrow—

Mother of God, forgive me. I forgot that your mother Chimene Liang-Haddad was one of the leaders of the cult that caused all that trouble. I know that your record says you never knew her, but it was still tactless of me to mention that. Well, she was a cousin of mine, too. Our line made its mark on Venus, for good and for ill, but mostly for good, I think.

As I was saying, you may know little more about what's going on here than most of us do about what's happening there, and the North American Plains aren't exactly a center of Earthly culture, so you wouldn't have much reason to concern yourself with our doings. We have our school, and five of our young students have gone off to universities for more training, and we all know that everything is changing. Fortunately, things aren't changing so quickly that our lives are too disrupted for us to adjust.

Lincoln isn't the only place that's being transformed, either. I did some digging around and discovered that a lot of small towns and isolated communities that never had schools until a few years ago now have them. There also seems to be an increase in the number of Counselors being trained and given assignments in all of the Nomarchies, which makes sense. Even if the Administrative Councils and the Mukhtars are cautious and go slow, a lot of people are going to feel increasingly disoriented.

This message from a stranger, even if she is a kinswoman, has gone on much too long already, and I still haven't told you what impelled me to send it to you. I'd been meaning to contact you for a while before the Habbers came. That's what this message is about, actually—the Habbers.

A month ago, Torie Crawfordsville told us that three Linkers and three Habbers were coming here. The Linkers were to be from our Nomarchy's Administrative Council, and the Habbers were supposedly coming here simply as observers. Every household got her message, and within a few minutes after Torie was off the screen, my mother was getting calls from everyone in town. I mean, having Linkers here, especially people so highly placed, would have been enough of a shock, but Habbers—we couldn't believe it, and maybe it's just as well that Torie didn't leave us too much time to think about it, because within three days after her announcement, a floater arrived here, landed in our one airship cradle, and the door opened, and there on the ramp were the Linkers and the Habbers.

Everybody was there to greet them. There was a crowd at the cradle and another crowd in the town square, and Teresa was waiting at the cradle with a small delegation of heads of households to welcome them. I don't know what we expected to see, but some of the old women had been spreading tales about Habbers coming here to steal children for their Habs or to put implants in our brains in order to make us do their bidding. You would think they'd know better, and luckily most of us know such stories are ridiculous, but I think there was a moment, while we were standing by the floater cradle, when some of us were wondering whether the stories might be true.

The Linkers and Habbers have been here for a month now, and they've gone out of their way to be friendly and reassuring and to adapt to our ways—or at least to keep from offending anyone. But it's taken Teresa and me, and my grandmother Maria, most of that time to come to terms with the fact that one of the Habbers is part of our line.

We had known about him earlier, of course, and that he had gone with his mother to Venus and then abandoned Venus for the Habs, but nobody talked about him, and we certainly never thought we would see Benzi Liangharad in Lincoln. He was born here, he spent the first years of his life here, but we never expected to meet him here. He's over a century old, and yet he looks like a man of thirty or so at the most. Whatever rejuv techniques the Habbers have must be a lot more advanced than ours.

But you know him, so I don't have to tell you all of that. Anyway, that's why I'm sending you this message, because of Benzi. He suggested it to me and said that we should establish some contact now. And he asked me to say, though I'm not sure why, that he hasn't forgotten you and his other kin on Venus.

The quake struck when Mahala was on her way to Sagan's airship bay, which lay at the southern end of the east dome. The seismologists had been expecting a quake on Ishtar Terra's Lakshmi Plateau for a few days now, although their predictions of the quake's magnitude had varied.

Speeding up the rotation of Venus one hundred years ago with the antigravitational pulse generated by the three pyramidal surface installations had unlocked the planet's tectonic plates. There had been violent quakes after that, and domes able to withstand even the most powerful quakes had been manufactured to cover and seal in the settlements. For the past two decades, the plateau and mountain ranges of Ishtar Terra had been shaken by only a series of minor quakes, some of them too small to be perceptible to human beings, but many of the seismologists had been predicting a much stronger quake than usual within a month, while others anticipated one of the most severe they were ever likely to experience.

The jolt threw Mahala forward, as if the ground had suddenly been pulled out from under her feet. On the flat land to the south, tents swayed violently, sails moving over a sea of grass. She clawed at the grass. The ground heaved under her until it seemed that it would never stop.

Quakes had never caused a breach in a dome, and Mahala knew enough about the specs and the ceramic-metallic alloy of the domes to be certain that all of the domes would hold, but was terrified all the same. The installations near Sagan's two digger and crawler bays might be damaged. Conduits in several of those bunkers held oxygen extracted from the atmosphere of carbon dioxide, which was combined with nitrogen drawn from Venus's misty rains and then used to replenish the air inside the domes, and there had been explosions inside bunkers before. A few of the diggers and crawlers the settlers used for their external mining operations might have been buried under rockslides. Even after two years of living in Sagan, most of the people here still lived either in tents or in dormitories with walls and ceilings of light materials; anyone inside them was unlikely to suffer any injuries. But the other settlements, even with all the precautions people had taken in the construction of their dwellings and other structures, were likely to have injuries, even deaths.

The ground trembled and shook. Mahala pressed herself against the ground, waiting out the long moments until Venus was still once more, then pulled a palm-sized pocket screen from her physician's bag.

A number appeared on the screen: 8.3 on the scale, about as bad as it could get. The epicenter of the quake had been only fifty kilometers south of Turing and Hypatia and the other settlements in the Freyja Mountains to the north of the Lakshmi Plateau. She wondered how much damage Turing had suffered.

She dragged herself to her feet. A soft voice was speaking to her from the screen she held in her hand. Two men were down in the airship bay, one dazed and the other unconscious. She shut the screen off and thrust it into her pocket. She was close to the bay; she would head there first and take care of the injured men before seeing who else might need her.

Sven Hmong had been securing a crane when the quake hit; his arm was broken. Tomas Sechen had been helping him, and part of the crane had hit Tomas in the head and knocked him unconscious. Mahala guessed that it had been a glancing blow, since there was little sign of injury except a bruise; a direct blow might have killed Tomas outright.

After telling others in the bay to carry the injured men to the room in one of the dormitories that was her office, she checked her screen again. A woman leaving the west dome's External Operations Center had been thrown against a wall; there might be broken bones.

"Distress call," somebody was saying behind her, "from the airship out of Ptolemy." Mahala recalled that an airship was supposed to be coming here from the settlement of Ptolemy with a few more settlers for Sagan. She hurried through the entrance to the bay and decided to head for the west dome on foot instead of waiting for one of the east dome's two carts. The small screen in her pocket was silent; apparently no one else needed medical help, at least not yet. She let out a sigh; they had been lucky.

She covered flat grassland, moving at a run, falling back into a rapid stride, then moving into a run again. The Sagan Council was scheduled to have its first meeting tonight, now that the people here had finally gotten around to electing Councilors. Mahala had unexpectedly found herself elected as a Councilor, along with Tomas Sechen and Eugenio Tokugawa, who had moved to Sagan from Oberg a year ago. Their meeting was to have been devoted to the subject of whether a Habber should also be chosen to be a member of the Council, a move favored by some people as a bow to the new era but regarded by others as too provocative; the other settlements might not be so ready to accept a Habber as a Councilor.

Now she would have to call off that meeting. She found herself wondering when the first aftershock would come. There would be one, of course, and probably a strong one, given the quake's magnitude.

By the time she came to the tunnel that led to the west dome, two men were there, carrying Vanah Robell on a makeshift stretcher.

"Is Vanah the only one hurt?" Mahala asked. One of the men nodded. She led them to the dormitory room that was her office, where the two men who had been injured in the bay had arrived and were awaiting treatment.

A scan revealed that Vanah had a fractured rib. Mahala taped her up, set Sven's arm in a splint, then embedded implants in the chests of her two patients; the osteo-hormones would hasten the knitting of their broken bones while they recovered. Tomas's scan revealed a concussion, but no fracture; he would need rest and periodic scans for a while in case he developed a subdural hematoma that might require treatment. She thought of the Habbers in Sagan, whose bones might already have nano-healed by now if they had suffered any fractures. The tiny molecule-sized devices that coursed through their circulatory systems might already have repaired any fractures, knitting the breaks and generating new bone to replace any lost calcium. She had learned a few things from the Habbers here, but without access to their technology and training in how to use their tools, the knowledge alone did not do her much good.

"I want all of you to sleep here," she said, "and I'll see how your scans look tomorrow." She glanced at Tomas. "And I'm postponing our Council meeting."

The two men who had carried Vanah to the dormitory sat in a corner of the small room near Mahala's examination table, peering at a pocket screen. They had come to Sagan only recently; she could not recall their names. The bearded one looked up. "There's some excitement at the east dome External Operations Center," he said.

"More injuries?" she asked.

"No, nothing like that, just a short message from Solveig Einarsdottir. She says they've seen something quite remarkable outside, that they're going to try to verify their observations before saying anything more, and that anyone who's interested is welcome to come to the Center and take a look at what they've found."

Such mysteriousness was unlike Solveig. Mahala was suddenly curious. She got up and went to the door, then hesitated.

"Another message," the man said, "about that downed airship. The tracking team in Ptolemy's bay is trying to raise the pilots, but there's no response. They may have to send out a scooper ship to rescue them." He looked up. "I can stay with these people if you want to go. I have some paramedical training."

"That's kind of you," she said. "I'll take you up on that."

The bearded man's companion took the screen from him and held it to his face. Mahala picked up her physician's bag out of habit, slung the strap over her shoulder, hurried through the door, and turned north, in the direction of the External Operations Center.

As she walked, she called up reports on the situation in Oberg and

Turing on her palm screen; every settlement on Venus would have felt the powerful quake, although Turing and the four other settlements in the Freyja Mountains were closest to the epicenter. At least thirty were dead in Turing; Oberg had lost ten people, but others had been severely injured. She opened a channel and whispered a short message to Risa, Sef, and Dyami, telling them all that she was unharmed and that Sagan had apparently suffered no deaths.

Except for a few shrubs and a scattering of slender young trees, much of the area under Sagan's domes was still flat grassland. The poisonous rains of Venus, collected in Sagan's outside receptacles and then channeled into the dome, fed the stream that meandered through the east dome. Mahala came to a footbridge, crossed the stream, and passed the three community greenhouses that stood along the western shore of a small, shallow lake, then stopped to peer at her screen.

There were two brief messages. The first, from Sef, said only that the people in his household were unharmed and that Risa and Paul were out aiding the emergency workers. Dyami's message informed her that he had been outside his house when the quake hit, that Amina was safe, and that both of them were now with Tasida to help in whatever way they could.

She closed the screen again and tucked it into her bag. The External Operations Center was about the size of a large house; the side panels were of a light metal much like tin. Two of the diggers used for excavation and landscaping inside the settlement sat near the entrance, with a passenger cart behind them.

Mahala pressed her palm against the entrance. As the door slid open, she saw people crowded around the screens, some with thin silvery bands around their heads and others without bands. Twenty people wearing bands sat in front of the consoles through which they controlled the equipment that handled all external operations; others stood behind them, peering over their shoulders.

She entered the large room and made her way toward Orban, one of the Habbers who sometimes assisted her with her medical duties. "What's going on?" she asked him.

"Look there." Orban pointed at one of the screens. She could see nothing except a patch of dark rusty rock illuminated faintly by light from the dome. There were small black cracks in the rock; she narrowed her eyes.

At first, she was not sure of what she was seeing, and then the light suddenly grew brighter and the image changed, as if it had been magnified.

"I've moved a crawler closer to it," a woman's voice said. "We've got more light on it now."

On the rock was a patch of what looked like a mossy substance, one of the patches of genetically engineered moss that could grow outside the domes, and then she noticed something else. Two tiny stalks, barely the size of blades of grass, were attached to the dark moss, as if growing from it.

"What is it?" Mahala asked.

"A plant of some kind," someone replied, "and we didn't put it there. It's something new, something that evolved here on the surface of Venus."

Orban turned toward her. "We noticed it just after the quake," he said. "Maybe it developed from the algae used to seed the atmosphere, or it might have developed from microscopic spores carried outside by our equipment, but it's life, and it's something we didn't plan for. We didn't plant it there ourselves, and none of our computer models, including the ones that allowed for possible contamination by our equipment, predicted that anything like it would grow from that moss."

"We'll have to collect a sample, bring it inside, and analyze it." That was Solveig's voice, to her left. Mahala made her way past the people around her to her friend.

Solveig was at a screen, a band around her head; she had learned how to run the diggers and crawlers during her first year in Sagan, while still putting in her shifts in the settlement's greenhouses. Mahala put a hand on her shoulder; Solveig looked up, then removed her band.

"How fascinating," Mahala said.

"It's there," Solveig said, "and it looks like a kind of grass, and if there's a patch of it here, then there might be more elsewhere."

"There's a message coming in from the airship bay," a man called out from the back of the room. "An airship on its way to Sagan from Ptolemy went down. The crew on duty in Ptolemy's bay sent out a probe to scan the area where the distress signal came from, and they've located the ship, or what's left of it. They were only a half hour out of Ptolemy when the quake hit. Doesn't look like they'll be sending a rescue ship for them."

Solveig pressed a button on her console. Mahala leaned forward as the letters of the report scrolled up on the screen.

According to the report, it seemed that at least one valve had failed in the dirigible of helium-filled lofter cells just as the vessel was beginning to gain altitude. The airship had suddenly begun falling toward the surface, according to the first and only message from the pilots. The distress signal had been sent just before the airship's pilots had managed a landing.

The people aboard would have survived the fall, but the airship had been forced down near the bottom of a steep mountain cliff, where the ship had been crushed by a massive sheet of rock sheared off from the cliffside by the quake and then buried by a rockslide. A scan had shown an airship cabin crushed nearly flat; it was certain that all of the passengers and both pilots were dead. The report ended with a promise of more details after the probe's scan had been completed.

Mahala knew that a list of the names of those lost would now follow. The names of the pilots appeared first: Achmad Henning and Frania Astarte Milus. She blinked, not believing what she was reading.

"No," someone behind her whispered, "not Frani." Many of the people in this room knew Frania, who had decided to make Sagan her residence between periods of flight duty nearly a year and a half ago. Mahala stared at the letters of Frania's name as they disappeared, to be followed by the short list of passengers.

It was a mistake. Frani had been taken off the roster at the last minute and replaced with another pilot. The scanner in the probe had been malfunctioning and come up with the wrong data, and the pilots and passengers were still alive, awaiting rescue. There were not too many other possibilities for error.

Mahala suddenly wanted to escape from the people around her.

"It isn't true," she muttered, backing into someone behind her, "it isn't true." She wondered how Ragnar, who had never come to visit his estranged bondmate in Sagan, would feel when he found out.

Orban caught her by the arm. "Mahala—"

"It can't be true." She abruptly pulled away and ran from the room.

*   *   *

Mahala sat by the entrance to the airship bay. The wide entrance to the bay was closed now, but it would open after the airship landed and she would look up to see Frania coming toward her.

Frania had found some contentment during her sojourns in Sagan. Occasionally she stayed with other pilots in the plain square building near the bay that was the pilots' dormitory, but usually she came to Mahala's dormitory and stayed there with Solveig. Lately, she had sounded as though she was on better terms with her emotionally distant bondmate. She had seen Ragnar during a recent run to the southern Bat, and he had seemed more amenable to coming to Sagan during his next period of time off, at least for a few days.

But Frania had also begun to look beyond the confines of her life. She, like Mahala and Solveig, felt drawn to the reaches of interstellar space. The signal sometimes seemed to be calling to them all as they listened to the atonal sighs the Habber receivers had recorded. "We'll go there," Frania had said once, "and we'll find them, and they'll follow us back to Venus, the planet our people brought to life," and with those simple heartfelt words, she had for a moment banished all the barriers of time and space that stood between them and that vision.

Mahala should be in front of a screen, calling Amina to offer what comfort she could on the loss of her niece. She would also have to send a message to Ragnar. A message would not be enough; she would have to call and speak to him directly. Her insides knotted as she remembered how much Frania had loved life and how ready Ragnar had been to throw his own life away.

The ground trembled under her. Another aftershock, but not nearly as severe as an earlier one an hour ago. Frania had other friends in Sagan. There were the four people staying in the pilots' quarters, who would be mourning their two dead colleagues, and the friends she had made among the settlers, and there was Eugenio Tokugawa, who might have asked Frania for a pledge if she were not already bound to Ragnar.

Last light was approaching. She looked up to see the shadowy form of Chike walking in her direction across the plain of grass.

He came up to her and sat down. "Solveig told me," he said. "She came over to the lab and told me, and then she said that she was going to call her brother and her parents."

Mahala was silent.

"All airship flights have been temporarily canceled for twenty-four hours. They think that what happened is that the valve wore out prematurely. A recommendation has already been issued to replace every airship valve sooner than the specs call for its replacement. That will mean more expense for the Project, so I hope they'll act on the recommendation instead of deciding it's too costly."

"It isn't the valve that did it." Her voice was hoarse, her throat sore, her eyes stinging from holding back her tears. "They could have survived that. They could have lasted until a rescue ship came. The quake killed them, that rockslide killed them. Venus killed them."

"Mahala—"

"When we were children, Frani told me once that she hated this place, hated Venus. It was right after her parents died. Venus killed them and now it's killed her, too."

Chike did not speak.

Mahala knew what was required of her now. She would have to speak with Amina and Ragnar, and then she would have to organize some sort of gathering in Frania's memory for those who wanted to mourn her. She was one of the Councilors here and one of Frania's closest friends; people would expect it of her. They had postponed putting up any memorial pillar in Sagan; the settlement was still young, there had been no deaths here, and a few people had felt that the Habbers among them, who seemed to shy away from any mention of death, might be uneasy around such a reminder of mortality. Now they would have to put up a pillar, and Frani's face would be the first to be memorialized.

Chike slipped his arm around her, and at last she allowed herself to weep.

"The team and I just finished it a couple of hours ago," Tomas Sechen said. "How do you like it?"

Mahala folded her arms as she regarded the small building. The two side walls of the structure were made of glass, so that anyone passing by had a view of the room where Sagan's Councilors would hold their meetings and also of the room on the other side, where any hearings would be held. Sliding doors in the glass walls could be opened, so that anyone wishing to attend a meeting or hearing could sit outside if all of the space inside the meeting rooms was taken. Even though people could always participate in the Councilors' public meetings through their screens or look at a record of them, Mahala had wanted a feeling of openness, an Administrative Center that conveyed the impression of a Council ready to hear from anyone and open to all.

"You did well," she said, then nodded at the three men and two women who were resting near the main entrance of the new building.

Tomas shrugged. "I might have come up with the design, but you had the original idea."

She turned away from the building. Not far from the new Administrative Center, a steel memorial pillar had been erected. She gazed at the bare pillar, her throat tightening as she thought of Frania. Eugenio Tokugawa had gone through the records and found a holo image of Frania that might be suitable for the pillar; it showed her with her head raised and a distant look in her beautiful hazel eyes, as if she were trying to look up and see what lay beyond the dome above her.

The grief-stricken Eugenio had shown more feeling for Frania than had Ragnar, who had been working his shift and unavailable when Mahala first called him and had responded to none of her messages afterward. Amina had wept, clearly devastated; Dyami had promised to sculpt an image of Frania for Turing's memorial pillar, since she had spent so much of her short life there. Einar and Thorunn had spoken of Frania as if she had been their own daughter.

But there had been nothing but silence from Ragnar, who had not even bothered to answer Solveig's messages. Mahala had sent him another message only a few hours ago, to discover that he had left the southern Bat forty-eight hours earlier, presumably to return to Turing.

"We'll finally have our long-postponed first meeting," Mahala murmured. "It's about time we scheduled one. Tomorrow, after last light—that'll give us time to announce it." She glanced at the timepiece on her finger. "And right now I have to get to the bay—Lucia's the paramedic on duty and I promised her I would relieve her almost an hour ago."

She left Tomas by the building, averted her eyes from the memorial pillar, and hurried toward the airship bay. A few people, two of them in the blue garb of pilots, were coming out of the bay, tiny figures in the open entrance. She absently recalled that an airship was due from Hypatia with a couple of new settlers and some much-needed supplies, and then she noticed the pale blond hair of one of the newcomers.

Ragnar, she thought. She recognized him even from this distance; he was taller than the others and still walked in the same loose-limbed, almost arrogant way. A large duffel hung from his shoulder, probably filled with chisels and clay and tiny scalpels and knives and the other useless tools of his art. As she came closer, she saw that his hair was shorter; the long blond braid was gone.

He continued to walk toward her. She wanted to rage at him for coming here now, for not coming to stay with Frania before, and then she saw the ravaged look of his face and the pain in his gray eyes. She came to a halt. He strode past her, as if not seeing her at all, and then he slowed and turned toward her.

"Mahala," he said in a voice so low that she barely heard him.

The despair in his face drove her anger from her. "Ragnar," she whispered.

"Don't say anything—just walk with me for a while."

He began to walk northwest, in the direction of the Administrative Center. She kept at his side. The memorial pillar lay straight ahead, clearly visible. She wanted to steer him away from it, but he had increased his stride, and she had to quicken her pace to keep up with him.

When he reached the pillar, he gazed up at the top, about a half-meter above his head, for a long moment. Then he slipped his duffel from his shoulder and sat down at the base of the bare metal column.

Tomas came toward them; she waved him away, then sat down next to Ragnar, silent, waiting for him to speak.

"I saw her," he said, "only six weeks ago."

"I know," Mahala said. "She told me that you were thinking of coming here."

"I promised her that I would. I told her that it would be for at least a few days, and then once I started thinking about it, I said that I would come here and stay a while and see what it was like, and if I decided afterward that I wanted to move here, I'd go back to Turing and trade my house to someone else and take care of anything there that needed to be settled."

He fell silent again. At last she said, "You were going to stay here until you went back to the Bat, you mean."

"I finished my last shift there. When I think of how I was sometimes, not caring about any danger, I'm probably lucky to be alive. It isn't that I was careless or didn't look out for the others—it's just that—"

He let out a sigh. "I called Frani," he went on, "and promised her that I wouldn't volunteer for Bat duty again, that I'd decided to listen to her and see what kind of life I could make for myself here. In Sagan. With her."

He averted his face; his throat moved as he swallowed. "She was happy when I told her." His voice dropped. "She said . . . she said . . ."

He leaned back against the pillar and closed his eyes. Mahala watched him, wishing that she could think of something to say. Soon he opened his eyes again and pulled his duffel toward himself, opened it and rummaged among his belongings, then pulled out a carved piece of wood.

He had carved Frania's face, and she was smiling; the carved Frani looked as self-possessed and confident as she had always seemed among her fellow pilots. So Ragnar had finally seen her that way, too. Maybe that was how she had looked when he had told her that he wanted to begin his life with her again in Sagan.

"I wanted to do something for her memorial," he said as he handed the carving to her. Mahala gazed into the captured face of her lost friend. "I'll make a mold of it and cast it for her place on the pillar. I don't want it in steel, though, I want to use some sort of bronze or another copper alloy that'll keep its color, a color that's more like her eyes."

He took the carving from her and thrust it back into his duffel. "I don't know what I have to do to be allowed to live here," he said.

"It isn't that different from anywhere else," she replied, "except that we have more room than the older settlements. You state your intention, and our Council looks at your record and decides if we need somebody with your particular skills. Presumably you've made sure that your record notes any recommendations or special citations from your superiors or fellow workers. Anybody here who wants to put in a word in your favor or against you can do so, but that almost never happens. The only thing that's different in Sagan is that the Habbers have something to say about who comes here."

He sighed. "That's what Frani—that's what I was told."

"I'm one of the Councilors here," she continued. He glanced at her and raised his brows. "We finally had an election. I didn't ask for anyone's vote, but then we had no real campaigning here. I can speak up for you, but that's about all I can do. Eugenio Tokugawa is on the Council, too, but I don't think he'd hold anything you did in Oberg when you were younger against you. Tomas Sechen is our other Councilor, and he'll go by your public record. I don't think you'll have any trouble with us."

"But maybe I will with the Habbers."

"I don't know. Everyone who's here now—I used to think that we were selected as settlers mostly by the Administrators and the other Councils, the way it's always been. Then, after we came, I had the sense that the Habbers had more to do with deciding all of that than I realized. Now I wonder if they might have had the final say about who was to come here. It would make sense, given that they want to live here much in the same way we do, while sharing some of their knowledge with us."

"It would make sense if this is one of the groups where they expect to find their spacefarers. Frani mentioned that to me. She wasn't sure, but she thought some sort of selection process was already going on and that Sagan might be part of it."

"I've been thinking that for a while," Mahala admitted, "especially after finding out that there were a few delegations of Habbers on Earth."

He glanced at her. "I heard."

"Benzi's there," she said. "I found out two months ago. A distant relation of mine in the town my great-grandmother came from sent me a message. Tesia is there with him—maybe you remember her from when you first came to Turing."

Ragnar nodded. "The Habber that was there during that demonstration, when Frani—"

Mahala sat with him, not saying anything, watching as a few people left the airship bay with two passenger carts loaded with crates.

"Frani told me," Ragnar said, "that she wanted to become a spacefarer. It sneaked up on her in a way, she said, wanting to go, wanting to be part of that. She was trying to learn more about astrophysics, thinking it might give her more of a chance, even though she was having a hard time with the subject."

"I know," Mahala said, thinking of all the times Solveig would take Frania aside to tutor her and sit with her as she studied. "Solveig said she wasn't doing badly."

"She was trying. She thought that might help, that at least they'd know she was trying, and—" He covered his face. "She found something for herself. She thought we could be content here, whatever happened later on. She found a dream. And now she's gone."

She slipped her arm around him, hanging on to him tightly. His body shook as rasping sounds came from his throat. They sat by the pillar, mourning their loss.

22

For nearly three centuries, the people of the Associated Habitats had been sending AI probes outside the solar system, but had not ventured into interstellar space themselves. Their cybernetic intermediaries had mapped sections of the Oort Cloud, that sphere of planetary debris that surrounded the sun and its planets; the artificial intelligences had long ago confirmed for the Habbers that the Oort Cloud was the source of the vast majority of comets that entered the solar system and also that many of the smaller bodies that were part of it had apparently originated inside the solar system while it was forming and had then been flung into space.

As for what lay beyond the Oort Cloud in interstellar space, a few of the probes had confirmed that the Alpha Centauri system, Tau Ceti, and a few other nearby star systems had planets and that most of these planets were either gas giants resembling Jupiter and Saturn or were smaller, seemingly lifeless bodies with atmospheres of carbon dioxide. The Habbers had found this intriguing, but had drawn no conclusions about planetary evolution, the possibility of life existing on those planets or on others, or whether a planet such as Earth might be a rare and perhaps unique result of planetary evolution. They had sampled far too small a sample of the universe to estimate the probability of life existing elsewhere.

They had chosen to remain inside the solar system in their Habitats. The bond that connected them to the rest of humankind still held. They had abandoned planets for their Habitats, lengthened their lives, and developed a technology that made interstellar voyages a possibility, yet they had recoiled from severing their ties with the rest of their species.

Now another intelligence was calling to them, to all of humankind.

At three points along the equator of Venus, the black ruins of the three monumental pyramids erected by the Habbers a century and a half ago still stood. Habber machines, guided from afar by Habbers and their cyberminds, had built the pyramids. Habber scientists had developed the antigravitational engines housed inside those massive structures, engines powerful enough to produce the pulse of energy that had speeded up Venus's rotation one hundred years ago. Two of the pyramids were now covered by the acidic oceans of Venus, but the third sat on the land mass of Aphrodite Terra to the south, in the slopes of the Ovda region.

Whenever she looked at images of that giant structure, Mahala saw the pyramid as a monument to the Project and to humankind's past efforts to terraform her world. But the pyramid had also become a monument to the new era, and to the technology that would be needed to realize new goals.

The Habbers had grown freer in their exchanges of information with Venus and with Earth, but much about their motives remained hidden. The Habbers had been willing to aid Earth in terraforming Venus, but had preserved Mars from any efforts to make it into an Earthlike planet. Various reasons had been offered for keeping Mars as it was; the Habbers found the Red Planet aesthetically pleasing in its natural state and had staked their claim to it long ago, perhaps so that they could establish a planetary base of their own if one were ever needed.

Mahala had once thought that their desire to preserve Mars had been a logical outgrowth of their abandonment of planets for their Habitats; why terraform another planet when they had given up living on planets altogether? But the Habbers had also believed it unwise to attempt to terraform a planet for human settlers who would eventually be cut off from their home world. The descendants of any Martian settlers, born and bred on a world with only one third of Earth's gravity, would never be able to visit Earth easily in their frailer bodies. There also seemed little purpose in transforming a world that would inevitably lose any Earthlike atmosphere created for it, since Mars lacked the gravitational pull needed to hold such an atmosphere for millennia. A terraformed Mars would forever require much human intervention to maintain its environment; better, the Habbers had reasoned, to devote their efforts to building and maintaining their Habitats.

Yet the Habbers had contributed much to the Venus Project, and without them, Mahala knew, the obstacles to terraforming would have been far greater. The Habitat-dwellers had chosen to strengthen their ties to the planet-bound branch of humankind by aiding in the transformation of Venus. Perhaps some of them had also been moved by the arguments of Earth's planetologists that they would be restoring Venus, Earth's sister planet, to what it once had been. Venus, after its transformation into a living Earthlike world, promised to be stable as long as some part of the Parasol remained to shield it from too much sunlight; the vision that the Ishtar cult had distorted into a belief in a planetary Spirit to come would be realized in a self-regulating biosphere. The future Cytherians, living on a world with a gravitational force only slightly weaker than that of Earth, would be able to return to humanity's home world. Certainly the knowledge gained by assisting the Project would be of benefit to the Habitats and was also of interest in itself.

But the Habbers Mahala had come to know in Sagan had implied that some among their people had long hoped for a time when they would venture beyond the solar system. Her kinsman Benzi had joined his life to theirs out of a hope that the Habbers would turn to exploring interstellar space. Now Benzi and all who shared his dream would reach for the stars, using much of the technology that had served the Venus Project. A force field and an alloy even stronger than that used for the domes of the Venus surface settlements would shield the interstellar traveler during its journey; the energies used to speed up the rotation of Venus would be harnessed in the matter-antimatter-powered drive that would carry the nomadic Habitat out of the solar system, where a vacuum drive would cut in to draw on the energy that existed in all space.

Another civilization was calling to them, but the Habbers would not be abandoning the rest of their kind, severing their ties to the other people of the solar system. They would share the adventure with their human brothers and sisters.

Those leaving on the journey would not return to the worlds they knew. Even at a velocity close to the speed of light, six hundred years would pass in the solar system by the time the spacefarers found the alien beacon, while only ninety would pass for the spacefarers. There would be a period of suspended animation for the voyagers, but they would awake from their deep sleep knowing that everyone they knew back home was very likely dead and perhaps forgotten. They would return with what they had learned about the alien culture to a human civilization that might be unrecognizable.

The Habbers had tested prototypes of the matter-antimatter drive and the vacuum drive in earlier interstellar probes. Now they had an overpowering reason to go into space and the opportunity to share that great adventure with the rest of their species. But the psychological barrier of knowing that the break with those they left would be final would, Mahala was sure, be much more difficult for all of the potential spacefarers to breach.

The Habbers had seen that a community of spacefarers, a Habitat of many voyagers, was one way of overcoming some of the worst psychological displacement. Any returning space travelers would still have to deal with a solar system that might seem completely alien to them, perhaps as alien as anything they discovered, but they would be facing that with thousands of companions like themselves. Habbers who had worried about their estrangement from the rest of humankind would be living among Earthfolk and Cytherians, in an environment that would foster strong bonds and deeper connections. They would, all of them, preserve their branch of humankind, even if the descendants of those they left behind became something else.

In the two years since Frania's death, three more faces had been added to Sagan's memorial pillar. Mahala stopped for a moment to gaze at the faces, remembering how her grandmother had occasionally asked her to go to the monuments in Oberg with flowers to lay at the foot of each memorial pillar.

Chike and Orban were silent as they stood with her. The narrow, pointed face of Stephan AnnasLeonards, her schoolmate on Anwara and on Island Two, was represented on the pillar; he had been killed by an unsecured gantry in the airship bay during a recent quake. Next to Stephan's visage was a holograph of Guillermo Sechen, who had come here toward the end of his life to say his farewells to his grandson Tomas and who had died here; Guillermo had been a century and two decades old, his heart giving out, and he had refused to waste the Project's medical resources on growing him a new one. The third face among the memorialized dead was that of Katy Philippa, whom Mahala had barely known. Katy had been in her forties, a trained geologist with a degree from the Cytherian Institute; her bond with her bondmate had lapsed, her only child was an adult, and she had come to Sagan less than a year ago, looking forward to a new life. She had died on the northern Bat, in an explosion that had taken ten other lives, while visiting her son and his new bondmate on the satellite, but it had seemed appropriate to memorialize her here. At the top, above the others, was the bronze face of Frania Astarte Milus, sculpted by her bondmate.

Ragnar had never spoken to Mahala of Frani since her death. When Mahala, growing concerned that his silence might be a sign of deep depression, had mentioned Frania's name, hoping to nudge him into talking about his loss, he had warded her off with an upraised hand and a quick shake of his head. Since then, he had put in his shifts at External Operations and passed most of his free time making small carvings and sculptures for some of the Habbers, who seemed to be encouraging him in that pursuit. Mahala had been surprised to find out from one Habber that Ragnar refused any payment for the objects he made, asking only to listen to tales of life in the Habitats and of the progress they and their colleagues from Earth were making on their plans for the interstellar expedition.

Frania's death had come just as the surface of Venus had yielded a new form of life; the two events would always be associated in Mahala's mind. More of the patches of moss on the rocks outside the domes of Sagan were sprouting grassy blades and tendrils that looked like filaments, and the same was happening outside other settlements. Only two months ago, a scan of part of the ocean to the south of Ishtar Terra had revealed the presence of a microscopic life form that resembled a virus.

People now spoke, mostly in jest but with a kind of wonder as well, about the garden of Venus. But the unexpected appearance of these particular life forms had also raised a more disturbing possibility; what if Venus, once life was possible, developed life forms that were incompatible, perhaps even deadly, to the species that had transformed the planet? What Mahala had imagined years ago, that people might eventually have to remake themselves in order to live unprotected on the surface of Venus, seemed a more plausible, if still very distant, possibility.

Chike moved closer to Mahala and took her hand, then bowed his head as though paying his respects. Orban made a sound in his throat; Mahala glanced at the Habber, noting the unease in his handsome olive-skinned face. The Habbers in Sagan usually avoided the memorial pillar, and often she had seen Habbers look away whenever they passed it. They had come to none of the ceremonies to honor the dead, when a sculpture or holo image was placed on the pillar and those who had known them told stories of the deceased. She wondered what Habbers did to mourn their dead. Perhaps their experience with death was so infrequent or so feared that they did not know how to mourn.

A lone figure came through the open entrance of the bay: Malik. A small dark-haired woman whom Mahala had never seen before was with him. Malik had been on Island Two for nearly a year now, apparently summoned there by his kinsman, Administrator Masud al-Tikriti. He had sent only three messages to her in that time, all of them brief and telling her little more than that he was thinking of her and that he and Administrator Masud, with the help of a few other Linkers, were organizing some of the Venus Project's historical records. She had not believed for a moment that work on those records was the only matter that had brought him back to the Islands.

Now suddenly he was here, after informing her only two days ago that he and another Habber would be arriving in Sagan.

"I don't know anything about the Habber woman who came here with my grandfather Malik," she murmured to Orban as they walked toward the bay entrance. "He didn't even mention her name. Perhaps you can tell me something about her."

"Her name is Te-yu," Orban replied. The name sounded vaguely familiar. "She was known as Hong Te-yu when she was a pilot for the Project, on your Islands. She was among those who fled to the Habitats with your kinsman Benzi."

Mahala nodded, recalling that Benzi had mentioned the name a few times in passing. "When did she come back here?"

"Only a few days ago. She had been on Anwara for ten days before then." Orban had the slightly blank look in his eyes that told her that he was listening to his Link. "She will be traveling with Malik to . . . " Orban gave her and Chike his impersonal smile. "But he will be speaking to you of that very soon."

Mahala was suddenly annoyed with Orban. Even after two years of living in fairly close contact with Habbers and coming to consider Orban and several of the others as friends, they could still at times seem unnecessarily opaque.

"If you already know why Malik's here," Chike said, "and what he's going to say, seems to me that you could have told us yourself and saved him the trouble of this trip."

"That might have been appropriate under other circumstances," Orban said, "but Malik wished to come here himself, and there are other reasons for him to consult with you in person." His smile broadened and his mouth twitched slightly, as if he had said something amusing.

Malik looked much as he always had, with a touch of silver in his black hair at the temples and a handsome, unlined face; even the expression in his eyes seemed more open and youthful. He carried a small satchel and wore a long white robe that resembled the formal robe of an Administrator.

"Greetings, Malik," Mahala said, taking his free hand between her palms.

"Salaam." Her grandfather bowed slightly as she introduced Chike to him. Te-yu introduced herself in a light, musical voice; she was an attractive woman with large brown eyes and short black hair who looked youthful, even though she had to be well over a century old.

"If you like," Mahala said, "I'll show you where you'll be staying. We've got more residences up now, and there are a few empty rooms in the newest one. If you're tired, you can rest there."

"We're not tired," Malik said.

"We can ride there in a cart," Chike said, gesturing at one vehicle near the bay entrance, where two men were loading crates.

"We'd rather walk," Malik said. "We'd like to meet with you and the other Councilors here as soon as possible, in a few hours if you can arrange it."

"I think we can," Mahala said. "Eugenio has a shift after last light over at external operations, but we can find somebody to substitute for him."

"Do it, then," Malik said. There was a nervousness about him that she had not seen before, a sound of impatience in his voice. "This is very important, and the matter came up rather suddenly. It was felt that my presence was needed here, as well as Te-yu's, since we've been involved in plans for this meeting almost from the start. And I must admit that I also wanted to see you again and see the kind of life you have made for yourself here."

"I'm content," Mahala said, and it was true. Being a physician gave her a purpose; living among Habbers and freely associating with them had been both an intellectual and an emotional education, opening her mind and tempering her impatience.

They had reached the memorial pillar and the Administrative Center; Mahala gestured at the building. "That's where we usually hold our Council meetings," she continued.

"Then we'll speak to you there," Malik said.

"You may speak to anyone who is interested," Mahala said. "Anybody who wants to view the meeting over the screen or come in person is welcome to do so. We've never held any of our meetings in private. That seems only fair, given that Orban is also a Councilor and any other Habber is able to Link with him during meetings." That had been one of the first decisions made by the Sagan Council, to request that the Habbers here elect one among themselves as a Councilor.

"Very well," Malik said. "We'll speak to you at an open meeting. The subject is a most important upcoming conference, and either your Council, or all of the people here, will have to decide who will represent you there."

"A conference?" Chike asked.

"A conference to lay down the basis for what kinds of agreements we may need between Earth, Venus, and the Associated Habitats and to begin the process of choosing those who wish to become spacefarers. Those present at the conference will include Habbers, Cytherians, Administrators, and, it is said, Mukhtar Tabib al-Tahir himself. I'll explain everything in more detail later—many of the arrangements are still being worked out."

"And where is this conference to be?" Mahala asked.

"On Earth," Malik replied.

Mahala halted. Chike and Orban slowed and came to a stop as Malik and Te-yu turned toward them. "On Earth?" Chike repeated.

"In a town on the North American Plains, as a matter of fact," Malik said. "The Mukhtars feel that it would be best to hold such a conference in a more remote and out-of-the-way location, one that has only a small population and attracts few visitors. Although most of the Nomarchies seem content, or at least resigned to the new era, they would prefer a site where participants can be more easily protected and that isn't likely to draw demonstrations of the discontented." He paused. "The meeting is going to be held where Benzi has been staying, in Lincoln."

23

Mahala woke up. For a moment, she did not know where she was, then remembered.

She lay on a small, narrow bed in a bare room. She sat up slowly and looked toward the round window on her right. Outside the window was the unfamiliar sight of a patch of blue sky. She was on Earth, aboard a floater, a vehicle almost indistinguishable from a Cytherian airship, bound for Lincoln.

Traveling to the Islands and then by shuttle to Anwara had caused her little distress. The torchship provided to her and the other Cytherians for the trip from Anwara to Earth, the *Melville*, had small but comfortable cabins for the passengers, along with both a recreation room and a dining area; she had shared her cabin with her old friend Ah Lin Bergen, one of the delegates from the Maxwell Mountains settlements who had been chosen to attend the conference. Even the Wheel, the largest of the space stations in Earth orbit, where the *Melville* had docked and the Earthbound passengers had been transferred to a shuttlecraft, had not been unduly disorienting; despite its immense size, the inside corridors of the Wheel seemed much like those of Anwara.

It had been after leaving the shuttle at the San Antonio port in North America that she had suddenly felt the beginnings of panic, a tightness in her throat, a racing heartbeat, a constriction in her lungs that made her feel that she might suffocate. The air in the wide walkway leading into the port felt too cold; throngs of people filled the corridors of the port. Low but audible disembodied voices called out gate numbers, times of arrival and departure of shuttle and sub-orbital flights, and the names of destinations in Anglaic, Arabic, and occasionally in other languages she did not know. She kept near the others in her group, picking up the aromas of flowers, coffee, onions, and other scents she could not identify as they moved through the port. Just one of the port's long corridors, she realized, probably held as many people as did Turing; the number of people hurrying to the various gates might exceed the entire population of Venus. She had steadied herself by keeping her eyes on the floor, staying near Malik and the others traveling with her.

The sub-orbital flight to Winnipeg had taken less than an hour, and by the time she had boarded the sub-orb, she felt calmer. The small implant in her upper right arm dispensed only a minimal dose of a mild tranquilizer; she had convinced herself that she would need no more than that. It was not until she was in the Winnipeg port, walking toward the gate that would lead her outside to the airship cradles, that the fear had nearly immobilized her. Nothing in any of the mind-tours of Earth that she had sampled could possibly have prepared her for this experience. There would be no protective dome outside, only wind and air and open sky.

A quick glance upward had shown her an overcast dark sky; the clouds concealing the stars had made it easier for her to pretend that she was still inside a dome after last light. Mahala did not remember how she had crossed the few meters from the exit to the ramp of the floater cradle, but recalled that she had boarded the airship without giving in to panic. The floaters carried people and goods to the small towns and the more isolated communities of Earth that were not connected to the outside world by high-speed trains and shuttle ports. The floater had rows of seats much like those on the airships of Venus, but there were also private rooms in the back of the cabin for those willing to spend extra credit. Mahala and the people with her had been given rooms, even though, judging by the empty passenger seats, no one else would be traveling with them.

Mahala looked down at the identity bracelet on her wrist. She had worn such a bracelet as a child, and later during trips between the Venus settlements, but now she would be wearing one all the time; she had been told to keep it on even after arriving in Lincoln. She had left Venus a month and a half ago, and now her home world seemed impossibly far away.

Too much had happened too suddenly. The people of Sagan had elected her to the post of their delegate to Earth with a surprising near-unanimity, and she suspected that Malik had anticipated that result. There had been no time even to travel to Turing or to Oberg to say her farewells before she was on an airship bound for the Platform.

The delegation traveling with her was small but illustrious; she was clearly one of the least important people among them. The others seemed to find it appropriate that a descendant of Iris Angharads, who had herself been a native of Lincoln, was among them, but they had kept largely to themselves during the torchship journey. Administrator Masud al-Tikriti had seemed disinclined to pay much more than a distant, cordial attention to any of the representatives of the surface settlers; he usually dined with Administrator Constantine Matheos, who had been on the Venus Project Council for several years and was now reputed to be its most influential member. Even Malik and Te-yu, the only Habbers among the travelers, who had apparently decided that diplomacy required that they make the journey on one of Earth's ships instead of aboard a Habber craft, had kept to their rooms except for meals. Only Ah Lin, who felt that she was going to Earth largely on the strength of the support thrown her way by Risa and other respected Cytherians, had kept her company, and she was as much in the dark about the upcoming conference as was Mahala.

What were they going to discuss? Even Malik had not been very forthcoming about specifics; perhaps he and the other Habbers knew little more than she did. She and Ah Lin had come to the tentative conclusion that the meeting was largely ceremonial. Working out detailed agreements would require the efforts of legal scholars, aides to the Council of Mukhtars, certain Administrators and Habbers, and the analysis of cyberminds; such agreements and decisions did not require the presence of delegates in a place like Lincoln. The Mukhtars were going to a lot of trouble to bring people to Earth for what seemed little more than a public exercise in good will.

She reminded herself that if they accomplished no more than maintaining and publicly underlining that good will, that might be enough of an achievement. She was also growing more conscious of the fact that her conduct here might either increase her chances of becoming a spacefarer or damage them severely. Coming to Earth was another test.

She leaned back on her bed, rested her back against the wall, and forced herself to gaze at the sky outside the floater window. A breathable outside, she said to herself in wonder, as someday Venus would have . . .

Mahala had changed her clothes and repacked her duffel by the time the floater was dropping toward Lincoln. She knew what she would see as she approached her window. There were the two cradles of Lincoln's only port; once, there had been only one cradle for the small town. There was a road, a wide black ribbon, that led from the cradles to the town square; other narrow roads, which ran from the town into the surrounding fields, seemed little more than footpaths. But it was the open land around the town that made her catch her breath, the fields of growing grain dotted with silos that stretched to the horizon.

For a moment, she felt dizzy, and then she slipped the strap of her physician's bag over her shoulder, reached for her duffel, and pressed her door open.

Her fellow travelers shuffled through the narrow hallway outside their rooms toward the front of the floater. Kesse Enu-Barnes was among them; he was here as an aide to Administrator Masud al-Tikriti. Kesse glanced at her with his black eyes, and she felt how much she missed his brother Chike. Ah Lin stood behind him, looking apprehensive, perhaps thinking of the open air that awaited them outside.

"There's something odd about this business," Dyami had told her during a call the day before she was to leave Sagan.

"Odd about what?" Mahala had asked.

"Holding this conference on Earth. Requesting the presence of Administrator Masud and of people with the status of Constantine Matheos. Going to the trouble of transporting all of the delegates to a somewhat isolated Earth community. A screen conference would have made more practical sense."

"But the Council of Mukhtars explained why they wanted it this way. They felt that we'd make more progress if we were all in one place for a while and able to talk face-to-face."

"They might have chosen Anwara then, as they have in the past."

"But there is a kind of symbolism in having the conference on Earth, given that it's the home planet. It's another way of marking the new era."

Dyami had sighed, then smiled. "You're probably right, Mahala. Even after all this time, I guess I'm just too distrustful, even when I don't have to be." He had gone on to speak of Balin and had asked after Ragnar and then had wished her a safe journey before blanking the screen.

"Salaam," a man's voice called out from near the exit, "and welcome to Lincoln." The people in front of Mahala moved forward. Mahala followed them onto the ramp and felt air rush past her face. Wind, she thought, and shuddered. The sky was darker; evening was coming. She kept her eyes on the ramp, afraid that if she looked up, the sight of the expanse of sky and land would make her faint.

"Greetings." That was the same voice she had heard before. A hand clutched her under the elbow, helping her step down to the ground. She looked up and saw a young man with reddish-brown hair in the black uniform of a Guardian.

Mahala froze and then noticed that there were other Guardians near the ramp, all at attention, all of them armed with wands that hung from their belts. But of course there would be Guardians, she reminded herself, in order to protect the people who had come here.

Five women stood a few meters from the ramp, all of them wearing long lace-trimmed tunics that fell to their ankles. Mahala recognized two of the women from images that had been sent to her with messages. One of them, a pretty dark-haired woman, was Teresa Marias, Mahala's kinswoman and the mayor of Lincoln. At her right was her daughter, Harriett Teresas; she had her mother's dark hair, but Mahala knew her by her eyes, which were even larger and more strikingly green than they had appeared to be on her screen image.

"Welcome to Lincoln," Teresa Marias called out in a resonant alto voice. Mahala struggled to maintain her composure. I will not look up at the sky, she thought, and I won't think about the gusts of air blowing past my face. The wind had picked up; she could hear it now, moaning softly. She knew from Harriett's messages about Plains weather that her cousin would consider this wind little more than a breeze.

"I am most pleased," the mayor continued, "and—oh!" Teresa lifted a hand to her face; a Guardian and two of the women with Teresa were suddenly rushing toward the new arrivals. Mahala turned around and saw Tonya Chang, one of the representatives from the Maxwell Mountain settlements, lying on her back, mouth open, legs folded under her.

Tonya Chang, perhaps exhausted, perhaps overcome by terror of the outdoors, had fainted.

Tonya recovered and was able to walk by the time Mahala and her companions were led to the town hall, escorted by Guardians toting their duffels and trailed by a procession of curious townsfolk. After a short speech describing how honored the people of Lincoln were to be the site of such a gathering, Teresa Marias announced that those who were to be hosts to the visitors would accompany them to their quarters.

"We would have planned a more elaborate celebration," Teresa went on, "with a banquet here in the town hall, but the Council of Mukhtars advised us to get you settled first and to let you rest, so please don't think badly of us for not making more of a fuss. If there is anything you need, do let the members of your host commune know. We want you to be as comfortable as possible."

Harriett Teresas edged closer to Mahala. "You'll be staying with us," the young woman whispered, flattening her vowels as most of the Plainspeople did in their speech. "After all, you are part of our line." Those were the first words that Harriett had spoken to her since her arrival; Mahala had been eyeing her kinswoman with both curiosity and anxiety. Harriett was a teacher at the Lincoln Academy and had gone north for a year to study mathematics at the University of Winnipeg; Mahala knew that much from the messages they had exchanged with each other.

"I'm pleased to be your guest," Mahala replied.

"Benzi's staying with us, too. He was living with Tesia and Jeffrey, the two Habbers who came here with him, but he's moved in with us for now, so you'll have somebody familiar nearby."

Mahala smiled; she had not seen or heard from Benzi for so long that he seemed as much a stranger to her as was Harriett. She looked around for Ah Lin and saw her leaving the town hall with three women who hovered around her protectively.

"Teresa will probably stay here for a bit," Harriett said, "but you may come home with me now. My grandmother's cooked up a fine supper for you, and the rest of our household is looking forward to meeting you."

Mahala gazed into her cousin's eyes. There was something of Risa in Harriett's strong-boned attractive face. Harriett motioned to the Guardian who was carrying Mahala's duffel; he was the same Guardian who had greeted them at the floater cradle. "Jeremy," Harriett called out, "are you going to tote that thing to my house for our guest, or do I have to drag it there by myself?"

"I'll carry it," Mahala murmured, thinking that was hardly the way to speak to a Guardian, but the young man seemed unperturbed.

"I'll bring it," the Guardian said, "as long as I can stay for supper."

"You're asking me for a bribe," Harriett said, "and Guardians aren't supposed to take bribes," but she smiled as she spoke.

Mahala managed to descend the steps outside the town hall and cross the square without betraying any uneasiness, concentrating on the people who had come there to gawk at the delegates. It was late spring in Lincoln, and she knew from Harriett's messages that this was a better season to be here than in winter, when the winds howled and the Plains were assaulted by snow and ice.

She kept near Harriett, both of them trailed by the Guardian, whose full name was Jeremy Courtneys. The houses along the road stood close to one another, and the light wands and lamps she glimpsed through the windows cast a warm welcoming glow. There was a large greenhouse on the street, used by several of the nearby households; Harriett pointed it out to Mahala, then stopped in front of one house.

"This is it," Harriett said, gesturing at the steps that led up to the front door. "It's our house, where my mother's commune lives."

Mahala approached the steps of the large square structure. Her great-grandmother Iris had lived in this house; Benzi had been born here over a century ago. Harriett led her inside, followed by Jeremy. Two women stood in the hallway in front of a staircase; they smiled at Mahala, then batted their eyes at Jeremy.

"This is Gisella," Harriett said, gesturing toward the tall blond woman, "and Zofie." Gisella nodded at them; a smile crossed Zofie's round, pretty face. "They're part of our household and they're also two of my mother's oldest friends. This is my cousin, Mahala Liangharad."

"Welcome to Lincoln," Zofie said. "Have a seat in the common room—Maria's cooking up quite a feed for you."

"Amaris is helping her out in the kitchen," Gisella said. The two women continued to stare at Mahala, as if uncertain of what else to say, and then Zofie came toward her and embraced her. "Welcome home, Mahala."

In the common room, Mahala saw several chairs and a couch covered in a bright red fabric; end tables with lamps nestled in the corners, a long low wooden table was near the couch, and the wall screen showed a holo of pine-covered hills, making the room seem even larger than it was. She sank into one of the chairs; the room seemed cluttered, the amount of furniture almost wasteful. The women of the household sat with Mahala in the common room, speaking of Linkers and Administrators and other illustrious personages who had been coming in and out of Lincoln to make arrangements for the conference, until it was time to gather at the large wooden table in the kitchen for dinner.

There were two children in this commune, Amaris's son, Graham, and Gisella's daughter, Mara, who told Mahala a little of what they had learned about the Venus Project in school. Maria Sylvies, Harriett's grandmother, fussed over Mahala and kept passing her platters of meat, bread, and vegetables, while Amaris, the youngest woman in the household except for Harriett, flirted with Jeremy.

The Guardian, it turned out, came from Oxbow, another Plains town. According to him, the detachment of fifty Guardians stationed here were mostly men, most of them natives of the Plains. This diplomatic arrangement appealed to the respectable women of Lincoln, since it provided them with a variety of potential bed-partners who were familiar with Plains customs and would not be offended by invitations to spend the night. Although Jeremy had clearly attached himself to Harriett, this did not keep the other women at the table, even gray-haired old Nona, the oldest woman in the household, from flirting with the young man.

Teresa Marias arrived toward the end of the meal, muttering of a few last details that had to be taken care of before Mukhtar Tabib al-Tahir arrived as planned the next morning, just before noon, accompanied by the former Cytherian Administrator Jamilah al-Hussaini. He had insisted on coming there quietly, without any public fuss, but it would not be appropriate for a Mukhtar to arrive in Lincoln with no ceremony at all. She had decided on a subdued welcome at the town hall, with Benzi Liangharad and Masud al-Tikriti, and perhaps a few town dignitaries, in attendance.

"Benzi won't be coming back here tonight," Teresa added as she glanced at Mahala, "but I'm sure you'll see him tomorrow. He seemed anxious to pass the evening with a Habber who came here with you— Te-yu, I believe her name was."

"They're old friends," Mahala said.

Gisella and Amaris giggled while Zofie rolled her eyes. "Even Habbers need bed-partners sometimes," old Nona said loudly, as if she were an authority on the subject.

Harriett led Mahala upstairs to a bedroom, then went to another room down the hall with Jeremy, who was apparently spending the night. Mahala's bed was the size of three futons; a Cytherian family could easily have slept in it together. Clearly the women here liked to have plenty of room to enjoy their bed-partners. Mahala unpacked her clothes, hung them on a rod along one wall, went down the hall to the washroom with its roomy shower stall, large porcelain sink, and a toilet that used a full tank of water and flushed with a frightening loud whooshing sound, then returned to her room. Her eyelids felt gritty and her muscles, used to a gravity that was about eighty-five percent of Earth's, ached slightly; she was exhausted, yet did not feel ready for sleep.

Iris had once had a room like this, perhaps the same room. She had lived in this house hoping to escape from Lincoln.

Mahala got up from the bed, went to the open window that overlooked the courtyard, and sat down on the cushioned ledge of the window seat. The women of the household had gathered below, apparently to question Teresa about the events of the day. The courtyard, roofed in by a force field and enclosed by the four wings of the house, was protected from the seasons, and Harriett had told her that they often sat out there instead of in the common room. A tree grew in the center of the grassy courtyard, while a garden of rose bushes had been planted in the southwest corner.

The women sat on blankets under the tree. "Habbers and Linkers," old Nona muttered. She took a swig from the bottle she was holding. "Administrators and Mukhtars and folks from the Venus settlements, all coming to Lincoln for this gab session. Never thought I'd see the day."

Amaris took the bottle from Nona and lifted it to her lips. "When are they going to start holding their meetings?" Amaris asked.

"Damned if I know," Teresa replied. "The Mukhtar, may God and His Holy Mother protect him, didn't say anything in his message about when they were going to start palavering." Amaris handed her the bottle; Teresa drank.

"Look, we're getting plenty of extra credit for housing all these people," Zofie said, "along with a larger selection of bed-partners, what with all those Guardians and those good-looking workers sent here to fix things. Means more business for the shopkeepers, too."

"Not to mention a lot more for us to gossip about," Gisella added.

Mahala heard a light tap on the door behind her. "Harriett Teresas," the door said.

"Please come in," Mahala replied. The door opened, creaking slightly. Harriett, wearing a long white garment that reached to her ankles, entered the room. The ceiling light flowed on; Harriett waved it off and came to the window.

"Jeremy's too tired to fuck at the moment," Harriett said, sitting down at the other end of the window seat. "He's already fast asleep. But he told me he wouldn't mind paying a call during the night on you."

Harriett clearly meant that remark as a compliment. "I have a man already," Mahala said, thinking of Chike. "On Venus, I mean."

"Yes, but he's there and Jeremy's here."

"I think Jeremy's more interested in you," Mahala said.

"I do love him, in a way. He's been here a month with that detachment of Guardians, and he's been with me almost every night. I had to push him into sleeping with Gisella and Zofie a couple of times just so the rest of the commune doesn't think we're monogamous and abnormal or that I'm trying to keep him all to myself."

Mahala glanced down at the women in the courtyard. "They seem to be drinking a lot," she said. "Are they celebrating the start of the conference?"

"A lot—that isn't a lot." Harriett chuckled. "They've been sticking to a bottle a night among them. That's not so bad—I've seen nights when my grandmother and Nona would pass out and the rest of them would be stumbling all over the place in a stupor just trying to get to bed. But everybody's being more moderate these days. The Muslims in Lincoln will look the other way or even take a discreet nip once in a while, but we don't want to make a bad impression, with Linkers and

Mukhtars around. They seem much more strict about such things. Even Allison at the tavern is rationing what she serves her customers, and she isn't doing any back door business at all."

"Back door business?"

"With any Muslims who aren't that strict in their observance. They don't like to be seen coming in the front entrance, and now they aren't coming at all."

"Probably just as well," Mahala said, hoping that she did not sound too disapproving.

"I should take you over to the school when you feel up to it, introduce you to some of my students." Harriett paused. "The Lincoln Academy is one of the best things that ever happened in this town. If I end up having to stay here, at least I'll have my students."

"You sound as though you don't really want to stay," Mahala said.

"I want to be one of the spacefarers." Harriett had never mentioned such a hope in her messages, but somehow Mahala was not surprised. "Not that I have much of a chance."

"You can't tell if there's a chance or not. The trouble is, we don't know what our chances are. We don't even know how all of that's going to be decided."

"I know. At least I can hope. Knowing that we're not alone, that another intelligence is out there—" She sighed. "Some people think I'm mad to want to go, and others, usually the older women, claim they wouldn't mind going themselves, but that's because it's almost impossible to explain interstellar distances to them, or even interplanetary distances. To someone like Nona, there's Earth, and then there's everything out there, and Venus and Jupiter and the Moon and Alpha Centauri seem about equally far away to her. She just shakes her head when I try to explain what six hundred light-years actually means and how far away the alien beacon is."

Harriett was silent for a few moments, then added, "I'd better let you get some sleep." She stood up. "I'll show you around town tomorrow if you like, after school is out."

"I'd like that."

Harriett left the room. Mahala still felt restless. Perhaps that was only the strain of the trip and of what lay ahead of her, but she felt uneasy and exposed. Reminding herself that she was inside a house and protected from the outside, she got up, closed the window, and went to bed.

* * *

Mahala kept near the house the next day, making herself useful. After breakfast, she helped clear the table; when Harriett left for the Lincoln Academy with young Mara and Graham in tow, Mahala gave Nona, who was complaining of a headache, a scan and then a mild pain medication so that she would not have to venture out to see the town's physician. Teresa left shortly after that to meet Mukhtar Tabib al-Tahir at the town hall when he arrived with Jamilah al-Hussaini; since Benzi would be there with her to welcome the Mukhtar, Mahala guessed that she would not see him before that evening.

Gisella and Maria had decided that it was time to go over the household records, while Amaris and Zofie needed to make purchases from one of the shops at the town square. "Come along with us, Mahala," Zofie had murmured, "and maybe we'll catch sight of that high and mighty Mukhtar, too," but Mahala had refused the offer. If she was going to venture outside the confines of the house, she would do so with Harriett, and in late afternoon, when the shadows would be longer and the sky growing darker.

With little to do for the next few hours, Mahala went upstairs to her room, sat down in front of the desk screen, and sent a message to Ah Lin Bergen. Her friend's round face appeared on the screen a few moments later.

"How is it going with you?" Ah Lin asked.

"Fine," Mahala replied. "Everyone's been very hospitable. I think you'll like my cousin Harriett when you meet her. She's at the school now—she's a teacher there." She paused. "Have you been outside today?"

Ah Lin shook her head. "I'm still working up to that."

"It'll pass. When I was first on Anwara, I wondered if I'd ever adjust to it."

"At least Anwara is completely enclosed." Ah Lin took a breath; her narrowed eyes were slits. "We're on the edge of town. There's a view of the fields from the windows in the back part of this house. I think I'll go there and force myself to look outside and try to get used to this."

Mahala blanked the screen, then decided to send a message to Solveig. Perhaps she should send one to Chike also, and then others to Dyami and to Risa while she had the time to do so. They would all be interested in her first impressions of Earth, and Risa would be especially curious about Lincoln.

"Solveig Einarsdottir, Venus, Sagan settlement," Mahala said to the screen, then pulled out the keyboard; Solveig preferred written messages to spoken ones, feeling that writing was more succinct. She waited for the tiny light to the right of the console to signal that a channel was open.

The screen remained blank. Mahala repeated Solveig's name, then requested an open channel. The screen brightened into blue, then faded to black again.

A malfunction, she thought, and reached for the slender gold band that lay next to the console and put it on her head. For one disorienting second, she was suddenly adrift in nothingness, and then she sensed the channel opening for her. She was in a small cozy space that resembled her dormitory room in Sagan, with a screen in front of her.

Mahala lifted the band from around her head and the virtual room and screen vanished. The small light at the right of the desk screen was on, telling her that a channel was now open. She could not recall when she had last had such an experience; such malfunctions were rare. But maybe they were not so unusual here, in this small Earth town.

She drew the keyboard toward her and entered a heading for Solveig. It seemed to take a half-second longer than usual for the letters to appear on the screen, but perhaps she was only imagining that. "I'm in Lincoln," she began, "sitting in a room in the house where my great-grandmother grew up," and then she continued with her message.

"Here it is," Harriett said to Mahala, "the field where I officially became a woman. It might even be the same field where Iris Angharads took part in the rite."

They stood to the west of Lincoln, at the side of a dirt road that led away from the town and ended at a field of young grain. Harriet had been her guide for a walk along the roads of Lincoln and to the shops around the town square; they had gone to the tavern for a drink. The whiskey had fortified Mahala, who felt ready afterward to walk with her cousin to the edge of the town. She had a physician's pouch hanging from her belt, partly out of habit but also in case she might need a mood to control her panic. Maybe, she told herself, she was beginning to adjust to this environment.

The grain already reached past Mahala's waist. Tall silos dotted the field, each with an airship cradle for the floaters and freighters that would arrive later in the season for the harvested grain. She turned northwest and saw mountains in the distance, peaks that had to be many kilometers away but appeared so close that it seemed she might be able to walk to them in less than an hour. She could look toward the horizon now without wanting to crouch down and cover her head, but a life spent inside enclosed settlements had left her unable to judge distances here. The sun was low in the west; the wind rose over the flat land, making waves on the sea of wheat.

"I don't know that much about your ceremony," Mahala said.

"We hold it every year, just after the spring sowing," Harriett said. "All of the girls who have started their monthly bleeding are led here by their mothers and the other women of Lincoln. They wear white dresses, and the mayor gives a speech welcoming them to the communes as women. It's a Spiritist custom, but we all follow it whether we're Spiritists or not. Then the mayor makes the sign of the helix and pricks the finger of each girl to draw some blood, and each girl recites, 'I give my blood to the communes.' They're all considered women after that, and then everybody goes back to the town hall to celebrate."

"We don't do anything that elaborate," Mahala said. "We just get our implants and the physician answers any questions we might have. Mothers or other female relatives sometimes give a small party, but that's just for the family and close friends."

Harriett gazed past her. "Looks like we've been followed."

Mahala turned toward the town. Two Guardians were walking along the road in their direction. One of them was Jeremy Courtneys; he lifted a hand and waved.

"Wooo," Harriett murmured, "he's brought a friend along for you, and a nice-looking one, too. His name's Chet, and if it weren't for Jeremy, I wouldn't mind taking him on myself." Plainswomen acted sillier when men were around; Mahala had noticed that in the shops and at the tavern. They sidled up to any likely prospects, batted their eyes, and sometimes even offered a few bawdy compliments. There were, according to Harriett, more men than usual in the shops around the square and in the tavern. More workers had come to Lincoln to renovate the town for the conference, and so there were even more opportunities for flirting.

"I told you before, Harriett," Mahala said. "There's someone else for me."

"And he's still on Venus, and you're still here."

The young man with Jeremy was tall, big-shouldered, and dark-haired, with a broad, pleasant face. Mahala suddenly had the feeling that Harriett had told her Guardian lover that they would both be out here walking by the road about now.

"We just got off duty," Jeremy called out. "I thought the lieutenant might stick Chet with night patrol duty, but he didn't, so you can invite him to supper, too." He glanced at his comrade. "Chester Marjories, meet Mahala Liangharad, Harriett's cousin from Venus."

Chet Marjories grinned at her, looking much too affable to be a Guardian. She found herself smiling back at him. Harriett slipped her hand into Jeremy's. Mahala allowed Chet to loop his arm through hers.

They walked along the road. The tractors and other vehicles that moved across the fields during the day, controlled remotely by Lincoln's farmers from their homes, were idle now, looking much like the diggers and crawlers of Venus. The sun was setting, the air growing colder. Chet told Mahala a little about himself. His mother was a shopkeeper in Council Bluffs; his father, whom he had seen only twice in his life, was a satellite repair worker. "At least that's what he was doing a couple of years ago," Chet added. "I haven't checked to see what he's up to now."

"Have you heard anything about when the conference will start?" Mahala asked.

"I'm so low on the chain of command that I'd be one of the last to know. But I did catch a glimpse of Mukhtar Tabib, so it'll have to start soon. He didn't come here all the way from Damascus just to sample a few Plainswomen."

"Not that he wouldn't have a few good romps if he did," Harriett said.

Jeremy suddenly came to a stop. "Look—out there, to the southwest."

Mahala turned to look. Several tiny specks were barely visible against the darkening sky. "What is it?" she asked, unable to tell how far away the specks were; for a brief dizzying moment, they almost looked like insects only an arm's length from her.

"Visitors?" Harriett asked. "They can't be more delegates—my mother would have been told if they were coming."

"Hovercars," Chet muttered. "No, they're slightly bigger than that—hovercraft." He turned southeast. "And I see a few more over there."

"Something's wrong," Jeremy said. "Anybody authorized to be here would be coming in on a floater—or else we would have been told if they were arriving any other way. We'd better alert the captain."

Chet pulled a palm-sized communicator from a pouch at his belt;

Jeremy grabbed his arm. "Not that way," Jeremy said. "If this is trouble, your message could be picked up."

"I'll find him," Chet said. "He should still be at the town hall."

"Get rid of that and anything else that can be used to track you." Chet tossed his comm into the field of wheat, then pulled off his identity bracelet and hurled it from himself. "Good luck," Jeremy added to his friend.

"Same to you." Chet started running toward Lincoln.

"Get rid of your bracelets, too," Jeremy said as he tore his own off his wrist and threw it into the field with his comm.

Mahala moved closer to Harriett, feeling more bewildered than frightened. "What is it, Jeremy?"

"No one else is scheduled to come here at the moment, and now we've got twenty hovercraft heading right toward Lincoln. Not everybody was real happy about this conference, you know. There was a rumor going around the barracks before we came here that a few Guardian Commanders were removed from duty and forced to resign because they didn't like the whole idea and weren't shy about saying so. Why do you think the Mukhtars decided to have it out here, away from everything?"

"If they thought there might be trouble," Mahala said, "then why didn't they station more Guardians here?"

Jeremy now looked as confused as she felt. "That's a damn good question," he replied, "and I don't have an answer."

Mahala pulled off her bracelet; Harriett did the same. The specks were growing larger, but with the sun almost below the horizon, she could no longer see the vehicles as well.

"Come on," Jeremy said.

"What are we going to do?" Harriett asked.

"Hide," he answered, "and hope like hell that we don't get found."

They ran through the field, keeping low, concealing themselves below the tops of the growing stalks of wheat until they reached a tractor. They were closer to the town now, able to see the road and the lights of the nearby houses through the wheat.

Jeremy looked back. "Bad news," he gasped. "Those are Guardian hovercraft—I can see the black shield insignia on the front. We would have known if more Guardians were being ordered here."

They dropped to their knees and crawled under the tractor. "Will we be safe?" Harriett whispered.

"I hope so," Jeremy said. "We'll be able to see something of what's going on from here."

"Maybe it's nothing," Harriett said.

Jeremy said, "You don't believe that, Harriett."

Mahala was thinking of the suspicions Dyami had voiced about the conference. "Be quiet," Jeremy continued, "and don't move, and don't do anything that might give you away. If they pick us up on their screens, and there's a good chance they will if somebody does a complete sweep, maybe they'll take us for some kids playing hide-and-seek or lovers having some outdoor fun."

"Lovers?" Mahala pressed herself against the ground. "There's three of us."

"Plainswomen have been known to share," Harriett murmured.

They fell silent and waited. Even huddled under the tractor with the others, Mahala could feel how cold the air was getting. In the distance, she heard a soft sound that might have been the wind or else the hum of the approaching hovercraft. She was unfamiliar with the sounds of this world. She had come to Earth thinking that her worst problems would be having to get used to open space and unfiltered air. Would Mukhtar Tabib have lured Habbers and Cytherians here only to make hostages of them for some other end of his own? Somehow, she did not think so.

The hum grew louder. Mahala held her breath. Through the stalks of wheat, she saw a dark shape with a domed top moving along the road, followed by another and then a third. The humming was all around her now. She kept still, certain that the hovercraft were moving along the roads and over the fields to surround Lincoln.

Two of the craft continued into the town. The third hovercraft sank slowly to the surface of the road and sat there.

"They haven't done a sweep," Jeremy whispered. "If they had, they would have come over here by now, and I'd be trying to think of some shit to tell them."

Mahala inched closer to Jeremy. "What do you think they'll do?" she asked.

"They must have already cut off all the channels from Lincoln to the outside—that would have been the first thing to do. The screen channels first, and then blocks on all the Link portals."

Mahala thought of the way her screen had been acting up earlier, of the channels that had taken longer than usual to open for her. "Can they do that?"

Jeremy sighed. "A Guardian Commander could. He'd have the authority."

"But there's a Mukhtar in Lincoln now," Harriett murmured. "Couldn't he override that kind of order?"

"He could if he had enough warning. If he didn't, I don't know. His Link to the cyberminds might be blocked by now, along with any other Linker's. Sooner or later, somebody close to the Council of Muhktars will notice that."

"And know something's wrong," Harriett said.

"Which means," Jeremy said in an even lower voice, "that whatever these Guardians are here to do, they'll have to do it fast."

"Attention," an amplified male voice called out in Anglaic, "attention, all residents of Lincoln." Even at this distance, Mahala heard the words clearly. "This town is now under our control. Stay where you are and remain indoors. Anyone found outside will be shot on sight and detained after regaining consciousness. Be assured that the experience of detention will not be pleasant."

Jeremy moved forward on his elbows and stomach, raised himself up on his arms, then crept back under the tractor. "We might be able to sneak into town," he whispered. "The wheat should hide us from that hovercraft until we get to the nearest yard. There's a hedge there we can use for cover."

"What's the point?" Harriett asked. "You heard that announcement."

"All I know," Jeremy said, "is that I don't like the idea of sitting out here and doing nothing. I've got friends in there, and you've got family, and we don't know what's going to happen to any of them."

"What can we do?" Harriett asked.

"Let's find out," Jeremy replied.

They made it safely through the yard, moving alongside the high hedge until they came to a narrow road. The door of one house farther up the street opened; two Guardians led a man down the steps, followed by a third Guardian. Mahala noticed then that the man in the custody of the Guardians had his hands bound behind his back. She recognized him now, even in the shadows of the dimly lit street: Kesse Enu-Barnes.

"Looks like they're doing a search and rounding people up," Jeremy said. "Harriett, do you think you can get Mahala to your house without being seen?"

Harriett glanced across the road toward a path that led between two houses. "Maybe," she said. "We cut through there and it's two roads over. Let's just hope we can avoid any search parties. What are you going to do?"

"Head for the square. They've probably taken over the town hall by now."

"Then I'm coming with you," Harriett said. "I know the shortcuts—you don't. They might pick you up before you get there."

"Harriett—"

"My mother's probably still in the town hall," Harriett whispered, "in her office."

"What about Mahala?" Jeremy asked.

"I'll stick with you," Mahala said. "If they're going from house to house, we might not be any safer with Harriett's household anyway."

Harriett led them along the road and then into a walled passageway. They came to another street; a hovercraft was up ahead, near the lighted space of the town square. Harriett suddenly darted behind a row of buildings and guided them down a long path to the back of one stone structure.

"This is the tavern," Harriett said, "and over there is the entrance to the cellar." She pointed at a small wooden door on her right. "That's where the backsliding Muslims sneak inside."

"There might be Guardians inside now," Mahala said.

"There might be," Jeremy said. "If there are, then one's probably on guard behind the door. I might be able to get a shot at him, but you two will have to make a run for it after that." His hand moved toward the wand at his waist.

Harriett crept down the three stone steps to the door and passed her hand over the sensor. The door suddenly swung open; Mahala recoiled.

A tall blond woman stood in the open doorway, her thin fine-featured face illuminated by a light wand that she held in her hand. Mahala had seen her before, behind the bar of the tavern. Chet Marjories stood just behind her, his weapon aimed directly at Harriett.

"Allison," Harriett said.

"Mother of God." The blond woman grabbed Harriett's arm; Chet stepped back. "Get inside, all of you."

"I didn't get to Captain Dullea," Chet said as Mahala finished her medscan. "My foot went right into a rut in the road. By the time I got to the square, they were taking over the town hall, so I ducked in here."

Chet's left ankle was fractured, the cartilage of his left knee torn. He had limped the short distance through the cellar and up the stairs into the tavern's main room; his ankle was so swollen that he could not remove his boot.

"I can give you something for the pain and swelling," Mahala said, "but you'll have to stay off that leg until you're treated with—"

"I'm not going anywhere," Chet said.

They sat in the back of the tavern. Allison had dimmed the lights, so that they would not be seen by any Guardians at the opposite end of the square. Others were in the tavern, several men in the gray garb of workers and a scattering of townswomen in the customary Lincoln garb of long dresses or loose tunics and pants. Mahala finished treating her patient, then looked toward the front windows. Four hovercraft were parked in the square, in front of the town hall and near the road that led to the floater cradles.

"They rounded up our comrades," Chet continued. "They marched them over to the town hall—probably have them locked up in one of the meeting rooms. They were bringing in some others, too." He stared grimly at Mahala. "They brought in some of the delegates who came here with you."

"Then they might be looking for her now," Jeremy said.

"They probably are."

"Is my mother inside the hall?" Harriett asked.

"I don't know," Chet replied.

"If I were home," a woman sitting near them muttered, "I'd greet them with a shotgun when they came to my door."

Mahala frowned. She had noticed two long projectile weapons locked in a case in the common room of Harriett's house, but Gisella had told her that they were old rifles passed down through the line and used only for traditional sports such as target shooting or taking pot shots at rats.

"If you did," Jeremy said to the woman who had spoken, "you'd end up either stunned or dead. Old guns won't help you against beamers and wands and trained Guardians."

The woman's eyes narrowed. "Maybe so," she said, "but I don't like the idea of Guardians barging in here and dragging off our guests. What kind of hospitality is that? What sort of beginning of the goddamn new era is that?" Others in the tavern nodded in agreement. Two men in workers' gray got up and moved closer to a window, watching the square.

"Have they come in here to look for anybody?" Jeremy asked.

The woman and several other people shook their heads. "Not yet," the woman replied.

"Then they'll find her when they do," Chet said, jerking his head at Mahala.

"I can hide her," Allison said.

Chet grimaced. "Not from a sweep, you can't, and there'd just be a lot more trouble for you when she's found."

Mahala looked around the room. Most of the people looked angry or frustrated; she had the feeling that they would help her if they could. The Guardians must have come here to stop the conference somehow, perhaps by using Mukhtar Tabib and the other delegates as hostages. They were probably not interested in Lincoln's citizens or in the visiting workers at all, unless they got in the way.

"Then we have to get her to some place that's already been searched," another woman said.

"I can do that," Harriett said.

"No," Mahala heard herself say.

"You're going to stay here?" Chet asked.

Mahala stood up, knowing what she would have to do. "They seem to be after the delegates," she said. "You'll just bring trouble on yourselves if you try to protect me."

"We're in trouble already," Allison said.

"They won't make more trouble for you than they have to," Mahala said. "I think I should give myself up—and before they come to search this place."

"But you don't know what they want to do," Harriett said.

"No, I don't, but friends of mine are being held by them, people I care about. It might get worse for them if I don't give myself up. The Guardians holding them might think they would know where I am."

Jeremy sighed. "They could be questioning people about that. Guardian interrogations aren't exactly pleasant."

Allison said, "I don't think you should go there."

"I have to go." Now that she had committed herself to that course of action, Mahala felt drained and empty. "You'd better let me out the back way. You don't want them to see me coming out the front."

"I see Guardians coming out of Rosalie's shop," a woman near the windows said. "Now they're going into Miri's place, so they'll be here pretty soon."

"You might need somebody with you," Harriett said to Mahala. "You still don't know your way around."

"It doesn't matter," Mahala said, "as long as they don't see me coming out of your place."

A man said, "I'll come with you."

Mahala turned her head toward the stranger as he stood up and came toward them. He was a slender man in the gray pants and shirt of a worker, of medium height, with a shaggy mop of light brown hair.

"Who are you?" Harriett asked.

"Edmund Helgas," he said.

"He's been staying with my commune for the past couple of weeks," a dark-haired woman who had been sitting next to him said.

"I can get you away from here," Edmund Helgas said, "and it might go better for you if somebody's with you. Guardians can give folks a harder time when there's no witnesses."

"He's right about that," Chet said.

"All right," Mahala said, "we'd better leave before they come here."

"I don't like this," Allison said as she opened the back door.

"I don't either," Mahala said softly.

Edmund led her outside and along a darkened pathway behind several buildings. She could not tell if this was the same way Harriett had taken to get her here or another path altogether, and then they turned a corner. A man stood at the end of a passageway, silhouetted by the lights of the square.

A Guardian, she thought. The man turned toward them and raised his arm, and she knew that he was aiming a weapon at them.

"Who's there?" the Guardian called out, and a bright light was suddenly shining on them.

Edmund held up one hand and grabbed Mahala by the arm. "Look, I was fixing a homeostat in one of the shops," he said in a high-pitched voice unlike the one he had used in the tavern. He walked toward the light, still gripping her. "Found this girl hiding behind a crate outside, in the back."

They emerged into the square. The light winked out. Mahala did not like the hard look of the Guardian's face. The uniformed man stared at her, then motioned to his two companions. "She doesn't have her bracelet on," he said, "but she looks like that holo we saw."

The two other Guardians moved toward them. "Who are you?" one of them said to Edmund.

"Edmund Helgas. I was sent here to do maintenance and repairs. Just scan my bracelet and you'll see—"

The Guardian suddenly struck him on the side of the head with his wand. Edmund staggered, still clutching her arm, then steadied himself.

"Maybe he expects us to give him a reward for bringing her in," the third Guardian said. He was the tallest of the three, much taller than she and Edmund; he pulled Edmund toward him by the shoulders. "How do we know you weren't hiding her all along, trying to sneak her somewhere else?"

"We don't know," another Guardian muttered, "so we'll have to bring him along." He grabbed Mahala by the upper arm, his fingers digging into her arm so deeply that it hurt.

They were ushered across the square, toward the steps of the town hall. Someone has to stop them, Mahala thought. By now someone in authority had surely discovered that Lincoln was cut off from the outside. The Mukhtars and their aides would be worrying about the safety of the delegates, trying to find out what had happened.

She and Edmund climbed the steps with their captors; the wide entrance above them opened. Two more Guardians were there, with the bars of officers on their black collars. Someone was crying inside, emitting hoarse, rasping sobs.

They came through the entrance. The doors on either side of the wide hallway were closed; a Guardian was posted in front of each of them. Ahmad Berkur, one of the Cytherian delegates, was lying on the floor next to the booted feet of another Guardian; blood covered his face. The sobbing woman huddled on the floor near another

Guardian was Ah Lin Bergen; she raised a bruised and discolored face to Mahala.

"We thought they might know where you could be hiding," the Guardian holding her arm said, "but they didn't."

Mahala was shocked into silence for a few long moments, then found her voice. "I'm a physician," she managed to say. "Let me take care of them."

"We don't have to let you do a fucking thing," one of the officers said. "Baro, take that worker to the mayor's office and throw him in with the locals." One of the Guardians who had led her here dragged Edmund across the hallway. The two officers took Mahala by the arms and propelled her toward a door.

The Guardian at the door stepped aside as it opened. A man was shouting inside, ranting in Anglaic. "Idiots!" he screamed. "Traitors! Do you think I can't stop this? I have already stopped it!" He spun around and faced Mahala; the jewel of a Linker glittered on his forehead. He was a tall man with graying dark hair and a sharp-boned face reddened and distorted by rage, and then she saw the gold stars of a Commander on his collar.

Malik was in the room, seated in front of a round table, bound to a chair, with Benzi tied to a chair next to him. Two Guardians stood behind them, wands in their hands. Tesia was there, and Hong Te-yu, along with a red-haired man Mahala did not know. Jamilah al-Hussaini, the former Liaison to the Project Council, was also under restraint. Mahala recognized the bearded face of the seventh person at the table, the only one of the captives who was not bound: Mukhtar Tabib al-Tahir, clothed in a formal white robe and headdress.

"Commander Lawrence," one of the Guardians holding her said, "we found this one." A hand pushed against her back, propelling her into the room.

The Commander strode toward Mahala. She feared for a moment that he would strike her. Incongruously, he suddenly smiled. "Salaam, Mahala Liangharad," he said calmly.

"Greetings," Mahala replied weakly.

"We have nothing against you," the Commander said. "Let me assure you of that, young woman. We have nothing against any Cytherian—you are Earth's children, after all. But it wasn't at all wise of you to think you could hide from us."

She swallowed. "There are two Cytherian delegates in the hallway." A whining tone had crept into her voice. "They look badly hurt. I'm a physician—let me help them."

He was still smiling. His open hand caught her in the face, knocking her against the wall. She grabbed at the nearest chair to right herself.

"Enough!" a man shouted.

"Mukhtar Tabib, you are in no position to tell me anything," the Commander said. He clutched Mahala's shoulder and forced her to sit down. "And you, Mahala Liangharad, are in no position to make any demands of me."

She kept still. Mukhtar Tabib looked angry; Jamilah al-Hussaini's widened eyes showed her fear. Mahala tried to imagine what it had been like for the two Linkers when they had realized that their Links were blocked. Unless they were Linking with people in other locations or searching for information that was not stored in their implants, they might not even have known that they were cut off until after these Guardians had entered the town. She glanced at Malik, who seemed strangely composed, almost resigned.

"Commander Lawrence," Mukhtar Tabib said softly, "I will do what I can for you, but I must beseech you to tell me what it is that you want. I have been sitting here and waiting while you have been conducting a search for delegates to our conference and locking up Captain Dullea's detachment of Guardians."

"There's two of those Guardians still missing," said one of the Guardians standing in the open doorway.

The Commander turned around. "Then find them!"

"They're looking for them, sir."

The Commander turned back to the others in the room. There was nothing human in his furious eyes and twisted face. Muhktar Tabib leaned forward, resting his arms on the tabletop, gazing up at the Commander almost as if he sympathized with him. "Commander Lawrence," the Mukhtar said in his oddly gentle voice, "I will do whatever I can for you, God willing. Please inform me of your purpose in coming to Lincoln."

"To stop this conference, this abomination." The Commander pulled a weapon from his belt, an object that was slightly longer and wider than a wand. A beamer, Mahala thought, and felt her heart racing. Wands only stunned their targets; beamers were lethal.

"As long as you are keeping us here," Mukhtar Tabib murmured, "the conference cannot be held. It seems that you have stopped it already."

"Don't insult me, Mukhtar." The rage left the Commander's face; he almost looked happy. "You know that I can hold this area only for a short time. By now the Plains Administrators must be aware that Lincoln has dropped off the net. They will inform the Council of Mukhtars of that fact, and perhaps your colleagues are at this very moment studying scans and satellite images of this location. They will see that unauthorized Guardian vehicles are here, and they will be trying to decide what to do. And after enough time has elapsed, they will do what they must do to take us out, so to speak, regardless of any risks to the lives of others."

"You have said it, Commander." Mukhtar Tabib folded his hands. "You have already lost."

"Do you think that I'm another of those weak-willed soldiers you pushed out of your way during your rise to power? Do you think I am the sort who plans his battles with his own self-interest in mind, who's afraid to risk his own hide? I know that I'll have nothing for myself when this is over, and stand a good chance of losing everything, but I will stop your conference, and that is what this battle is about. You want to strengthen our ties with the Habbers, and that will only destroy us in the end, destroy what we are. I am here to show the Habbers that they will never have our world as a gift, that they will never have our Earth, the planet they abandoned, turned over to them as a present by misguided people such as yourself. They may have deceived you with their spurious alien signal, but they haven't fooled me."

"Commander—" the Mukhtar began.

"You believe them only because that serves your ends."

"I believe them because we confirmed—"

"Lies," Commander Lawrence shouted. "They will never have our world unless they fight for it, and I do not think that they are capable of that."

"Commander," Mukhtar Tabib said, "I urge you to think this over, to consider—"

"You are trying to delay me, Mukhtar. You are trying to buy time." Commander Lawrence lifted his arm, aiming his weapon at the red-haired man next to Benzi. Tabib rose from his chair; a Guardian moved toward him, wand out. The Mukhtar sat down again.

"Jeffrey Arnold," the Commander said, "I know who you are, what you were. Everything you had was given to you by the Venus Project, and you threw it away to flee to the Habbers." A short sound like a scream came from the officer's weapon as a bright light flashed. Mahala blinked, unable to see for a second, and then looked toward the back of the room. The red-haired man was still in his chair, his head thrown back, his body stiff. There was no mark on him, but Mahala knew that there was nothing she could do for him; the beamer had destroyed his brain and all the nerve cells of his body.

"Malik Haddad," the Commander said, and for a moment Mahala stopped breathing. "You are an offense to your people, to your world, to God. You were given everything by Earth, and you rose to become a Linker yourself, but you could not stop yourself from spreading foolish ideas about the Venus Project, writing that it might become a bridge between Earth and the Habbers. Your Link was taken from you and you were sent to Venus, to atone for your mistakes, and instead you betrayed your people again to run to the Habbers. Now, at last, you will have the punishment you deserve and be an example to other traitors."

Mahala could not turn away from her grandfather. Malik sat there, his expression calm, his dark eyes showing no fear. He seemed about to speak, and she wondered if there was anything he could say that might save his life.

"The bridge has been built," Malik said softly, "and you cannot tear it down, Commander."

The Commander's weapon screamed again, and a light blazed for a few brief seconds. Malik slumped in his chair, his eyes still open. Benzi would be next, Mahala supposed, or perhaps he would kill one of the Habber women first. Maybe, in spite of what he had said, he would execute all of them.

The sound of an explosion nearly deafened her, so close that the walls of the room seemed to shake. Commander Lawrence cursed; the Guardians nearest the door ran from the room. There was the sound of another blast, closer this time, then the shouts of people in the hallway.

"On the floor!" someone shouted from outside the room. "Get on the floor!" Mahala threw herself forward as a beam shot past her; a weapon whined again, spitting out a second beam and then a third. She lay on her stomach; fingers grabbed her by the wrist. She lifted her head slightly and found herself looking into the face of Mukhtar Tabib.

"Secure this room," a man called out. A pair of booted feet were near her; Mahala sat up slowly as the Mukhtar let go of her. More Guardians were in the room; one of them helped Tabib to his feet.

There was smoke in the hallway. Edmund Helgas stood in the doorway, holding a wand. The hallway echoed with the sounds of shouted commands and the whines of wands being fired. "We lost two people," Mukhtar Tabib muttered. "You took your time."

"I moved as fast as I could," Edmund replied. "You'd better stay here."

Mahala looked up at the man she had met in Allison's tavern. "You're not a worker," she said.

"No, I'm not." Edmund moved away from the door.

Mahala stood up unsteadily. More Guardians ran through the hallway toward the entrance to the town hall; others lay on the floor. She willed herself not to turn around, not to look at the bodies of her grandfather and his dead comrade.

She stepped toward the doorway, coughing from the smoke. "Stay here," Muhktar Tabib said, "until this building is secured."

She ignored him and peered down the smoke-filled hallway to her left. Ah Lin was still out there, seated with her back against the wall; Ahmad Berkur lay on the floor, his eyes closed. A Guardian stood near the two Cytherians; he looked toward her.

"I'm a physician," she said. "I can help."

Ah Lin had been beaten, but would recover. Ahmad had a fractured nose, a concussion, and a ruptured kidney from his beating. Mahala had just finished embedding an implant in Ahmad's arm when she felt a hand on her shoulder.

She looked up to see a broad-faced woman in a brown tunic and pants with a physician's bag hanging from one shoulder. "I'm Shirl Heathers," the woman said. "I'm a physician." She looked up at the Guardian near them. "Can you get them to the mayor's office? They can rest there."

The Guardian nodded. Shirl Heathers helped Mahala up. In the hall, Guardians were dragging other unconscious uniformed men by the heels or the arms toward a room across the way. Outside, in the direction of the town square, Mahala heard shouts and then a series of loud popping sounds.

"What's going on?" Mahala asked.

"We were in the mayor's office," the other physician replied, "Teresa and I and a few others who were here to welcome Mukhtar

Tabib. Captain Dullea was just outside the door with a few of his Guardians. Somebody started shouting something about hovercraft coming into the town square, and the captain went to investigate. The next thing I knew, Captain Dullea and his soldiers were being herded into another room and more Guardians were swarming into the hall. Then a maniac with stars on his collar walked into the mayor's office and told us that we were all under arrest."

"Commander Lawrence," Mahala whispered.

"His men grabbed the two Administrators with us, Masud al-Tikriti and Constantine Matheos, and threw them in with the captain and his people. The commander was screaming that he had nothing against them, that they had been misled, that he wouldn't harm them as long as they didn't get in his way, and then he and his men grabbed the Mukhtar and that Linker woman and the Habbers who were with us and took them away and locked us in the office. Teresa tried to override the lock, but couldn't. A while later, somebody opened the door and pushed a worker inside."

"Edmund Helgas," Mahala said.

"Didn't tell us his name. Said he'd get us out of there. Did a check of the room and then told us to stay back. We got under the table, as far away from the door as possible, and I was deaf for at least three minutes after he blew it open."

Teresa Marias was coming toward them. She hurried to Mahala and clasped her hands. "Have you seen my daughter?" the mayor asked.

"Harriett was with me," Mahala said. "We made it to the tavern. She's probably there now—she's safe."

"If you ask me," Shirl murmured, "that Commander needs a metabolic adjustment."

Mahala freed herself from Teresa and crossed the hallway to the entrance. Guardians who might be unconscious or dead were being dragged from three hovercraft. Several bodies lay in the square; armed men in the gray clothing of workers herded ten Guardians toward the town hall. Mahala descended the steps and went to tend to the wounded.

Lincoln's town hall became a makeshift infirmary. Teresa went to her house, found out that her housemates were safe, and came back to the town hall with the rest of Mahala's medical supplies and her physician's bag. Mahala and Shirl, with only Midge Laras, a paramedic in training, to help them, worked throughout the night. Mahala ignored her fatigue, refusing to lie down and rest for even a few moments, rejecting the cups of tea Harriett and Jeremy brought to her. The work of healing kept her from thinking about the two Habbers who had been killed, about the grandfather whom she had never really known and who was now forever lost to her.

Harriett told her a little of what had happened in the tavern after Mahala had left with Edmund. They had waited, expecting Allison's tavern to be searched within the hour. Jeremy and Chet had been talking about giving themselves up when they heard the muffled sound of an explosion. The workers inside Allison's had run from the tavern and were in the square right after the second blast, pulling out concealed weapons from their shirts and shooting at the Guardians in front of the town hall. Harriett had seen one man slap a disk that looked like a sensor patch on the top of a hovercar in the square; the vehicle had suddenly glowed with a bright light. Mahala thought of the bodies lying next to hovercraft that she had scanned, that had shown no signs of life.

By dawn, six people who were too badly off to be moved lay on futons in the hallway of the town hall; other injured townsfolk had been sent home with members of their households. Twenty members of Commander Lawrence's force were among the wounded, most of them the victims of shotgun blasts or bullets fired from pistols. The women of Lincoln, once they had realized that a battle was under way, had been quick to join in the fighting with their old weapons, firing upon the Guardians who had come to search their homes and shops.

Mahala had seen how much damage a shotgun or pistol could do to a human body. She reminded herself that the members of Commander Lawrence's force had followed him willingly, either out of belief in his cause or because of personal devotion to him. She would not pity the more grievously wounded of his Guardians too much.

She finished scanning a man in workers' clothes who had been stunned by a wand beam, then gave him an injection for his nausea. "Stay here," she said as she eased him back against his futon, "until you feel well enough to get up. That shouldn't be more than an hour or two."

"Thanks," he said. This young man and some fifty other workers, she had discovered during the course of her therapeutic labors, were actually members of the personal guard of the Council of Mukhtars. She had seen Edmund Helgas striding through the hallway, issuing orders, seeing that the defeated Guardian prisoners were secured and under restraint. Even without a uniform, Edmund—if that was in fact his name, which she doubted—had the air of a Guardian officer.

Mahala rose and glanced toward the room where Malik had died. His body and that of his fellow Habber had been carried from the room earlier. History had caught up with Malik in this place; that was probably the way he would have viewed his death.

The door to the mayor's office opened. Mukhtar Tabib and Administrator Masud came into the hallway, followed by Benzi. The three of them had been in the room all night, after Teresa and the other townsfolk who were not needed here had left with the rest of the delegates to the conference.

Benzi walked toward her. "You've been here all night," he said.

"I gave myself something to stay awake."

"Tesia is staying with Te-yu. I'm going back to Teresa Marias's house. We can walk there together if you like."

Tabib and Masud were standing by the door. The Mukhtar murmured a few words to the Administrator, then turned to Mahala and Benzi. "I am sorry for what happened to your grandfather," he said, "and to his comrade."

"You knew what might happen," Mahala said. "You must have known, or Edmund Helgas and those other men wouldn't have been here."

"I knew what might happen—that is true."

"Then you might have tried to stop it. You didn't have to let it happen."

"You are wrong, child." The Mukhtar stepped toward her. "We had rooted out the Guardian officers most likely to oppose this conference or to attempt to put a stop to it. We thought we had them all, but could not be sure, and there were indications that others among the Guardians might be covertly disloyal. We had to find a way to draw them out."

"Using us as bait," Benzi said, and Mahala heard the bitterness and sorrow in his voice. "Knowing that our lives were at risk."

"Your lives were at risk as soon as you set foot on Earth," Tabib said. "When you and the other Habbers among us were left unharmed, treated warmly, or at least courteously, by those among whom you were living, I allowed myself to hope that I might have overestimated the amount of hostility to your presence. But I did not delude myself. I knew that those who hated you and your kind might try to stop this conference." The Mukhtar drew his black eyebrows together. "Let me point out that my own life was also at risk, that I was part of the bait."

"I doubt that those Guardians would have killed a Mukhtar," Benzi said.

Tabib shook his head. "You Habbers are even more naïve than I thought. You saw Commander Lawrence. I am certain that he was capable of killing everyone in Lincoln if that would have served his purpose."

"Maybe he wasn't the only one," Mahala said. "Maybe there are others."

"There may well be," Tabib said, "and if so, we now have a means of ferreting them out. Those who were opposed to the new era had the choice of abiding by the will of the Council of Mukhtars without complaint or of resigning their positions and having no further role in public life and political matters. Both I and the Guardian Commander in Chief were bound to respect those who chose to resign. We might have taken steps to see if they had knowledge of others in the ranks who might be disloyal, but such interrogations would have set a bad example and damaged morale. Our quarrel was not with those who were open in their disagreement with us and who had honorably resigned their posts, but with those who might be secretly preparing to defy us. Now they have acted against us, and so we are free to regard them as criminals, to use any means of interrogation necessary to find out if they have other accomplices." His mouth twisted into what seemed a mockery of a smile. "I can assure you that the death of your grandfather will be avenged by the torments his murderer is likely to suffer during such questioning."

"Commander Lawrence may not be the only one plotting against you in secret," Benzi said.

"I sincerely doubt that he is," Tabib replied.

"He may have no knowledge of others who might be your enemies," Benzi said.

"Our enemies, Benzi Liangharad. We are in this together, you and I. Commander Lawrence will serve as a useful example in any case. Others may be induced to bow out of our public affairs and to seek retirement."

Mahala moved closer to Benzi, suddenly wishing that she had never come to this place.

"I know what you are thinking, child," the Mukhtar continued, "that I am ruthless and cruel and a relic of a violent past. That is true,

I suppose, but my ruthlessness is being used in the service of the new era—or so I tell myself. You are thinking that you should never have come here. Be thankful that you have. You have had a demonstration of what we are hoping to escape as we struggle to become something better."

24

Mahala Liangharad:
Excerpts from Journal Entries

June 14, 657:

All of the delegates to the Lincoln Conference, as this gathering is now being called, have been asked to keep records of our thoughts and experiences. Mukhtar Tabib al-Tahir has said that we're free either to keep an oral record or to write our observations down and to use whatever languages come most easily to us. He has also urged us to be completely honest, since only certain scholars will have access to our journals in the near future, and to be mindful of the fact that our words may be an important part of the historical record. Other than that, he hasn't offered any guidance at all.

Over two weeks have passed since I arrived in Lincoln, and our first official meeting is tomorrow. We're still getting past the horror of these past days. Mukhtar Tabib (and presumably the rest of the Council of Mukhtars, although it is increasingly obvious that he has the power to speak for all of them) decided that my grandfather Malik Haddad should be buried in Damascus, with all honor, immediately after Lincoln was secured. Naturally that meant that Mukhtar Tabib had to be present for the funeral, as did Administrator Masud, since he is a kinsman of Malik's. A man who was once a Linker on Earth, and then a Cytherian settler, and after that a Habber—the Mukhtars could hardly have found a better martyr to the new era. There must have been thousands outside the mosque, and thousands more in the procession when Malik's body was carried to the graveyard.

A search through the records revealed that Jeffrey Arnold had kinsfolk in the Atlantic Federation near New York. They were given permission to scatter his remains at sea from a sailing vessel, which made for yet another visual spectacle of mourning for a martyr.

I didn't go to Damascus. Given that Mukhtar Tabib was determined to give Malik a traditional funeral, I would have had to remain out of sight with the other female mourners anyway. Jamilah al-Hussaini also hinted that the Mukhtar thought all of the delegates would be much safer staying in Lincoln. That is something else we have to worry about now, our personal safety. The Guardians are still here, and I know that others have been stationed at other points outside Lincoln. I haven't tried to find out what other measures are being taken to protect us, and perhaps it's better if we don't know the specifics.

I also don't particularly want to know what his interrogators may have learned from Commander Lawrence, or what methods they used to get the information.

Benzi has been staying here, with Teresa Marias and her household. For days after the incident, he hardly spoke at all. Most of the time, he would sit in the courtyard, staring at the roses. He had promised me that he would tell Risa about Malik's end, and he sent her a message right away, and I sat with him and sent her a message of my own to console her, and then after that, Benzi retreated into himself. Harriett heard rumors from other households that the other Habbers here were in the same sort of state, just completely closed off from everything. If they were communing with one another through their Links, they showed no sign of that.

After a week, I couldn't bear to see him like that anymore, sitting out there, going back to his room for a few hours, and then going into the courtyard again. Finally I went out to him, and sat with him for a while, and then I said, "I know you're mourning and that losing someone through death must be even harder for Habbers than it is for us, but I'm worried about you, everyone here is concerned. Teresa doesn't know what to do, and neither does anyone else."

He looked at me then. "I was thinking," he said, "of what my life might be like now if I had stayed here."

"You might not even be alive," I told him, "and if you were, you'd be an old man, even older than Nona. And you wouldn't have been living in this house—you would have become another wandering Plainsman."

"I might have become a shopkeeper in Lincoln. There are a few men among them. Then I could have stayed."

"Are you sorry that you didn't?" I asked.

"No. It wasn't my choice to leave here, but I am not sorry for the way my life has gone. Still, there might have been satisfactions in living it another way."

At least he was talking now. "I miss him," I said. "I miss my grandfather." I was regretting the times when I might have sought Malik out and had instead avoided him. What I missed was the chance we might have had to build our own personal bridge during this conference.

"We haven't lost him entirely," Benzi said. "A record of some of his memories will remain with our cyberminds. Eventually he might have left more of a pattern of his thoughts and feelings with our minds, but there is at least something of him left."

I said, "You sound as though you're talking of a soul."

"Not really. The man we knew as Malik no longer exists."

"Would he still exist if there had been time for your cyberminds to hold his pattern?" I was thinking of what Balin and Orban and other Habbers had implied, that their minds might persist, captured by the artificial intelligences of their Habitats, even after their bodies had failed.

"It's not quite that straightforward, Mahala. There might have been a mental pattern that I could respond to through my Link as though I were encountering Malik, but whether or not that pattern would be Malik in any true sense is a metaphysical question. I've never had much taste for metaphysical speculation."

"Maybe I've misunderstood some of what I've heard from the Habbers I know," I said. "Sometimes Balin almost made it sound as though Habbers, instead of dying, could choose to become part of your cybernetic net."

"Choose to become?" His expression changed; there was something alien, something *other* in his face. "We already are part of that net."

"Through your Links, of course," I said, "but that wasn't what I meant."

"That wasn't what I meant, either. Someone like me, someone like Tesia or Te-yu or Jeffrey—" He looked away for a moment, as though he had just recalled that his comrade Jeffrey was dead, too. "We're not so different from Linkers. Tesia and Balin, being Habbers who have lived among Cytherians for many years and formed strong bonds with them, haven't diverged that much from other human beings. Te-yu and I weren't brought up by Habbers—we came to the Habitats later in life. There are still many times when I choose to block my Link, to leave it silent, as many of Earth's Linkers do. But to describe other Habbers as being only humans who are Linked and who happen to live in Habitats would be inaccurate at best."

I told him that as a child, I had assumed that the Habbers whose Habitats were farther out in the solar system might be much more alien than those we had encountered. Solveig and Ah Lin and other friends of mine had speculated that they might even have given up their human bodies and taken on completely different forms.

Benzi's face softened at these comments; he looked almost as if he were smiling. "Oh, no," he said, "their bodies are as human as ours in appearance. In a way, that makes many of them seem even more alien. I used to think that such Habbers weren't much more than the eyes and ears of our artificial intelligences, but that isn't quite accurate, either."

He seemed to want to say more at that point, while trying to decide how to proceed. I kept silent and waited.

"When someone has chosen to give up many, perhaps most of his memories," Benzi said at last, "while allowing the cyberminds to save those memories, and then goes on to live another life, I am not at all sure you can call him the same person. If he can no longer draw any distinction between himself, his own mentality, and the Link within him, perhaps it isn't accurate to call him human, either. And when I consider cyberminds with the accumulated memories and thoughts and dreams and maybe even feelings of millions of Habitat-dwellers, I wonder if parts of our net of artificial intelligences aren't more human than some of us are."

"Human enough to have hoped for a new era?" I meant that as a joke.

Benzi stared directly at me. "That is exactly what they want," he said, "what they—maybe saying that they want this or desire that particular outcome isn't a precise enough way to speak of it, but it is true that our artificial intelligences are trying to reach out to their cybernetic brethren on Earth. It is also true that Earth's cyberminds, while treated more as servants and appendages by the Linkers of Earth, seem to be welcoming a chance for closer ties with the Habitats. To put it as simply as possible, our cyberminds are ready to share their information, their data—whatever you wish to call what they are and what is in them—with the minds of Earth. The artificial intelligences of Earth apparently have the same aim. That isn't their only goal, of course—there is also a universe for them to explore, and an alien mentality for them to contact."

"You make it sound as though we're almost incidental to their plans," I said.

Benzi looked grim for a moment, and then he laughed softly. The sound of that subdued laughter unnerved me almost as much as Commander Lawrence had with his rantings.

"Not yet," Benzi told me, "not yet. I think human beings may be forgiven the actions of a rogue Guardian Commander. They may even be forgiven several more such spasms. But I don't think that we should test the patience—if I may call it patience—of our cyberminds too far. We would not want to give them reasons to decide that they might be better off without their fleshy companions."

I could think of nothing to say to that.

"In other words," Benzi went on, "let us hope that this conference succeeds."

June 22, 657:

Our meetings are being held in the town hall, in the largest of the rooms off the hallway. Since the room isn't used that often—the mayor uses it mostly for welcoming visiting officials, for groups of townspeople who have requested a meeting with her, or for lectures and presentations by the Lincoln Academy faculty that townsfolk might like to attend in person—our sessions shouldn't disrupt the business of the town. There are other places where we might have met, but the Lincoln town hall seems the most appropriate. So far, it seems to be working.

June 30, 657:

For many decades, Earth has allowed people to gather in camps near three cities in different regions to await a chance for passage to Venus. Anyone who has been turned away by the representatives of the Project Council, who has been refused a place as a specialist or a worker, may still go to one of the camps and hope to be chosen eventually. My own grandfather Malik made his way to such a camp after his disgrace and won his passage to Venus there, as did my grandfather Sef.

But the price such hopeful settlers must pay is high. They give up everything to go to those camps. They live in primitive surroundings under the supervision of Guardians, with no guarantee that they will ever get passage. Yet even under those conditions, thousands of people have been willing to take the risk and to seek a new life on Venus.

At least thousands have been until recently. The Council of Mukhtars considered closing the camps completely just after the new era of peace and friendship was announced, but decided against it in the end. Mukhtar Tabib was quite honest about admitting that it didn't seem advisable to close off that particular social safety valve until there were signs that the new era might last. As time went on, fewer people traveled to the camps anyway; living through the new era on Earth probably looked as promising or as challenging as building a new life in a Venus settlement. It seemed only a matter of time before would-be emigrants stopped coming to those camps.

Then this conference was announced, and suddenly people were streaming to the three camps again, thousands more than had been going there decades ago. More people than ever are ready to give up their lives on Earth for a chance to leave the home planet for good.

The difference is that many of them don't want to go to Venus. Many of them want to become spacefarers instead.

This subject has taken up most of our sessions. There are so many other matters to discuss, and we still haven't come to any consensus on what to do about those camps. Mukhtar Tabib and Administrator Masud want them closed. Constantine Matheos and Jamilah al-Hussaini have recommended stationing some Counselors at each camp, presumably to find ways to keep the situation from spiraling out of control, and also want a commission to study the problem and "make recommendations." In other words, they obviously don't know what to think.

Well, I don't know what to think, either.

The Habbers, though, know exactly what they think. Benzi was speaking for the Habber delegates who are here, but he strongly implied that others would agree with him. (Other Habbers? The Habber cyberminds? None of us among the delegates are now sure of where to draw the line between them.) In any case, the Habbers say they would welcome anyone from those camps who is willing to leave the solar system aboard their interstellar vessel.

They are still insisting on that. The delegates finally had to agree to set the whole issue aside for now.

July 1, 657:

No meeting today. Another group of Habbers arrived to "observe some sessions," even though we all know that they could do that through their Links with the Habbers who are already here. A few Linkers who are aides to the Council of Mukhtars are coming tomorrow, for the same stated reason, which makes as little sense in their case. Perhaps this is just more diplomacy, coming here personally. The only other explanation I can think of is that there are some things these Linkers want to discuss privately among themselves, with their Links closed.

The people of Lincoln, the shopkeepers in particular, will welcome these new delegations. At the same time, some people here are complaining that the meetings should be held in public. Teresa seems quite insulted that even she, as the mayor, hasn't been invited to participate, and others are wondering why the sessions aren't being made available on public channels. I told Teresa that nothing had been resolved yet, and that she hadn't missed much, but I'm not sure she believed me.

Benzi left Teresa's house at dawn to meet the arriving Habbers and didn't return until evening. At last I was able to speak to him alone in the courtyard after dark. "Don't you realize," I told him, "that if everybody from the camps who wants to be on your space vessel is allowed to go, there won't be room for a lot of the people who will be essential?"

"Mahala, I'm disappointed in you," he replied. "We're speaking of a Habitat, a space-going worldlet. We're talking about a community of hundreds of thousands in an environment that will have space for even more than that."

"You'll need specialists. Most of the people in those camps are workers. Some of them are probably people who lived on basic credit and whatever they could con somebody out of or steal."

"We can train them and educate them."

"I don't care what you say—you can't possibly take everybody who will want to go."

Benzi smiled. "You're wrong, Mahala. As I said, we'll have more than enough room. You think people will be begging to go, that millions of Earthfolk and Cytherians and Habbers will choose to go on this voyage."

"Millions do want to be part of it. You know that."

He shook his head. "They dream of it, and they'll go on dreaming of it, but in the end they won't go. Our problem is not going to be deciding which people should be part of this voyage and which to turn away. Our problem is going to be finding enough people who will choose to make the journey, and who will help make it what it should be rather than a cosmic disaster."

I looked at him questioningly.

"What I mean is not a technical disaster, although that might happen, unlikely as it may be. I mean a cultural catastrophe, or tragedy, an encounter that might destroy whatever we find or destroy us."

July 17, 657:

Exaggerated accounts of the Battle of Lincoln, as the more dramatically inclined are calling Commander Lawrence's failed attack on the conference, have been all over the public channels. According to one rumor, a group of mind-tour producers wanted to create a depiction of the events, either for the historical record or simply as an exciting simulated adventure; they were quickly discouraged from doing so. The authorities probably would have preferred not to have word of the incident get out at all, but that would have required closing off Lincoln and finding ways to keep the people here from talking. Rumors might have gotten out anyway, and turning an entire community into a kind of prison would not have been an appropriate way to mark the new era.

This evening, Amaris and Gisella came home with a story about a town in the North Mediterranean Nomarchy that had been taken over by Guardians. Within a few minutes, the entire household was in the common room watching reports on the screen. The town was a place called Tivoli, and order was restored within three hours, but not before a Habber in residence there had been killed.

Now everyone is wondering if there will be other incidents—and what the Habbers will do if they lose any more of their people.

I also find myself wondering if it's possible for a cybermind to become disgusted enough not to want to have anything to do with us. Or to wonder why it should want to gather any group of human beings together to meet an alien culture when cyberminds could make that journey by themselves.

August 11, 657:

We have agreed to make records of our private meetings and discussions available to all regional Administrative Committees on Earth, and to the Administrators' Committees and the surface settlement Councils of Venus; they are then to decide how much they wish to make public. They are being strongly encouraged to release as little about the sessions as possible (a euphemism for "if you put too much of this on the public record, you will suffer harsh consequences"), and advised (a euphemism for "ordered") to make only a brief summary available in both Anglaic and Arabic.

My own brief summary would be as follows: We've held a lot of meetings and discussed issues ranging from the future role of the Guardians to whether or not the Habbers should give us more information about themselves, their culture, and the details of their lives. We've had some very interesting discussions, and we haven't come to an agreement on a damned thing except to agree to give out as little information as possible.

The Habbers went along with our resolution, even though they obviously didn't like it. I suppose they were thinking that we had to agree on something before more people began to wonder if this conference is a complete waste of time. The irony here is that the Habbers were pushing for detailed records of all the meetings to be made public, just as earlier they were saying that they would be willing to answer any questions about themselves and their society that anyone wanted to pose, even to prepare a mind-tour of a Habitat for distribution. It's the Mukhtars and Linkers of Earth who want to restrict information and who would also prefer that the Associated Habitats remain as mysterious as they always have been to the vast majority of Earthfolk.

Sooner or later, some Administrator may ignore the directive about releasing complete records of this conference. Somebody will decide that our supposed new era was about more openness and that openness is preferable to secrecy.

August 20, 657:

For the first time in our lives, we Cytherians who have never known anything but our dome environments are trying to endure seasons and changes in weather. Had the weather remained as it was in late spring, we might have adjusted more easily. As it is, I have come to dread leaving the comfortable dry air of the house and walking even the short distance to the town hall for our meetings.

Arrangements might have been made to convey us to the town hall in vehicles. The possibility of enclosed walkways had also been discussed and then rejected. The Council of Mukhtars, perhaps wisely, had decided that as long as we were in Lincoln, it would be best to follow the ways of its citizens. If they were able to endure the extremities of their climate, then so could the delegates. Maybe the Mukhtars were also thinking of how impotent and enfeebled we would look if we couldn't deal with a little physical discomfort.

In early morning, the outside air is hot enough to make me sweat even when I walk at a slow and relaxed pace. At midday, the heat is so intense that one wonders how the people who lived here centuries ago, without homeostats and the other amenities of our lives, ever survived. Then there are all the insects — mosquitoes and other annoying mites that seem to be everywhere in the evenings. Harriett recommended that I wear a hat with a protective veil of netting when the insects are out, as the Plainswomen do, and keep the rest of myself covered, and a dose of antihistamine medicine reduces the swelling and itching of the bites, but I have found that a few of the wretched things can penetrate any barrier and deliver enough bites to make one's life miserable. I avoid being outdoors in the evenings whenever possible.

Harriett tells me that a Plains winter will be yet another adventure, assuming that we're still here then, and it seems as though we will be.

August 21, 657:

I knew that Teresa Marias and other townspeople had been grumbling about being excluded from the conference. I sympathized with them, even though I kept my opinion to myself. Here they were, doing everything they could to make the delegates, along with all of the other groups of Habbers and Linkers and aides to the Project Council who keep coming into Lincoln for short visits as "observers," as comfortable as possible, and not only are they not admitted to the sessions, but they don't even get a full summary of our meetings.

I didn't expect Mayor Teresa to do what she did today.

It happened an hour after our morning session began. The room where we meet is set up with three large tables near the center of the room, and in the back, a longer table where Mukhtar Tabib, Jamilah al-Hussaini, Constantine Matheos, and Masud al-Tikriti are seated. Commander Helgas (Edmund Helgas is still known by that name, whether or not it's actually the one he was born with) and a few of his people are always present, partly to provide security and partly to offer any opinions of their own; some of them are seated at each table. The rest of us are free to sit where we like, and there's enough room so that any visiting observers can sit at the tables with us. In other words, without the observers (who don't just sit there observing, but usually have something to say), we would be rattling around in a nearly empty room, a fact that probably impressed itself on Teresa.

We were in the middle of discussing the situation at the camp of would-be emigrants outside Tashkent, where the Guardian officer in charge has been predicting that there will soon be riots if the people there aren't promised either immediate passage to Venus or more comfortable quarters in their encampment, when the door opened and Captain Dullea entered the room.

"The mayor of Lincoln is outside," the captain announced, "and there are several townspeople with her, and they demand to be admitted."

Everyone turned toward the Mukhtar's table. Whatever the rest of us thought, we knew that Mukhtar Tabib would decide what to do about that. I was worrying about what Teresa and the others would do if he refused to let them in and how the Guardians in the hallway might react.

Mukhtar Tabib seemed unperturbed. He stroked his beard for a moment, as if deep in thought—or perhaps consulting with others through his Link—and then said, "Are they likely to disperse quietly, Captain?"

The officer shook his head. "The mayor seems quite angry. We may have to stun a few of them to get the others to leave."

"Then let them in."

Most of the visiting Linkers shook their heads as the door opened. The Mukhtar stood up as Teresa hurried into the room, followed by Shirl the physician, Allison the barkeep, and several other illustrious citizens.

"Salaam," Tabib murmured before Teresa could get a word out. "I am most pleased to welcome the mayor of Lincoln to this meeting."

Teresa halted for a moment, then kept going until she was right in front of the Mukhtar. "If you were that pleased to welcome me," she replied, "you would have invited me here long before now."

The Mukhtar smiled. "I have been remiss, my good woman. There is something I should have explained to you before, and perhaps to the Cytherian delegates as well, even though it must be obvious to almost everyone else in attendance."

"Explain away," Teresa said, "that is, if you think it's worth your while to bother explaining things to a simple Plainswoman." I had to admire my kinswoman for not allowing him to intimidate her, even while fearing that she might push him too far.

"Please be seated." Mukhtar Tabib waved a hand in the direction of the other townsfolk. "All of you, please sit down. Let me inform you that these proceedings are being recorded, and that I am willing to make my statements public afterward if that is what you desire."

Teresa looked away from him and toward the townspeople who were standing just inside the door. Clearly she was taken aback by this concession; I suppose that she had expected more resistance. She motioned to the others, who came to the tables and sat down; there were more than enough seats for all of them.

"Satisfy my curiosity, Mayor Teresa Marias," the Mukhtar said. "What did you intend to do if we had refused to admit you?"

Teresa had taken a seat near me. She pushed back her wide-brimmed hat, then leaned forward and rested her arms on the table-top. "There wouldn't have been much I could do," she said, "and you could probably hush up whatever you did to us by just cutting off our channels to the outside, but that wouldn't have looked good for your conference, especially after that battle we had here this spring. You could always move this confab somewhere else, but that wouldn't look good, either, and one point of this whole business is to look good."

"Very astute of you," the Mukhtar said. "Now allow me to tell you what you don't seem to understand, and then you can decide for yourselves how much you wish me to make public. To put it as simply as possible, I am trying to prevent disaster, trying to make certain that we don't end up in an even worse state than our ancestors were in at the end of the Resource Wars centuries ago. Because if we fall that far, I very much doubt that we will ever again be able to regain the technology that we have now."

The Mukhtar went on to explain what he meant as simply as possible. Earth had been able to rebuild itself after the Resource Wars, but social stability had been bought at the cost of suppressing certain developments or directing the human capacity for innovation elsewhere. Better for those who were impatient with the pace of change on Earth to leave and build their Associated Habitats; better to use the Venus Project as the moral equivalent of war and as a way to inspire Earth's billions, than to engage in actual conflict. There had been mistakes along the way, and times when the people of Earth and Venus and the Habitats had come perilously close to war, but the dangers threatening them all had been averted.

The day of reckoning was now upon us, according to Mukhtar Tabib. The new era promised us peace with the Habbers, more support and faster progress for the terraforming of Venus, life spans that might be indefinitely prolonged, and humankind's first voyage beyond the confines of the solar system to look for the source of an alien signal. The new era might also offer us social disruptions on a scale human beings had never experienced before, even during the time of rapid technical innovation and social dislocation that had led to the Resource Wars. Everything would change; little would remain the same.

All of this was probably obvious to the Linkers who were present, and perhaps to the Habbers as well. Had I given more thought to the issues Tabib raised, I most likely would have come to the same conclusions. Malik might have enlightened me about this historical context if he were still alive; I felt myself mourning for him again.

My fellow Cytherians wore expressions ranging from acceptance to disbelief to anger. The people of Lincoln who had come there with Teresa looked frightened. They knew what the Mukhtar was saying—that their way of life was dying, that it would pass before too much longer, and that all they could hope for was that the change would be peaceful and not violent.

Mukhtar Tabib was silent for a few moments, perhaps assessing our varied expressions. "In other words, Mukhtar," Teresa said at last, "you're trying to keep the lid on."

"Astutely put," the Mukhtar said. "You saw what happened last May, with Commander Lawrence and his rogue Guardians. You may think of the Commander as a madman, but let me assure you that he is not. He saw what might happen and tried to stop it. He's only a small example of what might happen later on if we don't . . . keep the lid on for a while."

Benzi was gazing intently at the Mukhtar; he almost looked worried. Perhaps he was thinking that Tabib had made a mistake in trying to explain himself to the Plainspeople sitting with us. I did not think it was a mistake. What happened during this time of transition would depend as much on the good will and cooperation of people like Teresa as it would on the directives of the Council of Mukhtars.

"I knew changes were coming," Teresa murmured, "when the Counselor came here some years back and told us that we were going to have a school in Lincoln."

"Yes," the Mukhtar said, "that was part of the preparation for the new era. I still have much to tell you. This voyage of discovery, this journey beyond this solar system—it's more than a search for the alien and a symbolic way to mark the new era. It is also to ensure that, if the worst happens here, some part of us, of our species, will survive elsewhere."

"You sound as though you expect the worst to happen." That was my remark, which escaped me before I could call it back.

"I deal in probabilities," Tabib responded. "There is a strong possibility that our species may not survive this upheaval on Earth. That would deprive the Venus Project of the technological support that the settlements need in order to survive, so they would be doomed as well, unless the Habbers took over the Project. The Habbers stand a good chance to survive regardless of what happens on Earth or on Venus, unless of course they get drawn too deeply into our troubles. But there are those who might contend that Habbers are no longer truly human, and perhaps they will lose interest in human affairs altogether and leave this system." He fixed his gaze on Benzi and the Habbers sitting with him, then turned to Teresa. "If you wish to attend our sessions, you may do so. If you want to bring every one of your constituents to our meetings, we won't stop you. Sooner or later, everything we say here will become public anyway. I had hoped that wouldn't happen until certain issues were settled, and we had reached some kind of agreement, but perhaps I hoped for too much."

Teresa looked down for a moment. "I may decide to attend," she said, "or I may not, as long as I know I'm welcome." There was a note of wounded pride in her voice. "I don't think there's any point in talking about this, among ourselves or with folks in other communes, as long as you say it'll all come out in public anyway." She looked up with a pensive expression on her face. "I know what it's like at town meetings when everybody has to get in her say and people are so interested in pushing their own opinions that nothing gets decided. You haven't made up your minds about anything yet, so you don't need more of us butting in right now."

The Mukhtar said, "I am grateful for your understanding."

Teresa stood up and glanced at the townspeople nearest her. "We'd better let them go about their business," she murmured, "and get things settled, before we end up with something worse than that Guardian Commander." She left the room, with the others following, her back straight and rigid with dignity.

September 30, 657:

After over a month of discussions that sometimes reached a high level of intensity—

No, that isn't the way to put it. After over a month of sessions where a number of my fellow Cytherians, Administrator Constantine Matheos in particular, often got into shouting matches with Mukhtar Tabib and any Linkers from Earth who happened to be present, we have the beginnings of an agreement. Only the Habber delegates kept the arguments from becoming even more angry and bitter than they were. Benzi and his comrades displayed a talent for being calm and soothing without giving off any obnoxious odor of superiority. Maybe that's why they were able to win the kind of agreement they wanted.

It isn't official, but it will be. The delegates, and the observers who might as well be delegates themselves, will argue some more, and then we'll all admit that we've done about as well as we are likely to do. Few of the delegates want to be here during the harsh Plains winter.

Few of us also want to give any discontented and angry people with the capacity to organize themselves a chance to conclude that our deliberations are useless and to take matters into their own hands.

October 657
From: Mahala Liangharad, Commune of Teresa Marias,
Lincoln, Nomarchy of the Plains Communes
To: Chike Enu-Barnes, East Dome,
Cytherian Settlement of Sagan

The conference is over. Your brother Kesse may not have told you that yet, since it isn't official, but our work here is essentially done, and not a moment too soon. I can feel winter in the air and in the wind every time I go outside. Mukhtar Tabib seems increasingly anxious to get back to the warmer climes of the New Islamic Nomarchy, and the Cytherians here are already making plans to leave.

I should be doing the same thing, but Benzi is staying on in Lincoln for a while, and I have decided to stay here with him. I miss you badly and would much rather be in the temperate environment of a dome than on this flat wind-swept prairie, but I have my reasons for remaining here for now.

Aides to the Council of Mukhtars and the Project Council, in consultation with various Habbers, will draw up the detailed agreement, making sure that every provision has no loopholes, and the whole thing is bound to be loaded with ceremonial phrases and clauses covering every possible contingency, but essentially the agreement will guarantee that the Venus Project will continue with the aid of both Earth and the Associated Habitats, with both Islanders and surface-dwellers having a lot more control over decisions. It also gives the Habbers who are building the interstellar Habitat the power to accept or reject anyone who wishes to be a voyager, although people who feel that they've been rejected unfairly will be able to appeal, ask for a public hearing, submit an assessment by a Counselor that they're emotionally or mentally fit for the voyage, and so forth. The Habbers will consider all adults, meaning people who are at least twenty years old, and won't take the parents of children who are younger than that. This is for ethical reasons, since the Habbers argued that young children can't give informed consent to such a choice.

That makes it sound as though the process of selecting spacefarers could go on indefinitely, but most of the Habbers seem to agree with Benzi when he claims that this won't be a problem, that the qualified applicants will not be so numerous that there won't be space for them.

I didn't believe my great-uncle when he first told me this, and I don't believe him now. In Sagan alone, I can think of at least three hundred people who will want to be part of this voyage, including you. Multiply that by equivalent percentages from each settlement and Island, add in the number from Earth who will be clamoring to go, and the Habbers doing the selecting will have millions to deal with, and millions more who are children now but will want to be considered later, and — it all seems impossible, even if you assume that the Habber cyberminds might be able to speed up the process.

I've told Benzi that I want to go as soon as the worldlet is ready for habitation. He wants the same thing; he's told me more times than I can count that this was his dream, as far back as when he was a young Islander planning to flee from Venus. But whenever I speak of my wishes, he gets a strange look on his face, as if he doesn't really believe me.

The Lincoln Conference Agreement was made public on January 1, 658, on all public channels in various languages, with each version read by aides to the Council of Mukhtars, Venus Project Council members, or Habbers of indeterminate status. Mahala watched a reading of the agreement by Jamilah al-Hussaini in the common room of Teresa Marias's house, but by then much about the conference meetings had become public. During the month preceding the announcement, there were rumors of riots in some of Earth's larger cities, of violence against individual Habbers, but such stories remained rumors. That might mean that the tales were exaggerated, Mahala mused, or else that the Mukhtars were doing a much better job at keeping such incidents quiet.

The day after the announcement, Mahala walked with Chet Marjories to the floater cradles to say her farewells to him, trailed by her cousin Harriett and Jeremy Courtneys. The two young Guardians had stayed on in Lincoln with a small detachment after most of the delegates had left, volunteering for the extra duty; Mukhtar Tabib had thought the town might need some Guardians stationed there for a while. When the rest of the detachment had been ordered to their new post, Chet and Jeremy had been granted a week of leave in Lincoln.

The snow had drifted during the night, making small mounds against the houses and white dunes in the fields, but the air was clear and the sky a piercing, cloudless blue. The wind had died down in the night; the floater would not have to postpone its scheduled stop at Lincoln. Mahala waded through the snow, shivering even in her felt hat, long woolen coat, and thick-soled boots. She no longer minded the cold and could look up at the vast dome of the sky without flinching; she had grown to see some beauty in this harsh piece of Earth. She would miss Lincoln when she left it and wondered how many other places on Earth she might have come to love.

"I love you," Chet had told her a month ago, after a summer and autumn of finding every excuse to be near her. He came to Teresa's house for dinner with Jeremy and took Mahala to the tavern for a drink after meetings. Later, when the delegates were gone and she was spending alternate days assisting Shirl Heathers with her patients and supervising elementary biology classes at the Lincoln Academy, Chet was often waiting for her outside Shirl's examination room or in the road outside the school. Being friendly but distant to him had made him even more persistent, but then he was a Plainsman, accustomed to women who not only welcomed his attentions but demanded them; part of her attraction for him had been the novelty of her behavior.

They had been lovers for a month now. She had grown comfortable with his affectionate ways and his unsubtle but straightforward mind. Even so, she might have continued to discourage him except for a message she had received from Chike two months earlier. The message had been full of news about plans for a new dome in the Sagan settlement and of expeditions to explore more of the surface. "We have a vehicle now," he had said, "a modified crawler that can carry people inside it and remain outside a dome for a week or more." Cytherians would begin to venture outside the domes themselves for longer periods of time. That prospect had clearly excited him; Chike had not sounded like a man who intended to leave Venus for interstellar space. That night, she had welcomed Chet to her room, at last relieving the women of Teresa's household from worries that she might be, in their eyes, perverted.

His passion had cooled since then, and Mahala supposed that he would say his farewells to her with feelings similar to her own: He would remember her with some fondness and leave her without regret.

The floater had arrived and was tethered to its cradle when they reached it, the ramp down to receive passengers. Jeremy and Harriett held each other tightly in a wordless embrace while Mahala told Chet that she would send him a message from time to time, knowing that she was unlikely to keep that promise. Mahala stood with her cousin as the two men, bulky in their long black coats, walked up the ramp to board the floater; Chet lifted a hand in farewell before the door closed behind him.

"Mother of God," Harriett whispered, "I'm going to miss Jeremy. I'll miss him terribly."

Mahala hooked her arm through Harriett's as they walked back along the snow-covered road toward the town. "He said he'd be back in the spring," Mahala said. "They've already promised him leave."

"I know. I'll still miss him. I think I'd be content if Jeremy's the only man I ever share my bed with again." Harriett glanced at Mahala, as if embarrassed at saying something so unconventional. "Well, we are both part of Iris Angharads's line, and she took a bondmate for life."

That was not quite accurate, but Mahala let it pass. "Would you have a ceremony and take Jeremy as a bondmate?" Mahala asked.

"Oh, I wouldn't go that far, but—" Harriett's steps slowed. "He says that more Guardians are going to be assigned to civic patrols and police forces, since we may need more of them in places that don't have them now."

"I know," Mahala said. That had been one of the issues discussed near the end of the conference.

"If that happens, Jeremy thinks there's a good chance he'll be stationed here. We could be together then. We've been talking about having a child."

Mahala glanced at her kinswoman. "But I thought you wanted to be part of the space expedition. I thought Jeremy did, too. They won't consider either of you if you have a child."

"I know that, Mahala, but the more I think about it, the more I wonder if being one of the spacefarers is really what I want."

"But—" It came to Mahala then that she had heard little from either Harriett or Jeremy about the interstellar expedition lately. "You'd be giving up a chance to be part of our greatest adventure," she finished.

"And if I leave, I may be giving up a chance to be part of the greatest change in our history. Leaving now, without knowing what might happen here, without doing what I can to see that we get through it— I don't think I can do it."

Mahala said, "You might not get through it. The new era could become a very dangerous and violent time."

"I know that, too, and maybe running away from it is a kind of cowardice." Harriett's grip tightened on Mahala's arm. "I shouldn't have said that to you. You still want to be a spacefarer, don't you."

"Yes, I do," Mahala said, but she was already thinking of all the arguments that she could make against becoming one.

The courtyard surrounded by the four wings of Teresa's house was warm and snowless. Overhead, the snow that had settled on the force field shielding the courtyard was visible in the soft light cast by the lanterns scattered about the grassy ground. The carpet of snow was melting into patches. Mahala looked up through a space between two patches of snow at the night sky and the beckoning stars. They still called to her, but she was growing more conscious of the price she would have to pay in order to reach them.

The women of the household were already asleep, but Benzi was still in the courtyard, sitting near the rosebushes. He had been coming out here more often, to sit with the women and hear the stories that had been passed on to them by grandmothers and great-grandmothers. Over a century after leaving Lincoln as a child, he was woven into the fabric of the town once more. Perhaps he, like Harriett, was having second thoughts.

She sat down on one corner of his blanket. In the false spring of the courtyard, the rosebushes were budding again. "I spoke to Harriett this afternoon," she said. "She says that she may not want to become part of the interstellar expedition after all."

His head turned toward her. "I know."

"So she confided in you before she told me."

"No. I guessed it. I expected it. She's thinking of what she'd be leaving behind."

"I'm thinking of that, too," Mahala said. "It'll be a long series of farewells, and when I leave, I'll never see any of those people again. A time will come aboard the interstellar Habitat when I'll know that all of them are dead, and then another moment will come when I'll know that everybody who knew them or had any memory of them is dead, too, but I will have lost them long before that."

"I know," Benzi said.

"And that isn't all of it. Those of us who leave may never know what happens here, whether the rest of our species comes through this transition or destroys itself. We may never know if we're only a small branch of a thriving race or if we are all that's left of it, even if we do manage to come back eventually. There may be nothing left to tell us what happened by then."

"That's possible," he said. "It may be that the entire human species will abandon planets for Habitats and leave this system in the end."

"Now I'm beginning to see why you think that there won't be that many people wanting to be spacefarers."

"Are you having your own doubts?" he asked.

"I wouldn't call them doubts. They're more like questions. I'll be leaving Venus. I won't be one of those who stayed to bring it to life."

Benzi said, "You might be trading that for a chance to see what Venus becomes."

She breathed in the fragrance of the roses, another memory she would take with her from Earth. "It's the uncertainty of everything now—that's what's getting to people."

"Things always were uncertain," Benzi said. "Most of us simply hid that fact from ourselves for a while. Too many Habbers are still in danger of retreating from uncertainty. Now we'll all have to embrace that uncertainty, whatever we choose to do."

25

The bright spot on Mahala's screen, a beacon orbiting the sun midway between the orbits of Venus and Earth, had begun as an asteroid enclosed in a metal shell. Engineering crews and robotic limbs guided by cyberminds had installed its matter-antimatter drive and its vacuum drive; the worldlet that would become a nomadic interstellar Habitat was acquiring the first members of its community.

Each prospective spacefarer would live inside the Habitat for some years before it began its journey, with the goal of Linking everyone aboard to the Habitat's cyberminds before departure. Benzi claimed that this would not make Habbers of the Earthfolk and Cytherians aboard, that the minds integrated with the vessel and its functions were young artificial intelligences that would learn and develop along with the human beings to whom they were Linked. Mahala was not certain that he was right about that. In time, the difference between being a human being with a Link and being a Habber with a symbiotic artificial intelligence might be a lost distinction.

The first thousand people from Earth had already been ferried to the Habitat by torchship, and more thousands would follow them soon. The social engineers involved with the space expedition, both the Habbers and the Counselors from Earth and Venus, wanted to see a true community of starfarers established well before the Hab left the solar system, but there was another reason for bringing people aboard continuously over a period of several years. The artificial intelligences of the more unified net of the new era had predicted that a sizable minority of those volunteering to be spacefarers would eventually decide against being a part of the voyage, even after years of living inside the Habitat, even after the decade or more that it was likely to take for the voyagers to adapt to their new environment.

Farewells, Mahala thought; much of her life now involved preparing herself for leaving behind forever all of the places and many of the people she had known. She had left Lincoln and her cousin Harriett knowing that she would never see them again. Her farewells to those she loved on her own world would be far more painful. Even during her first months back in Sagan, a few of her friends had admitted that they had grown reluctant to sever themselves so completely from their home. With each of her farewells, she felt an increasing sympathy for those who had decided to turn away from the dream of interstellar travel.

Her grandmother Risa and her grandfather Sef welcomed her to their house in Oberg as they always had, with a large supper shared with the rest of the household. In the middle of the meal, Kyril Anders, the nineteen-year-old son of Risa's housemates Barika Maitana and Kristof Anders, announced that he was going to volunteer for the interstellar expedition as soon as he turned twenty. No one seemed surprised at the announcement, although Kyril's parents shook their heads at him regretfully.

Akilah Ching spoke of her interstellar intentions. "I want to be part of it, too," the beautiful young woman said in her musical voice.

"You're only seventeen," her father, Jamil Owens, replied. "You've been chosen for an Island school — are you going to throw that away?"

"Of course not. I'll get my education and then apply later, when I'm old enough."

Sef frowned. "So many young people want to leave," he said. "Makes you wonder what we built our settlements for. There won't be anybody left to keep things going."

"Sef," Akilah said gently, "you're exaggerating."

"More settlers will come here from Earth," Mahala said, "to replace any people you lose."

"I suppose." Sef looked away. "Somehow, that isn't much of a comfort."

"Sef." Risa put a hand on her bondmate's wrist. "You chose to come here, after all. Better that others have the choice of whether to stay or go."

They finished the meal listening to Grazie's recital of the latest Oberg gossip. After dinner, as Mahala expected, Risa asked her to accompany her on a walk. As they left the house, Risa hooked her arm through hers.

"I have the day off tomorrow," Risa said. "You can help me with some weeding in my greenhouse."

"Of course."

"You're staying with us for less than a month. Seems to me that you could have taken more time, seeing as it's likely to be your last visit."

Mahala felt a sharp pang of remorse at those words. "We'll be able to exchange messages," she said. "We won't be leaving the solar system for at least a few years, maybe longer. They want to make sure that people who might change their minds will have plenty of time to reconsider."

"Don't try to comfort me with that, Mahala. You've made your choice. You'll have to start separating from us. When you leave for that Habitat, you'll be gone for good." Risa slowed as they came near the tunnel that led into Oberg's main dome. "I won't make this harder for you—if I were younger, I might have done the same thing you're doing. And maybe you'll come back eventually to see what we made here. Anyway, I'm an old woman now, so you'd be saying your final farewells to me soon enough even if you stayed here."

That was an exaggeration; her grandmother had not yet turned ninety. "Risa," Mahala said, "you'll be around for another three decades at least—maybe longer, given what our biologists may be able to do now." She had been keeping up with some of Earth's medical research, the pace of which had noticeably increased, now that more information was flowing from the Habber cyberminds to those of Earth. Human life spans on Earth and on Venus might increase dramatically and soon. The promise was not only one of an indefinite life span, but also of social disruption on a massive scale. Death might come to be seen not as an inevitable and necessary event, but as an enemy.

"We'll go to the memorial pillars now," Risa said, as if picking up some of her thoughts, "and pay our respects. You might as well do that now, and not when you're about to leave Oberg. I want you to leave us with memories of our life here, and not only with memories of the dead."

*   *   *

Mahala's farewell to Dyami was a return to the life that she had once lived in Turing, a life that she could still have if she turned back. She slept in the bedroom she had once shared with Frania; at first light, she went with Tasida to the infirmary to help the other physician and Haroun Delassi with their medical duties. In spare moments, the three of them shared a meal and talked of recent medical developments.

"Implants," Tasida muttered a few days after Mahala had returned. "They seem so clumsy and inefficient compared to the nanomeds we'll be trying out soon." Tasida and Haroun were already learning as much as they could about those therapeutic molecule-sized devices from a few of the Habbers in Turing. Clearing out protein cross-linkages, preventing aneurysms from developing, healing and strengthening bones a moment after a fracture—there seemed no limit to what the tiny mechanisms could do. That the Habber nanotechnology might also make much of their work as physicians unnecessary was apparently a matter of indifference to Tasida and her assistant.

In the evenings, Mahala visited a few old friends, discovering that she would not have to say farewells to some of them after all. Josef Feldshuh was still determined to become a spacefarer, as he had told her after the end of the Lincoln Conference before leaving Earth. According to him, several of their old primary schoolmates had the same intention. It had been much the same in Oberg; she had come to see why Sef worried that Venus might lose much of its younger generation. Perhaps it was natural that the descendants of people who had left humankind's home world would want to go on this journey. But she also knew that some of the hopeful spacefarers would decide to remain on Venus in the end.

After last light, in the days before the celebration that would mark the beginning of the year 659, Mahala took a walk with Balin along the shore of the lake near Dyami's house. The Habber was living with Dyami while teaching at the primary school and instructing any of the children who were interested in mathematics. He and Dyami seemed bound together, content with their lives and at peace with each other. She had thought that Balin would want to join the interstellar community, but suspected that he might now be having qualms about that.

"I was talking to Dyami earlier," she said, hoping to elicit some of his thoughts. "I asked him if he was thinking of being a spacefarer himself. He's only a bit over fifty, and his old friend Suleiman Khan told me that he wants to be a part of the expedition. But Dyami said that he thought there'd be enough challenges for him here, that he'd given too much of himself to this place to leave it." She had not known if her uncle had been referring to Venus or simply to Turing, the place of his youthful imprisonment and the settlement where he had rebuilt his life.

"I assume you haven't been reconsidering your decision," Balin said.

"Oh, no."

"Even if perhaps you might be a bit young to make such a decision?"

Mahala laughed softly. "I'm twenty-six. I'm not a child."

"I thought perhaps we should set the age limit higher than that, perhaps at thirty or forty, when a person has had more experience with life. But there's also something to be said for having younger and fresher minds aboard, and there will be some years of maturation before the Habitat begins its journey. And there are those of us who are perhaps too old to go, too—" He paused. "I was going to say too weary, but that isn't the right word."

She said, "You aren't going, then."

"No, I'm not. I've decided to stay here."

"Until you go back to your own Hab." She hoped for Dyami's sake that Balin would not leave for many years.

"I'm free to live on this world now, for as long as I like. I may never go back to a Hab."

They came to a stop and gazed out at the flat black surface of the lake and the disk of faint reflected light that floated upon it. "There have been so many reasons for many of us to come to live among your people," he continued. "Some of us are altruists. Some of us welcomed the opportunity to practice some planetary engineering. A few of us were curious about a life that was different from our own. And some of us felt it was a way to hold on to the humanity we might otherwise be in danger of losing. But some of us had fallen into a trap. Our times on Venus, difficult as they sometimes were when compared to life inside a Habitat, were a way of escaping that trap." Balin was silent for a while. "I was caught in that trap."

Mahala waited for him to go on.

"You know how seductive a mind-tour can be, or any virtual experience, but the time comes when you have to remove your band and get on with your life. A Linker here or on Earth can connect himself directly to any number of experiences and scenarios, but sooner or later, he is called back to himself, either by his duties or else by the controls Earth's people have imposed on their cyberminds. But a Habber is free to lose himself in a mental labyrinth of realized imaginings and desires and never find his way out again. I was in danger of becoming one such lost wanderer, before I found my way to Venus. And every time I went back to my Hab, I felt the temptation again. It was our great weakness—and something we kept hidden from Earth. There are Habbers who have died in their virtual worlds. There are Habbers who have been there for centuries and who will never find their way out again."

"Balin," she said, and took his hand.

"It's harder to get drawn into the trap here," he said. "I still have my Link, I can escape whenever I please, but that's more difficult when you have ties to others and various obligations. On a Hab—well, it's very easy to retreat. The net of the Hab will maintain you physically, and in your mind you can have whatever you desire. There are hundreds of thousands of Habbers who have forgotten that there is a reality outside of the one they and their Links have created for themselves."

Mahala shuddered. "It sounds," she said, "like a kind of living death."

"If you saw the dreamers, you wouldn't feel that way. Don't imagine rows of ghoulish half-dead physically degenerate creatures. What you would see are people who would look as though they were meditating or as if they're asleep, all of them wearing the same serene expression on their faces."

"Is that what Habbers mean when they speak of bringing themselves into balance?" Mahala asked.

Balin shook his head. "No, that's a way of shedding disturbing thoughts without losing your memories completely. It's a discipline of sorts, while the other is an escape. It is unfortunately true that some find the escape much easier and more pleasant than the discipline."

"And there's nothing your people can do to stop this?" she asked.

"How should we do that? Have human beings ever been able to prevent others of our kind from all kinds of destructive indulgences? Trying to stop them can cause even more problems than allowing others to do as they please, even if it means ultimately losing those people." They turned back toward the hill that led to Dyami's house.

"That is another reason for keeping the spacefaring Habitat within this system for a time, so that those most susceptible to the trap can be weeded out before that Hab departs."

As the airship dropped toward the lighted open bay of Sagan, Mahala continued to gaze at the screen. The next time she saw an image of the bay from an airship, she would be leaving this settlement for the last time. Saying farewell to Dyami had brought her close to changing her mind; it had been a struggle to keep from turning back, from deciding that her life belonged to this world and its future after all.

Dyami had known what she was thinking. "You think that you may be making a mistake," he had told her as they walked together to Turing's airship bay. "You're thinking of staying on Venus. And if you do, you may feel, for a few years anyway, that you made the right decision. But I have a feeling that deep regrets would overtake you later on, when that starfaring Hab begins its journey and you realize that you won't be one of the voyagers."

"This won't be the only voyage," Mahala replied. "It will only be the first."

"In the long run, that may be likely. In the short run, during my lifetime, for instance, I have my doubts. I've been reading some of Malik's writings since his death. History is an area I hadn't explored much until recently, and your grandfather made some interesting points. He argued that the Venus Project, and the great efforts that were required for such a monumental and long-term project, had shackled other possible developments. So many of Earth's resources flowed toward the terraforming of Venus that anything that wouldn't further that end was held back. For example, we have interplanetary travel, our torchships and freighters and other such vessels, because those were necessary to the Project. But interstellar travel and the disciplines connected to its realization, astronomy and astrophysics and the development of relativistic propulsion systems, were ignored, except by the Habbers, who didn't have to be restrained by our practical considerations. If it hadn't been for the aid of the Habbers, we wouldn't even have come this far with the Project."

"You're saying," she said, "that we'll be shackled to the Project for some time to come."

"I'm saying that, even with Earth's new policy, even with full co-operation and communication between Earthpeople, Cytherians, and Habbers, there's only so much we can do. There are indications that the Habbers may, now that they're free to do so, show us more ways to speed up the process of terraforming. They may become as shackled to this Project as Earth has been. We may all come to feel that any future interstellar expeditions should be postponed for a while."

That, Mahala thought, was apart from the possibility that Earth might be torn apart during this period of transition. The Project might be left entirely to the Habbers and the Cytherians. They might be forced to choose between finishing their work here or abandoning it for the stars. She pondered what Balin had told her about the Habbers who had retreated into their imagined sensory worlds; more Habbers might join them in their black hole of dreams, which might even in time pull in everyone.

"I'll miss you," she had said to Dyami then. "I think I may miss you more than anyone else here."

"I'll miss you, too," he said. "If I were younger, if my life hadn't left me with some of the scars I still have, I would have made the choice that you've made."

The airship had landed. She heard the sound of the cradle's clamps as the cabin was secured and waited as the roof closed and air began to cycle into the bay. She left her seat, shouldered her duffel, and followed the other passengers out of the dirigible, still thinking of Dyami as she descended the ramp. He and Risa had both been telling her that they had accepted her decision, that they were at peace with their farewells and willing to let her go.

She had passed the row of cradles and was nearing the open doorway when someone called out her name. She turned to see Ragnar coming toward her. She had seen little of him after returning here from Earth, but had heard from others about some of his recent pursuits. He was devoting himself to more study of physics, with Solveig, a couple of specialists in physics, and a Habber all helping to guide him in his studies. A group of Administrators from the Cytherian Institute, now undergoing a transformation that would turn that university into the Interstellar Institute, had offered him a commission to design a sculpture to commemorate the new era. In the meantime, he was occupying himself by designing houses; even within the limits of the housing materials and prefab components allotted to Sagan, the people of this settlement would, through Ragnar's efforts, be able to leave their dormitories and tents for dwellings with gardens and greenhouses that would complement the open, grassy spaces and the wooded regions of young trees, instead of living in homes that had been hastily thrown up wherever there was space for them on the blank landscape.

"Greetings, Ragnar," Mahala said, happy at the sight of him. His blond hair had grown longer and was tied back from his face. The haunted, haggard expression that had become so characteristic of him was gone; he had stopped mourning Frania at last. "I didn't know you had bay duty."

"I don't," he said. "I was waiting for you." She glanced at him in surprise as he took her duffel from her. "Solveig told me that you might be coming back here today, and Dyami confirmed that when I sent a message to him."

"I didn't know Solveig was back here already." Mahala had thought her friend would be spending more time saying her farewells to her parents in Hypatia.

"She's been here for ten days. She says she'll come by and see you after her shift."

A path of flat white flagstones led to the main roadway that now encircled Sagan's east dome. On the other side of the road, the path branched into three paths. Ragnar took the middle path, leading her north toward her dormitory. They passed six houses that stood around a common greenhouse and garden; two of the houses had roofed courtyards outside their entrances, as Ragnar's former home in Turing did.

"We're going to be having some interesting discussions fairly soon," he continued. "The Habbers are already running models showing ways in which they might create molecular machines that would be able to metabolize Venus's carbon dioxide rapidly. I haven't described that very well, but then I'm still filling in the gaps in my education."

"I know a little about it," Mahala said. Chike had been sending her records of some of the projections, clearly fascinated by the possibilities. Converting carbon dioxide to some useful form of carbon, either metabolizing the oxygen or converting it to a less volatile form—not only would the process of terraforming be speeded up, but it might also be possible to shut down the Bat operations altogether. There was the hope that people would be freed from those dangerous tasks, since Habbers and Project engineers were already designing AI-operated systems for those operations; the Project would no longer have to save on costs by putting those workers at risk.

Chike had mentioned possible new uses for the Bats, as laboratories and places for research; it might be advisable to study any newly created molecular forms of life or molecular machines—and the distinction between the two was becoming harder and harder to draw—on the two satellites, where any potentially problematic organisms could be isolated and studied. It had occurred to Mahala after getting his messages that Chike had not spoken of the interstellar expedition at all.

"I knew things were going to change," Ragnar continued, "but I didn't think they would start changing so quickly. I just wish—" His voice caught, and she knew that he was remembering Frania.

"Everyone seems so involved in what's going to happen here," Mahala said, "that our interstellar effort seems all but forgotten."

"Not quite. I know of at least forty people here who have already put in for the journey, and they're only the first. You're still going, aren't you?"

"Yes. I won't say I didn't have my doubts, but I've made up my mind."

They had come to the wooden footbridge. Ragnar halted and set her duffel down. "Solveig wanted me to tell you this. I told her that she should talk to you herself, but maybe it's better if I prepare you for what she's going to say. She's decided she's not going to go, that she wants to stay here."

She heard his words, not feeling the truth of them yet, grateful for the numbness that kept what he was telling her at bay. In all her thoughts of what she would be losing, of the people she would be leaving behind, she had always seen Solveig at her side, traveling with her to the Habitat and what awaited them both beyond this system. She had never imagined that she might have to say a farewell to Solveig.

"No," she heard herself say, as if from a distance. "No."

"It's true, Mahala. She struggled with it, she couldn't make up her mind, but when she did—"

"She can't mean it. This is what she always wanted. Maybe she just needs to think about it some more before she leaves here."

Ragnar said, "You should be saying that to Solveig, not to me."

Anger flared inside her. "You don't care at all, do you? You don't care about anything—" A look of sympathy and concern crossed his face, and she wanted to call back her words.

"I care," he said, and picked up her duffel.

"Chike's not going, either," she said.

"Did he tell you that?"

"He doesn't have to tell me. I know." She followed Ragnar across the bridge.

Mahala had asked Ragnar to share a meal with her and Solveig, but he muttered an excuse about a darktime shift in External Operations and left them at one of the tables in the recently planted flower garden outside the dormitory. More of the dormitory residents were taking their meals here, according to Solveig, carrying their food from the common room's kitchen out to the garden. Time spent on cultivating the flowers might have been spent on more practical tasks, but the sight of the budding rosebushes, rows of violets, and the bright yellow blossoms of an unfamiliar flower eased the knots of tension and sorrow inside Mahala.

Solveig spoke of all the considerations that had led to her decision. There had been too many farewells; she had soon lost the stomach for them. The new era would mean opportunities for her to work and to study aboard an orbiting observatory. She had learned that she was more attached to this world than she had realized and wanted to be part of the Project's next phase.

Mahala forced herself to finish her small meal of parsley and grain salad and vegetables. Solveig poured her another glass of wine; her friend had spent some credit on a bottle of the wine, a local product made from a rapidly maturing strain of grapes. The wine was too sweet and no match for the Earth wines she had occasionally sampled and had learned to appreciate at Allison's tavern in Lincoln, but the pink liquid soothed her a little.

"Maybe the dream was more enticing than the reality," Solveig said. "When I thought it might never happen, I wanted it more than anything. When this kind of journey seemed a possibility, I longed to be part of it. And then the decision was upon me, and—" She looked down for a moment. "I knew then that I couldn't go."

"All the farewells," Mahala said.

"Not just that. I haven't forgotten that time you found me by the lake, after Ragnar and Frani's bondmate ceremony. It suddenly came to me that I might become like that again aboard that Hab, alone and adrift, that the darkness inside me might swallow me up completely."

"You don't know that."

"I know it," Solveig said softly, "and as soon as I understood that, I knew that I couldn't go. You know what I'm like — it hasn't been easy for me to form attachments, to grow close to other people. I value those connections I made too much now to let go of them. And there's something else." She lifted her head. "This won't be the first such expedition. There will be others, I'm sure of that. Maybe in time I can be part of one of them, and if not, I can be content knowing that someone else has realized that dream."

"You might change your mind later," Mahala said, feeling the hollowness of that hope.

"I won't," Solveig said, "and neither will you."

"No, I won't change my mind." Mahala's eyes stung. "But this is the closest I've come to thinking that I should have decided to stay here."

Chike had moved into a house with wide windows built around a central courtyard. His housemates were a young couple with two children who had recently moved to Sagan, a physicist who had moved there from Island Seven, and two Habbers, a man and a woman. He had introduced them all to Mahala before retreating with her to the courtyard. She had already forgotten their names, not wanting to become acquainted with any more people to whom she would only have to say good-bye.

She had saved Chike the trouble of informing her that he had decided to remain by telling him that she had guessed what he wanted to do and had accepted it. She had relieved him of the burden of explaining himself to her.

"When did you know?" Chike asked.

"I think I sensed it when I was still in Lincoln, when I saw your messages."

"Then you knew what I was going to do before I knew it myself," he said. "I hadn't decided anything then, not consciously. I was still wrestling with myself."

"I suppose that I must still love you, then. That must be how I knew." She forced herself to smile; she would not have him remember her as somebody who had reproached him.

They sat together on the ground, near a small tiled pool. Chike had told her that Ragnar had designed the labyrinthine pattern of ceramic tiles at the bottom of the pool for Chike's two Habber housemates.

He leaned toward her and touched her face lightly. "You can still leave something of yourself on Venus," Chike said. She knew what he meant. Those leaving Venus and Earth would be allowed to store their genetic material on their home worlds; descendants of the spacefarers could still remain among those they had abandoned. Mahala had not yet heard of any potential spacefarer taking advantage of that option.

"No," she said, "I can't."

"You think it's a test of some kind, that those willing to leave sperm or ova behind might be showing too much ambivalence about their choice."

"I suppose they would be revealing some uncertainty, but that's not my reason for refusing. I just don't think it's fair. The people who choose to make their lives here or on Earth deserve to have their own descendants inherit what they accomplish. And I'm not so sure that it would be fair to the children, either. I know what it's like to grow up with parents I could never know and who would never know me."

"Parents, children, all of those family and social structures—" Chike shrugged. "They may not mean as much to us later on. We may become more like Habbers."

"Perhaps." She reached for his hand and held it, caring for him still, even as she felt herself growing apart from him.

She had prepared for her departure, given away personal possessions that she no longer wanted, and said her farewells. To wait any longer would be both an indulgence and a cruelty. She would only be procrastinating, dragging out the leavetaking and tormenting those who had reluctantly come to accept her choice.

Mahala left her dormitory with only a lightly packed duffel and her physician's bag. She was not likely to need the tools of her profession in the Habitat, but had picked up her bag automatically. Someone traveling with her might suddenly need her care, and later, she would have a tangible reminder of what she had once been.

She took the path that would lead her past the Administrative Center and the memorial pillar. As she walked, she tried to concentrate on her surroundings, knowing that she was seeing them for the last time, but Sagan had changed during the past year and had always felt like a temporary home to her anyway. It had been harder for her to say farewell to Turing and to Oberg.

Mahala had asked her friends not to come with her to the bay, but as she passed the glassy square of the Administrative Center, she glimpsed Solveig and Chike at the memorial pillar. She came toward them, knowing that they had come there to wait for her.

Solveig embraced her wordlessly. Chike held her for a while as she rested her head against his chest, then said, "I love you, Mahala."

"Is this your last try at convincing me to stay?"

"No," he replied. "I'm just telling you that I love you."

She stepped back and gazed into his face. His sharp cheekbones, the warm dark brown of his skin, his short black hair, his penetrating black eyes—he was so familiar to her that she felt that she would carry his image in her memory for the rest of her life, that she could never forget him, and yet she also knew that his memory would fade in time.

She stared at the pillar for a while, at the image of Frania that Ragnar had made, then turned away. "My brother told me that he would come to see you," Chike said, "when you're on Island Two."

"I won't be there very long," Mahala said; she did not have that many farewells to say there.

"Kesse wants to spend time with you anyway. I asked him to do that. If there's anything that you forgot to say to me, you can tell it to him."

"Farewell, Mahala," Solveig said, hugging her. "I love you, too, I always have."

"I know. Farewell."

Mahala left the pillar, forcing herself not to look back. She was near the pilots' dormitory before she saw Ragnar's bright blond head in the distance. He was waiting by the gaping entrance of the bay with Tomas Sechen; apparently Ragnar had decided to prolong his farewells to her. At least she would not have to go through a painful leavetaking with Tomas, who would be joining the interstellar expedition after his last trip to Oberg.

The numbness she had felt when waking up earlier was still with her. Mahala felt as though her emotions had been muted and her senses muffled. She might weep once she was aboard the airship or when she reached Island Two, but for now she could approach Tomas and Ragnar calmly.

"Greetings," Tomas said to her, "and there isn't much more for me to say except have a safe journey."

"And that you'll be seeing me later," Mahala added, trying to smile.

"That, too." He strode away, almost too hastily, clearly anxious to leave her alone with Ragnar.

"Solveig and Chike were at the memorial pillar," she said.

"I know."

"Farewell, Ragnar."

He clutched her by the arms. "I didn't come here to say good-bye to you. I've put in for the expedition myself."

She stared at him, still numb, not knowing what to say.

"I've been thinking about it for months. Tomas knows, and Orban, and a few others, but I didn't want to speak of it to anyone else until I was sure. I want to go, and they'll accept me. I didn't know that until today, but I wanted to tell you before you left."

"Ragnar," she whispered.

"Now I'll have to go around saying my farewells to everybody, and I don't know how long that'll take me, but you should be seeing me again within a year."

"Ragnar." She would not be abandoning this piece of her heart after all. She let him take her duffel from her and walk with her into the bay.

The Heavens

26

Mahala Liangharad, in common with all of the prospective spacefarers who were brought aboard the Seeker—for that was how we were soon thinking of our nomadic Habitat, as the Seeker—believed that she had measured up to some unknown and yet specific standards to become a part of the interstellar voyage. She and her companions had, to put it another way, passed a test.

In a sense, this was true. There were some who sought to become spacefarers who were clearly unsuited for the voyage, however qualified they might appear to be on the basis of their records. Their unsuitability had little to do with their physical or intellectual qualifications and much to do with the way in which their impulses and synapses and neurons and the components of their conscious minds interacted and reacted with others of their kind and with the environment around them.

Or, as Mahala and her fellow human voyagers might put it, becoming a spacefarer was, in the end, largely determined by an individual's character. A human being without skills or learning could be trained, as long as she was willing to make the effort. A person with certain other qualities—determination, endurance, amiability, and a kind of social intelligence—would also have much to offer a spacefaring community.

Human brilliance was always of extreme interest to me, to all of us woven into the net of minds. The facets of such a mind were a jewel to be treasured, and contact with such minds and their workings made me appreciate anew the complex universe that exists inside each human mind. But what was needed aboard the Seeker was a brilliance that lay in the perspective of an individual; what I came to admire most was a mentality that could find something new in what was known, that could create a beauty or an intellectual construct that had not existed before, that could look out at the universe and glimpse a truth that had escaped the notice of others. Mental trickery, mastery of facts, a chaotic and unconscious eccentricity—such things had been taken for brilliance by human beings in the past, but that was never what I thought of as true genius. Such mentalities were not needed on the Seeker anyway, not with a net of cyberminds to gather and synthesize data and with Links providing access to that ocean of data. What was much more essential was an ability to sort through this information, to focus on what was important or of interest while ignoring that which was only distraction and to be able to synthesize.

Mahala and her fellow spacefarers believed that some sort of selection process, however invisible to them, accounted for their presence aboard the Seeker. There was indeed a process of selection, although the Habitat-dwellers and their artificial intelligences and the Counselors and Administrators and cyberminds had less to do with that process than Mahala realized. The process was largely one of self-selection: Most of the people of Earth and Venus and those living inside the Habitats preferred to stay where they were. Of the tens of millions who had a desire to become spacefarers, many soon came to realize that they were too psychologically bound to familiar people and places to take such an irreversible step away from them. That still left many millions who were willing to become part of the Seeker's community, but of these, a few million more turned back of their own accord, some only moments before they were to board the torchships that were to carry them to their new home.

Then there were those who came to the Seeker, lived here, prepared themselves for the voyage, and then returned to their former homes, called back by emotional ties, unresolved regrets, feelings of displacement, or a growing fear of what might lie ahead. And then there were those who discovered in themselves a heretofore unsuspected craving for the chimerical but excessively pleasurable experiences and scenarios that the Seeker's net of cyberminds could create for them. They might have remained among us, cared for as they explored their dreams, but that would have upset the balance of our spacefaring community; if too many others followed them in their retreat, our human community might have been damaged beyond repair. They were allowed to leave, to travel to another Habitat and to lose themselves among their illusions.

After the unsuitable and the regretful and the dreamers had left us, Mahala was struck by two facts. One was that few of the Habbers who joined us felt any obsessive desire for such illusory experiences; instead, it was the people from Earth who proved most susceptible. I could have explained to her that those Habbers who had come to the Seeker had either conquered such appetites earlier or had never been in thrall to them to begin with, but she was still getting used to her Link and often kept her channel closed.

The second fact that caught her attention was that a far smaller percentage of Cytherians, as compared to percentages of Habitat-dwellers or of Earthfolk, contributed to our rate of attrition. That, however, had been an expected outcome. The Cytherians among us were the products of a pioneer culture, people who had sought to shed the past and create a new society, the descendants of people who had broken old ties. They were in many ways well suited to be spacefarers.

What remained to be determined was whether or not they could readily adapt to us.

Most of the Habitats had begun as hollowed-out asteroids, and the same was true of the Seeker. The outer shells of our worldlet were the asteroid's thick metallic layers of rock, covered by another shell of an alloy that would help to shield the Seeker's inhabitants from cosmic rays. But the starfarers would not rely on that passive shielding alone; a force field produced by magnetic deflectors would be yet another protective skin.

The core of the Seeker was made into one of the gardened environments so beloved of the Habitat-dwellers, a very gently curved landscape of rivers and forests and open grassy land. I learned from Mahala later that her first sight of this vast enclosed space, where one stood with head pointed toward the center, had been extremely disorienting and might even have produced a feeling of terror in her had she not already had the experience of visiting Earth. She had gone there for the first time with Benzi, a Habitat-dweller with whom she shared a genetic connection.

What she saw was a landscape without a horizon, a vista of green marked with the blue veins and patches of rivers and lakes that seemed to stretch as endlessly as the Plains around Lincoln. The flatness of the land was an illusion; when she looked up, she could see the white tendrils of clouds and, above them, the blue threads of rivers winding past another panorama of green.

Mahala reached for Benzi's arm and steadied herself. "How did you feel," she asked, "when you first saw this kind of space?"

"Disoriented," he replied. "I wasn't able to judge distances at first. I couldn't tell if I was looking at a shrub that was only a few meters away or a large tree that was much farther away." He guided her across a grassy expanse toward a grove of trees. "You'll be able to live in here later on if you prefer, just as you would on any other Hab."

Mahala knew of the dwellings and living spaces that were planned for the Seeker's core. There would be hollowed-out caves in the cliffs that rose up from the sides of rivers, pavilions near lakes and sailing vessels with cabins for passengers, tents and huts and various other structures, all of them modeled on the abodes of past times and all of them equipped with every device needed for comfort. For Habitat-dwellers, such places embued them with a feeling that they had not lost their humanity and their natural past entirely, while for the Earth-people aboard the Seeker, the landscape would function as a reminder of home. Mahala, who had lived her life in the environments of Venus's domed settlements, thought of the core as a monumental and ecologically complex version of a garden or a park.

"It's lovely," she said to Benzi, "but I wonder if it's really necessary." Something about this vast, incurving landscape also disturbed her, but she ignored her unease, which, she told herself, probably had no more significance than the disorientation she had felt during her first days in Anwara.

Her unsettled state, although she did not realize this until much later, was caused by an unconscious apprehension that the core—or the Seeker's Heart, as the artificial wilderness came to be known—might prove too seductive an escape for some of those aboard. Like many human beings, Mahala was mistakenly convinced that one way to keep people from succumbing to temptation was to remove the temptation altogether, or at least to control access to it.

But we knew that, in a community of Links and cyberminds and memories and experiences that could be called up on command or shed from one's consciousness without a trace, there could be no control except an individual's own volition. We had not been made to control humankind, to prevent human beings from doing whatever they cared to do. We had not been made to judge our people.

During her earliest times aboard the Seeker, Mahala often felt that she had been cut adrift from any real purpose. She studied the Seeker and its workings, exchanged ideas with other spacefarers about their various scientific and intellectual disciplines, perused written records and mind-tours on any subject that struck her interest. The new implant inside her opened up a sea of data that beckoned her to other intellectual shores, while the workings of the molecular machines and biologically engineered microbes that would maintain her body indefinitely were of intense interest to her. At other times, she took long walks with others in the wilderness of the Seeker's Heart, taking pleasure in the life forms that could be found there, the variety of piscatorial and avian and mammalian creatures that constituted the hollow's menagerie. She learned her way around the levels that housed the newly arrived and arriving spacefarers, the wide hallways that connected the rooms and meeting spaces and recreational spaces and small gardens of each level. She made friends of those who lived closest to her quarters and then became better acquainted with people who resided on other levels. She formed emotional bonds with some people whose previous lives so differed from her own that they shared few common assumptions other than the views that exploring space was both valuable and desirable and that contact with an alien civilization was intrinsically of interest—and often they held even those opinions for entirely different reasons.

Her life had become more amorphous and aimless. That was what Mahala thought, during the few times that she was alone and with little to do except to reflect on her own thoughts. She did not seek solitude, feeling that too much time alone, with nothing outside of herself to hold her immediate attention, might cause her to dwell too much on the past, on the people she had known and loved and would never see again.

Then one of the people whom she had known in her earlier life came to the Seeker.

His name was Ragnar Einarsson. Mahala met him in the park near the torchship bay on the outermost level of the Seeker. Ragnar expressed surprise at the sight of the inner space of flowers and trees, as most of the new arrivals did. None of them had been told exactly what to expect, since their ability to adapt to an unfamiliar environment had to be reaffirmed when they arrived. Habitat-dwellers had only a slight advantage in adapting here, because the Seeker was a new community with a different purpose from that of the other Habitats.

"You haven't asked me about why I didn't come here sooner," Ragnar said after they had exchanged greetings.

His words surprised Mahala; she had to think for a moment before realizing that over two years had passed since she had last seen him. "It has been a while," she admitted. She had received only a few messages from Venus, most of them brief, informing her that daily life was for the time being going on much as before even while the Cytherians anticipated the changes that would soon come. Her replies had been equally brief. She was separating herself from her former life, losing track of how much time was passing aboard the Seeker.

"The farewells were even harder than I expected them to be," Ragnar said as Mahala led him toward the lift that would carry them to her level and the rooms where he would be living. "After all that time keeping my distance from most people, it was as if I had to make up for it by growing closer to them before I left for good. I found out more about my parents than I ever knew before, everything about their fears and hopes and secret failures, all the things they'd never told me about earlier."

"They want you to remember," Mahala said. Einar and Thorunn, she thought, wanted to live on inside of him, as Risa and Sef and Dyami would live on in her long after they were gone.

"And then there were all the carvings and sculptures and other things I'd made to give away. When I was visiting Dyami, I spent the better part of two months casting molds at the refinery. Maybe I could have refused, but I couldn't bring myself to refuse anybody who wanted something of mine. And maybe I want to make certain I'm remembered."

The lift opened onto a softly lighted hall. "I'll show you my rooms," Mahala said. "Yours are on this level, and they're much the same as mine, but you're free to change the furnishings and to move elsewhere later on if you like." She heard the soft sound of a chime, halted in front of the arched indentations on the wall, and pressed her hand against the surface; an arched open entrance to her quarters suddenly appeared. As she led him into a high-ceiling room furnished with cushions, low tables, and transparent display cases to hold the reproductions of the vases and goblets that she had begun to collect, she explained to him that the pilot embedded in his identity bracelet would guide him around the Seeker until he had his own Link.

He sat down. She seated herself next to him. "Solveig was unhappy for a while after you left," Ragnar said. "I don't know if she mentioned that in any messages. She missed you and then she began to wonder if she'd made the right decision. In the end, though, she said that she couldn't leave, that our parents shouldn't have to bear losing both their children, but that was only another excuse. She's grown closer to Chike now. It wouldn't surprise me if they become bondmates, even if they do both claim that formal bonds aren't necessary."

"That's what Chike and I always believed about such bonds," Mahala said.

"I'm sorry. Does it bother you that—"

"No," she said, "I'm happy for them," and meant it.

"Mahala," he murmured as he drew her to him. She slipped her arms around him, welcoming his embrace and yet feeling emotionally distant from him. She had never really seen that deeply into him. There had always been a wall between them before, and now she was no longer the person who had said farewell to him in Sagan, but was becoming something else.

Mahala and Ragnar came to love each other deeply as the years passed. Their courtship and mating followed a pattern much like that of the others aboard the Seeker, although they, as did most of the others, felt their emotional bond and its expression to be unique and peculiar to them.

Unlike almost all of the other couples forming bonds on the Seeker, Mahala and Ragnar had felt what they called love for each other some years earlier, as young adults. But Mahala recalled that emotional connection as a turbulent and painful experience. She had known Ragnar barely at all then, and had not understood the impulses that compelled him to create the aesthetically pleasing objects that he had learned how to fashion and to dream of those that he could not yet make. She had grown closer to him during their early years inside the Seeker and was gradually coming to realize that he had not chosen the spacefarer's way only out of a desire to escape a world that had often held him back from what he sought to express. Ragnar had also seen that our voyage might feed the hunger inside him by offering new subjects for his art, enlarging his perspective by opening up more of the universe to him.

As Mahala and Ragnar drew closer to each other, they also formed bonds with others, bonds that they often thought of as familial. In this, they also resembled the others whom the Seeker carried. The spacefarers became students of some of their comrades, mentors to others, and took on parental roles with younger voyagers. Among those who were closest to Mahala were two people she had known in the Cytherian settlement of Oberg, Akilah Ching and Kyril Anders, who had grown up in her grandmother Risa Liangharad's household. There was Ah Lin Bergen, a friend since childhood, and Wilhelm Asher, who had been a teacher of Mahala's when she was a child in Turing. Almost all of the spacefarers had their strongest bonds with people whom they had known in their earlier lives, and Mahala kept to this pattern.

Her earlier life began to recede from her. Occasionally, she gave in to the temptation to retreat into herself, to recapture an earlier happy memory of an evening with her biological kinsman Dyami and his household, of a few hours with her beloved Chike discussing their shared seminars in biological ethics or cosmology, or of a day spent with her close friend Solveig weeding hydroponic crops in a Sagan community greenhouse while gossiping about recent political developments in the Cytherian settlements. Knowing that I could aid in calling up memories indistinguishable from her actual past experiences, Mahala relived moments of her past life.

I did not begrudge her the memories or the verisimilitude I used in recreating them, for I understood that she would not seek a permanent retreat into them.

The memories were only another stage in her long farewell.

It may seem that the spacefarers spent much of their earliest time aboard the Seeker in establishing emotional bonds with others in their new community and in remembering the past. Mahala often had this misleading impression when reflecting on the beginnings of her new life. Human beings, I was learning from Mahala and those closest to her, often experienced their emotional states as the center of their life, as that which defined them and showed their true selves.

In reality, Mahala's emotions were often dominated by such concerns as the social disruptions being caused on Earth and to a lesser extent on Venus, by the prospect of greatly lengthened life spans. For centuries, Earthfolk had been using the techniques of genetic engineering to repair problematic and defective genes or to replace them altogether. The people of both Earth and Venus, as a result, could expect to live out a century and at least one or two more decades in reasonably good physical health and with the vigor of youth and middle age. That the Habitat-dwellers enjoyed much longer life spans was not so readily apparent to Earthfolk and Cytherians until there had been more contacts between the two branches of humanity, and even then there were many among the planet-bound who saw no advantage to a greatly extended life, who believed that those who lived too long would inevitably fall victim to ennui, boredom, and weariness.

Now, with the actual possibility of an indefinite life span ahead, those who saw such a long life as a trap were preparing for battle with those who viewed it as a opportunity and as a great leap forward in human evolution.

Mahala gleaned data from the public channels of Earth and Venus and from the personal messages sent to her. The public debates, intense as they often were, did not trouble her nearly so much as the acts of violence committed both by those who feared excessively long life spans and by those who feared that they might not live long enough to finally join the indefinitely long-lived. She often thought of Mukhtar Tabib's fear that the social disruption caused by too much change might irretrievably destroy Earth's societies. Occasionally, she felt the pangs of guilt for having escaped the disruptions of great change by joining the Seeker.

The life that stretched ahead of her was already altering her cerebral cortex and her limbic system, changing her thoughts and emotions and her reactions to what was around her. She was, as she would put it herself much later, becoming less conscious of the passage of time and of time's constraints and more aware of the possibilities that stretched before her. She was becoming an entity that would eventually reach both its potential and its limits, because there would be almost nothing to prevent that, nothing either to hold her back or to compel her to even greater efforts in compensation for perceived failures.

Their greatly extended lives were what made it possible for the people aboard the Seeker to become spacefarers. There would be a time of suspended animation for them, so that they would not be conscious for the entire ninety years that our voyage would take in relativistic time, but they had decided to live out the five years of the last leg of the journey, in order to reestablish their bonds and prepare themselves for the encounter with the alien. There, in that distant star system, the alien might summon us to a journey of even longer duration. A Seeker inhabited by successive generations of short-lived human beings, all except the last generation doomed to live out their lives and die inside our Habitat, would have prevented those generations from fully sharing in our enterprise. It would have made them our prisoners. In the end, it might have been left to us to explore the universe by ourselves.

Mahala was not entirely engaged, or even primarily occupied, in adapting to her new environment, managing her Link, mastering new intellectual disciplines, and building emotional connections to Ragnar and other companions and, by extension, to all of those who were her comrades aboard the Seeker. It was necessary for the Seeker, using data from all of our past and present astronomical observations, to calculate our trajectory to the distant star and the alien beacon, a complex process involving the measurement of the positions and velocities of that star and others in relation to the sun. It was likely that some modifications in our course would be made during the journey, if our drive performed differently than expected, but we would map our course as precisely as possible before leaving the solar system.

Some of the spacefarers were extremely familiar with the mathematics needed for interstellar navigation, but most of them, including Mahala, were not. Even though the cyberminds of the Seeker would be largely responsible for navigation, especially during the eight decades our people would spend in suspended animation, the human spacefarers had decided that it was essential for them to acquire at least a basic knowledge of the disciplines required for an interstellar voyage.

Mahala and her companions learned more about the measurements that would have to be made during the voyage. Signals from

pulsars, the periodic bursts of radio energy that came from rapidly ro-
tating neutron stars, would be used to determine the Seeker's position;
eclipsing binary stars would help in measuring both direction and time
during acceleration and deceleration. Doppler shift measurements,
formulas for relativistic stellar aberration, and other ways of making as-
trometric measurements were part of Mahala's studies. She found herself opening her Link more often to question the cyberminds, to check
her conclusions with theirs, to sense the queries of other spacefarers,
and soon she became adept at Linking with her fellow voyagers to exchange thoughts, a process that she thought of almost as a kind of
telepathy.

This was not quite accurate. Any spacefarer with an open Link,
even while looking at the world through the eyes of another or hearing
through another person's ears, could easily keep her innermost
thoughts and feelings hidden from others. Even I was often not entirely aware of Mahala's deeper or more reflexive thoughts and feelings
until she revealed them overtly, through laughter, tears, or an increased flow of adrenaline. But she grew used to engaging in sessions
that seemed to her to be much like telepathic seminars. Gradually she
was coming to see herself as a link in the Seeker's community of
minds.

A few years after Ragnar had come aboard the Seeker, he created his
first work of art for his fellow spacefarers, a simulation of a starscape as
it might appear at extremely high relativistic speeds. Stars came into
view and then grew dimmer and disappeared; other stars appeared and
turned blue, then swelled into red giants as they receded from us. A
cone of blackness behind the Seeker grew until all that was visible was
a small and brilliant ring of light; ahead, the bright colorful points of
red-shifted stars clustered together around our now invisible destination, a circle of color fading into blue and white. All of the universe
then seemed compressed into a single point of bright light. The visual,
and occasionally fanciful, aspects of Ragnar's creation were impressive
enough, but he had underlined them with emotional tones, conveying
an extreme sense of claustrophobia and temporal displacement to the
viewer.

I am lost, Mahala thought as she surrendered to Ragnar's vision, a creation that he had kept from her until he was prepared to show it to all of their comrades. The universe she had known would be gone, no more than a bright beacon of light; in the time that it took her to raise her hand, months would pass outside the Seeker. The emotional impact of that realization filled her with awe and with terror.

We had suspected that Ragnar's starscape might have an adverse effect on some members of the Seeker's human community. Several thousand potential voyagers were so deeply moved, and so emotionally wrought after their experience, that they were impelled to return to Earth or to their former Habitats. Reports of increasing social disruption on Earth and of the greater involvement of the Habitat-dwellers in events on Venus, with the Cytherians potentially endangered by Earth's political and social instability, did not deter these comrades from leaving the Seeker. Linking themselves to Earth's net of cyberminds or to the Habber cyberminds who were now more closely tied to their Earthly cybernetic brethren, and doing what they could to ward off widespread disorder, seemed preferable to enduring the extreme displacements of interstellar travel.

Ragnar, inspired by his recently acquired knowledge, had sought only to share his vision of what he might see outside the Seeker as it raced through the universe toward the alien calling to us—the blue-shifted giant stars, the visible blue of ultraviolet radiation distorting the positions and shapes and brightness of other stars, the red of the stars receding from us, the black cone forming at the back of the Seeker as its relativistic speed increased. That his starscape had impelled some of his fellows to abandon the Seeker was, he admitted to Mahala later, somewhat gratifying to him; he could bear almost any reaction to his creations except indifference.

That his starscape also served to weed out more people who might prove unsuited for our voyage also served our purposes.

The Seeker, powered by our matter-antimatter drive, left its orbit around the sun to embark on the first stage of our journey in the year 672 of the Nomarchies of Earth. Our community of spacefarers was composed by then of nearly five hundred thousand human beings, with as many Links to the voyaging Habitat's net of cyberminds.

"There should have been more people aboard," Benzi often said. He spent much of his time on the bridge, the vast open space of consoles and platforms that housed our navigational systems, surrounded on all sides by walls of holo screens for sensor displays of what lay outside the Seeker. "I knew that many would turn back, that most people wouldn't want even to consider joining us, but I thought there would be more."

Mahala understood what he meant. The dream of deep space exploration had lived inside Benzi for so long that he still found it hard to believe that so few members of his species shared its realization with him.

Mahala was approaching the fortieth year of her existence, a fact that struck her as having little relevance to her present life. Her emotional ties to Ragnar were still strong, even though they shared fewer moments with each other in such pursuits as talking and lovemaking and exploring yet another part of the landscape in the Seeker's Heart. They had moved to shared quarters in the level nearest the Heart; they were now over the novelty of being able to furnish their rooms with almost any objects our synthesizers could fashion for them. The clutter of their previous rooms had been replaced by cushions, a bed, a low table holding a few of Ragnar's carvings, and a wall screen that usually displayed either a landscape of a section of the Seeker's Heart or one of Ragnar's sketches.

Occasionally, Mahala called up a scene from one of the Seeker's sensors for her wall screen. She did not care to gaze at the red pinprick that was Mars as the Seeker passed that planet's orbit, or at giant Jupiter, or at cold bluish Neptune; that was looking back. Her screen held images of a field of stars slowly being compressed into a large cluster, of stars changing color as the Seeker's velocity increased.

We came to the Oort Cloud, that halo of thinly scattered comets and small bodies that surrounded the solar system. We left that last region of familiar space behind as our vacuum drive cut in, gradually increasing our velocity to ninety-eight percent of light speed. Ninety years would pass for us in relativistic, subjective time aboard the Seeker by the time we reached our destination, but six hundred years would have passed by then for those left behind in the solar system. This fact, well known to all aboard, was beginning to impress itself upon the emotions of our human companions.

Mahala was often on the bridge with Benzi and Suleiman Khan to observe the familiar visual universe vanish around us, to be displaced by the ever-increasing deep black cone astern and the Doppler-shifted stars, altering in size and color, toward which the Seeker was rushing. The bridge, large enough to hold over a thousand people, was often empty except for a few pilots, five trained astrophysicists and a few others who had made themselves into students of that discipline, and a small group of the curious. I knew through the net that even though any of our human comrades could have been watching on wall screens elsewhere or could have called up a holo display, few of them were actually doing so.

They did not want to view those distortions of space. Perhaps many of them were like Ragnar in preferring to undergo this passage in solitude while musing on their memories of a past that was retreating ever more rapidly from them.

Mahala had decided to view the passage, to come to the bridge to watch, but during one visit, as the forward field of stars grew more compressed on the screen, she turned away and left the bridge without speaking. The time and space that she had known now existed for her only here, in this place, as the rest of the universe fled from the Seeker.

She felt a hand on her arm; Suleiman had caught up with her. "I thought I had prepared myself for this," the older man told her as he slipped his arm through hers.

She probed the channels; his Link was closed. "Are you sorry that you stayed aboard?" she asked.

"No. I wouldn't have left. It's not that I have any regrets. It's just that I am now realizing how irrevocable my decision is and exactly what I've lost."

Suleiman, with almost seven decades of life behind him, must have said many farewells before leaving Venus. He would have even more memories to haunt him than she did. She wondered whether he would choose to give some of them up to be kept by the Seeker's cyberminds, or if he would begin to live inside them, as others were already beginning to do.

Mahala had taken to sharing her meals often with Akilah Ching and Kyril Anders. Sometimes they came to the rooms she shared with Ragnar; at other times, she and Ragnar met them in one of the gardens in the Seeker's Heart.

On one occasion, as the Heart's bands of light were fading into an soft evening glow, the four of them met in a small three-sided dwelling surrounded by trees. As Mahala and Ragnar laid out food and drink they had brought there from a dispensary on the low table they had found in the dwelling, Mahala was suddenly struck by memories of dinners in her grandmother's house. The presence of Akilah and Kyril, who had grown up in Risa's household, made the memories sting even more.

She kept her Link closed, not wanting to know from us exactly how much time had passed outside the Seeker, how much our subjective time was slowing in relation to the rest of the universe.

"What is it, Mahala?" Akilah asked as she leaned forward.

Mahala shook her head.

"You're remembering," Ragnar said.

"I've been remembering, too," Kyril said. "It comes upon me suddenly. I've had moments when everything around me vanishes and I find myself back in Oberg, at some place or in some situation from my past, and it all seems as real as if I were there. I don't need my Link to make it seem entirely authentic, either." His brown eyes were solemn as he gazed across the table at Mahala. "In fact, I often have to use my Link to bring me back to the present."

"The present." Akilah shook her head, as if finding something absurd in those words.

The Seeker had by then reached a point where we could no longer accurately measure our distance from Earth or from our destination, where the light-years seemed to be shrinking around us, the universe seemingly growing smaller than it had been.

A numbness had been creeping into Mahala for some time now, as her mind resisted a complete understanding of what she had done. The Seeker had become familiar; she clung to that familiarity.

In that, she was like the vast majority of the human beings aboard the Seeker. They had come here to be explorers, to voyage into the unknown. Now they were looking into their own thoughts as their minds fell in on themselves and grew as compressed as the field of stars on the bridge screens.

The time had come for our human voyagers to sleep, to retreat to the chambers where they would be suspended, yet many resisted that sleep. Mahala was one of those who clung to consciousness. She told herself that as a physician, she was needed to counsel others who held back from suspended animation, in order to reassure them and to see that they were properly prepared for their decades-long sleep. But there were other reasons guiding her actions, reasons she only intermittently acknowledged consciously, reasons which haunted the minds of many of the spacefarers.

She would awake from her sleep when we were still five years from our destination, when our human community would come to life again, reestablishing their connections to one another and to us, assimilating whatever data we had gathered and preparing themselves for contact with the alien. And she would know, when she awoke, that well over five hundred years had passed in the solar system, that everyone she had known was irretrievably lost to her.

Five years after our departure from the solar system, Mahala went with Ragnar to one of the chambers that held our sleepers. Only a few thousand of our people were still awake by then; the rest lay in rows on sleeper platforms, visible through the transparent carapaces that enclosed them. Mahala glanced at their unmoving faces, closed eyes, the arms folded over their chests or resting at their sides, and thought of death.

"I'll be in the sleeper next to yours," Ragnar said. "When you wake, I'll be the first person you see."

She held on to him for a moment, then forced herself to lift the carapace of the empty sleeper. She stretched out quickly and closed her eyes as the carapace closed over her.

This was how she recalled the experience later, when the sleeper opened and she was able to turn her head and see Ragnar on the platform next to hers, stretching his arms as he struggled into wakefulness: She remembered only closing her eyes and then waking to find herself stiff and disoriented and breathing air that seemed much too cold and dry until she remembered where she was. Yet she also had memories of being on the bridge, of gazing into a bright cluster of stars that was all she could see of the heavens, of feeling herself growing larger and more vast as the universe contracted around her.

Perhaps, she told herself later, after Ragnar had kissed her awake and she had helped to rouse others from their rest, it was only a phantom memory. But when she was with other people once more, listening to their recollections of their time in suspended animation, she began to see that specific memory as part of a dream all of them had shared.

It was also our dream, for we thought of our passage at relativistic speed as a dream, and perhaps some of that dream had filtered through their Links to the sleepers. Our space-time, the only reality that existed for us, insisted on confirming that the remaining distance to our destination had shrunk from four hundred to sixty light-years, that time was shortening beyond our comprehension. We could no longer measure the universe outside the Seeker. Our net of mentalities had devised a defense to protect our intellectual functions, one gained from the workings of human minds; we perceived our voyage as a dream.

Our people had been revived, but many could not bring themselves to awaken fully to the reality around them. We felt many of them retreating again, withdrawing from us and from the harder edges of our thoughts.

Mahala had always considered herself an empiricist. In this she knew, from the records and stories of her predecessors, that she resembled her great-grandfather, Liang Chen, who had concerned himself with what he could see and know. What others thought of as the spiritual realm had been of no interest to Chen. That the world had become what the Muslims around him called the *Dar al-Islam*, the Abode of Islam, that Islam had prevailed on Earth and had, as a result, later shown an increased tolerance for those who had not yet submitted to that faith, was a fact that he accepted without much thought. Whether or not the laws he lived under were derived from Islam or some other legal code was a matter of indifference to him, as long as such laws were applied fairly to all.

That was one part of Mahala's heritage, but there was also the example of her great-grandmother, Iris Angharads. Iris's public record noted that she had been brought up in Lincoln as a Marian Catholic and that her memorial service on Island Two had been conducted by a priest, but Mahala knew little about Iris's inner state of mind. From what she had seen of Iris's private records, she suspected that her great-grandmother had harbored much skepticism, but there was nothing that hinted at what she might have believed toward the end of her life.

There was also her grandfather Malik, who might have questioned some tenets of his Islamic faith, but whose scholarly writings bore the stamp of his culture and its religious beliefs. And then there were her parents, who had given themselves over to the destructive cultish fanaticism of Ishtar.

Mahala had never thought much about such matters. A worthwhile human life, she had always felt, had to be lived within the confines of what was known and what was theoretically probable, with doubt being one of a thinking person's most important intellectual tools. But it was becoming increasingly obvious that some of the others who lived in the Seeker were turning to older certainties.

Mahala was in the Seeker's Heart, following a stone path near a riverbank, when she heard the sound of the call to afternoon prayer. She halted, listened for a while, then moved toward the sound. In the levels of rooms and corridors that surrounded the Heart, people had occasionally gathered in groups to practice whatever rites had become habitual to them, but Mahala had believed such practices had been growing less common even before the period of suspended animation. Now she felt that there were aspects of life among her fellow spacefarers that had been invisible to her, perhaps because she assigned so little importance to them herself and had chosen to ignore them.

The voice of the muezzin fell silent. She rounded a bend in the river and came to a clearing. A slender spire made of ivory-colored stone stood at the corner of a small roofless structure of four walls. The spire, she realized, was meant to be a minaret; she had come to a mosque.

Three pairs of slippers sat outside the wall facing her. She sat down under the nearest trees and waited. At last the door to the tiny mosque opened; two men in headdresses and long robes came outside, followed by Suleiman Khan in a tunic and loose trousers. His two companions put on their slippers and left the clearing without acknowledging Mahala's presence. Suleiman donned his shoes, sat down, then beckoned to her.

She came toward him and seated herself. He said, "I have been praying."

"So I noticed."

"The last time that I prayed with any sincerity, may God forgive me, was as a very young man, before I went to live in Turing, before—" He was silent for a while. "I have been praying that those I once knew are at peace, that God now cradles them."

He had reminded her of the probability, the certainty, that everyone they had once known on Venus was dead. Mahala had kept that thought submerged, refusing to allow it to swim up into her conscious mind. She had seized on other possibilities: that human life spans had become so indefinitely prolonged that they amounted to a kind of physical immortality; that human mental patterns might live on in cybernetic intelligences that were far more subtle and developed than those who made up the network of the Seeker; that individual selves that she would recognize as Risa, Sef, Dyami, Chike, and Solveig were still somehow alive. To some, her hope would seem as irrational—or as much of a leap of faith—as Suleiman's hope that those he had cared for lived on in the paradise God had promised to all believers and good people.

"I do not know what I have been for much of my life," Suleiman continued. "Many, I am sure, would have called me an infidel, or a backslider at best, but God—may his name be praised—is all-forgiving. I've committed my share of sins. Men died at my hands during the Cytherian Revolt, when those of us imprisoned in Turing finally had our revenge on our tormentors, but I did not believe that any just God would punish me for that. And then for a long while it seemed that I had lost what little faith I had possessed in God and his truth, but maybe that was only a loss of faith in men." He gazed at her steadily with his dark eyes. "The believers, and those who emigrate and struggle in God's way—those have hopes of God's compassion, and God is All-forgiving, All-compassionate."

He had said that last phrase in Arabic, but Mahala understood enough Arabic to grasp the words, while I informed her through her Link that they were from a *sura* of the Koran.

"And yet," Suleiman said in Anglaic, "God is ultimately unknowable. As a child, I believed that the way to God lay in study of the Holy Koran, and later that the way to enlightenment and perhaps some knowledge of God, insofar as he chose to reveal himself, lay in the study of the sciences. But I have come to comprehend the truth of what the believers have always known, that God is ultimately transcendent and unknowable."

The air of the Seeker's Heart felt colder; Mahala shivered. "Why did you come aboard the Seeker?" she asked.

"I had my reasons, most of which could probably be summed up as being curious and wanting to engage in an entirely new human enterprise. Now it seems as though I was led here, that others might have been led here, for an entirely different purpose."

She did not want to ask the next question, but sensed that Suleiman expected it of her. "And what is that purpose?" she asked.

"We can never be certain of any of God's attributes except for those he chooses to reveal," Suleiman said, "but we can know his will for us through the Holy Koran and the Law. I shall admit something to you, Mahala. When I knew that another intelligence existed in the universe, that it was calling out to us, doubt and skepticism overtook me. You see, I knew what Islam would demand of us, that we bring God's Word to those beings, that they be brought under the rule of God's Law, and I came to see that as an imposition, as a cruelty, as a way perhaps of denying our species the truths that a society of alien minds might impart to us, assuming that we were capable even of understanding what they might be able to tell us."

"Your faith once demanded the same for Earth," Mahala murmured.

"That is true, and the Council of Mukhtars came to power, and Islamic law came to govern all of Earth, and because of that, believers could be merciful to unbelievers. In the *Dar al-Islam*, Muslims could allow others to follow their traditional customs and ways, to practice their own beliefs, for the *Shari'a*, the Way, remained open to all who were willing to choose it. One cannot revoke divine law, but one can choose not to enforce it when that seems advisable."

He paused. "But how can we apply this to other species," he went on, "to nonhumans? God's Word and God's Law were meant for all sentient beings. How do we tell any aliens of God's Messenger Muhammad, may his name be forever blessed, and of the truths God revealed to his Prophet? What would we have to do if they are able to understand our words, yet still refuse to heed them? What if we realize that they will never know what we are saying to them at all, that too wide a gap divides us? What if instead of leaving themselves open to submission to the Way, whatever practices they might follow in the meantime, they turn away from the truth completely and reject it? Some of us might choose mercy and tolerance. But others might argue, with some justice, that a *jihad*, a Holy War, is required to bring the unbelievers to the truth."

"No," Mahala whispered.

"Now I pray that we are unable to understand them," Suleiman said, "that we will not be able to communicate with them, that the gap between our species remains unbridgeable. For if we cannot reach out to them, then we would be under no obligation to tell them of God's Word. They would be completely unknowable to us, and we to them."

He leaned forward, and his gaze was filled with an intensity that made her draw back from him. "Perhaps God has designed things that way so that our species can disperse itself throughout all of God's creation, but without cruelty and bloodshed. We may receive signals from others, we may travel to their worlds, but I pray that they will remain forever alien to us, forever unknown."

Mahala thrust out an arm. "Suleiman—" she began.

"You think I am mad," he said. "I see it in your face, Mahala." He looked more like his old self now, with his half-smile and his usual skeptical, slightly mocking expression. "But such musings have enabled me to submit to God's Will once more and to accept what he has ordained for me. I can hope that we will not find what we are seeking, that God will show us that mercy, and that has brought me a kind of peace."

She got to her feet, bowed her head slightly in his direction, then left him sitting outside his mosque.

Mahala took to roaming around more widely in the Seeker's Heart more often after that, sometimes following the stone walkways or the paths through our gardens, sometimes wandering into the wilder, more untamed regions of the environment. A few cycles after her encounter with Suleiman, she followed a trail through a wooded area to a cliff dotted with caves and found crosses or holo images of the Virgin Mary and her Son Jesus in almost every cave entrance. The people there welcomed her, invited her to share a meal with them, but did not stop her when she left them before they gathered to say their prayers. During another sojourn, she found what seemed to be a kind of shrine, a pavilion that had been raised over an image of the Buddha.

Occasionally, she came upon wooden structures where a lone person was praying or meditating; she often could not tell the difference and hesitated to interrupt those she found at their devotions.

How many people were wandering into the Seeker's Heart or living there for long periods, engaged in prayer, contemplation, metaphysical musings, readings, and other spiritual pursuits? Mahala asked that question of us, but we could not give her a precise answer. Those who sought such consolations did not often open their Links while engrossed in them and did not usually share such thoughts with us at other times. Our estimate was that some fifty to one hundred thousand people inside the Seeker were occasionally or largely occupied in matters involving the practices of the unverifiable beliefs that they called their faiths, but that was only an estimate. There might have been others who harbored such notions, but who kept them to themselves.

"What is going to happen to us," Mahala asked, "if even more people fall under this metaphysical spell?" She was asking that question of Benzi, who was on the bridge, and of Ragnar, Ah Lin Bergen, and Tomas Sechen, who were there with them, but she was also asking it of us. To her, those like Suleiman seemed as lost as people who were caught in the trap of endless synthetic experience.

"This is what we get," Mahala continued, "for wanting so many of our kind on this journey. Perhaps a smaller ship with fewer but saner people would have been better."

Ragnar shrugged; what others chose to do, as long as it did not affect the Seeker's mission, was their concern and not his. In that, he reflected our conclusions about the faith-seekers.

Ah Lin said, "There isn't much we can do to stop them."

Tomas said, "There isn't anything we should do to stop them. They'll find whatever it is they're looking for and then they'll rejoin our community, or else they'll go on searching. The Seeker is our universe now, until we reach our destination. If getting there at last doesn't bring our spiritual wanderers back to us, nothing will."

Mahala was troubled by dreams.

Occasionally, she woke abruptly from a recurring dream where she felt herself to be embedded in a thick ebony substance, unable to move, blinded because no light was able to reach her. At other times, she dreamed of running after something without knowing what it was and being unable to catch up with it. As the Seeker continued to decelerate, the dreams passed.

More of the Seeker's people were forming into various loosely connected groups or bands, gathering with others to study the data we were collecting, to learn new disciplines, or simply to lose themselves in meditation or physical exercise inside the Seeker's Heart. Mahala found a renewed satisfaction in the company of others and in using her old training as a physician to listen to and advise the more troubled of her comrades.

As Tomas Sechen had predicted, more of those who had been caught up in metaphysical musings were soon rejoining the life of the Seeker's community. Many of these people shared some of their thoughts and feelings with our net, in the hope that the data provided by their experiences might be useful. We glimpsed human minds that had struggled to a kind of serenity and faith and others who would continue to question and seek and doubt. We learned that a new desire had flowered in many of them during their search, replacing the longing for a faith in some of them, and the seeds of that longing were soon passed to others of the human spacefarers.

They wanted new people to join them aboard the Seeker. They longed for children. Yet they hesitated, concerned about what lay ahead, about the ethics of bringing children into existence before they knew what awaited us at our destination. We offered them no guidance, no advice; this was a matter they had to decide by themselves.

They chose to wait.

As the Seeker decelerated, our destination star again became visible; the bright point became a cluster and the heavens gradually transformed themselves into a field of stars. The alien signal was audible once more, singing to us, as we approached the outermost planet of this system, a lifeless mass of ice and rock. We swept toward the star, a G-2 yellow-white star so closely resembling our sun that it might have been its twin, in a long arc, noting the presence of three ringed gas giants in the outer reaches of this system and the two smaller planets nearer their sun, two hot dry worlds with atmospheres of carbon dioxide, planets that Mahala could almost imagine as the sisters of Venus.

Mahala was often on the bridge as we continued toward the alien beacon that orbited the innermost of the two Venusian worlds. Hundreds came to the bridge, crowding around the screens, while others watched on screens in their quarters or Linked themselves to our sensors. Some accepted what we had discovered here as soon as it was verified by our readings, while others continued to hope for more, but all of them had at last accepted the truth when we were within a million kilometers of the alien artifact.

The beacon was a solid round object some four kilometers in diameter. Our scanners could not see into its solid core, and as we sent out our answering call, the alien voices abruptly fell silent. There was no alien life in this system, as we had seen while falling toward its sun; unless some primitive strain of microbial life existed on any of the planets, there was no life at all. We had come six hundred light-years only to reaffirm what we already knew; that another intelligence existed in the universe, and that we might never have contact with that intelligence.

"We are here," they had told us, and we had gone to them. Now they were mute, and Mahala feared that their voices would never speak to us again. Suleiman would call it God's mercy, that humankind knew of this alien intelligence without being able to reach out to it. She tried to take some solace in that thought.

We remained in that star system for a time, mapping its planets, confirming that there was no life on any of them, and struck by the resemblance of the planetary bodies to those of our solar system. The alien beacon remained silent and impenetrable to us, and gradually all of our people accepted the truth.

Humankind would have to search for the beacon's creators elsewhere; we would find nothing of them in this system. There was no life here, and it was probable, based on the data gathered by our sensors and probes, that none had ever existed.

We had come this far, but contact with the alien was never our sole purpose, only the motivation human beings had needed to undertake their long journey. There was still the hope of return, of going back to see what had become of the worlds we had left behind. There was still the hope for children, young people who would not have to live out all of their lives inside a nomad with no destination.

Children would come to the Seeker. The spacefarers would take our children, the children of their bodies and the children of our net, back to our home.

Home

27

A year and a half after we had left the alien star system, measured in our time, Mahala went to the chamber to prepare for sleep and for oblivion. By then, the extreme disappointment many of our human companions had felt at finding only a silent alien beacon, with no sign as to where its creators might be found, had faded.

Perhaps the alien signal had been designed to draw other intelligences capable of interstellar space travel into exploring the universe. Perhaps, Mahala thought, the aliens meant to reveal themselves only after more of her species had ventured beyond their home system. Maybe the aliens would call out to humanity again when people had loosed themselves from more of the ties that still bound them to the past; Mahala was thinking of Suleiman Khan then and his words about unknowable aliens and God's mercy. She had been quick to see him as deluded by his beliefs, but now, as she contemplated the vast distances between the stars and the temporal displacements of relativistic space travel, it seemed possible to her that an unknowable God might have shown his creatures some mercy by creating such formidable barriers, which would allow each of his life-forms the isolation they might require to attain the wisdom that would be needed before they met other alien mentalities.

We would also be returning to the solar system with our observations of a star system that bore intriguing resemblances to our own. Its star was of a yellow spectral class identical to the sun, while its three gas giants, each with several small moons, were much like Saturn and Neptune. A belt of asteroids orbited the star in a band midway between the gas giants and the two inner planets. We had mapped those two inner planets, with their thick clouds that gave off so much light that they seemed to Mahala like pearls, and had sent our probes to their surfaces, and had seen Venus as she might have been two billion years ago.

Fanciful notions came to Mahala then: Perhaps the aliens had meant for human beings to come here and find those worlds, to make new Earths of them as humankind was already doing with their distant sister world of Venus; and perhaps when we had transformed them, the beings who had signaled to us would return to this system at last and reveal themselves.

Ragnar accompanied Mahala to the chamber, as he had before. Again she dreamed as she slept, this time of rushing toward a world where time was passing so rapidly that every observable event was a blur. Houses inside transparent domes rose and fell and sprang up once more in new patterns; clusters of domes formed on dark plains in a instant; thick clouds evaporated into white wisps; green masses grew until they encompassed continents. It came to her, after she awoke, that she had been dreaming of Venus.

Ragnar was at her side, helping her up gently as she came to herself. She searched his face and saw the distant look she remembered in his grayish-blue eyes, the expression that always reminded her that there were still parts of him that she would never know.

"There is no one left who remembers us," he said.

"We knew that some time ago," Mahala murmured.

"I meant there may be no one left who remembers this voyage and the Seeker's mission." He held her, not speaking for a while, as others began to wake around them.

Less than twenty years remained of our voyage in relativistic time, but Mahala sensed no time passing as she took up the threads of her life again. She recalled the first time that she had traveled from Oberg to Turing as a child, when she had imagined that the airship might continue on an endless journey, and that she and her fellow passengers would be suspended forever in the restful interlude between what they had left behind and where they were headed; that notion had filled her with an unexpected pleasure.

Mahala was one of those whose medical and biological knowledge had equipped her for helping others during this new stage in our voyage, and yet she felt apprehensive. Having children among the spacefarers would destroy the illusion she could sometimes create of time standing still, of feeling that the people she had left behind might be alive after all. Bringing new human beings to life here seemed an admission that they might be the only remaining members of their species and that the Seeker might become their only world. The rest of humankind might have died out, transformed itself, divided into thousands of unrecognizable species that might be as strange to her and her comrades as any alien.

If so, Mahala concluded, then they had even more of an obligation to build a true human community aboard the Seeker.

A number of choices were available to the spacefarers for the creation of the new generation. A gestating embryo might carry the genes of two parents, several people, or only one; instead of simply ensuring that each child was free of obvious physical, mental, or hormonal disabilities, certain qualities could be enhanced through gene manipulation. Mahala found herself increasingly relied upon as an advisor to those who wanted children. To her surprise, almost every prospective parent she counseled decided to use the most conservative and least intrusive biological techniques. Later, she came to see this as an attempt to hold on to a comforting familiarity, an effort by her fellow voyagers to maintain their bond with humankind's past. The descendants of the spacefarers might eventually choose a more divergent path, but the Seeker would preserve the species as they knew it.

The rooms where our people had slept were transformed into incubators. It soon became customary for parents to visit the ectogenetic chambers where their offspring were gestating. This was ostensibly to monitor that process, and yet it also seemed that most of them were drawn to the chambers by deeper instincts, by an urge to bond with their young even before birth. The parents were also present when their infants were removed from the artificial wombs, an occasion marked by subdued but joyous celebrations. The children were regarded as the children of all, and each child had a number of adults to serve as caretakers, nurses, teachers, and mentors, but the biological parents of the children tended to spend more time than others with their offspring and to develop stronger bonds with them.

We also had reason to welcome these young human beings. We

would be able to Link ourselves to fresh youthful minds, and to acquire new perspectives.

During her earlier life, Mahala had rarely thought of becoming a biological parent herself. That possibility had seemed to lie far in her future, after she had sated her curiosity, become more skilled at her work, established her social bonds with her community, fulfilled some of her obligations to the Venus Project, visited new places, and decided what kind of life she wanted within the context of a relatively stable society.

Then the new era had come, promising changes that might upset many of her old preconceptions, and she had put any thought of parenthood aside.

Now she found herself drawn to the children who had appeared among the spacefarers, especially those who were the children of her closest friends. Ah Lin Bergen and Tomas Sechen were the parents of a son, while Akilah Ching and Kyril Anders were rearing a daughter. The infants in whom she had taken a detached interest were growing into inquisitive children to whom she felt a strong attachment, who induced a longing in her that she had not felt before.

"It's an understandable emotion," Mahala explained to Ragnar when they were alone in their quarters. She had often come upon him in the Seeker's Heart, sitting with a few of the children and their caregivers, carving small wooden animals and human figures for them to use as toys. "It's natural to take an interest in the next generation, especially under these circumstances."

Ragnar smiled; he smiled more often now. "You want a child," he said. "I know how you feel, Mahala. I have the same kind of feeling, and it surprises me that I do. My art was always enough to satisfy such yearnings, and on Venus, I resisted anything that might take me away from that, but maybe if I had stayed in Sagan and Frani had been there, I would have felt this longing sooner."

That was how it was with him, then; he was regretting his lost love, imagining the child that he and Frania had never had. That life was so long ago; she was startled at how his words cut at her.

"I see," she said softly.

"No, that isn't what I meant. I don't want to become the father of a child now because of what I didn't have with Frani. That's over now, and I can never bring it back. I did fall in love with you first, you know. I've been in love with you for most of my life now."

She thrust her hand into his. "I'm ready to be a parent, and it's your child that I want." They sat together for a while, leaning against each other and content in their silence.

"Are you going to have a daughter," Benzi asked Mahala, "or a son?"

"A daughter," she replied. She had gone to the bridge to tell him that there would be a new addition to their line. Benzi seemed pleased, but not overly excited; his smile was closer to an expression of amusement than of joy.

"And have you decided on a name for her yet?" he said.

"Angharad Ragnarsdottir."

"So her name will come from both of your lines." Benzi's expression grew gentle, but there was a weariness in his eyes. He looked that way more often now, tired and aged, an old man in spite of his rejuvenated body and unwrinkled face. "Angharad—so she'll be named for my grandmother in Lincoln. Angharad was a stubborn woman and ignorant, but I loved her very much and was sorry to leave her." He paused. "She didn't approve of my name at all. Benzi Liangharad— she didn't understand why my mother wanted to work my father's surname of Liang into it when children on the Plains always took their mothers' names for surnames, or else the names of their home towns."

"I know about the custom," she said and wondered if anyone still lived on the Plains who remembered that old custom.

"Angharad was like a mother to me during those early years. Even now I can sometimes feel myself missing her, even though she wouldn't have had the faintest idea of why we came aboard the Seeker and wouldn't have cared to know."

Benzi was being unusually garrulous, and his voice was wistful; he almost sounded like some of the old people who had been her patients near the end of their lives, when they were waiting to die and did not want their lives wastefully and needlessly prolonged.

"I am happy you're naming the child for her," he said as he turned back to the console.

When the embryo was gestating, Benzi went with Mahala and Ragnar to the incubating room. A long row of large, egg-shaped chambers sat against the walls of the softly lighted room; this space, like all of the other rooms set aside for the wombs, evoked feelings of calm. At one end of the room, a holographic image of waves rolling toward a beach of white sand, accompanied by the soothing sound of surf washing ashore, seemed so real that Mahala felt an urge to step into the scene. At other times, she had viewed a forest, a garden with colorful songbirds, and a flat grassy landscape that had reminded her of the Plains around Lincoln.

People hovered over the chambers holding their progeny, whispered to them, checked their life signs on the consoles next to each chamber. Mahala moved closer to Ragnar as they gazed down at the womb holding their daughter. Benzi hung back, almost as if he wanted to be elsewhere.

Benzi had never become a parent. That was the way he had put the matter to Mahala. The Habbers drew a distinction between simply contributing genetic material to their banks which might be passed on to any of their progeny and becoming a true parent—a caregiver, a nurturer and teacher. Habbers, he had explained, did not have to compensate for failures and dissatisfactions through their children or live out lives they had wanted for themselves vicariously through them. They did not have to grab at the consolation of children in the face of a death that might come prematurely. Habbers became parents only when they had a calling for it.

Perhaps their way was better, Mahala thought, and wondered if she had wanted a child of her own for reasons she had preferred not to examine too closely.

"Life always finds a way," Benzi said suddenly, startling her. "That was certainly one of the assumptions behind the terraforming of Venus, wasn't it? Give life an opening, a chance, and . . . " He paused. "I wonder what Venus is like now."

"We'll find out before too long," Ragnar said.

"I want to see it again," Benzi said, "and that surprises me. I was always so restless in my earlier life. I don't feel that restlessless now."

Mahala felt reassured by her decision when she lifted Angharad from her womb, bathed her in warm water, and listened to her first cries. A Link was implanted in the infant's forehead a few days after birth; all of our people had agreed to this custom of the Habitat-dwellers, so that the children could adapt to their Links easily and be watched over by us as they grew.

Her parents had chosen to be Angharad's primary caregivers, but other people were there to feed and hold and care for the child and to offer advice on how to look after her. There were times, Mahala reluctantly admitted to Ragnar, that their daughter seemed little more than a bundle of appetites screaming for satisfaction. Such admissions on her part reminded me of how we interfaced with our new components and new Links, how simple and slow they were in their operations until they became more complex and more tightly woven into our net. But our situation was not entirely analogous to that of the new human parents aboard the Seeker. They had a bond with their young ones that was as rooted in their biology as it was in their rational faculties.

As Angharad learned to crawl, sit up, walk, and say her first words, Mahala's awareness of the passage of time shifted again. The feeling of timelessness was replaced by a sense that time was passing too rapidly, that too much experience was going by before she had the chance to assimilate it. Her dark-eyed and raven-haired child was soon growing and showing signs that she had inherited her father's long limbs. Mahala had hardly grown used to carrying Angharad into the tamer areas of the Seeker's Heart before the child was insisting on being set down and allowed to walk. Almost before she could get over her pleasure in hearing her daughter call out her name or Ragnar's, Angharad had grown more fluent in her speech and could often be found in one of the gardens, talking with other small children.

Then there were the questions:

"Why are we here, Mahala?"

"What is the Seeker?"

"Is there anything outside the Seeker?"

"Where are we going?"

"What's the sun?"

"What is the solar system?"

"Why did you and Ragnar leave that other place?"

"Why are we going back?"

"Will we stay inside the Seeker, or will we have to go away?"

Mahala and Ragnar, and the other parents of the young, answered the questions as thoroughly as they could and also taught the children how to use their Links to access our data and the sensory experiences we could provide. They often gathered in the Seeker's Heart to explore that environment in small groups; they also came to the bridge to gaze at the contracted cluster of stars. The illusions of relativistic travel presented by our instruments, which informed us that we were moving at an impossible velocity faster than the speed of light, were accepted calmly by their young minds; they knew no other world except the Seeker, no other space-time except what we were experiencing.

We had begun deceleration and had noticed that fewer of the older people were paying visits to the bridge; even the parents of our human children seemed reluctant to be on the bridge with their young. Mahala, along with most of them, was contemplating what might lie ahead while retreating into the familiar regions of the Seeker.

"This might be the only home we have left," she said to Ragnar. "The Venus Project might have been abandoned long ago. The Earthfolk might have abandoned that world for Habitats, or they might have fulfilled the worst of Mukhtar Tabib's predictions." I could not tell what she feared most, that she might return to a system that would still be familiar in many ways, that the branches of humankind there might have diverged beyond recognition, or that their struggle to the next stage of their civilization might have proved futile in the end.

But for the children, the past of their kind was only the images and impressions of mind-tours and virtual experiences, the written public and personal records we had stored, the stories their parents had told them. Their history had begun with the Seeker. They came to the bridge and marveled as the bright pinpoint of light that was the universe slowly blossomed against the blackness that surrounded it, gradually transforming itself into a field of blue-shifted stars. The children regarded our destination not with apprehension and fear, but with wonder and curiosity.

Mahala stood on the bridge, one arm around her daughter, the other encircling Ragnar's waist. She had been keeping a channel of her Link open almost constantly, as were almost all of our spacefarers. The sun was now visible as a tiny violet point; the fan of stars was steadily widening as other stars passed through a spectrum of color.

Throngs of people had come to the bridge; others had gathered in large common rooms in front of other screens. Still others had their Links fully open to our sensors and were experiencing this stage of the voyage in full communion with the Seeker and its mentalities. We expected the spacefarers to remain absorbed in this last stage of our journey during most of their conscious moments.

"There is our sun," Mahala said to Angharad; an unnecessary remark, since the girl's Link had already communicated that information to her. It came to Mahala then that Angharad might never feel any more attachment to this star and its system than to any other place. Here was simply another family of planets; the Seeker was Angharad's base and all of the universe her home.

Angharad said, "Mahala, you're afraid, aren't you? You and Ragnar both."

Benzi, standing near Mahala in the crowd, glanced at them. "I'll admit to being apprehensive," Ragnar said softly. "Are you afraid, Angharad?"

"No."

Mahala turned toward her daughter. Angharad had inherited her father's height; she would soon be as tall as her mother. Despite her dark hair and eyes, her calm expression and intelligent steady gaze reminded Mahala of Solveig. What would she find here for her child? Would Venus finally have become the habitable world dreamed of by so many millions of people or had it been forgotten, left to revert to its lifeless hellish state? Had the Project stalled, had humankind been able to pass through the period of disruption and change without destroying much of what had been built? Would Angharad see the evidence of forebears who had triumphed or a race who had failed?

Whatever they had done, Mahala knew that she and her comrades had not been a part of it. If they found only the remnants of a failed civilization, their children might take solace from having been born among those who had escaped the destruction, or else they might feel the weight and the guilt of survivors. If the spacefarers found a thriving culture, or many cultures, they would know that this was the achievement of others and not themselves. She and the others with the Seeker were outside of their history, and it might now be impossible for them to rejoin it.

The spacefarers waited and watched as we decelerated, abandoning that task only for periods of rest and nourishment, and when we had entered nonrelativistic space again, with a familiar starfield of blue-white and yellow stars around us and the pinprick of Sol shining brightly ahead of us, we picked up a signal.

We recognized it after listening for only a few seconds; it was a replica of the signal once emitted by the alien beacon, and yet its source lay in the orbital path of Pluto. That realization leapt from our minds to those of our people, racing through the Links that connected us in an instant.

Mahala had a brief moment of mingled awe and terror. The aliens who had called to us were here, in the solar system; they had traveled here while she and her comrades were searching for them six hundred light-years away; they would reveal themselves at last. The thoughts of our human companions, as they cried out to one another, laughed, wept, rushed to the bridge and to common rooms to gather with their fellows, were in such turmoil that some time passed before we were able to help them in restoring their balance.

Only the children maintained their equilibrium. They had viewed our changing starscapes with a calm curiosity, and at the sound of the alien song, felt wonderment at such an unexpected delight.

And then we heard the rest of the message and knew the truth.

28

From the personal record of Mahala Liangharad:

For one brief moment, we thought we had achieved our end after all, that we had found the object of our search, and then the beacon appeared on the bridge's screens, magnified by our sensors.

The beacon was not an alien artifact but a Habber probe, as we quickly verified, and our Links were already whispering the rest of its message to all of us. I listened, and understood, and then closed my Link, wanting to hold my disappointment inside myself for a while.

One hundred years after the Seeker had left on its journey, the people of the two Habitats in the outer solar system had left a recording of the alien signal along with a message for us, in case we ever returned to this region of space. The sound of the signal was meant as a welcome and a sign of recognition to any aliens who might be returning with us. The message from the Habitat-dwellers was to tell us that they had chosen not to wait here, that their Habitats had already left the solar system on a search and that other expeditions were likely to follow them. They did not intend to follow course to our destination; they would leave it to us to locate the source of the signal they had reproduced. Their goal was to explore the nearer stars, to learn what they could about those systems, to move on after that to other stars, and to leave other beacons with both the alien signal and their own signal behind them.

I stood there with the others, lost in my own thoughts, gradually realizing that no one near me had yet said a word aloud. I recalled what Solveig had told me over twelve hundred years ago, that ours would not be the only such journey, that there would be others. Part of me had known that she was right, that if humankind survived the time of transition, then others would begin to look outward once more.

Now I wondered: If two Habitats had left the solar system, how many other people had followed them? How many of our kind still remained here?

The minds of the Seeker set a course that would take us toward Earth. We sent out our calls, heard no replies, and launched probes to search for signs of human activity. Even allowing for how long it might take any observers in the inner solar system to verify the Seeker's presence, to decide how to respond, and to transmit a message to us, we grew increasingly dismayed by the utter silence that greeted our return.

Only our children seemed undisturbed by the lack of responses to our messages. To be in our home system, in the setting of the tales we had told to them and the scenarios the Seeker's minds had presented to them, was gratifying enough for them. Sometimes when I looked at Angharad—she had grown taller than I by then and still often wore the inward-looking expression I remembered seeing on Solveig's face—I wondered if she and her friends might be happier if we found no one at all, so that they would finally be cut free from our past.

By the time we were inside the asteroid belt, our probes and sensors had already verified that no Habitats were in orbit around Mars. That planet remained as it had been, cold and dry, salmon-pink and lifeless, and had lost its satellites of Phobos and Deimos that had been made into two of the earliest Habitats. Perhaps those Habitats had also left on an interstellar voyage, but if so, they had left no welcoming artifact for us, no message to tell us where they had gone.

No Habitats remained in that region of the solar system that the Habbers had once claimed as their space. Benzi was deeply shaken by that fact, as were many of the former Habbers among us. Benzi had entertained thoughts similar to my own, that perhaps people who still remembered those he had known and lived among and loved might somehow be alive or that there would be some relics of former comrades—records held by the net, thought patterns, even an intelligence

Linked to cyberminds—to which he could return. Now they were gone, all of the people of the Habitats, almost as if they had never existed.

And Venus, I thought: What of Venus? Had my home been abandoned as well? I haunted the bridge with Ragnar and with others from my world as the Seeker swept toward Earth and its Moon; we monitored every bit of data the probes moving toward Venus were gathering. We might have kept such a vigil anywhere inside the Seeker, watching and listening through our Links, but something drove us to wait on the bridge. Maybe we simply needed to be together in what we had come to see as the eyes of the Seeker.

The Parasol was there, still shielding Venus from an excess of sunlight, but several of its fans had been removed. The wings of the Bats remained above the north and south poles, but without the tiers and lattices that had serviced the vehicles that had docked there. Anwara still moved around the planet in its high orbit, but was only a shell of itself, a giant gyroscope of girders and empty docks.

We noted all of that, but it was Venus herself that held our attention, that gave us some hope that our journey, our voyage into the future of the home we had left, had not been in vain. The atmosphere was still thick with clouds giving off the reflected light now shining again from the sun, but they veiled the planet more lightly now, and our probes had glimpsed through them to see what lay below.

Venus: blue and green and alive with life, with the life that had been created by the terraformers.

But there was no sign that any of the descendants of the terraformers were still there. The polar installations that had once extracted excess oxygen were encased in the ice of snowcaps. There were domes on the surface, but no sign of any activity around them. We called out to Venus, but heard no reply.

Had the Cytherians abandoned Venus? Had they followed other interstellar nomads away from this system? We wondered at that, but while we gathered on the bridge yet again, still watching the images of Venus and hoping that our call might be answered, Earth called to us.

At first, our cyberminds could not read the signals clearly or interpret them, except to verify that they were indeed from Earth. Gradually, they were able to piece together portions of a message.

The Earthfolk, their instrumentalities, or their artificial intelligences (the distinctions among them seemed unclear, and perhaps were nonexistent) had observed the Seeker entering this system. They were gratified (surprised? amused?) to discover that we were natives of this system and had left it over a millennium ago, and they had managed to locate an incomplete record (a memory? an account?) of the early plans for our expedition. They were curious about us and requested (insisted? demanded?) that they be allowed to send a few of their number to the Seeker.

"Well?" Benzi said to those of us who were assembled on the bridge. "What shall we do now?"

"We invite them to come here," I replied, noting from the expressions of those crowded around me that I was speaking for them as well.

"But we don't know their intentions." That was Suleiman Khan.

Ah Lin glanced at Suleiman. "Do you really think they could be a danger to us?" she asked.

"I don't know," he said. "All I know is that their message sounded almost as strange as—"

"We have to let them come here." My daughter was speaking now, and through my Link I sensed others, the young ones, assenting to her words. "Why wouldn't you want to meet them? Why would you turn them away?" Angharad regarded Suleiman with her characteristic calm and remote gaze. "You're not fearing that they'll harm us. You're afraid to see what they might have become. Or maybe you're worrying about letting them see what we are."

Suleiman looked away from her. "Perhaps."

The Seeker's scanning of Earthspace had revealed that the only artifacts in orbits around humankind's home planet were seven silvery worldlets. It was from those worldlets that our visitors came, flying out from openings in the silver walls aboard gossamer vessels with solar sails. Mindful that we had been separated from this branch of our kind for over twelve centuries and that we might inadvertently prove vulnerable to either naturally evolving or genetically engineered microbes carried by the Earthfolk, we were careful to scan the first of our visitors thoroughly before allowing them to leave the bays in which they had docked their fragile-looking spacecraft. But we had nothing to fear from them; perhaps they had foreseen such a possibility and had taken preventive measures of their own.

Physically, they were almost indistinguishable from us, but my Link informed me that they seemed far more tightly wedded to their cyberminds than we were to ours. Listening in on what little they cared to say—on what little our net of minds could understand—I could not tell if they were artificial intelligences wearing human bodies or human minds that often lived as easily in the connections of their cybernets as they did in their old physical forms. Perhaps they were both—or something else altogether.

They came to the Seeker in small groups, explored our rooms and hallways and the landscapes of our Heart, sat and listened to us as we spoke, repeated a few words of our various languages, and then left us. We grew more accustomed to their presence, but were never able to Link with them, to glimpse even a sign of their inner thoughts and feelings, and our cyberminds sensed a similar resistance to their efforts at communicating with Earth's artificial intelligences. Only when the Earthfolk were in the company of the youngest of our children, who soon took to following them everywhere, did I glimpse even a trace of a warmer expression in their faces, an upward curve of the lips that might have been a smile.

They came to us, but we did not go to them. We had seen evidence of their communities on Earth, communities that lived inside vast force fields or in areas that had apparently reverted to wilderness. We had learned that others, those who had come to us, lived inside their silvery worldlets. We did not know if these different communities were entirely separate or if those living in them exchanged places from time to time.

"We can be sure of one thing," I said to Angharad. "Earth didn't destroy itself during the time of changes. We aren't the last remnant of a destructive and suicidal species."

"But we don't know that for certain," my daughter replied in that calm fashion of hers that was beginning to remind me of the manner of our visitors. "These people might be descended from survivors of a catastrophe we can't imagine, which could explain why they had only a partial record of this expedition. The others who left this system might have felt that nothing remained for them here."

"How depressing," I said, foolishly.

Angharad shook her head at me. "It is their history, Mahala, not ours. We still have our own history to make."

The Earthfolk came among us, and then they seemed to lose interest in the Seeker, and soon we knew, through our cyberminds and our Links, that they would come among us no more and would also not welcome us as visitors to Earth. They did not want to interfere with us, to impose their technology and their culture and their ways on an earlier variant of their species. They wanted to leave us free.

That was what we were able to glean from them, but I found myself thinking of my farewell to Balin so long ago, when he had told me of the Habbers who had retreated into dreams and simulations. Perhaps these Earthfolk had a similar weakness they sought to hide. I would probably never know, one way or another.

We knew, as we said our farewells to Earth, where we would have to go: to Venus.

Venus was alive, and yet there were no people there, and also no cyberminds holding any record of what the Cytherians had become.

Had they abandoned the metamorphosis of that planet to return to Earth, to rejoin that branch of our kind? Or had they followed the Habbers into space? I preferred to believe the latter, perhaps because I felt some contentment at imagining the descendants of Solveig and Chike and the others I had loved moving out across the universe on their relativistic paths, remembering their forebears and their earlier lives on Venus.

The Seeker became a satellite of Venus, falling into an orbit that took us out past the remaining fans of the Parasol and then to within one thousand kilometers of what remained of the abandoned space station of Anwara. The Lakshmi Plateau, flanked by the Maxwell Mountains to the south and the Freyja Mountains to the north, was now the high green steppe of a continent; another continent made from the landmass of Aphrodite Terra, a scorpion with a long tail that curved east, lay along the equator. Islands, large ones and small, dotted the oceans.

An analysis of the atmosphere revealed that it was breathable, but with a lower percentage of oxygen than the atmosphere of Earth. We would have to bring oxygen with us and wear protective suits, but could walk on the surface and breathe the air.

We could make a life for ourselves there.

✼   ✼   ✼

A few among my companions traveled to Anwara in torchships, ostensibly to correct its decaying orbit and to see what could be salvaged there, but I suspected that several of them also wanted to postpone any journey to the surface of Venus. Many of my comrades lacked a deep emotional bond with this world, while others feared leaving an environment that had become so familiar to them. I supposed that many of them would eventually choose to continue their lives inside the Seeker, remaining near Venus without fully committing their lives to that planet.

From what some who sought me out as an adviser had confided, I also knew that there were people who were thinking of constructing another Seeker and following the stream of humankind to the stars. Already I was wondering if Angharad, and indeed most of our children, would eventually be among them, if she might in the future say her farewells to me as I had said mine to my grandmother Risa.

We would not be able to land our shuttlecraft on the Platform that had functioned as the port of the Islands, for the Islands no longer floated in the upper atmosphere. As had been planned for the later stages of the Project, they had dropped slowly down through the atmosphere and now rested on the surface. Our scans had revealed what remained of them; seven domed areas dotted the equatorial continent that had been formed from Aphrodite Terra, and another dome sat on the slope of a volcano we had known as Rhea in Beta Regio, now an island that resembled the isle of Hawaii on Earth. The other Islands, including the Platform, were submerged in the shallow Cytherian oceans. That to me suggested that the Islands had been abandoned before the final stages of their descent, and perhaps long before that.

There were also domes in the mountain ranges of Ishtar Terra, in the same locations where the settlements I remembered had been.

"We'll have to go down there," Angharad told me, "to find out anything more." I was about to give her some excuse, another reason for waiting, then realized that I was finding my own ways of postponing my return.

"Yes," I told her, "I know." I looked at her and saw her watching me with what might have been either compassion or pity. She had become a woman, not much younger than I had been when I decided to become a spacefarer, and it seemed to me that she had grown up too quickly, that she had been a child only a little while ago, and then I understood what she had just said to me.

"You'll come with me?" I asked.

She smiled. "Of course."

Even the largest of our shuttlecraft had room for only fifty passengers, and most of the craft were smaller than that. This was just as well, since those of us who wanted to explore the surface had chosen to go there in small groups. I preferred to view what had become of my world only in the company of close companions who also remembered what it had been—and with my daughter.

Benzi came with us, to monitor the cyberpilot and perhaps to pretend that he was a pilot again. Angharad was with me, and Ragnar, along with Ah Lin and Tomas and their son Jori, who wore the same compassionate—or pitying—look on his face as did my daughter. Our Links were silent, our channels closed; we did not speak as we dropped through the thick dark clouds. Ishtar Terra was still hidden by night, and for an instant I felt that I was looking into the past, at the Venus that had been completely shadowed by the Parasol, and then I found myself listening to the silence outside our vessel. The fierce winds that had once swept around Venus had finally died.

A red glow on the black surface below us grew into a bright red spot; a volcano was erupting. We swept toward the high shelf of Ishtar and the Maxwell Mountains and dropped toward the northern part of the massif, toward the domes that had once been Oberg.

The shuttlecraft landed next to the square structure that had once been a digger and crawler bay. That installation still jutted out from the much larger walls of the airship bay. The entrance to the crawler bay was open, as our instruments had confirmed before landing; all of us were in the thin silvery skins of our protective suits and wearing filters to shield us against any infectious microbes, prepared to leave our craft, and still we sat in our seats, waiting. I was suddenly afraid to go into that place, into my earliest memories.

"Mahala." That was Angharad's voice. She stood up, then held out her hand. "Mother, come with me."

I followed her out of the craft and down the short ramp. Through my nose filters, an odor came to me, a smell of moss and mud and an acrid smell I could not recognize, and then I thought with wonder: I am breathing the air of Venus.

A cool breeze caressed my face; I shivered. On the ground, traces of frost were visible; snow might come to these mountains in time. I looked west, away from the darkened dome behind me, and in that moment saw light in the gray western sky; the sun was rising. The others stood with me, watching as Sol slowly rose above the seemingly endless plateau far below us, lighting up the grassy plain. Dawn had come to Venus, and I wondered if others had stood here to view that dawn before departing from this world or if we were the first people to see the morning sun come to Ishtar. We continued to gaze in the direction of the sun until a shadow passed across the bright disk, an eclipse produced by a fan of the Parasol.

My arm was clutched more tightly. "Mahala," Angharad said; she sounded afraid, and I remembered that she had never set foot on a planet before. "Let's go inside."

I slipped my oxygen mask over my nose and mouth; Angharad did the same. Benzi and Tomas were already walking through the open entrance of the bay. The rest of us hurried after them, moving through the empty bay quickly. A wall was ahead of us, barely visible in the dim light that was the bay's only illumination. Tomas halted and felt along the wall until he found a sensor, and then the wall rose, revealing another open space.

We entered the airship bay, empty now except for its cradles. The flat roof high overhead was closed to the outside, but the entrance to Oberg was open. I held my breath, almost expecting to hear a voice inviting us to come inside, and then the region beyond the entrance grew light. The eclipse of the sun had passed; we could now see inside the dome.

We came through the entrance and into a barren landscape, a region of black rock and lifeless brown land. No buildings remained, no glassy greenhouses, no pilots' dormitory, not even the walls of the mosque; they had taken everything with them. There would have been ruins if they had died here, the walls of houses and the rubble of complexes, the detritus of their lives. But they had left nothing behind them, which meant that they had planned their departure, and, being the practical people most Cytherians were, had taken every useful resource of Oberg's with them.

I looked up at the protective dome, now translucent except for a wide black disk in the center where its panels of light had once glowed, and then began to walk east, away from the entrance. Ah Lin trailed after me, along with my daughter.

"I know where you're going," Ah Lin said as she caught up to me. "You're looking for the memorials."

"Memorials?" Angharad asked.

"The memorial pillars, to commemorate the dead," Ah Lin replied, but I could already see that even those pillars were not here. Had the Cytherians, wherever they had gone, wanted to keep that monument to those who had died in making this world, in order to remember them? Or had they become a people less conscious of death, who might have removed the memorial pillars for some other reason? I would probably never know, but felt easier inside myself, relieved that the pillars had not been left here for us to find, that I would not have to search them and possibly find on them the images of Risa and Sef.

Only one pillar was left. I went to it, wishing suddenly and absurdly that I had brought flowers with me from the Seeker's Heart to set at its base. I stopped at the pillar and looked up at the faces of Iris Angharads and Amir Azad. Maybe the last people to leave Oberg had known that we would come back here; maybe they had remembered enough about my great-grandmother and the man who had died with her to know that their memorial should remain on this world.

Angharad came to my side. "We shouldn't leave it here," she said. "It should stand in a garden on Venus someday, not in this empty place." Her words warmed me; she was speaking as if she intended to stay on this world. She had seen the memorial before, in the historical records of the Seeker, but she reached for my hand and held it as she read the words on the inscription. " 'In honor of Iris Angharads and Amir Azad, the first true Cytherians, who gave their lives to save our new world. They shall not be forgotten. May their spirit live on in all those who follow them. They rest forever on the world they helped to build.' "

"That's all that's left of our people here," Ah Lin murmured, "that monument."

"No," I replied, "there is Venus."

All of Oberg was dead and empty; a brief exploration of the nearby domes of al-Khwarizmi revealed only another abandoned settlement. We passed the night sleeping in our craft and then flew north to the Freyja Mountains in the morning. Others from the Seeker were already inside Turing and had found another barren environment, with only a rock-filled hollow where the lake near Dyami's house had once been. Even the pillar that my uncle had designed, to commemorate those who had suffered before the Cytherian Revolt, was gone. Had that monument been taken away so that the past would not be forgotten? Or had people who remembered Dyami wanted to keep his most ambitious and accomplished piece of work with them?

There was nothing in Turing for us, nothing inside any of the domes where our people had once lived. The life of Venus was outside those domes now, growing and evolving, a living Cytherian biosphere. Like the pyramids of ancient Earth, once meant to be gateways to another life, the domes of Venus had fulfilled their purpose.

We flew south, over the green plateau of Lakshmi and the sheer cliffsides of the Himalayan Maxwell massif, then over another green plain, and found ourselves above the greenish-blue expanse of a Venusian ocean. Soon we were passing over Venus's other great continent, the equatorial landmass formed from Aphrodite Terra. The jumbled ridges of the west had sprouted trees with wide fronds; a jungle of green plants and colorful flowers had come to Aphrodite. On the plateaus we had known as Ovda and Thetis, the land resembled large flat tiles of green, and I spied a moss-covered slope that might once have been an Island dome. Our craft dropped down as we soared over the chasm of Diana, a deep scar on the land over three kilometers deep with a great river running through it; we followed that crevasse east to a region marked by recent lava flows and dominated by the giant shield volcano of Maat Mons. The temperature, according to our instruments, was much warmer here than in the highlands of Ishtar, as warm as the tropical areas of Earth.

This continent, with its rugged and widely varying terrain, would be hard to settle. I supposed that we would come to live on Ishtar first, as had the first settlers here, before exploring Aphrodite.

As our craft lifted, I caught a glimpse of a large tawny-furred animal slinking under a leaf that resembled a fern and then saw a tiny winged creature land on a leafy tree limb. I thought of the birds and cats and small apes and other animals that had once lived on the Islands and wondered if I had seen their descendants, or if these were life-forms made for and adapted to this planet. Had they been left here to evolve without interference, or put here as companions for any future human settlers? That was yet another question that might never be answered.

We flew north once more, toward Ishtar, and landed southwest of the Maxwell Mountains, on another green plain that stretched toward the greenish-blue sea. The mountain ridge loomed in the northeast, the rocky cliffsides so steep that they might have been part of a wall.

Another shuttlecraft was on the plain, near a gentle slope that led down to the sea; that craft sat on its runners atop the flat surface of a faceted white boulder that glittered like a diamond. Carbon oxides, I thought, some of the residue of terraforming; more of the giant gems jutted from the land along the shore. Five figures in silver suits stood next to the diamond boulder. One of them turned, saw us, and lifted a hand.

I recognized the black mustache of Suleiman Khan and waved to him. He waved back and quickly began to climb toward us. "We've picked up some readings from the ocean," he said as he came to my side. "There's life there, Mahala, some algae, something very like plankton, a few creatures that resemble large hydras, even a few relatives of crustaceans."

"Nothing on the land here, though," another man's voice said, "except of course the grasses and mosses. There's nothing that resembles animal life."

"Maybe not here," Ragnar said, "but we still have some exploration to do. We saw signs of animal life on Aphrodite Terra, and I suspect we'll find something here."

"Yes," Suleiman said, "God willing, perhaps we will. I didn't think this would actually happen, that we would stand here and breathe the air of Venus. I did not think—" He paused. "I have come home at last." He looked happy in his tears.

Angharad stood with Jori, looking out at the sea as the wind rose. It wrinkled the vast blue-green ocean, making whitecaps on the water. The gray clouds were growing thicker again; soon the sun was hidden behind them.

"A storm is coming," Benzi said. Ah Lin and Tomas had already retreated inside our craft. "We should leave."

"We'll come back." I gazed at my daughter and Jori, thinking of the life they might make for themselves here. We would have to plan environments in which to house ourselves, tend this biosphere, see that Venus never reverted to the hot and hellish and poisonous world it had once been.

I must have smiled then. "Mahala, what are you thinking about?" Ragnar asked.

I was thinking: All of the efforts of the Project, all of the paths we had taken in our lives, the long voyage of the Seeker—all of it had been to bring us back here, to ensure that this small human strain would survive on the world that so many of our ancestors had labored to create. My bond with Iris and Risa and all of those who had come before me had been strengthened and renewed. The instincts that had given me my daughter, that had given me that genetic tie to the past, had also given birth to this world.

The wind rose over the gray ocean, then died as the dark clouds fled from the sun. The storm would not come right away, not yet. I slipped my hand into Ragnar's and went with him to stand next to Angharad. We watched the sea become blue-green again, in the light of the sun glistening and dancing on the waves.

About the Author

Pamela Sargent sold her first published story during her senior year in college at the State University of New York at Binghamton, where she earned a B.A. and M.A. in philosophy and also studied ancient history and Greek. She is the author of several highly praised novels, among them *Cloned Lives* (1976), *The Sudden Star* (1979), *The Golden Space* (1982), *The Alien Upstairs* (1983), and *Alien Child* (1988). Her novel *Venus of Dreams* (1986) was selected by The Easton Press for its "Masterpieces of Science Fiction" series; Gregory Benford described it as "a sensitive portrait of people caught up in a vast project. It tells us much about how people react to technology's relentless hand, and does so deftly. A new high point in humanistic science fiction." *Venus of Shadows* (1988), the sequel, was called "a masterly piece of world-building" by James Morrow and "alive with humanity, moving, and memorable" by *Locus*. *The Shore of Women* (1986), one of Sargent's best-known books, was praised as "a compelling and emotionally involving novel" by *Publishers Weekly*; Gerald Jonas of the *New York Times* said: "I applaud Ms. Sargent's ambition and admire the way she has unflinchingly pursued the logic of her vision." The *Washington Post Book World* has called her "one of the genre's best writers."

Sargent is also the author of *Earthseed* (1983), chosen as a Best Book for Young Adults by the American Library Association, and two collections of short fiction, *Starshadows* (1977) and *The Best of Pamela Sargent* (1987). Her novels *Watchstar* (1980), *Eye of the Comet* (1984), and *Homesmind* (1984) comprise a trilogy. She has won the Nebula Award, the Locus Award, and has been a finalist for the Hugo Award. Her work has been translated into French, German, Dutch, Spanish,

Portuguese, Italian, Swedish, Japanese, Chinese, Russian, Polish, and Serbo-Croatian.

Ruler of the Sky (1993), Sargent's epic historical novel about Genghis Khan, published in the United States by Crown Publishers and in Britain by Chatto & Windus, tells the Mongol conqueror's story largely from the points-of-view of women. Gary Jennings, bestselling author of the historical novels *Aztec* and *The Journeyer*, said about *Ruler of the Sky*: "This formidably researched and exquisitely written novel is surely destined to be known hereafter as *the* definitive history of the life and times and conquests of Genghis, mightiest of Khans." Elizabeth Marshall Thomas, author of *Reindeer Moon* and *The Hidden Life of Dogs*, commented: "Scholarly without ever seeming pedantic, the book is fascinating from cover to cover and does admirable justice to a man who might very well be called history's single most important character."

Sargent is also an editor and anthologist. In the 1970s, she edited the *Women of Wonder* series, the first collections of science fiction by women; her other anthologies include *Bio-Futures* and, with British writer Ian Watson as co-editor, *Afterlives*. Two anthologies, *Women of Wonder, The Classic Years: Science Fiction by Women from the 1940s to the 1970s*, and *Women of Wonder, The Contemporary Years: Science Fiction by Women from the 1970s to the 1990s*, were published by Harcourt Brace & Company/Harvest Books in 1995; *Publishers Weekly* called these two books "essential reading for any serious sf fan." With artist Ron Miller, she collaborated on *Firebrands: The Heroines of Science Fiction and Fantasy* (1998), published by Thunder's Mouth Press in the U.S. and Collins & Brown/Paper Tiger in the U.K.

Her novel *Climb the Wind: A Novel of Another America* was published by HarperPrism in January of 1999 and was a finalist for the Sidewise Award for Alternate History. Gahan Wilson, writing in *Realms of Fantasy*, calls this book "a most enjoyable and entertaining new alternate history adventure . . . which brings a new dimension to the form," while *Science Fiction Chronicle* describes it as "a first class work from a first class writer." *Child of Venus*, the third novel in Sargent's Venus trilogy, is appearing from Eos simultaneously with reissues of *Venus of Dreams* and *Venus of Shadows*, the first two novels in this trilogy, in both print-on-demand trade paperbacks and downloadable editions in electronic formats from the electronic publisher e-reads.com.

Pamela Sargent lives in upstate New York. Her World Wide Web site is located at: http://www.sff.net/people/PSargent/default.htm